The Accursed

Austin Harper

Cover art by Gwendolyn Powell

CONTENTS

Copyright 2

Chapter I – Esteri 5

Chapter II – Tius 18

Chapter III – Delphina 31

Chapter IV – Esteri 43

Chapter V – Piru 55

Chapter VI – Acacia 67

Chapter VII – Esteri 80

Chapter VIII – Piru 101

Chapter IX – Tius 113

Chapter X – Ukko 129

Chapter XI – Avina 142

Chapter XII – Esteri 154

Chapter XIII – Acacia 167

Chapter XIV – Tius 180

Chapter XV – Delphina 193

Chapter XVI – Esteri 205

Chapter XVII – Ukko 221

Chapter XVIII – Tius 234

Chapter XIX – Ulfr 248

Chapter XX – Esteri 258

Chapter XXI – Avina 271

Chapter XXII – Erikis 281

Chapter XXIII – Tius 288

Chapter XXIV – Acacia 300

Chapter XXV – Esteri 313

Chapter XXVI – Ulfr 321

Chapter XXVII – Delphina 328

Chapter XXVIII – Piru 345

Chapter XXIX – Esteri 353

Chapter XXX – Avina 373

Chapter XXXI – Ulfr 392

Chapter XXXII – Acacia 407

Chapter XXXIII – Esteri 426

Chapter XXXIV – Acacia 444

Chapter XXXV – Esteri 465

Epilogue 483

CHAPTER I

Esteri

Esteri Piritta Metsaa Kalest, First Princess of Kalest and heir apparent to her father's throne, was having another rotten day. Like so many days before, she went through her routine mechanically and without purpose. Hours were wasted in formalities and receiving the latest reports from around the world – meaningless gossip of the lives of well-to-dos in other kingdoms, not a one of which today or any day before for as long as the princess could remember portended anything for her nor for Kalest itself.

Even her time in the library, learning the history of her nation and her world, had become less than satisfying – the sins of the past always seemed to repeat themselves despite the best efforts of people far wiser than her or anyone living. The more she learned, the more she dreaded what would be her time: all the prattling of spies and embassies said nothing, but the inexorable count of time said that sooner or later there'd be war. Maybe not this year, but before she was laid to rest, almost assuredly.

History repeating itself did not put Princess Esteri in a good mood when it came to dinner with her family. Faintly, she remembered the days of her youth when her father had smiled and laughed and her mother had sat across from her and humored the young princess. This day, though, as every day for years, she would sit in a nearly silent hall where her father cast icy glares from place to place and her stepmother made her displeasure that the fruit of her womb would not inherit plainly known. Only her half-brother was tolerable now, and he was just a child.

All the same, she had no choice but to attend. When the sun was low in the sky and its light streamed across the high table and cast its white cloth in faded gold, the family assembled once more for their bitter ritual.

This time it was Delphina – Queen Delphina Anu Metsaa Kalest – who was the first to break the silence. It usually was.

"I trust your lessons were satisfactory today, dear?" she said, talking obviously to her own son.

"They were fine," Tuoni said around a mouth of food. "But I bet Esteri gets to learn all the fun stuff. Right, sister?"

Esteri winced. The last thing she wanted was to be brought into the conversation.

"Oh," Delphina said, tone icy and flat. "Yes, I completely forgot to ask her about her day. How clumsy of me."

"It's quite alright, highness," Esteri replied, refusing to address the woman as mother. "Your silence gave no offense."

Delphina pointedly looked away. "Now that was uncalled for. Apologize, young lady."

Esteri's cheeks burned. She should have known better than to rise to the bait. She reached for her chalice, taking it from the food taster and quickly claiming a sip of wine, the action giving her a moment to think of a response.

Of course hers would be warm. She signaled for ice – at least they were close enough to the mountains to have some brought in this time of year.

She looked up from the disappointing chalice and feigned surprise. "Why, I don't know what you mean me to apologize for. I was myself giving forgiveness for the breach of protocol, as you wanted."

Delphina turned her head in a disgusted motion, "It must have been your ingratitude," she said, "that drove your mother to an early grave."

The server returned, pouring a measure of ice water from his pitcher into Esteri's chalice. For what wasn't the first time, the princess was glad that the cups were metal – she wasn't a strong young woman, but when pushed she had once broken a fine crystal glass flute when so provoked.

Esteri took a sip of the freshly chilled wine.

"Speechless, I see," Delphina said. "I suppose not even you can defend such blatant breaches of common courtesy towards someone who has done nothing but love and nurture you for ten years now."

Esteri drained half her glass. Her father, King Piru Rekorius Metsaa Kalest, was hiding his face in his hand as he often did when this happened. She would get no help there.

"Really," Delphina continued, "I don't know what Kalest is going to do the day it finds someone like you sitting upon the throne, may that not be for many years yet, so utterly lacking in courtly graces and good manners. I have tried my best to teach you but I suppose sometimes it is simply impossible to change a person's nature."

Esteri gripped the arms of her chair, not in rage for that was fading along with the memory of Delphia's most dire accusation, but because she felt as though the room had suddenly begun listing to one side.

"I suppose that for the good of the nation, I shall have to see if I can find any tutors stricter than those we have already tried. If you have any love for your father or your people you will try to take to their instruction and become a proper princess who respects her elders when they try to make small talk at the dinner table. Do I make myself clear?"

The heaving of the room had only gotten more intense, now decidedly unnatural. Though Esteri knew she was sitting still, she couldn't shake the feeling that she was spinning about, nor that it had somehow, suddenly, become infernally hot.

"I don't..." she began, finding the words hard to form, like her mouth was full of cotton. "I don't feel so good."

"Nor should you," Delphina said, "for if you have any shame then now would be a proper time to display it and the first stop along a long path towards the lowest bar of being a presentable young lady. Now apologize"-

"I'm serious!" Esteri shouted, and tried to stand.

That was a mistake. As soon as she was on her own two feet she lost her balance in a fit of vertigo. With one hand, she caught the tablecloth, pulling it her direction, her goblet clattering to the floor beside her head and her plate falling and shattering near her hip. She looked as the wine flowed across the stones of the dining hall, and her mind reached its verdict on this sudden illness.

Poison, it had to be. But the food taster... hadn't tasted the ice water. She struggled to find a way to move, even crawl. She could have hours or she could have minutes, it was impossible to know. If she could get to the doctors...

There was shouting all around her, and she could barely see as she began to crawl in what she hoped was the direction of the door. To hell with poise and dignity, it was her life on the line.

Esteri felt someone grasp her ankles, and another set or hands at her shoulders. Her first instinct was to struggle, but then she heard her father's voice.

"Quickly!" he said. "Get her to the doctors. I don't care what they're in the middle of, this is what we quarter them for!"

Esteri stopped trying to move on her own and let herself be carried. It felt like she was falling the whole time, and she couldn't see the world around her as anything more than a whirl of colors, but she had enough wits left that as far as she could tell her vision wasn't dimming. She forced herself to keep her eyes open, too afraid that if she closed them, that might be the end.

Eventually, she stopped moving, though what she saw didn't stop tossing back and forth. She felt something soft behind her back, and the room around her was white – she thought she could make up familiar shapes of the quarters accorded to the palace's medical staff.

8

"Let me through!" an old, familiar voice shouted. "Let me through!" It was Doctor Markku, who had attended to no few of her scraped knees, colds, and other needs as she had grown. Some part of her felt relieved – if anyone she knew could cure what ailed her, it was Markku.

He shooed out what must have been a crowd and then took her wrist and checked her pulse as he spoke

"Can you hear me?" he asked.

"I can," Esteri managed. Talking was easier than she had expected it would be, though her words were terribly slurred. "Can you help me?"

There was a long, uncomfortable pause.

"I won't lie," Markku said. "I don't yet know, because I don't know what you've been poisoned with. Your skin is deathly cold, and that narrows it down. What can you tell me about your other symptoms?"

"The world's spinning," Esteri answered.

"That narrows it down as well. Anything else? How fast did it start, do you know?"

"Right away, I think," she said. "And it's like my mouth's full of cotton."

"That rules out Maiden's Tears," Markku muttered, "and shadowbloom and... That rules out a lot."

"Do you know?" Esteri pleaded.

"I think..." he said. "Little princess, I think I have one more question for you. Can you feel the tips of your fingers?"

Esteri tried to tap each of her fingers to her thumb.

"They kind of sting," she said.

Again, Markku fell silent. Esteri waited a moment with bated breath, but then could take no more.

"What is it, Markku?" she asked. "You can cure me, can't you?"

"I'm sorry, my little princess," the old doctor said. "If this is any toxin I know, and I suspect that it is, it is Wolf's Breath. For that all I can do is give you a measure of poppy extract, the sort that numbs all senses and gives fantastic dreams. If you want it, that is the most I can do. Otherwise the pain in your fingers and toes will spread throughout your body, as though you were being devoured by a wolf, it's said. There is no antidote that I have nor any I can brew."

Esteri closed her eyes. If she was going to die, she could at least take solace in the darkness under her eyelids rather than the nonsensical whirl of the room around her.

"Is there any chance I can simply survive?" she asked. "That I didn't drink enough to kill me, just to make me sick?"

"Slim," the doctor replied. "If the pain spreads past your wrists and ankles, though, it won't stop."

Already Esteri could feel a tingling along the palm of her hands and in the arches of her feet, and at her furthest extremities the slight sting was slowly turning into an angry ache.

"Then I'd rather be able to feel at least until then," she said.

"You are very brave, little princess," Markku said. "Your mother would be proud."

"You were at her bedside in her last days, right?" Esteri asked, though she knew the answer already. "How... how was she?"

"She never wanted to leave you behind so young," Markku said, "nor to leave your father... but by the end, she was at peace."

"Because some day I'd be a good, wise queen, right?"

"That's very right."

"Then I think she might be disappointed in me right now," Esteri said with a wince.

"If there is anything you wish me to do for you," Markku said, "I am ever at your service, pitiful as that might be."

Esteri tried to think. Markku was a very wise man, but he didn't know everything and Esteri herself spent more of her waking hours with books than with people. In all the pointless, repetitious history of the world, there had to be some time when it looked like everything was lost and yet salvation was found.

"Just... tell me a story," Esteri said. "I can't see and I... I think I'll be better if I can hear someone's voice."

"Once upon a time," Markku said with a heavy sigh born of sorrow and not of unjustified frustration as she so often heard from her father and queen Delphina, "there was a little girl who was lost in the deep, dark woods. She could not remember what she was trying to find, or where she came from, or even who she was. The woods were all she knew. That, and that she was lost."

Esteri's toes and the tips of her fingers... they felt like something was biting down on them, like they were being pierced by wicked teeth, the pins and needles and pricks and jabs of the earlier stages transformed into a wicked agony. She grasped the edges of the bed and curled her toes and tried not to show how she gritted her teeth.

Battles played over in her head, even as she listened to Markku's story. In the sphere of war, fantastic reversals were well known, but that did not help her. Had no one important ever been sick or wounded and lived for some great reason? Esteri struggled to remember; were she speaking the truth would have been on the tip of her tongue.

"One day, a little bird alighted on a branch near the girl. 'Are you lost too?' she asked, and the bird cawed, 'No, for we birds can see over the tallest trees and always know the way to fly back home.' And the little girl then asked the bird if it had ever seen her home. Again it answered no, but this time said that it did know the home of another human, who was sometimes kind to birds and fed them scraps."

The tingling was at Esteri's wrists and her ankles, she thought. She couldn't tell just how high it went up her arms or her legs, for the pain further down and away was vicious and made it hard to feel anything less.

Thoughts came to her mind about mysterious persons in the pages of history, monsters and tyrants that had survived so many attempts on their lives that dark magic was suspected. If dark magic was what it would take to survive, Esteri thought, she would pay its price – but then, she would have to know what the magic was.

"The little girl asked the bird to show her the way to this place where another human lived, for in all her wanderings in that forest, she had never seen another human, nor any place where a human might live. The bird obliged, and flitted from branch to branch in one direction, letting the girl follow along close behind."

Esteri's fingers bit into her palms, even as the poison seemed to gnaw her hands to ribbons yet never tear them such that they could not feel. She thought she felt the tingling in her forearms and her calves, that portent of what had been pronounced as certain doom. At the very least, the progress of the worst had not slowed in the least since it first began.

All the same, she remembered one more monster who now survived as ink upon parchment – the Everking Adalric the Butcher, once warlord of Arynias. The mad monarch they said was immortal. He drank the blood of enemies and ate the flesh of his children for a hundred and fifty years. When he died, his countless enemies had to hack all his limbs from his body, and his head did not die until it had spent several days on a pike, taunting his killers. But before that, he had been a child with the bleeding sickness that ran in the lines of Arynias nobility.

What had changed that, what had made a dying child immortal, was an alchemist's potion.

"When the little girl reached the place the bird lead her to, she found a small cottage, and its inhabitant, who was a little boy. Now the little girl,"

"And the little boy," Esteri said, "after many trials in the great forest fell in love with one another. From that place, they slowly tamed the forest, and the birds lead many other people to them, who carved roads between the trees and raised their own houses in wood and in stone. Those were the first people of Kalest and the boy and the girl were their first king and queen. My ancestors."

"So you do remember," Markku said. "I was wondering if the tale was as new to you. Do you want to hear something else?"

"I'd love to hear everything," Esteri said, "but first I need your help. It's gone past my wrists. I can feel it."

"What would you have me do, little princess?" Markku asked, clearly dreading the answer. Well, Esteri thought, perhaps he should, though she doubted it would be the one he expected.

"The Cursed Potion," Esteri said. "Do you know how to mix it?"

"I do," Markku replied, "but... I don't understand."

"Even the dying," Esteri replied, "live on as the Accursed if they drink it, and I'd rather live as a monster than die as a human if that's what it takes."

"You're certain? I cannot say I know what will become of you should you take it, if you will live and if you will remain Esteri."

"I'll live," Esteri said, "and some day I'll be a strong, wise queen and make my mother proud, but not if I don't take that potion soon. Please, Markku, you said yourself there was no medicine for this."

"I will do as you ask," Markku said. "You are a very brave girl. I have to believe it will work as you say."

Esteri didn't know if she believed herself, but she had made her choice, to become one of the Accursed in the hope that it would save her life.

The Accursed were a part of history that repeated again and again. Whether they were properly humans who had drunk an alchemical brew to turn them into something more, or monsters that had been born as humans was a debate on which there was no agreement. Most of the time, they looked like ordinary people, though they were stronger, faster, and more resilient. They also stopped aging and gained magical powers, the nature of which could never be predicted. Many went violently insane.

Time and again when nations went to war with one another, one or more would dredge up the recipe for that potion in the hopes of creating an army of obedient monsters. Sometimes they were successful and sometimes their creations turned their new power against those who created them, but never did anyone have a plan for what to do when the war was over. After all, they never died any but violent deaths, so people couldn't simply wait for their sins to vanish.

At other times, kings and despots attempted to study the potion in hopes of discovering an elixir of life that would not turn its drinker into something inhuman, or to refine the formula so that when war came again they would be able to control its results. Or they hunted the Accursed and tried to suppress and destroy the knowledge of the potion's creation, though somehow it always survived. And now and again someone else brewed up the thing and drank it, for power or in madness or fear of death. Their fate was always uncertain.

Supposedly, when once or twice a century the Accursed were driven from civilized lands, those few of them that survived the purges gathered in the mountains. Would she be driven there, from her home and family as a monster? Perhaps she could conceal her condition, at least for long enough that her father would believe she was still human at heart.

"Markku," she called through gritted teeth, "Markku, I have a request."

"Yes?" he answered.

"There is no one else in the room, is there?"

"No one. I shall have to leave shortly to procure the Æther. If you want me to have someone come in, I can."

"No," Esteri said, "I'd like the opposite. Tell no one what we are doing or have done, whether I live or die."

"You mean to hide the results?"

"If I live, yes."

"I do not think it will be easy," Markku said, "but not even the king shall hear of this."

Though the agony that Esteri assumed gave the poison in her blood its name was steadily creeping up her limbs, she breathed a little easier at that.

She did not hear the footsteps of Markku leaving the room moments later, nor those when he returned, for Esteri turned all her thought to suppressing the urge to cry out in pain. She closed her eyes tight, clenched fists, and writhed upon the cot on which she was laid, trying in vain to make it hurt less. The air of a spring evening was stiflingly hot upon her skin, and even with her eyes closed she doubted she could stand steady on her own two feet.

Esteri felt a hand behind her neck.

"The potion is ready," Markku said. "Are you?"

"I hope," Esteri choked out. She felt a rim of glass pressed to her lips. She pursed her lips and soon felt a warm, bubbling liquid touch them. She steeled herself and began to drink – the concoction tasted like blood and bile and pungent weeds, but she forced herself to swallow until it stopped flowing. This, she thought, was the remedy for her lack of foresight.

A moment later there was a new pain, fire spreading along her veins, out from her heart and stomach alike. Esteri screamed and, as it burned away the gnashing and the vertigo, lost consciousness.

***

Esteri awoke in darkness. There was a single candle in the room, on her bedside table, and it was burning low. From outside the near door, she heard her father's voice

"I still do not like this," he said. "Markku should have reported something before retiring if what you said is true."

"If the waiting is what bothers you," Delphina replied, "you can make doubly sure yourself, or allow me the honor of securing our future."

"I will not hear that," Piru replied, "for whether she lives or dies serves our aims just as well. Lysama will still be blamed. The armies will still march."

The relief at waking up at all that Esteri had felt had faded. She might have expected Delphina of trying to kill her, making some attempt to guarantee Tuoni's inheritance... but her own father? War with Lysama? What was this madness?

"And I have told you that it is not enough," Delphina hissed. "For there to be this war the people must demand it, and they think of the girl as they did her mother, so if she dies nothing less than retribution will be accepted. But if she lives? They are likely to see it as nothing more than part of the great game they think nobles play. You may raise an army to extract a price, but it will march without its heart in the fight and be beaten."

Her father was worryingly silent. Even as Esteri listened intently for every word, she rose from the bed as quietly as she could. There was a window in the room, and she was on the first floor... slowly, quietly, she drew back the curtains and opened the latch.

"You know I am right," Delphina said. "This morning you had the resolution to do what your country needed you to do. Have you lost it now? Have you forgotten that all who live in Kalest save one shall gain from this? What right does Esteri have to deny the people the happiness they do not even know they can have?"

Esteri did not wait to hear any more – she leapt out the window and into the hedge below.

Though she did not regret her choice, she quickly found that it may not have been the wisest, as her fine dress became tangled in the branches. She tore free, but was quickly obliged to shed it down to the slip below.

The air was cool and fresh, blowing down from the hills at her back. The palace grounds were removed from the city below. If her father really did mean to have her killed, then nowhere within Kalest was safe. If the rumors of Accursed colonies in the northwestern mountains were true, perhaps she could there wait for her father to regain his senses...

It occurred to her that she should probably have felt worried about the whole matter, horrified that her family had conspired against her, and especially that she ought to be full of trepidation for the uncertain path ahead, which she had to walk with nothing but a slip and some jewelry to her name.

But the night air was cool and the wind blew at her back, and every fiber of her being felt alive. She felt nearly light enough to fly, strong enough to fight, fit enough to run to the horizon and back. And there was a large part of her that, as she walked away from the palace that was her home, dearly wanted to do all those things, to test the limits of her new self. This was a curse? It felt like the greatest blessing that could be bestowed.

Slowly, Esteri's instincts took over. She could almost feel her path, west by northwest, and her speed picked up as her caution, her fear, her horror at her place in the world evaporated.

Esteri of the house of Metsaa, heir of Kalest, once dying and now Accursed, bolted into the night.

CHAPTER II

Tius

A great, dark claw smashed into the ground where Tius had been moments before, shattering the stone to rubble. Half a dozen yards away, he materialized from the dart of smoke he had become, but was still too slow. The shadowy figure was upon him in an instant, grasped him by the neck and lifted him into the air.

Tius darted again. It was like blinking – for a split second, his world was black, but when his eyes opened again he was in a different spot, what should have been far enough away.

Inky tendrils lashed at him before he found his bearings, locking around his arm and then yanking him towards his opponent. He blinked again, passing through the figure and out the other side.

"Enough!" Tius shouted. "That's enough!"

The shadowy figure sighed as her monstrous form melted back into the body of a sixteen-year-old girl. A slip of a girl at that – Avina ate like a bird, at least compared to most other Accursed, and it showed. She was a head shorter than Tius and lissome at best.

Avina brushed the last remnants of writhing tendrils down into long, black hair.

"Done so soon?" she asked. "You need to work on your form. I could have killed you at least two times out of every three."

Tius rubbed his neck. "You play rough," he said. "I've had enough for now, and need to head down the hills eventually anyway."

Avina pouted. "All right then," she said, "but maybe we could do something else when you get back? Or have another go at it, you know?"

"Right," Tius. "Maybe if it's not too late and my neck isn't too stiff."

"I'll hold you to that," she said with a smile. "See you, Tius."

Avina skipped quickly down, and disappeared around a bend.

"You know," Hathus called from his perch partway up one of the nearby crags, "she'd probably stop thrashing you if you'd give her any other moment of your time."

"Lay off it," Tius sighed.

"Come on," Hathus replied, hopping down onto the more or less flat ring of stone that served as their 'arena.' "She likes you."

Hathus looked like a rather young and tall Kalesti man, with brown eyes and brown-blonde hair. For most intents and purposes, that was what he was, save for the fact that he was over fifty years older than he looked. Though he was among the youngest Accursed other than Tius and Avina, both of whom were something of special cases, and also among the youngest seeming, he seemed to delight in 'acting his age,' that being seventy-two, when it would annoy whoever he was around the most. His supposedly insightful moments were part of that.

"Really? Because she also scares the crap out of me."

Hathus laughed. "If that were true you wouldn't keep sparring with her. Anyway, she's sixteen – a woman in every country in the world except maybe Hyperborea and gods alone know what they do."

"And I'm old enough to have been here when she was two."

"It's sweet, the little girl growing up for you."

"It's creepy."

Hathus shook his head, "Ah, what do I know about the problems of the young? I can't even remember when I was sixteen anymore, I must be getting senile in my dotage. But if I weren't, I'd probably remind you her parents have a couple centuries between them."

Avina was strange in a number of ways, other than her personal mannerisms and ability to go from demure young lady to demonic behemoth in a matter of seconds, and most of it stemmed from that fact. The vast majority of Accursed were sterile, both with humans and with each other. Avina's parents, though, proved after what he had heard were many, many years to be not quite that way, which made the girl herself even more of an aberration: a second generation Accursed. No one, at least in the colony, knew when or if she would stop aging, nor if her powers, which already far outstripped any other, had reached their peak.

"Well," Tius said, "maybe by the time I have a century, or even half of one, under my belt, the idea won't feel so strange."

"Suit yourself," Hathus said, "but I only really meant that if you'd play cards with her or something she might not be so eager to break your neck, though it would be a lot less fun to watch."

Hathus began to walk the path back to the heart of the colony himself, but then stopped and looked back over his shoulder.

"By the way," he said, "I didn't just drop in for a lovers' quarrel. Radegond wanted me to tell you that she covered the north face yesterday and brought down a deer, so she's expecting you to either deliver some results in the south or at least stay out there until you feel your hunting skills improve. So I guess either you're bringing dinner or missing your date."

"Bitch," Tius muttered. "It's easy for her to cover ground when she can fly. And what's she stockpiling for anyway? Winter's over."

"That's your problem, not mine. I've got the weak knees and a bad back and rotten teeth."

He grinned with his perfect teeth.

Tius waved Hathus farewell and headed down the other

trail towards the wild mountainside. The south face, being the most exposed to human sight, wasn't home to much handiwork of the Accursed: they planted berry bushes and trees that bore fruit or nuts in the region and made small goat-paths down through the brush, but little else, for it was better if ordinary folk did not know where exactly their colony was, or some ill turn of politics in Kalest or Tyrvad could see an army on their doorstep. That made it hard for new Accursed to find, but in these peaceful days they were very rare. Accursed from the colony went down into towns sometimes, hiding their nature and origins, and Tius himself had been the last one anyone had even heard rumors of.

Tius circled down the mountain, and into the verdant brush. There was no point looking for game in the upper reaches of it, though; Radegond would give him hell if he didn't at least patrol down into the foothills, so he'd have to carry anything he brought down that far and back.

The lower hills had many paths through them – game trails and goat-paths, and very few of them led up to the colony. The unfortunate part was that there were also very few branches that led down into the flatlands, so it was easy enough for travelers to get lost. The chances of running into a human were decently high, so using magical abilities was strictly off limits. Of course, that was a bit less annoying for Accursed who didn't have abilities about motion and travel.

Tius couldn't complain too much, though. Not only was he the youngest Accursed other than Avina, but he'd signed up for the detail. The opportunity to, now and again, talk with someone from outside was refreshing, even if he resented the other duties it implied.

In one of the more open areas halfway between the flatlands and the upper slopes that the Accursed more often frequented, Tius felt something off. At first, it wasn't obvious. He noted a few broken branches – several, in fact, as though someone had stumbled upward, carving a new path through the brush with great effort and, knowing the foliage, probably a little pain. There wasn't any similar path leading out of the clearing, but there was a large stone there, which he suspected that someone could be camped behind, out of his sight.

For a moment, Tius hesitated – whoever might be there was stubborn and trekking up the mountain, which meant whoever it was, was either dangerous, desperate, or insane. On the other hand, Tius was convinced that he could handle himself in any of the troublesome cases, and having someone to talk to and maybe lead down to the flatlands would take the edge of the tiresome patrol task and let him claim to have done something useful.

Tius rounded the rock, and what he saw surprised him. It was a young woman, perhaps as old as Tius had been when he took the Accursed potion. Her long, blood-red hair was in a loose braid and dirty, twigs and leaves from what must have been her forced passage through the brush stuck in it. Her fair skin was covered in dust, and her bare legs and face had many fine red scratches from stray branches, her knees scraped by what must have been more than a few falls.

The strangest thing was her clothing. The woman had a large and shabby coat, of the sort that even the poor city folk kept for when it was raining, and this might have been older than she was. Beneath that, she wore what looked to be a fine silk slip such as rich ladies would beneath their dresses, and a number of pieces of fine jewelry: a velvet choker set with Lapis Lazuli and a longer necklace of twisted golden wire with crimson gems, no few rings that sparkled with gold and silver, rubies and sapphires, bejeweled earrings, and bracelets and anklets of precious metals besides. It was as though some lord's daughter had stripped off her fancy dress and thrown on some beggar's shabby things instead.

Though her current state, battered and dirty, was more like the coat, her bearing seemed to Tius to be closer to what was underneath. Even asleep in the dirt, she had a proud look about her, such that he hesitated again considering whether or not to wake her. After a moment, though, Tius recalled that he could not exactly leave her to her own devices without discerning her intent, and reached out and shook her shoulder.

The woman didn't budge.

Tius shook again, and called out to her quite loudly, but she did not stir in the least. At this, and now quite worried, he checked her pulse and was able to find it. She was, at least, alive... but if it was exhaustion that she was sleeping off, he had never seen its equal in severity.

He could, he realized, leave her to her own devices with that. She was in such sorry shape that she didn't present the least threat to the colony, and Radegond couldn't fault him for doing nothing about her. He mused as to what the others would do: Radegond would likely leave her, or take her jewelry for the cause. Hathus would likely wait around until he decided he was too old for such trifling, and Erikis was hard to predict, for he warned often against getting involved in human problems while insisting on finding a way to get news from their world. Avina... Avina had never been human and didn't hold a high opinion of them, so whatever she did or didn't do, she certainly wouldn't help.

But Tius wasn't like his friends and compatriots. Even if it was the right thing to do, he couldn't live with himself if he left well enough alone. She was in such a sorry state that she didn't present a threat, but that meant she was in such a sorry state that she would probably die on her own, and it wasn't in him to just let that stand, or rob her of her valuables and hope the gods spared her life.

"I am going to be in so much trouble because of you," he said with a sigh, then bent down and, one hand behind her back and another behind her knees, picked her up and began his ascent of the mountain, back up to home.

***

"I'm sorry," Tius said. "I couldn't just leave her."

"I understand." Gelvira replied, "but beyond even the obvious problems, what you did was reckless. If she was hurt, moving her alone like you did could have made it worse."

Gelvira, Avina's mother, had to some extent adopted the entire colony as her family. She wasn't the oldest in real years, nor life experience before she made the fateful choice to take the potion, but alone of all of them she had both a desire to look out for everyone and a calm, reassuring manner. With the mild censure from her, there was sure to be trouble from everyone else.

"I..."

"It's fine," Gelvira said. "Your heart was in the right place, and if we just keep her in the dark, you can lead her down the mountain once she's recovered, and she will probably think us nothing than an odd little village. In fact, I'd be willing to keep this our little secret, though I'd have to make some preparations before"-

"Mom, why's another girl in my bed?"

Gelvira covered her face with a hand as Avina walked in, seething.

"Who is that girl?" she demanded, looking right at Tius. "Why is she here?"

"It's alright, honey," Gelvira said. "It won't be for long."

"But it's my bed and I'm tired!"

"You can use my bed for now," Gelvira said.

Avina folded her arms. "It's not the same. Why can't she use your bed?"

"Because," Gelvira replied, "Tius found that poor thing on the mountain. We don't know for certain that she's not one of us until Erikis gets back but it's safer to assume that she isn't, because that's much more likely. And what does my bedroom have that yours doesn't?"

"... A window."

"That's right. A window. One that looks out onto the commons, where most people don't care to be subtle with their powers."

Avina huffed, then turned to Tius.

"Why'd you bring a smelly human up here anyway? You know they're bad news."

24

"She wasn't waking up, so I thought she'd probably die out there on her own. I couldn't just leave."

"Yeah, you could," Avina said. "It's easy, you turn and walk the other way."

"It's not that simple"

"Of course it is! She's a human, right?"

"Look," Tius said, "you said yourself you were tired. Maybe if you take a rest, things will make a little more sense to you later."

"But she's in my bed!"

"I'm sorry about that, but your mom said it wasn't a good idea to move her."

Avina marched over to the unconscious girl.

"Did she get into a fight with a wildcat, you think?"

"Actually," Tius replied, "the bushes."

"Really? Bushes did that to her? Humans are really fragile."

"Most of us are too, Avvy."

"So when's she going to wake up and get out of my bed?" Avina asked.

"We don't know," Gelvira said. "It could be moments or days. Frankly, I don't know what's wrong with her. Maybe she was just on her feet for days on end and finally passed out, or maybe she hit her head and we could even lose her still. All we can do is watch and wait."

"And only two of us have silk sheets – me and Tius. And I'm really used to them."

Tius suspected that Avina was just being difficult. When Gelvira had met a trader in the lower woods and bought a couple bolts of silk while steering him away from the colony, she did indeed make bed covers and sheets for Avina first and Tius himself second, but by Tius' estimation they weren't any better than the goat wool that most people had, and might be worse when nights were cold.

"If that's what's important," Tius said, "you can rest at my place. I'll sleep outside or something. I'm fine in the dirt and it's my fault."

"Really?" Avina asked, brightening. "You don't have to do that for me."

She looked back at the girl.

"She's got a lot of jewelry. Maybe she'll give us some! That'd make it worth our while, right? Do you see me in the choker or the dangly necklace?"

"I hadn't"-

"And what's wrong with her hair?" Avina continued, not listening to the previous answer. "Is it bleeding or something? You said she hit her head, right?"

"Actually," said a new voice, entering the conversation, "it's rare but normal for humans to have red hair, though except in a few noble families it's usually more orange than bright crimson."

"Erikis!" Avina shouted, starting with a jump. He was probably the only living thing that seemed able to intimidate her.

"I thought you weren't coming back up until tomorrow," Tius said.

"Plans changed," Erikis replied. "May I approach?"

Gelvira nodded, motioning for Avina to step away from the sleeping girl.

Tius watched carefully as Erikis approached. He was both the informal leader of the colony, being the oldest of the Accursed there by far, and probably the most powerful member of it on a personal level. As far as Tius could remember, he'd never displayed the full extent of his abilities, but could probably hold his own against Avina with what he'd shown.

The vast majority of the Accursed looked young, having been young soldiers or young and stupid when they drank the potion, but Erikis was, in his own way, simply ageless – smooth-faced and possessed of long, platinum-blonde hair that he claimed was the high fashion of Hyperborea when he lived there, but with a bearing and countenance that at all times hinted towards his real age in ways that those with only a few centuries behind them did not.

"Well," Erikis said, maintaining his level inflection, voice deep and free of any accent, "the good news is that this young lady is most certainly one of us, so we don't have to worry about what might have happened from leading a normal human all the way up here."

"And the bad news?" Tius asked, knowing that such was portended.

"I left the lowlands early because war is once again brewing in the world," Erikis said. "Do you want to know what over?"

"I'm going to assume it matters."

"The Rose of Kalest, so they say, was drugged and kidnapped by spies from Lysama. Kalest, naturally, threatens war if she is not returned to them, safe and sound."

"What's a Rose of Kalest?" Avina asked.

"In short," Erikis said, "I believe it is her. I could search through her belongings for some token that would prove it, but that would be quite rude."

Avina folded her arms across her chest. "I'm not a child. I want the full answer."

"May I?" Tius asked.

"Of course," Erikis replied, "though I shall correct any factual errors."

"When I was a human in Kalest," Tius said, "the queen was a very kind woman who gave food and money to the poor. The people, and I mean all of us, really loved her, and called her the Ruby of Kalest because she was rich and shining and, of course, it was a ruby because she had bright ruby-red hair."

"The giving, of course," said Erikis, "was a very token effort, something I would not expect young Tius to know. But it was the first anyone near the throne had done in living memory."

"Anyway," Tius continued, "eventually the king and queen had their first kid, a daughter. The entire nation celebrated, because there was a new heir, and since the little girl had bright red hair too, they called her the Rose, since a baby was soft and fragile like a flower."

"And," Erikis added, "no lesser gemstone than the mother's

would suffice, so they had to title her after something else."

"So if this is her," Avina said, "shouldn't she have a palace or something? Why is she out here? Why would she take the potion?"

"That," Erikis said, "I do not know. I suspect we shall have to wait until she wakes up to find out the truth behind the tales."

Avina sighed. "So there's nothing else to do about her right now?"

"Not in particular," Erikis said. "I'll stay here and watch over her if your parents don't mind, and would thank you to not make too much of a fuss about this matter until we know more."

"All right," she said. "You don't have to go back down the mountain, do you, Tius? Want to head to the arena?"

"I'm tired and sore, Avina," he replied. Avina looked up at him, clearly doing her best to produce big doe-eyes and not doing a terribly good job of it. Tius sighed. "But you know, we could do something else if you're really not tired anymore."

"Really?" she asked, eager. "Like what?"

"We'll figure something out," Tius said. He had a few ideas, but shuffled uncomfortably, remembering what Hathus had said and worrying that Avina might have other ideas.

"All right." Avina said with a smile, "Let's go."

They stepped outside, into the fading afternoon. The central 'square' of the Accursed colony was a small plateau with some of their houses and the most important buildings around it. Sheltered on three sides by mountains and on the fourth by a long, shallow, and tree-covered slope before a drop-off, it was essentially invisible until you reached it, as were the paths to the arena and the springs, and other clusters of dwellings or storehouses that the thirty-some Accursed of the colony used on a daily basis.

It was a stark, austere place, but Tius wouldn't have traded it for his old life back under any circumstances; it was home in a way that the gutters and hovels of the city had never been, and it was home to the best friends he had ever had.

"You're not mad at me, are you?" Avina asked.

"Hm?"

"I know you hate it when I say nasty things about humans. And she wasn't even one of them after all that, anyway."

"We all were humans," Tius replied. "Well, all but you. And some of us still like to think of ourselves that way."

"Why?"

"Well," Tius said, "because the humans call us monsters, or think of us as something less, and we'd like to believe we aren't."

"But that's just the thing," Avina said. "Humans are mean. They drive us out of their lands and force us to live in the mountains, right? And they'd kill us if they could, even Erikis says so and he knows better than anyone."

"A lot of humans would, yeah," Tius admitted. "Enough that we can't let them all know we're here. But that doesn't mean that every last one of them is bad. After all, all of the rest of us used to be them. We didn't grow consciences because we took a potion."

"And that's why you brought her up here, right?"

Tius nodded. "That's right. I'd like to think I'm a good person, and that somebody I help out will be at least willing to be one, too."

"I'm glad," Avina said. "I just thought you thought she was pretty."

"Hey!" Tius protested, "I wouldn't put us in danger for that. You know me better than that." He punched her lightly in the upper arm.

Avina smiled. "You're right. Sorry for doubting you like that."

***

A few hours later, the two of them were staring at a game board.

"I don't get it," Avina sighed. "It's fun, but if I stare at little black and white rocks like this for much longer, I'm going to go crazy."

"It's okay," Tius said. "It's late. We can pick up in the morning if you like."

"You can pack it away," she said. "I'll beat you one game or another, but not this one."

"Hey," he said, "I still can't handle Radegond without a handicap, and you keep refusing to take one."

"That's different," Avina said. "She's got a whole hundred years on you or more."

"Well-"

"Tius!" a voice called. It was Frideger, Avina's father.

"What is it?"

"Boss man says the Rose girl is waking up. He seems to think you should be there."

"Right," Tius replied. He turned to Avina. "You should probably come too. You might get to sleep in your own bed."

"No thanks," Avina said. "I'm dead tired. I'll see you in the morning."

Tius followed Frideger hurriedly out of the building and to the other end of town. Inside were Erikis and Gelvira, Frideger and Radegond waiting in the adjoining room out of sight.

Tius ignored the others and walked over to the bedside. The red-haired young woman, Rose of Kalest or no, was indeed beginning to stir.

"Hey," he said softly, calling to her, "hey, can you hear me?"

After a long, sluggish moment, the woman nodded slowly, then opened her bright, blue eyes.

"I... Where am I?"

"A village partway up the mountain you collapsed on. You're... among friends. I'm Tius. And you?"

"My name is Esteri Piritta Metsaa Kalest," she said

So it was true – the Rose of Kalest and heir of house Metsaa was among them.

CHAPTER III

Delphina

Queen Delphina Anu Metsaa Kalest paced up and down the hallway, glowering at the shadows that lingered just outside the reach of her candle. He was late, and that would not do. When she spoke with the ambassador again, she would ask for the man's head on a spit, at least after the job was done. She doubted she would get it, nor did she particularly want it the way she wanted that wretched girl dead and buried.

Briefly, she paused and inspected herself in reflection of a painting's protective glass. She took a breath and watched her face resume a dispassionate frown. Lightly, she touched the little crows' feet at the corners of her eyes and they smoothed and vanished. Small magic, the one real good turn her ancestry had done her it seemed, but it appeased her vanity. Sour at the paltry nature of that inheritance, she went back to pacing.

Miserable Hyperboreans. They had done her a good turn in the past, and Delphina knew that she owed them much of her current position, but at the same time she understood very keenly why her mother had broken ties with her ancestral homeland and all its other scheming agents. They told her very little and probably seldom shared with each other the intricate details of their schemes.

"Majesty," a smooth voice said from the shadows.

"Ulfr, I presume," she replied.

"The same."

"Step into the light, Ulfr," Delphina ordered. "I want to see who I'm talking to."

A tall man approached, into the range of her candle light. Ulfr was in many ways what one would expect from a Hyperborean man: light eyes, hair that was somewhere between silver and gold and fell to his shoulders, and dressed in fine silk clothes that displayed the wealth of his nation without the gaudy weight of jewels or great masses of precious metals.

But Delphina, being half-Hyperborean herself, had known enough of their kind to pick out subtle differences: Ulfr carried himself with the poise of a functionary but the power of a full ambassador or even more, and in his half-smile and tawny amber eyes had a cruelly hungry look that Delphina did not in the least appreciate.

"You," she said, as haughty as possible, "are late, and that is a very dangerous thing to be when you meet with a queen."

"My sincerest apologies, O Delphina, queen of mortals," the silver-tongued Ulfr declared, "but your doctor was quite stubborn in his silence and it took far longer than I anticipated to extract the necessary information."

"Markku?"

"He will recover," Ulfr said, "more or less."

"What did you learn?" Delphina demanded. "What went wrong with the poisoning?"

"Nothing went wrong in the poisoning itself," Ulfr replied. "It seems that your stepdaughter is now one of the Accursed. The transformation does at least temporarily remove most vectors for mortality."

"Well, then," Delphina said, "I was lead to believe that you were going to dispatch her. Will that still be possible?"

"While I do not fear any one of the Accursed," Ulfr said, "this revelation means that the girl shall be taken alive."

"What?" Delphina shrieked, "You expect me to abide such treachery?"

At that moment, she could have killed Ulfr had she lacked the proper restraint; her marriage to Piru was happy, but the people of Kalest were still wedded to their precious 'ruby,' and the memory of that woman, who had once stolen Piru away from Delphina, lived on in the form of her daughter Esteri. Even on the most trivial of subjects, Delphina was not a forgiving woman, and of all subjects this was the closest to her heart.

"Don't let it trouble you, my lovely queen," Ulfr said. "We do not intend to return the child to her station. It is simply that your husband's pedigree is so close to ideal for our purposes, so unless you are willing to give up your own son to the cause..."

"You cannot be serious!" Delphina hissed. "Or did you think I would be willing to pawn off my flesh and blood?"

"I did not think you would be," Ulfr replied. "You are far too honorable a lady. As such, I shall find the girl, and personally conduct her to Hyperborea for inspection. If she fails, she will die. If she is what we need, her purpose will also cost her life. So really, it is only a delay in her demise and a change in my part in it."

"So," Delphina said, mollified, "what is this going to mean for me?"

"Your most radiant highness," Ulfr said, "the girl's trail is unfortunately cold, seeing as I was not here to track her until today. I expect that there might be... incidents... regarding your husband and your war before I manage to reach her. After all, the cursed ones can travel very quickly over land, and that is in the best case scenario."

"And?"

"I imagine that his highness will either want her back or want her dead when he finds out what she is and where."

"How long do I have?"

"I suspect until he awakens," Ulfr replied, "though I could buy you some time by making the doctor disappear."

"That won't be necessary." Delphina replied, steeling herself. "I propose that you handle the girl while I handle starting the war. I can convince my husband to keep what's happened more or less a secret."

"I hope you're right, majesty. For your sake."

At that, Ulfr stepped back and seemed to melt again into

the shadows.

Delphina's rage had subsided. That wretched girl was as good as dead and certainly would never be her problem again, but there was a point of worry that remained: the aims of Hyperborea.

Delphina realized she would have a lot of work to do. Not only did she have to keep her husband resolute and unyielding in his devotion to ruling over this world, but she now needed to reread the journals her mother had left her, and discern the truth behind Ulfr's words. She did not think that he had lied to her, not exactly, but she did think that she needed to know more about Hyperborea and their game.

***

"So," Delphina said, rubbing her husband's shoulders, "that's the way it is?"

She had been fortunate. After her late night she had slept in, but Piru had come to her after hearing Markku's story. Ulfr had been right about that much: after having it no doubt tortured out of him, he thought to tell someone who might be less hostile towards the princess thereafter.

"Even so," Piru said. "My daughter... she lives as a monster! How can I abide this, that it happened because of my decisions and that I must now come to terms with it?"

"It is all for the best," Delphina replied, "so long as Lysama can still be blamed."

"You say that," Piru replied, "and I know that it is true for my people, but my dear, I am not just a king, I am a man."

"And as a man," Delphina said, "it is given you to make the difficult choices that this world throws upon us."

"And I have. I have made choice after choice, and all of them lead only to further heartache."

Delphina kissed him on the neck. "Not all, I hope," she said. "You've made many wise choices, in your life and your reign, though I agree you deserve some ease. That's part of what the entire campaign is about."

"Bitter work for a better future, I know."

"Not just that," Delphina said. "You can leave war to the generals. You'll have more time for me and our son once our efforts are in their hands. You'll relax, and enjoy some of the finer things in life, and when the campaign is done we can tour the vineyards in what used to be Lysama, and maybe even Indris."

"Even so," Piru said, "I must do something about Esteri. I cannot simply ignore her."

"I agree wholeheartedly," Delphina said, "but you can delegate that as well. Hyperborea has eyes and ears and hands in every country, but they favor us in Kalest the most, for I, its queen, am of their blood. We could involve the ambassador, and then there would be nowhere in the world that she could hide."

"I am done in this matter with their assassins," Piru declared firmly. "I never should have used their venom. There were other ways to provoke the people to war, there must have been."

"You can't worry about that now, dear"-

"I do not," Piru said, "but I have taken their advice for my daughter a time too many. Delphina... I am sorry Delphina, but I want to see her again. Just once, to look in her eyes and know if she is still my daughter or if she is a monster that wears my daughter's skin. I will not rest easy until I know that much."

"Who else can you trust?" Delphina demanded, harsher than she intended. It was not hard for her to dote on Piru, nor for her to forgive his occasional slights to her feelings. She was strong, and would be as strong as she had to be to stay with him, but this was entirely too much for her composure. "The ambassador already knows what was intended, if not what transpired. You cannot trust that to a general, nor can you trust in the skill of a common bounty hunter to bring an Accursed here, nor his honor in bringing her in any state you would like to see."

Piru was long silent, looking down at his hands with sorrow in his eyes. He would smile again, Delphina told herself. He would forget the Rose and her mother the Ruby and they would be happy together, at the top of the world. But that was not today. Today, their hearts ached.

"There is one," Piru finally said.

"Really?" Delphina asked. "Who?"

"You are my wife and by that token a Metsaa," Piru said, "so I suppose it is your right to know the story. Many generations ago, so many that I know not for certain their count, Kalest had a young queen. Lysama warred with us in those days, thinking she was too weak to hold the throne. The queen had help – one of the great lords of the land by her side negotiated treaties with Tyrvad and what was then the Indris kingdom to turn the tables on Lysama, and a young knight of peerless skill on the field of battle broke their armies.

"The queen loved them both in different ways: she had great respect for the Lord who had done so much for her, but loved only his deeds. For the knight, though, she held the burning passion that both men held for her. Politics wedded her to the Lord, but he never saw her bed because she pined for her champion.

"The way I have heard it told, one of the chambermaids of the queen attempted a solution, to dose the knight with the Cursed Potion and turn him into a monster that would be thrown out of high society, and the queen could forget him. But the chambermaid did something terribly right: the potion did not seem at first to change the knight, and indeed though it was claimed to the world that the Queen's first child belonged to her husband, all three knew who was truly the father.

"The Knight, though, over years watched his beloved queen begin to fade from the beauty of her youth, and her husband slide into the ruin of great old age. But he was standing still, unchanged despite the years. Like the Accursed, he was frozen in the moment he had drunk the foul potion, but somehow it had taken his mortality without turning him into a beast of magic.

"Eventually, as it became more and more obvious that there was something different about him, he retreated into the forest, telling only the queen and the son he knew to be his where he was going. Since then, in times of great or personal need, we who are his descendants have visited him for the counsel he can give thanks to his great many years, or more rarely to beseech his supreme skill that only countless lifetimes could grant.

"This man... Esteri is my child, and thus he is her grandfather of grandfathers as well. I can trust his honor and his skill beyond all others. I shall ask him to recover her for me."

Delphina considered the matter. She considered it a problem of the highest order, a factor that she could not have expected and even knowing of it could not predict. If anyone could outpace Ulfr to his prize, it would be this immortal man, and if the immortal brought Esteri back there was no certainty Delphina could ever be rid of her without losing Piru.

"If I may say," Delphina replied, "I think there are some flaws in your plan. The first is that if this man is as honorable as you say, he will not think kindly on what we have done, which necessitates some deception. Namely, we must hope he can find her from Lysama, because that is where we have told the world she will be."

"And a second?"

"A second is that while the hunt for Esteri is no doubt very important, it seems a waste of such a talented and powerful man as this one. Therefore, I think you should bring him here for the war in whole. An immortal is the perfect thing for ruling the world, especially when no doubt Lysama and the other nations will dredge up the potion eventually. Let him prepare not only to find your daughter, but to fight the Accursed... In fact, let him pass his great skill in fighting them onto a legion of our soldiers, so that we do not ourselves have to wield monsters."

"Well," said Piru, "you are right, as usual. It will delay his efforts, though, and who could say what might happen in the intervening time? If she is now a monster she could hurt the people and reveal herself and through that our plans. If she is still my daughter, she could herself be hurt."

"Patience, dear husband," Delphina said. It was easy to counsel patience when what she desired was for this immortal's hunt to be indefinitely postponed – or at least put back long enough that Ulfr would find the girl first. "We can only do so much here and now. Will finding your immortal take long?"

"I will be gone from the capital for two or three days," Piru replied.

"Then for today, you had best make sure affairs here are in order," Delphina said, "among the generals, among the servants, and particularly..." She laid back on the bed. "Right here in this room."

***

Much later, Delphina stood in the wings, watching as her husband prepared for his brief absence in a critical time. The grand hall was largely empty – only the highest generals were part of this council.

"My liege," said General Rikhard, with his usual excessive formality and a salute, "may I ask why we have been summoned here?"

"If I did not intend to tell you," Piru said, "I would not have summoned you. On the morrow, I will be leaving the capital. I shall be going alone and I expect to return the next day or the day after that. In the meantime, matters of nations are reaching a head, and I will expect you to react to them rather than waiting for me to return."

"And," said General Katri – Kalest's only female general, whom Delphina quite respected for that distinction – "I am to assume that you do not intend to simply leave probable courses of action up to our discretion?"

She was still a soldier, though. No way with words.

"Quite," replied Piru. The king had little patience for formalities at times like this. "The most likely event is that the Indris Confederation either agrees to help us in our war with Lysama, agrees to grant our armies passage through their lands, or refuses to do either. In any of the cases, our armies will shortly march into Indris."

"Majesty!" Katri gasped. Many of the other generals also seemed uncomfortable with the idea, and why shouldn't they be? They were generals, and all five of them noble-born. They were raised on stories of the nobility of knights, of justice and honor in battle. Such a move as to refuse the Confederation's sovereignty, no matter how sublime a stroke of tactics, was anathema to that school of thinking. Thankfully, Piru had not chosen the generals to promote and include in this venture hastily or foolishly, and Delphina was confident that they would be, overall, either flexible in their morals or at least obedient to their king.

"In the first two cases, we shall naturally march directly there, and unless trouble arises, through on to our true foe. In the last case, I have made it clear that I will hold the Confederation complicit in my daughter's kidnapping should they refuse us even passage through their borders. We cannot afford to take the strongholds in the mountain passes – your own advised me that such a campaign would take months in the best of cases, while a march through Indris territory would allow us to sweep into Lysama from the south, where they have no fortifications and do not anticipate attack."

The generals nodded sagely. That, they could accept. Their king would consider Indris' failure to render aid itself an act of war, and he let them believe that Indris already knew that such was the case. They could accept that. They could do that, any of them.

"You will march due west until the mountains appear on the horizon," Piru continued, "and then turn south, staying out of what Lysama can sight from their fortifications and giving Indris spies little time to report our hostile movements back to the masters. I entrust this duty, the punitive campaign against Lysama and if necessary against Indris, to generals Sauli, Rikhard, and Tahvo and their forces. General Katri and her forces are to go as well if Indris proves hostile. If Indris cooperates, Katri and her forces shall remain here, as shall General Anselm and his forces."

It was a good plan – Katri commanded entirely cavalry and thus could reinforce the front if the situation went sour, and Anselm was an old hand at playing defense and of all the generals the most likely to make some objection to ensuring the final conquest of Indris and Lysama. Delphina knew it was a good plan because it was her plan. Oh, the abstracts of marching and fighting, who should give battle where – those were all Piru's. But when it came to determining the use of people, Delphina felt herself unequaled.

"If all goes well in my venture, we shall have reinforcements for the major sieges in Lysama in any case. I do not expect the march shall have to begin these next few days while I am away, but if it does, General Sauli is to be considered the first among you, and you are to follow his orders in the field as though they were my own. Is that clear?"

In unison, all five generals gave a solid, "Yes, sir!"

That was a good crop of soldiers, Delphina thought, leaning against the pillar. There was the lock-step obedience she expected, the willingness to do whatever was asked if Piru simply twiddled his finger. Delphina considered herself loyal to her husband, but she did not go that far.

"Excellent," Piru said. "I will speak with General Sauli privately. The rest of you may leave."

The four dismissed saluted, and shouted for glory to Kalest. In that, Delphina thought, their wishes would be granted.

Once they had departed the marble hall, Sauli spoke.

"And the queen?" he asked.

"What about me, Sauli?" Delphina asked. "Do you object to the presence of one of your sovereigns to the other?"

Of all the generals, Delphina knew Sauli the best, in that she had known him before he was a general and she was queen.

The man rather despised her now, though he would never say that he did nor why. Delphina imagined, owing that his bitterness had only appeared after her marriage, that he may have been slighted when she pursued the king over him, but that thought only amused her. Let him burn with envy – he never would have stood a chance in any world.

"I merely noted, highness," he replied with venom, "that his majesty said he wished to speak with me privately."

"And this is private," Delphina replied. "Have you forgotten that I share the King's bed, privy to the words he speaks as he dreams? I daresay that if a matter weighs heavily on his highness' mind, I am likely to already know it."

Delphina smirked as Sauli stood in place, the good little soldier, fighting to restrain any anger at her sly barbs from showing on his face.

"Would you like me to predict what orders you will receive?" she asked.

"I believe," General Sauli said, "That is between me and his majesty."

"It is fine," said Piru. "Delphina does already know what I am to say, and you can be confident that she will know sooner or later what you have to say as well."

"I see."

"I have further orders for you, in the event that Indris is somehow cooperative. If that happens, you are to establish an occupation of key confederation cities. It will be best if their armies are convinced to march on Lysama and we can take possession while their soldiers fight our war, but if we are simply allowed to pass, we must still take pains to secure our position."

"Devious," Sauli said. "The Confederation will not be prepared for such a strike, but I must wonder if Tyrvad and Arynias will stand for it. Katri and Anselm have a sizable force under their banner, but not enough to guard two fronts."

"I have prepared for that. Our allies will ensure that retribution comes slowly, if it comes at all. By then, Lysama and

Indris will be firmly under our control, and we can redirect our efforts, along with fresh recruits."

"If you keep going like that," Sauli said, "you might just end up ruling the world before you're done."

"That would, of course, be ideal."

"I would be out of a job," the general joked.

"And a good thing, too," replied Piru. "You could find yourself a wife rather than being stuck on the march half the time."

Sauli smiled. "Perhaps. I shall be sure, then, to execute your orders with the utmost efficiency. Lysama, and Indris as well, shall fall under our banner."

"Then you may go."

Sauli gave his own salute. "For the dominion to come!"

CHAPTER IV

Esteri

Esteri felt a warm, soft bed beneath her, silken sheets wrapped around her body. She breathed a sigh of relief. She was back at home, in her own bed, and none of the horrible things she remembered so clearly had ever happened. What a vile nightmare! Yet, it felt so real. She remembered so many sensations so vividly, the separate agonies of poison and potion each ravaging her body, the thrill of running free into the night, reborn. She remembered the thorns and branches that scratched at her skin, the stench of the hovel from which she had stolen a coat to cover somewhat her worrisome lack of dress, the bone-deep weariness after running and walking for days on end, climbing a mountain that seemed made of thorn-bushes, and finally the moment of relief when she had slid off to sleep when her body would simply go no further.

It was dark out, Esteri could guess that much without opening her eyes, but she was no longer tired and had the sneaking suspicion that there was someone in her room. Likely a chambermaid picking up and dusting, but...

The more Esteri thought, the more she realized that there were still a few things wrong. The air smelled clear and cold as it did in the summer palace up in the mountains, and held none of the perfumes of any of her regular abodes. Lamp oil, sage smoke, some meaty odor perhaps, a hint of damp foliage somewhere near, none of these were normal. The thought occurred to Esteri very quickly, as the haze of sleep faded from her mind, that she could very well be somewhere quite alien, and all her nightmares a grim reality.

To shut her eyes to that world or to open them? It was no question at all – Esteri could not sleep forever, so which life awaited her, that of the princess or that of the fugitive, she would have to face it sooner or later.

Esteri opened her eyes.

She was in a small room, lit by a single clay lamp on the top of a squat, sturdy, and rustic chest of drawers, and she was not alone.

"I..." she stammered to the nearest of the four other figures, a young man with sandy brown hair, bright blue eyes, and a kind smile. "Where am I?"

"A village partway up the mountain you collapsed on," he said. "You're... among friends. I'm Tius. And you?"

"My name is Esteri Piritta Metsaa Kalest," she said. She realized she should have thought it foolish to give her real name, much less her full name, but somehow it didn't bother her. It just seemed somehow natural, right.

"It's as I thought," one of the others said. He was a man with long, platinum-blond hair, a narrow frame, and a hawkish face. There was something about him that made Esteri uncomfortable, though she quickly wrote it off as a passing resemblance to the Queen, meaning he was likely of Hyperborean extraction. Oddly, Esteri felt she could not rightly place his age – he should have looked young, but there was something about him that just felt old. She put it out of mind, guessing he could not be past his thirties.

"Under normal circumstances," the Hyperborean man said, "I would prefer to stay out of national politics, but when Tius carries it up the mountain to our home, I cannot ignore it. So tell me, what happened to bring you to our village?"

They already knew her name, Esteri thought, there was no point keeping the truth from them. The only people the full truth could hurt were her father and the queen, if even them. She wished she understood why this all had happened. She remembered it had to do with Lysama, and probably war, but that raised more questions than it answered in her mind.

"I am here because I was obliged to flee my home," she declared. "An attempt was made on my life by the order of Queen Delphina and with the blessing of my father, King Piru. I would now be dead had fate not conspired to save me."

"Interesting," the Hyperborean said, his expression and tone perfectly neutral.

"I," Esteri began, and then hesitated. Would she really tell these people how she had survived? Her instincts were insisting she should the same as they had told her she should give her full name, and for that matter the same way they had told her which way to run. She decided to trust them. "I live only because I drank the Cursed Potion as an antidote to a vile poison that would have killed me. I accept what I have done, but if this makes any in your village uncomfortable with my presence among you I shall leave immediately, though I would much appreciate clothes better suited to the road, and at least a meal as I have not had but scraps since I fled the palace."

Another of the people around her spoke – this one a woman somewhat older than Esteri herself, with bob-cut black hair, dark eyes, and a motherly bearing.

"Don't worry yourself about it," she said. "We're all... a little different here. I don't know how you managed to find your way right to our doorstep, but you did. I'll get you some dinner."

The motherly woman hurried out of the room, and Esteri knew where she was. The Accursed Colony. For something that she had thought to be nothing more than a rumor, she had found it with remarkable ease and accuracy. Was that the way with all of the Accursed? Did they call to each other somehow, was she drawn here from the moment she drank that potion?

Esteri sat up, pulling the sheets around her as she did, painfully aware her slip was somewhat tattered and perhaps a bit sheer.

"Thank you all for your kindness," Esteri said. "I had hoped to find this place, though I cannot truthfully say that I know what I will do now that I have." She looked up at the young man. "Tius, was it?"

"Yes, your majesty," he said.

"No majesties here," Esteri replied. She did not expect these people to know protocol but did think they might trip over their own two feet trying to follow it, and felt it would be better if no one bothered. "Esteri will do, 'princess' if you wish. I have lost my claim to my birthright, more or less, and this will be harder for everyone if titles and address are an issue." She looked about the room. "I mean that for everyone."

"I'm sorry," Tius said.

"No..." Esteri sighed. "I just wished to thank you for bringing me up here, that's all." She took off one of her rings and handed it to him. "Here. For the service you rendered me." Esteri didn't like feeling indebted to anyone, much less someone that she had only just met. Now, at least, they were even. She turned to the once-Hyperborean. "And you, sir? I would guess you are the village head man."

"More or less," he admitted with a shrug, "though by my reckoning it would preferably be less. My name is Erikis, and I am the oldest of us. Forgive me if I don't provide an exact number, I stopped really counting when it hit a thousand."

"All the same," Esteri said, "I would ask your permission to remain here for at least a brief while and prepare myself for my next move. Things are changing in this world, and I wish to ensure that they change for good rather than for ill."

"We have a rule here," Erikis replied as the motherly woman came back with a small bowl full of a brown stew, "and that is that we always do what we can to help each other. Now, judging by the fact that you are starving"--Esteri had already begun to eat, ignoring manners--"and were quite firmly unconscious, I have a feeling you are in no fit state to aid the community, but that does not mean we will not help you. Perhaps if you could tell me more of your situation?"

Esteri gulped down several great spoonfuls of what tasted like venison, then spoke.

"There is a lot to tell," she admitted. "Do you think I could have a moment to compose my thoughts?"

"Of course," Erikis said.

"Is there anything you need in the meantime, princess?" Tius asked her.

"I'll be fine for now," Esteri said. "Thank you again."

Tius and the woman bowed, and all three turned to leave the room.

"Oh!" Esteri said. "Miss...?"

"Gelvira, ma'am."

"Is there any chance I could borrow a change of clothes?"

"Certainly," Gelvira replied. "I'll find you something nice."

***

Esteri ran her fingers through her hair, trying to work out the knots. Dressed in the rustic garb Gelvira had lent her and still covered in dust and scratches, she was not ever going to be presentable by the standards of court, but she could try at least to look a little less like a beggar. After all, these people now held her fate in their hands, and Esteri did not like the feeling.

And yet... she had to trust on them. Otherwise she had nothing, and no way to help herself. So how to ensure that trust? Well, had they really meant her ill, Esteri suspected that she wouldn't have woken up at all, much less with all of her jewelry still in her possession. Even her signet ring, which had been in the pocket of her shabby coat rather than on her person, was untouched.

She thought of the three of the Accursed she had met. Tius seemed more or less like a normal young man, Gelvira seemed somewhat older than she appeared in her habits, and Erikis... even letting the thought that he was ancient settle in, there was still something about him that was off.

Esteri steeled herself. He was the one with authority, so she was going to have to deal with him. She didn't expect much, but she did hope that she could at least buy some supplies and change her jewels for coinage so that she didn't have to walk days on end with nearly nothing to eat again.

There was that, at least. While Esteri wasn't exactly comfortable with her condition, she had to admit it had its advantages. Before, she doubted she could have gone a day without food or on her feet with as few complaints. It was no wonder any more why the potion kept surfacing... it had an allure to it that almost made up for being something other than human.

Esteri had seen her reflection since her change – she looked no different, save for the dirt and such, than she had before. And even Erikis, old by his own account, could be mistaken for a normal person. She had expected quite the opposite, having read many tales of the damned who shambled forth to war, massive and deformed bodies ready for battle, or at the least the madmen that glowed with inner fire or whose limbs twisted with vile contortions.

Perhaps only the fortunate survived?

Esteri shook her head, adjusted her bodice yet again, and then looked towards the door.

She strode out confidently into the room to which the others had retreated to find a small sitting room of sorts: a couple chairs, a few more around a table, and Tius seemingly sleeping in one of the more upholstered of the lot.

It was late, she reflected, bottling up her annoyance at not being able to make an entrance, and they had not slept as she had. Still, it seemed rude to keep a princess, even a beggared princess, waiting.

Upon scanning the room and realizing that, yes, there was no sign of Gelvira nor Erikis, nor anyone else for that matter, she took a seat in what looked to be the second most comfortable chair in the room, that being the one positioned next to Tius' own. She reflected that like the bed and the clothes it may have been quite quaint in appearance, but was more than serviceable.

A thought stuck her.

"Tius?" she asked in a plain speaking voice. "Can you hear me?"

There was no reply. He was quite soundly asleep.

"Good," Esteri said with a smile. "I'd hoped you'd be able to hear me out."

She took a deep breath.

"How do you deal with this curse, Tius? It's the strangest thing. It feels so much like a blessing, a gift, deep in my blood. There's... power there. Something that I was always meant to have, something that fills me yet leaves me hungry for more. And I'm afraid of it. I'm afraid that who I am now is balanced on the edge of an abyss, ready to fall forever."

Esteri sighed. She could never have said such things for a waking soul to hear. She had to be strong. Strong when her mother died, strong when her father remarried, strong as she came of age, strong as she prepared to some day lead her nation, and now strong as she had to leave that life behind. There was no room for being afraid, not where anyone could see it.

"I don't know," she said. "Maybe it will all work out for the best, but somehow I doubt that. No matter what I look like, I'm someone, something different than I was. I can't ever really go back to what I had before, especially not when daddy... when my father conspired to have me killed."

The memory of that still burned, and Esteri did not want to believe that what she had overheard was true. She didn't want to believe that her father could offer her up as a sacrifice, or scheme to bring the world to war. Her father had been a good man. He had loved her. It all had to be Delphina's doing, and yet... the fact remained he had known and hadn't stopped her, even if it was.

"And yet... you seem to be living here just fine. Removed from the world, maybe, but you looked happy enough. I admit, I haven't seen much of your world, but it doesn't look so bad, what I have seen. Perhaps some day I'll even come back here, since I've got all the time in the world and no place in it anymore. I've got to go to Lysama first, since heavens know somebody has to set the record straight, but after that? I'm not sure what else I could do. I'm going to live basically forever if I understand this right, so it would seem a shame to..."

To just end it. The thought had crept into Esteri's mind more than once since becoming a monster, the thought that she had survived for some reason, and when that was done with she could lay down and accept her fate. She didn't know how to do anything else, but with enough time she was sure she could learn. Still, it was a hard thought to put away, especially when going to warn Lysama and reveal herself to the world meant that even if her stepmother didn't manage somehow to get her killed, the Lysamans, or even an angry mob, could.

"I wonder what life you left behind," Esteri said after a lengthy silence. "You don't look like you were a soldier. Neither does Gelvira, for that matter. You two must have had friends, family, a home. You must have had people close to you, and places in the world that you had to let go of in order to start over here. What were they? How did you manage?"

Naturally, Tius made no reply. That was something Esteri might be able to ask him later, as saying it out loud she was honestly quite curious.

"Well," she said, "maybe you'll feel like telling me some time soon. Until then, I guess what I'm trying to say is that I don't know what the future holds to me. I know I have to face it and yet I don't know how I'm going to. I guess I'll just have to find out one day, one moment at a time. Maybe I'll live, and maybe I'll die, and maybe I'll turn all the way into some ravening beast, but it's not like I can see the future."

She closed her eyes and tried to imagine it.

"The future looks pretty bleak," she said. "There's war on the horizon, and death, and pain, but that can't be all there is to it. Castles bathed in flame and lands cracked in the grasp of great black arms. All that is there, but there has to be to be something more, some light behind it all."

Esteri sighed.

"Why is death all I can think of? I'm alive, and as long as that's true, I can do something to change at least my own future, right? Well, I'll start when Erikis gets back. I don't want to trouble your village or bring trouble to it, so I'll get on my way to Lysama just as fast as I can."

Esteri looked over Tius. Still slumbering soundly, oblivious to everything that she had said, which was exactly the way she wanted it. Somehow, her burden felt a little lighter now. Monster or Accursed or whatever she was, Esteri was still determined that she knew what was right, and if it killed her, fine. If it didn't, she'd find a way to live.

"Thank you for listening," she said. "We'll talk again some time, I'm sure. Probably when you're awake."

***

Erikis entered what Esteri guessed was under an hour later, with Gelvira and two others, presumably important persons or decision makers of the village. One was a severe woman named Radegond who looked somewhat older than most of the Accursed did, her dark brown hair in a tight bun and her cold blue eyes applying withering glares wherever she looked. The other was a young-looking man named Frideger with a slight pot belly, short-cropped black hair, a short full beard and moustache, and a jovial manner.

To keep from waking Tius, though he seemed to sleep very soundly, Esteri had insisted on speaking outside.

"I have decided what I mean to do," she said. "My father intends war against Lysama, with my loss as the cause. Therefore, I must go to Lysama by the quickest road, both to warn its leaders and to unravel the web of lies that is no doubt being spun regarding my life or my death."

"I see," Erikis said.

"To that end, I would ask you for supplies for my journey. Food and clothes, primarily, and if you have them, maps by which I could find my way and a compass to use with them. I am willing to pay with the jewelry I wear, the exact terms of which I am sure we can negotiate further when I see what I would receive."

"I thought you might ask something like that," Erikis said,

"and I have a counter-proposal. Keep your jewels. You are one of us, and war is sure to affect us all sooner or later, so we will aid you for the asking, and what's more"-

"What's more," Radegond interrupted, "is that you're a snot-nosed child and even Tius has at least a decade of combat training on you, so if you expect to live for five minutes in what is likely to be the middle of a gods-damned war zone, you are going to need to spend some time learning your abilities and limits, and you are still going to need an escort."

Esteri balked. How was she supposed to reply to that? On one hand, the tone and insults would have another noble-woman, in her own palace, calling for guards. On the other, it constituted an offer of aid she guessed, so was she to accept it with the ridicule?

"Thank you, Radegond," Erikis said, covering his face with his hand. "That is, to put it in a very particular tone, the situation. We would like to spend a week or so instructing you, and if you would have our aid, would not send you alone into danger."

Esteri breathed a sigh of relief. That she knew how to handle.

"I accept your kind offer," she said. "I would like to begin my instruction as soon as possible, and would also appreciate being introduced to whomsoever is to accompany me on my journey."

"Well," Frideger said, "as to that second bit, the four of us will be coming, and maybe three more, depending on what they'd like to do. Tius, you've already met, and I don't think he'll say no."

"And the other two?"

"We'll introduce you tomorrow." Gelvira said. "One is a young man named Hathus, He's really a dear, though he likes to act his age, which is to say seventy something, so you should be prepared for that." She paused, and took Frideger's hand. "The other is our daughter, Avina. It's her room you're borrowing for the moment, though you're welcome to stay as long as you're here. I'm sure we can work something out."

An entire family of Accursed? Esteri supposed it made sense: if one of them was put in a bad situation, those close to him or, Esteri suspected, her might make the choice to join their relatives in exile. But Gelvira looked so young! It was hard to believe that she could have an adult daughter, as Esteri guessed Avina had to be from the size of her bed and the fact that she was going on this journey rather than being left back, possibly with her mother as well. Perhaps they had simply adopted the girl...

"I'll be looking forward to meeting both of them," Esteri said.

"I'll make sure to get them for your training, then," Radegond said. "We start at dawn with basic hand-to-hand combat, and since we've got precious little time to get you into shape, we're going to go straight through to dusk with few if any little breaks, so if you think you might not be able to keep up for twice as long, you'd better get some rest first."

"Thank you, miss Radegond."

"Don't thank me until we're through," she replied. "You'll probably be singing a different tune then."

Radegond left, stalking off into the night.

"Is she always like that?" Esteri asked.

"Not always," Gelvira said, "but when she's thinking business, she is."

"I see," Esteri said. "Should I take her advice?"

"Maybe not right away," Frideger replied. "We can go back inside, and I'll fix you a drink or two. If there's one thing we can still do up here as well as they do in the flatlands, it's brew with what we've got."

"Thank you," Esteri said. "It's a very kind offer."

By her estimation they could also cook, though she had to admit that her hunger, which still wasn't quite abated, could have played a part in that.

"Now dear," Gelvira said, "perhaps we should leave that off for later." She turned to Esteri. "I may love my husband, but

53

his desire to make alcohol out of anything that grows is a little strange, and neither he nor anyone else can guarantee the flavor of a particular grog or spirit. They're different every time."

Esteri nodded, though not entirely sure what was meant by that.

"Trust me," Frideger said, "I know how to brew. I've practiced it longer than any human has been alive."

"And if your concoction is especially good," Erikis said, "then the princess will awaken hung over and just in time for Radegond's ministrations."

"Oh, there is that," Frideger admitted. "I suppose you'll be wanting a stiff drink after, rather than before."

"Well, then," Esteri said, "we shall see what tomorrow brings rather than worrying about it right now. I may not be particularly tired, but I'll take your words to heart."

Esteri had not been afraid of Radegond and what the dawn would bring before, but now had to admit some serious misgivings.

CHAPTER V

Piru

King Piru Rekorius Metsaa Kalest rode from the gates of his castle in search of a myth. Ukko the Immortal was as much a legend as he was a man, though the tales that were told throughout Kalest applied many names to what were no doubt his deeds. Sometimes a man, sometimes a monster, sometimes a spirit of the woods, it was hard to separate the tales that had been invented from those that had their basis in fact.

His origin, while a secret of House Metsaa, was known in a twisted way to the wider world, stories of an ancient queen who loved a noble knight, and of the knight's vanishing from the world. They gave it a hundred reasons, the entertainers who sang and spoke sometimes in the halls of the palace at invitation, and the scholars who recorded and categorized story after story. None of them guessed the truth, for it was far too preposterous to imagine.

And then there were other tales, those that Piru knew to be based on his interventions in the past, or at least suspected that they might be. Stories of a warrior that emerged from the morning mist to fight on behalf of Kalest and vanished back into it at the battle's end, or similarly elusive champions that rescued princesses or put down rampaging, monstrous Accursed.

Piru had met the man once – in his youth, his father had taught him a path through the ancient forest that sat at the heart of Kalest, a remnant of days before nations and kings that had never been marred by fire or axe. It was a terrifying, haunted place, and a mere few steps into its border, it felt like the civilized world was so far away that you would never again reach it.

Supposedly, all of Kalest had once been covered in a great forest like that, called the Birds' Wood for only the birds or those guided by them could find their way. What was left was not that tangled; there were signs and landmarks and the steady tell of a compass or the sun that would eventually guide a stranded traveler to its borders... but it was easy to believe the ancient tales.

There, somewhere close to the heart of the forest, was the dwelling of probably the oldest creature in the world. The dwelling, on the outside at least, looked the part, made as it was of unmortared, cyclopean stones weathered by eons in the forest and lashed together by the roots of twisted and ancient trees. Magnificent, in its own way, and timeless.

When Piru had been brought to the place as a child, his and his father's host had not been in, but royalty being royalty they had made themselves more or less at home. The interior of that abode was less alien than Piru's youthful imagination had wagered; though most of what was within was made from bone or pelts or dead-fallen branches, they were fine enough things to be familiar to a prince, and why should they not be? Their owner and no doubt maker had ages more than any tradesman to perfect their manufacture, even if the skills he had learned in his first life were those of war.

When their host had returned, young Piru had been twice shocked; once, on seeing the silhouette in the doorframe, massive enough to fill the great portal side to side; the second, when the figure stepped through the door and was revealed to be a more or less ordinary man carrying a dead deer across his shoulders.

Ukko, as Piru remembered him, was very strange. He did not look to be the massive brute that one would expect from the ancient hermit of the forest, but instead a man who could have been at home in the courts of Kalest, slender though strong, clean shaven with light brown hair that fell between his shoulder blades. He regarded the world with a kind smile and spoke with a soft voice, and though he had no doubt seen the events of any day so many times before, he seemed to take great interest in the news of the world that was brought to him, and even in the paltry chaos of simply living.

Piru and his father had stayed as Ukko's guest that night, though, which afforded Piru a chance to see another side of their host and ancestor. The young prince woke in the middle of the night, thirsty, and in searching for some convenient source of water happened upon Ukko in practice, behind the old and megalithic structure. Upon a stone dais, he set a great branch that must have fallen somewhere in the forest, and in his hand held a long, single-edged sword with a subtle curve. As Piru watched from the shadows. Ukko struck the branch a mighty blow, and as it fell another and another. Before the last piece had struck the earth, Ukko had made so many cuts, each flawless and precise, that Piru had lost count of them.

Though he seemed ready to repeat the demonstration and though Piru was certain he had been silent as the dead, Ukko turned to him, asked after his needs, fetched the water and sent the young prince back to bed. All the same, young Piru had not slept quickly, for he heard the faint echoes of more shows of skill that no mortal could ever hope to live to replicate.

This was a man, Piru mused after recalling that night, who could alone turn the tides of a battle, even a war. There could be no doubt that Delphina, knowing only a fraction what Piru himself did, had been right – with Ukko helping them, Kalest's armies could bring the world to heel beneath a single banner, and if he was able to transmit even a fraction of his skill to a class of mortals, there would be no need for the vile potion that had won wars and ruined lives over countless generations past.

These were Piru's thoughts as he reached the border of that

ancient, nameless forest, largely unchanged. Part of that was due to an old and long-standing edict of the royal family that only dead wood could be gathered from the forest, though such orders would likely not have held if not for the fact that the trees were too knotted and gnarled to make good boards or planks, and most of the peasantry held the place in reverent fear, thinking it haunted.

For the latter reason, the branches on the edge of what was considered the haunted forest were decorated. Effigies made from carved bone, twigs, straw, and strips of cloth were hung from the boughs of the old trees. Every village that bordered the forest had their own reasons for the practice. Some made dolls in the image of those missing or deceased, hoping that the supposed spirits of the forest would recognize them and either send them home or lead them on. Others, fearful of the alleged supernatural happenings, hoped the tiny, crude fac-similes would distract whatever lived within those darkened woods from approaching and possibly spiriting away real humans.

As with most peasant superstitions, it was all rubbish, of course. But as with most peasant superstitions, there was no point attempting to educate the masses out of it: they would always do things their way, and it hurt no one to allow them to do it.

Piru did not know which superstition held on the southern side of the forest, by which he meant to enter, but he did know that the peasantry held their monarch with enough reverent awe to not question why he rode towards the 'haunted' place, nor would they likely challenge him when he emerged in the company of another.

With some difficulty, he found the path he had been taught, starting at a great obelisk of stone embraced by a twisted tree that grew about it. Carefully, he took his bearings, and when he was not looking at his compass or for the next landmark along the path, his eyes darted between the shadows that lin-gered beneath those branches even at midday. Piru was not superstitious. He did not fear wood-spirits or the like. But, at the same time, he was not a fool and did at times fear wolves, the likes of which very well might patrol in the darkness.

But no wolves emerged from the shadows, and not too long after dusk, Piru reached the great, cyclopean dwelling.

"Ukko!" he called. "Forefather of Metsaa! I am Piru, son of Jyrki, and head of the house of Metsaa. I would have words with you."

A moment later, Ukko the Immortal emerged from his dwelling.

It struck Piru then, that he had not realized as a child just how young was the face of this ancient man, how vibrant his form. Esteri had received without immediate revulsion suitors with no fewer years than showed on her ancient ancestor. And to think this was his face after he had already accomplished many great deeds! Were all men in those days stronger sooner than they were now, or had Ukko always been something far beyond ordinary folk?

"I take it that there is ill news abroad," Ukko said, wistful, "or I might have expected another visitor. All the same, I welcome any news that comes to my abode. Come in, please."

Piru nodded, and followed Ukko inside. The hall was essentially as he remembered it, even as large as his childish perspective had imagined when so many other things seen as gigantic through a child's eyes might be small in truth.

"It is as you say, ill news," Piru said. "War is on the horizon."

"Is it now? Well, then, it's no wonder you've come. Most of your ancestors have, when the winds portend war." He walked over to the fireplace and lifted a small pot from it

"There's no reason to rush the evening, though," Ukko said. "I've found some of the plants in this forest make a fine herbal tea, though I confess it is a little different every time. Would you like some?"

"I would thank you for the hospitality," Piru replied, "though this is a very serious matter."

"I am sure," Ukko said, "and we shall certainly discuss it by the night's end, but perhaps you would indulge me with how your life has run since last we met? I assume from the flecks of grey in your beard that it has been many years, and you are now king." He poured hot water into a pair of small cups of polished stone. "Have you a queen? An heir? I should like to meet a child again. You are always so... unexpected."

"I am king," Piru said, "and have had two queens in my time, and a child by each."

"Now that is unusual," Ukko said. "There must to be a tale to it."

"Not much," said Piru, mood quickly darkening. "Aliisa, my first wife, I loved very dearly even from before I saw you last, but a sudden sickness took her from me ten years past. I thought my heart would never mend, though custom said that with but one child I should wed once more. Delphina... she is a wonderful woman, mostly, and I fear sometimes I do not treat her as she deserves for her patience and devotion to me."

"And in all of time," Ukko replied, "I shall never hear another story like that. I should love some more details, for the lives of the young are ever-new, but it seems the matters that brought you here weigh very heavy on your heart, and you would speak them sooner rather than later."

"It does not just have to do with war," Piru said. "At the heart of the matter is my elder child, Esteri. That, and not the clash of nations, is what first and foremost brings me to beseech your aid, grandfather-of-grandfathers."

"Tell me," Ukko said, interested and far less upbeat than previous.

"Esteri was stricken by poison," Piru said. "Perhaps meant for her, perhaps meant for any of our house. While she rested on her death-bed, the doctor that attended her mixed for her a draught of the Cursed Potion, for no other medicine in this world could even hope to bring about her survival. I know not what has or has not changed within her, though, for she was spirited away from the palace that very night, likely by the same agency that sought her life."

Ukko seemed to consider this. He sipped his tea, but his eyes did not for a moment leave Piru. It seemed in those moments as though Ukko could see everything, and though Piru dearly hoped that it was not so, neither was the deep remorse carved into his face a lie. He regretted his decision the moment he saw his daughter stricken and he would regret it until the day he died.

At last, Ukko spoke.

"It is a grave matter," he said, "and I can see why this portends war. I trust you have some evidence as to what force made such a strike."

"It is Lysama," Piru said, "Our ancient enemy, possibly in league with Indris."

"And what shall you do?"

"For the good of the world," Piru said, "I would end our pointless struggles for all time, and raise a single banner for the lands both east and west. I would see this war be the last bloodshed between Kalest and Lysama, and reign over the lands from a united throne."

"A noble goal," Ukko admitted, "but you must know that you are not the first to attempt it. In this world, as I have seen, there are things that happen only once, the pleasures and pains of single days, what makes one man laugh or another weep, a faint smile or a single tear – they shall never come again. And then there are the things that happen time and time again, the clash of nations, the cycle of wars and peace, and each time it is always the same."

Ukko sighed.

"How many times have I seen banners raised for conquest? How many times has this continent been rendered awash in blood? And after how many years do the same borders stand, or emerge swiftly from their alteration? I have lost track."

"What, then, would you counsel me to do?" Piru asked. "Am I to let be this offense? To wait until it is Lysaman banners being planted on Kalesti soil?"

"You can only do what you feel is right," Ukko said. "Though it pains me to learn of this, your pain at your daughter's fate can be no less, and for mortal men the dream of a lasting peace might be achieved. Perhaps, if you are triumphant, it will last for your time, and the time of your children before the peace is fractured and war rages again, before Lysama rises from its ashes and once more locks blades with Kalest."

"I ask you, lord Ukko, to aid me in this venture," Piru said, "to emerge from this forest and lift your sword on the behalf of Kalest. I have seen what I feel must be only the barest demonstration of your skill. Just as nations war in this world each half century or so, you must know that every time they resurrect the vile potion that turns men into monsters, and in so doing they create weapons from their populace. I do not wish to do this to my people, to repeat the sins that kings before me have indulged in, but I am not so foolish to think that we will not have to fight monsters."

"And I?"

"I would ask you to teach some fraction of your skill to mortal soldiers, that they might battle even the feral and unreasoning of the Accursed without themselves being bound to the same fate. And there is one more matter... if my daughter lives, it is likely she is now in Lysama. I... I want to see her again, whatever she has become. I would trust you to bring her to me if you find what has become of her, as she is of your blood as I am of your blood."

"I will do this for you," Ukko said. "It has been long enough since I have walked the world beyond these unchanging woods. Though my methods shall be my own, I shall teach others to fight the Accursed while remaining human, and if it is in my power I shall return young Esteri to her father's arms, if she is as I am or if she is a monster or if she stands anywhere between."

Piru could not help but be relieved. He had feared that Ukko would not stir, and that Esteri would be lost to him. Now, at least, he had hope that she could be returned. Perhaps, if she had not been too bitterly turned, Ukko could take his distant granddaughter under his wing. He seemed to long for company, and Piru could not help but feel that facing eternity alone would be difficult.

"I trust we can leave for the palace tomorrow?" Piru asked. "War does not wait for any man, no matter how good his herb teas."

"Of course," Ukko replied. "Are you tired from your journey, or would you stay up a while longer and speak that I may listen?"

"It is not too late," Piru replied.

"Then perhaps," Ukko said, "you might indulge me by telling me of your daughter and her mother?"

***

The return to the palace was somewhat slower, as Piru had, hoping to avoid strange suspicions, taken only his own horse. Ukko had been good company, adapting rather well to human society and the company of other folk that he had long been without, though any hope Piru had about maintaining a low profile was lost in Ukko's gregariousness and interest in the world.

Still, they had stayed at the residence of the town mayor, requisitioned a second horse, and made it to the capitol around midday of the third day since Piru had left. In that time he had been gone, no catastrophes had occurred. Indris had sent no reply, though scouts near the border had sent birds and seemed to think that Indris would side with Lysama. That was, perhaps, good news. Piru could better justify the invasion if Indris threw in their lot with the faction supposedly in the wrong.

As the sun sank low to the horizon, Piru had settled the affairs of state and was able to attend directly to Ukko, and whatever he might require in order to fulfill the tasks set to him. A small study had been made ready for what Piru hoped would be a brief discussion. The king sat upright in a high chair, while Delphina, present owing her central place in creating so many plans for war, draped herself against the nearest wall. Ukko entered none too far, and bowed to his monarchs.

"King Piru," he said, "and you must be her majesty Delphina. Truly, you are at least as lovely as I was lead to believe."

Delphina laughed. "Such flattery no doubt earned you the position you now enjoy," she said, "but in this generation I'm afraid it will get you nowhere."

Ukko nodded. "I would expect not," he said, and again faced Piru.

"Tell me," said Piru, "what will you need to train my soldiers to fight the Accursed?"

"I would ask this," Ukko replied. "Make it known that there is a need for volunteers for a task of great danger and equally great importance, both among the military as it is, and among the commoners who might be expected to enlist when war comes. I shall take the first hundred to reply."

"One hundred?" Piru asked. "So few?"

"And few of them will see the training through," Ukko replied. "The most dangerous of the Accursed are beasts many times the size of a man, possessed of unnatural strength and swiftness and seething with dark sorcery. Against such abominations, only a rare few can stand and win. To bring more is not only to sacrifice those needlessly, but to risk the lives of the few, who will no doubt attempt to save their doomed comrades."

"I see," Piru said. "Are you sure it is the first hundred that you want? I could see to it that the recruiters turn away those who are unfit, if you tell me the mark of such people."

"If there are not enough among the one hundred most swift to devote themselves to a purpose that endangers their life more keenly than ordinary soldiering," Ukko replied, "Kalest has fallen upon dark times, but I shall take another hundred then."

This time it was Piru's turn to nod sagely. He was not sure he understood, but then he was sure that he did not know best of this matter. He had hoped for a legion trained and ready to cut down the Accursed of Lysama, but if a company would serve better, than a company he could accept.

"It will be done," Piru said. "Announcements will be made tomorrow. I do not doubt that your hundred shall arrive very quickly thereafter. Kalesti blood still burns hot in these times, and hotter still at the affront we have suffered."

"Thank you," Ukko said. "I should also like some sort of accommodation. Though I might be comfortable resting my head wherever is convenient, I doubt that shall be the best for your palace."

"Go to the majordomo," Piru replied, quickly describing the man and where to find him. "And if he doubts you, then send him to me and I shall straighten the matter out immediately."

"I look forward to this service," Ukko said. "For the first time in long years I am in the living world, and for Kalest I will make the most of it."

Ukko bowed, as befitted the setting of an audience, and with Piru's leave, departed.

"Well," Delphina said when he had gone, "He has a silvery tongue, but he is not alone in that. You are certain this old blade of Kalest is not dulled with rust?"

"Quite supremely certain," Piru replied, "for I have seen him at work. If anything, there has been the opposite effect."

"Well then," Delphina said, "we have nothing to fear, do we? He will give us a weapon to best whatever Accursed Lysama can create, and likely find your daughter as well. Just as planned, correct?"

"Just as planned," Piru repeated, though he did not feel it. This plan was deeply flawed, and its contingencies and amendments made up the greater sum of its action. The pieces were falling into place, and Piru could see that, but somehow the slow assembly of such titanic machinations felt a hollow victory.

It was nothing, he told himself as Delphina had told him countless times before. The gnawing emptiness would fade away like morning mist when their schemes reached fruition. And, indeed, the ends were very bright. A single continent beneath a single banner, a legacy that he could leave for his children and grandchildren to rule in peace and prosperity. Ukko had doubted it, but at the same time Ukko himself had said that the specifics differed, and Piru did not want to believe that humanity was shackled to fighting the same wars time and time again. This time, it would be different. This time, they would change the course of the future.

But some wounds did refuse to heal. Aliisa haunted Piru's memory on dark nights, when he was alone with his thoughts, and now Esteri stained his soul, and whether she lived for eternity or died swiftly she would remain a blemish there forever. Would the blood shed in the name of unification be the same way? Would Ukko's prediction come back to haunt his descendants?

Piru did not wonder such things for very long as Delphina embraced him and whispered promises of the glories to come and enticements of more immediate reward into his ears. The subject was very shortly put out of his mind, but some splinter remained: he would wonder again, and perhaps never be satisfied.

CHAPTER VI

Acacia

Acacia woke up, as was usual, with great resentment for the sun intruding on her rest. As was usual, she reached a pleasant demeanor once her eyes were wide open, and took her time greeting the morning. She dressed in her best clothes – leather trousers, a white blouse, a bodice of dark tanned hide and brown jacket – braided her raven-black hair on either side of her head, and pulled on her boots after making sure that nothing had crawled into them during the night.

She looked over the room that she rented and smiled. She didn't care about the smells that wafted up from the alleyway, the rats that scrabbled in the walls, the creaking boards or the sticky door. The sun was shining and the people were bustling down below in the street. It was going to be a beautiful day.

Like every other day, she thought about whether she'd go to the market or not. The market was where work was, and so many lovely people knew her name and treated her like a friend. She could haul barrels of apples or crates of potatoes and get a few coins for her trouble, or sweep out the bakery's floor and get something warm and sweet for lunch. That was what she usually did, because it was the way she knew to live.

But Acacia always thought about doing something else, as the two fine swords that sat crossed on her dresser attested. She was happy helping her friends in the market, and she was happy to rest her head in that tiny upstairs room, but part of her had always longed for a grand adventure. She had dreamed of joining the army since she was small, as the years she saved up for her blades and the time she spent idly practicing with them attested, and ever since the Princess had been taken and war seemed to loom close, soldiers marching in the streets of the town and riders coming and going from the grounds of the palace in the hills just outside, those dreams had worn much more heavily on her mind.

She had tried to enlist once. They told her she was too young, or at least too small. Acacia had grown since then, and with war on the horizon they couldn't be too picky, could they?

But Acacia's stomach was empty and her coin purse was light. Maybe today wasn't the right day. If it was, Acacia thought that she would know for sure, rather than being left guessing. Thus, she set off for the market with a bright smile and a spring in her step. She offered a 'good day' to anyone she knew and some folk she didn't. She worked hard hauling sacks of flour for the bakery, giving the butcher's children rides on her back, or sorting fish from the river for Mister Karppinen, who sold them battered and fried in oil from a shop on the high road.

Around midday, Acacia had some coins in her pocket, a fillet of the best fried carp in her hand, some new memories and even a new friend. Today was a good day, she thought as she enjoyed her lunch, and it wasn't even close to over yet.

Acacia watched as a rider in bright armor and a great crimson cape galloped down the high road, and then stopped by the fountain in the square where it met the market street.

"Hear me!" the great man bellowed. "I speak with the words of our sovereign, King Piru, that all may hear!"

Acacia perked up, listening intently. She wasn't the only one, though many of the shopkeepers kept going about the business expecting that the king's words would not apply to them. The messenger unrolled a scroll and began to read from it, bellowing every word.

"In these dark days for Kalest," the messenger declared, "there is need for anyone brave enough to accept a new assignment within its glorious army! The danger will be great!" He paused for effect. "But greater shall be the import of what you brave few who answer the call of your king will do for your nation! Grave injustices against crown and people alike shall be redressed, and graver transgressions prevented! And none shall question that those who walk this path shall stand among Kalest's greatest heroes! All those who love their country, who would lay down their lives for their honor and for their homes, should report to the mustering grounds in the shadow of the palace this day! For the glory of Kalest!"

Acacia didn't wait any longer. She stood up, stuffed the rest of the fish in her mouth, and bolted up the high road. She had to get her swords! Today was the day!

"There is a true Kalesti!" she heard, the messenger's booming voice fading in the background. "Will you sit by..."

Acacia didn't stop running. She felt like she had to hurry, but at the same time she couldn't be happier. Today was her chance, her great big chance to be a hero. All she needed to do was get there.

By the time she reached the mustering grounds, swords at her hips, Acacia was out of breath, heart pounding in her chest. She hadn't remembered how far it was up the high road, but she hadn't been willing to change her pace once she got started.

"I'm here," she told the guards at the gates between breaths, "About the message... something really important... for the kingdom?"

One of the guards looked to the other, "Those new orders? How many volunteers did we get them already? Is it a hundred?"

"A hundred and nine," the other guard replied. "I don't think anybody's going to make a fuss about number one hundred ten, even if she is the first from the city."

"How'd they want us to handle newcomers, again?"

"Just send them along," the second guard replied with a shrug, pushing open the gate. "I think they're going to do the paperwork after they see who makes it through day one." He turned to Acacia. "Third terrace up, and the second yard to the left. You're alright? Got your breath again?"

Acacia nodded. "I should be fine."

"Good," the guard said, "because you'd better run to get there before Lord Ukko starts. If you don't make it"-

"Thanks!" Acacia called, having already bolted forward.

She darted through the first terrace, up the stairs to the crossing of the second, and then up again. She looked to her left – and crashed into someone right in front of her. Acacia and the stranger went down immediately. She tried to catch herself, but the best she could do was hit the ground rolling and try to get her feet back under her. Even that didn't quite work, and she was left sitting on the stone.

"I'm sorry!" she cried, "I'm sorry! I wasn't looking, and"-

There was a soft laugh, and Acacia looked up and saw who she had run into – a young man in an odd uniform, with long brown hair, who seemed to be quite amused by the entire matter.

"It's fine," he said, standing slowly. "As long as you weren't hurt, at least."

"I'm okay," she said. "I'm sorry, the guards said I had to hurry, so I did, and I probably still have to hurry or I'll be late!"

"Hurry where?"

Acacia, standing herself, focused. "Third terrace, second yard on the left. I have to get there fast because they said something about there being over a hundred volunteers and having to be there before a 'Lord Ukko' starts, so I should really"-

"It will be fine," the man said. "I'll walk slowly, so you can get in line. I wouldn't want to lose someone so eager to serve her country."

"I..." Acacia hesitated. "You're Lord Ukko?"

She put a hand over her mouth to stifle a gasp. Perhaps he was older than he looked, but... he couldn't even be as much as thirty, not even close! She'd expected a grizzled old sergeant, not someone she might have grown up with.

"I'm so, so sorry, sir! I'll make it up, I promise!"

"As I said," Ukko said, "it's fine. The both of us are no worse for the wear. Now, hurry along – but not too fast!"

***

Acacia stood in her place, in the back of the eleventh file, at attention and saluting, when Lord Ukko walked onto the field.

"At ease!" he called. Acacia's eyes darted to the professional soldiers in earlier files, and she quickly adopted their stance.

"You are no doubt the swiftest soldiers to swear your devotion to the crown," Ukko said, "even in the face of grave danger. You may not know what you have been called for, so I will tell you. Over the next weeks, as Kalest prepares for war, I will train you to fight the mightiest, the most devastating of the Accursed. If anyone here cares for his life too much to take those odds, leave now." He paused, but not a soul budged.

"Good," he said, "though many of you will still be leaving – indeed, I should be greatly surprised if even a dozen of your number join me on the field! These weeks I will cull those who stand before me time and time again, starting today. I asked for no more than a hundred trainees, but it seems that I have got a hundred ten. I will decimate your number before the sun sets! Only ninety-nine, less those who feel the training is too hard, or who find they have reservations about our mission or my command, will stand before me tomorrow! One in ten will be dismissed."

There was some shifting in the ranks, and Acacia, though she tried her best to stand perfectly still, knew exactly why. She wasn't the only one afraid of being dismissed. If Ukko threw her out, which he might very well do if she didn't make a good second impression, would the regular recruiting officers even take her? Or would they say that she'd failed to pass Lord Ukko's muster, so why would she pass theirs?

"I will assess as best I can your skill and your character. I will determine if you have what it takes to battle the monsters our enemy will create, and my decision on the matter is both final and absolute. Is that clear?!"

"Yes sir!" Acacia called back in chorus with the men and women before and beside her.

"Good!" Ukko called. "I see many of you have brought your weapons of choice to the yard. That is good, but you will not need them today. There are sufficient practice swords in the racks along the western wall. You will use one each today, and I will take the time to examine the personal skills only of those who will be retained into training."

The trainees waited.

"Obtain your weapons and pair off!" Ukko commanded. As one, the trainees saluted, shouted "Yes, sir!" and went to the western wall.

Acacia, being in the far-western file, was one of the first to grab a wooden training sword and start scanning the field for a partner. Solders were pairing off very quickly, and standing face to face, ready for the command to start.

Someone tapped her on the soldier.

"You," a gruff voice said.

"Yes?" Acacia asked, turning to face it. The speaker was, by his uniform, a regular in the army, and he was massive – perhaps half again as broad as Acacia, muscles bulging beneath the sleeves of his shirt. He might have been the largest man on the field, though he had some competition from taller sorts.

"Fight me," he said.

Well, Acacia, thought, she needed a partner anyway, even if he was one of the more intimidating available. That much meant that if she won it would shine out the brighter, and if she lost maybe she wouldn't be faulted badly enough to be sent home today.

"All right," she said with a smile. "My name's Acacia. What's yours?"

"None of your business," he huffed. "Get ready."

How rude, Acacia thought. Well, if he didn't want to give his name, it was no skin off her back. They walked out and staked out a position with enough clearance on every side for a spar.

Moments later, Ukko spoke again.

"I see everyone is in position," he said. "The basic rules of this are to fight to the yield, or until I say otherwise. Conserve your strength! I do not need the pinnacle of your ability, and anyone who cannot fight for a few minutes does not stand a chance. There will be exercises until the sun sets or very nearly. Begin!"

Immediately, Acacia's opponent swung, but she was just a hair faster, jumping back from the massive, horizontal slice. He was faster than he looked though, and though she recovered quicker he was upon her too swiftly for Acacia to mount an attack of her own.

Nimbly, she dodged one strike, parried another and a third, but Acacia knew that she couldn't keep it up forever. If she had a blade in her other hand, she could hold him at bay and cut like she had been taught to, but the rules of the match were one weapon only.

With a mighty yell, Acacia's opponent made another strike. Acacia raised her blade to parry, but his follow-through came down with his strength and no small portion of his weight, driving her to the ground.

Once on her back, Acacia knew she had seconds only. She planted her free hand, and swept her legs across the field, knocking her opponent's out from under him while working to get her feet under her again. He fell hard, and they both struggled to right themselves.

Acacia was on her feet first, and took a defensive stance, ready for the fight to start again. As her opponent stood, he made a clumsy swipe at her, and Acacia replied with a cut to the back of his hand, hopefully not too hard.

He growled in frustration, and redoubled his offense. He gripped his sword in both hands and swung furiously, what little he lost in switching technique more than made up for in brute strength.

Acacia began to worry. He was so strong... if he made a

clean hit, he could do real damage, even with the light wooden practice sword. Was this how soldiers usually trained? She couldn't spare the moment to look at another pair to see.

Unwilling to risk herself by attacking in the openings he left, Acacia focused entirely on deflecting strikes, turning them harmlessly away. No matter how often she did, though, the next was swift coming, and she only had to make one mistake.

Finally, after an overhand chop drove her back and left him off balance, Acacia took a knee and dropped her sword at her feet. She was going to get hit eventually, and if she wanted to last the day it was better to just lose before it happened.

"Enough," she said, "I"-

A mighty blow struck her in the shoulder and sent her sprawling.

Stay down, Acacia told herself. He'd realize what had happened.

Another blow struck her in the side, and she folded in on herself reflexively. A third, quickly after, cracked across her back only her lack of breath kept her from crying out in pain. Acacia curled up tight, and wrapped her arms behind her head. Don't scream, protect your neck and your head. She told herself to be strong and wait it out, but feared as another blow hit her, and another after that, that it was not going to stop.

And then, a pause where the next blow should have been.

"Drop your weapon, soldier!"

Acacia lifted her head to look, and saw Ukko as well as her opponent standing over her. With one hand, he had caught the massive man's wrist, and was holding it above his head. Her opponent's face was filled with stark fear, and when she saw Ukko's, she understood why – there was such a dark rage in his face that Acacia herself, spared from the raining blows, felt a new and different fear just to witness it.

Her opponent let go of the training sword.

"In what world," Ukko demanded, "does a soldier of Kalest batter an unarmed foe so unmercifully? In what world does he even strike after a sparring partner, for the gods' sake, has yielded?"

Acacia's opponent was silent, unable to muster any reply.

"Who is your commander?" Ukko roared.

"Y-you are, sir."

"I am not!" he bellowed, in a voice that might be heard as far as the market street. "Nor will I ever be! The likes of you dishonor Kalest by daring such craven deeds while wearing its colors!"

The large man cowered before such fury.

"Who is your commander?" Ukko repeated.

"I... I serve under General Anselm. N-no more specific assignment."

"And," Ukko said, "General Anselm will hear of this. If you have lied to me, then your king shall hear of both offenses, and then you will suffer not only whatever discipline Anselm provides, but the full force of Kalest's law. If I were you, I would pack your bags and pray that a discharge is the worst that can be dreamed up."

Ukko released the man's wrist. The trainee took a few steps back, rubbing it with his other hand.

"Get out of my sight!" Ukko bellowed. "And hope you never stray back into it!"

"And you, soldier," Ukko said, speaking softly and looking at Acacia. "Can you stand?"

"I think so, Sir," she replied, and slowly struggled to her feet, aching deep inside.

"Good," Ukko said. "Since we now have an odd number, I would like you to wait for the next exercise, if you feel fit to continue."

"I do, sir," Acacia replied hastily. She did not, but she wasn't about to let the pain keep her from going forward until the sun set. Even if this was what it took, Acacia wanted to last, wanted to make herself a hero and not just wash out after a single day.

Ukko looked about, and Acacia followed his gaze. The

pairs nearby were staring in her direction. In fact... the yard was silent, not the clatter of wood against wood to be heard anywhere.

"There is a seat by the western wall, if you want it," Ukko said quietly to her, "otherwise the south is in the shade." He turned outward again. "As for the rest of you, I do not recall telling anyone else to stop their exercises! Begin again!"

***

Acacia watched the others spar for a round. For most of them, it was a very practiced form, moving back and forth, making occasional taps with their swords, taking a knee if driven too far back. Some time later, another fighter was dismissed, though with far less wrath than before – Acacia didn't catch the reason.

She was paired with the other orphaned trainee, and tried her best to emulate what she had seen the others doing: slow, steady, and controlled. Sometimes, perhaps more often than not, she was forced to her knee, but sometimes she earned the upper hand. Though her back and her body ached fiercely, no doubt slowing her swings and her steps, Acacia did not surrender without at least giving a good account of herself, and paired inevitably against a real soldier, she felt some pride in that.

All the while, Ukko paced between the rows, and when Acacia could take a chance to see, sometimes he was watching a pair, other times speaking to them, or ordering particular exercises. As the afternoon grew later, partners were switched and new drills started, most of which the others knew instinctively, but some of which were utterly alien to Acacia.

It felt like the half day training there lasted forever, and by the time Ukko called a full halt to the proceedings, Acacia barely knew how she was able to stand. The strain after that first beating hadn't been much but at the same time she hadn't had a real chance to recover. Her spirits were lower than she could easily remember, because she was almost certain she was one of, if not the weakest soldier there. As she stood at attention in about the middle of the formation, knees slightly trembling, she watched Ukko begin at the first file, walking up it and down the next.

He spoke to each soldier in turn. Occasionally, one saluted and left, and other times he handed the soldier a folded paper. Finally, he came to her.

"Your name, soldier?"

"Acacia, sir."

"Acacia. Good." He held out one piece of paper. "You can take this to the medics. I want someone to make sure you aren't too badly hurt after what happened."

She took it.

"Thank you, sir."

At least Lord Ukko was a kind man, Acacia reflected. She'd regret only that she failed, not that she tried at all.

"And this," he said, holding out a second paper, "take to the Quartermaster. You'll need to be fitted for a uniform."

"Sir?" she asked, taking the folded note.

"Welcome to Kalest's army, Acacia."

Acacia wanted to jump for joy, but neither her weary bones nor her place in line would allow it. Instead, she simply stood a little taller, took her eyes from the ground and focused them straight ahead, and began to smile as Ukko moved on to the next soldier in line.

When he was done, all the ninety-nine left were dismissed, to go about their business as the sun sank below the horizon. Acacia left the practice yard limping but elated, wondering what her first order of business was to be. She wanted to see the physicians, but what if they ordered bed rest? Should she get her uniform first?

"Hey," a voice called from behind her. Acacia turned. There was one of the other trainees, a woman perhaps a year or two her senior with bob-cut blonde hair and grey eyes.

"Oh," Acacia said. "Hello."

"Whew," the other woman said, "that was some show earlier! Name's Maria, by the way, you?"

"Acacia."

"Acacia, great. I'm really surprised you were able to get up! That rat bastard was almost as strong as I am, and he wasn't holding a thing back – I was just a few pairs away, you see, saw the whole thing."

"What's going to happen to him, anyway?"

Maria shrugged, "He's going to be really glad he's under Anselm, who'll go by the book and not a letter either way. Most of the other generals could get really creative with punishments, probably involving beatings before the discharge, and Katri would probably have him hanged."

Acacia blanched a bit.

"Anyway," Maria said, "you must be made of iron to have held out the whole day after that. How about you come with me, and we go get a drink somewhere?"

"I kind of have to get a uniform, and... iron?"

"Yeah!" Maria slapped her on the shoulder, with sting bitterly. "Everyone saw it! And for somebody who's not trained military, you did a heck of a job. I'd like to see what you can do when you're not beat half to death."

"Thanks," Acacia said with a smile. "I've practiced a whole lot. I've always wanted to join the army."

"Well," Maria said, "you're in good company, and frankly if what we saw today is anything to go by, we're in good company too. I don't know how Ukko got a command like this so young, but at least he was good enough to see it too. Not that it was hard."

"Thanks." Acacia said, shifting slightly. "I... couldn't really see it myself. I was so sure I was going to be sent home." She looked up at the darkening sky, then back to Maria. "Where can I find the Quartermaster anyway? I doubt they'll be open too deep into the night."

"I'll take you right there," Maria said. "Who knows, maybe they'll have something in your size right away and we can hit the tavern anyway?"

"Maybe," Acacia said, "but I should see the doctors too. To-morrow after training?"

Maria laughed. "You've got it, but take my advice... ask for Markku if he's there, though he usually staffs up in the palace proper, or Kyllikki if he's not. They'll treat you right."

Acacia smiled, and walked up the terraces with Maria. She'd still be sore tomorrow, she knew, and likely the day after, and that wasn't even counting how she'd feel after a whole day doing the same or more. But, at the same time, she'd make it. Battered and bruised or no, today had been a beautiful day.

CHAPTER VII

Esteri

Esteri woke up in near darkness, being shaken, and at first having a difficult time understanding that she had left her dreams behind. She hadn't woken up in the night that she remembered, nor could she recall exactly what she dreamed, only that it was awful and made her dread sleeping again almost as much as she wanted whoever it was to stop shaking her.

"What in the names of all the gods have you been doing?" a harsh voice shouted. Radegond, probably. "I need to know!"

"Doing?" Esteri croaked, sitting up and pushing herself away from Radegond. Her voice was strange – had she cried out in her sleep so often as to give herself a hoarse throat, or was it just the mountain air? "I was asleep."

"That's patently"-

Radegond sighed and backed off "No, it's fading now," she said. "I'll want an explanation later but it doesn't look like you hurt anything, so you'd better get dressed and ready for training."

"Hurt anything?" Esteri said. Her voice was normal again, "Fading? What are you talking about?"

"Get dressed," Radegond ordered, walking to the door. "I'll explain when you're out."

Esteri threw on her borrowed clothes quickly. Still too tight in places and too loose in others, but there was no time to waste adjusting over and over what really had to be tailored if it was to be any good. She stomped out into the common room, where Radegond was waiting.

"There," Esteri said. "Do you think you could explain why you were shaking me?"

"Follow me," Radegond said, and started to lead out the door. "I'll talk as we walk. The others should already be there."

They stepped out into the morning mist, and Radegond began to speak.

"You were warping fiercely," she said. "For most of us here, we look like humans at the best of times. Those who don't, don't tend to live long enough to get found by Erikis and make it up the mountain, even if they want to come. But we still end up looking like monsters, usually when calling upon the power endowed in us by that potion, but sometimes just when we get angry, or fight, or things like that. We call the change warping, or being warped, and it's usually temporary."

Radegond paused.

"Your eyes are still jet black all the way through," she said. "They might clear up like the rest of you did, by the time we get to the arena, by the end of the day, or if that was your first time warping at all, they might not ever change back."

"What did the rest look like?"

"It's not important," Radegond said. "We'll probably find something else that makes you warp today and then you can look in a mirror. I want to know, though, what could have caused it if you weren't calling on any power."

"Could fear?" Esteri asked. "I was having a nightmare. A rather dreadful one, I think, though I can't really remember it."

"That might," Radegond admitted, "though if you can remember anything else, I would hear of it."

"Not right now, no," Esteri said.

A few minutes later, they rounded a path to a sheltered area with a broad, flat ring of stone and a few seats carved into the drags at the edges, though one of the people in the arena, Hathus she guessed from what she had been told, had climbed somewhat higher into the rocks to find a perch.

Tius was there, waiting for her, and so was a rather small young woman with straight, waist-length black hair. Even compared to the other Accursed, she was relatively young, frozen at fifteen, perhaps sixteen unless Esteri missed her mark. Avina, she guessed. The girl looked somewhere between Lysaman and Aryniasian, so she might have been at least related to her 'parents.'

"All right!" Radegond barked. "All of you get in line this instant!"

The other three jumped, and Esteri followed suit as quickly as she got the picture.

"Now," Radegond yelled, "we've got a green trainee among us and not a whole lot of time to turn her into something else, so I expect you all to take this seriously and show her what it means to be Accursed. To that end, Esteri, Avina, step up."

Esteri took a few steps forward, as did Avina, who was smiling broadly.

"Here's how this is going to work right now," Radegond said, "and I'm only going to tell you once, so pay attention!"

Esteri tried to stand a little straighter so it was clear she was focused on Radegond. She'd seen soldiers standing in line before, she could do the same thing.

"Esteri," Radegond called, continuing to shout in tones that made Esteri more shocked she wasn't cursing, "you are stronger and faster than you expect, and tougher too. Those scratches you had last night are already gone, so don't worry about scraping your pretty little princess knees or bruising your oversized royal bosom, you got that?"

"Yes, ma'am?" Were the personal shots really necessary?

"As for you, Avina," Radegond yelled, "I expect to see some gods-damned control. You're not a little kid anymore, you need to stop acting like one and throwing temper tantrums in the ring! If you so much as go for a low blow, I am going to have you dig latrines just so I can have you muck them out, got it?"

"Yes, ma'am," Avina sighed. Well, at least Esteri had gotten the proper reply.

"Now," Radegond said, "this first bout is just going to be a demonstration. Your goal, both of you, is to pin the other woman to the ground, and I mean that without drawing blood or otherwise doing permanent damage."

That didn't sound like a demonstration, Esteri thought, nor did it sound quite fair – Avina was half a head shorter and quite a bit slimmer than Esteri herself, so even if she did have a better technique, it wouldn't count for everything in a contest like that.

Radegond walked to the edge of the ring, and the two men had also backed off, to the crags around it.

"You will begin on my mark."

Avina walked slowly to a position, and Esteri took up one opposite her. Keep a wide stance, she told herself. She'd overheard something about being harder to knock down that way, and while she expected to be able to win, she didn't expect that Avina would make it easy on her.

"Mark."

Before Esteri could move, the air rippled in front of her. Reflexively, she turned her head and closed her eyes, holding her hands out in front of her. There was a light burst of wind, and then something struck her in the chest, hard enough to knock the breath right out of her. Esteri toppled backward, onto the hard stone. A force pressed down upon her chest, and she could barely breathe. She opened her eyes, and standing over her, holding her firmly to the ground with one massive, taloned hand, was a monster. It was at least twice Esteri's height, purely black like condensed shadows, with overlong arms and legs and its massive hands, the creature being shaped vaguely like a human woman, arms and legs and head in roughly the right places, the waist the narrowest part of its frame.

And that face! That face might have been what horrified Esteri in her nightmares. Its mouth was simply a gash in the lower half of its face, the edges a jagged mockery of predatory teeth in the same sable as its skin and the interior faintly glowing with a crimson light, not unlike a gourd carved into the caricature of a frightening face. Esteri could make out no nose, and its eyes were deep sockets that blazed with blood-red fire. Upon its head writhed innumerable tendrils, alive like snakes and twisting in the air about it seemingly impervious to gravity.

It was Avina, Esteri realized.

"That was too easy," she said, the voice that issued from that horrible face a twisted mockery of Avina's youthful girlish tones. "I'll tell you what – your arms and legs are still free, so it's not over yet. If you can lift one of my fingers, I'll give you another go."

Esteri caught her breath, and it was all she could do to not cry or scream. Her heart was pounding in her chest, cold sweat covering her brow. She could barely think – she reminded herself that she was safe, that this thing was really just a girl like her, that Radegond would sooner or later call a stop to the bout, but it didn't help. Every sense, every instinct, wanted her to run, but she was trapped and unable to escape.

She had to fight.

Esteri's arms were trembling, but she reached up and placed her hand on one of Avina's great, dark claws, the one to the left of her head and began to push. At first, she couldn't give the effort much strength, but as she closed her eyes, shutting out the sight of what Avina became, she was able to give it her best. Her palms stung and she tried to brace herself against the ground to get a better shot at it, but all the same the talon might have been Kalest palace for all that she could raise it.

Then, Esteri heard something from deep inside her: a faint, wet sound. The claw started to yield, but then Esteri opened her eyes. Crimson veins, lit from within almost like Avina, were spreading across her hands and arms. In moment of panic, she let go.

"Close," Avina said. The tendrils that had replaced the girl's hair lashed out. One grabbed each of Esteri's wrists and held her hands outstretched while another set coiled around her legs and bound them together. "But point for me."

"Enough," Radegond said icily.

Avina released Esteri and stood tall, her form melting swiftly back into the girl she had been before. Slowly, cautiously, Esteri stood up.

"What was that about?" Esteri demanded of Radegond. "I didn't even have a chance!"

"No," Radegond said with a sigh, "you didn't, though I'd hoped you'd hold out a little longer. I'm used to people who have at least some experience using their abilities before they come here, and you don't even know what yours are, so I suppose I should apologize for that. Still, I think there's something you can learn from this."

"And that is?"

"Whatever we may look like," Radegond said, "doesn't really have a bearing on how dangerous or skilled we are. It's true for humans, twice as true for Accursed, and ten times as true for Avina. The point being that you need to forget what you're capable of, because you might be capable of anything. It's unlikely, but for all any of us know, you might have been able to win that."

Esteri looked down at her arms. They were normal now, but somehow she felt stronger, as though the world weighed less. Was it just knowing she could push herself, or was she still changing under the skin?

"Also," Radegond said, "fear doesn't seem to make you warp. Even your eyes are back to normal."

"That's good, right?"

"It means we have a mystery on our hands," Radegond said, "but that's neither here nor there. And the nightmare could still play into it; if you were reacting to something in your dream and could recall what, we might learn what you're capable of."

"I'll try," Esteri said, "but it's probably lost."

"If it is, that's unfortunate," Radegond replied. "It's hard to know how to teach you unless we know what you can do. Some Accursed seem to know by instinct, others only discover what, if anything, they got beyond the strength, speed, and toughness when they're in a situation that requires it."

"What are all your..." Esteri struggled for a word. "Abilities, anyway?"

Radegond nodded. "An intelligent question," she said. "Take a seat. You're going to be in the ring a lot, so don't get used to it. Hathus! Get down here, you're against me."

"I don't know," Hathus said in a creaky voice that Esteri couldn't help but feel was faked. "You know my old knees"-

"Cut it out and get down here! And Tius..." Radegond paused. "You know what, just make a demonstration."

"All right," Tius said. He walked over to Esteri. "Good morning, Princess."

"Good morning," she answered, pleased to be actually be given human treatment. "I take it you have something to show me?"

"Of course," Tius said. "See those rocks up there?"

"Yes."

In a split second, Tius vanished, and a wisp of oily smoke darted, swiftly, up to the rocks, where Tius reappeared, now standing in place. He waved to her, and then the wisp darted back, and he materialized in front of Esteri again. Black veins crawled along his skin, and his eyes had changed to awful red-orange irises and jaundiced whites. Apparently, Esteri was not able to keep her shock from her face, and he turned his head away.

"There," he said. "It's a neat trick, but I think Radegond and Hathus are about to start up."

"All right," Radegond said, "Hathus and I will now perform a combat demonstration. Please focus on what we're doing. Try to put yourself in our position and think of what you would do. If you experience any strange feelings of ability, please point yourself away from other people. When I was a mortal, I had to deal with a whole squad of new-fledged, and we did lose men to accidents. Hathus!"

"Yes?"

"I expect you to come at me with everything you've got, because I expect you know how to pull your blows. Begin!"

Radegond threw her cloak to the ground, which seemed to be a signal. It took only a second for Esteri to see why. Massive wings of stretched skin ripped from her back as Radegond gave a nearly inhuman shriek. She snapped the wings open, the action sprinkling the ring with droplets of blood, and leapt into the sky.

A moment later, a gout of flame followed her. Esteri looked, and saw Hathus, one arm now noticeably bulkier, black and knotted as though covered in thickly braided, ebony ropes. At the end, there was no hand, but a tubular mass. He made a punching motion, and that end spat out more fire, streaking into the sky at Radegond.

Radegond, in the air, dodged and weaved, and finally dove back towards the ground, Hathus throwing a blast of fire upwards at her as she came in. For a moment, Esteri couldn't see what had happened, but when the smoke cleared they were both picking themselves up. Radegond flared her wings, knocking Hathus back to the ground. He threw fire again before trying to rise, engulfing one of her wings, both of which promptly shriveled and vanished from sight, In the confusion of that, Radegond pounced, and held Hathus' warped arm to the ground. She had won, Esteri saw, but at what cost? Her back looked like a bloody mess. Though some of the damage might have been warped lesions, slowly evaporating, there was certainly real blood there.

"That was a... fascinating display," Esteri said as they picked themselves up, "but there are some things I don't understand. Your back is slick, and the wing..."

"Will be whole the next time I conjure them," Radegond replied. "As for the blood, that's just an unfortunate side-effect of being what I am, and nothing to concern yourself over. Now that you have seen what we are capable of, we must discover your limits and if possible your abilities. I trust you do not have any feelings of power, or instincts that speak to you?"

"No," Esteri said. "I don't know any more than you do."

"In which case," Radegond said, "in my experience it seems to be that combat is the surest way to draw what is in you to the front. As you have seen what we all are capable of, I will permit you to pick your opponent for the time being."

Esteri thought about it. She certainly had no desire to face Avina again. Radegond? Radegond was in command, which meant that barring natural ability she was almost certainly the best. And Esteri didn't have any expendable limbs for Hathus to set on fire. That left Tius... perhaps he would have a little mercy?

"Tius," she said, "shall we?"

"If you wish, Princess."

They paced out into the ring.

"Again," said Radegond, "the point is finding your limits. If you think you can do something, even for a second, attempt it. I'd trust Tius to get out of the way. Begin!"

Esteri took a readied pose, as did Tius. It seemed like neither one of them wanted to make the first move,

"I said begin!" Radegond barked.

Esteri made her move, lunging forward in an attempt to shove Tius over. Rather than anything else, he did his magic and darted out of the way... and out of sight. Esteri spun, only to find that he was right behind her. She threw a punch, and he smoke-dashed again, this time off to the right.

"Stop fooling around!" Radegond shouted

Clumsily, Esteri charged for his position, only to find as she got there that Tius seemed able to jump practically through her. The trail of smoke parted around Esteri in its brief existence, and she nearly lost her balance spinning to follow it.

This time, Esteri approached slowly, carefully, stalking forward. Was the goal still to pin him to the ground? She guessed it was, Radegond had not mentioned anything else.

"What's the problem, Tius?" Radegond demanded, "Are you worried she's going to cry home? Scared of pissing off the pretty princess?"

As Esteri looked for an opening, her mind looked for an endgame, and she came to the realization that her choice of opponents was very, very awkward. Perhaps if she could just knock him down in the first place, that would be enough?

"Get on with it!" said Radegond. "If you can't do this properly, I'll pit her against someone who can!"

Tius struck, or at least tried to, Esteri jumping out of the way quick enough to avoid him. She threw another punch of her own, aiming for his chest. She didn't know exactly why, but it felt like the right thing to do, and Radegond had harped on listening to instincts.

After that, the strikes came quickly. Tius didn't seem to want to try a grab any more than she did, but now he was on the offense. Each time he tried to hit her, or bowl her over, Esteri was fast enough to block, or dodge out of the way. It was exhausting, but at the same time it wasn't exactly hard – she almost felt like she was moving before he was.

Esteri didn't know how long the odd dance continued; it could have been minutes or mere seconds on the outside. Finally, Tius made a very clumsy push, and Esteri grabbed his wrist. Somehow, she felt a faint spike of fear, as though she was making a dire mistake, but she pulled and sent him toppling over. All she had to do was keep him on the ground for a second – a knee in the back wouldn't hurt that much and wouldn't hurt her pride. She lunged.

Esteri fell face first to the ground when Tius simply wasn't there. A split second later, she could feel him push his hands down between her shoulder blades – he was beside her, and while not stronger than Esteri expected, stronger than he looked. She was quickly borne to the ground.

Esteri could have fought back up – she knew it, and she was sure Tius knew it as well, but the last thing she wanted was to end up in a more compromising position. There had to be a better exercise. She held still.

"Tius," Radegond said, "that was miserably sloppy. What kind of excuse… oh."

Radegond was staring at Esteri. For that matter so was Erikis, just behind her. When had he arrived?

"Interesting," she said. "Your eyes again. I wonder what it means."

"I have a few ideas," Erikis said, "but for now I think you should give the poor girl a break. She's not used to this sort of treatment."

Radegond folded her arms. "How is she supposed to get used to it if she stops after just two bouts, one of which was hardly a demonstration of anything?"

"She is not to be punished unfairly for your history as a drill sergeant, Radegond. Esteri is both one of us, and royalty."

Esteri tuned out the argument.

"Princess?" Tius said. She looked towards him. He was offering a hand to help her up. Esteri took it, reflecting that at least the boy had manners, even if he cheated.

"Is this normal?" Esteri asked quietly, brushing herself off.

"Basically," Tius said. "Might as well wait in the shade, the two of them can go at it for some time if there's a real disagreement, and sometimes even if there isn't."

Esteri nodded, and started to walk back to the edge of the ring alongside Tius.

"Do I look alright?" Esteri asked. "Not that that's what's most important, mind you, but if I'm going to make myself known again, I need to be presentable."

"You look fine," Tius said. "I mean lovely... I mean, ah, whatever I'm supposed to say to royalty. I mean your eyes are back to normal."

"Thank you," Esteri said. "That's what I wanted to know."

She looked around. Hathus and Avina were crowding around Radegond and Erikis, seemingly with their own arguments to add.

"So," she said, "I don't think you were a soldier, Tius. How did it happen with you?"

"Me?" he asked. "Pure stupidity. I found about the potion, brewed it, and drank it. There's not a whole lot to it."

90

"Really?" Esteri asked. "Why?"

"Why what?"

"Why would you take the potion deliberately? It seems odd."

"Like I said, I was stupid."

Ester said nothing, but looked him in the eye. She never learned how to fight at court, but she had learned how to read people, and if he thought he was being subtle about evading the question, he was dead wrong.

Tius looked away, avoiding her gaze.

"And more than that... I was a thief. Small time, mostly, snagging bread or fish from the market when your mother's handouts just weren't enough to keep my stomach from aching, but I knew some people who were a lot deeper on the wrong side of the law, and once in a while they persuaded me to come along on a house job for a part of whatever I carried out. We raided an Alchemist's mansion, you see... I took a lot of the chemicals, and glassware, and a few books. My friends took most of the easily moved stuff as their share, so I was left with half a laboratory that I couldn't fence anytime soon. I had nothing better to do some days, so I read a few of that Alchemist's books."

"And?"

"And one of them talked about the potion, and the Accursed. How they could become monsters but how they could also stay basically humans, but with new abilities. I thought that with that kind of power, I might be able to make it in the world somehow, carve myself a new life. The powers that be weren't exactly friendly to me already, so unless I basically killed myself I couldn't make my situation any worse. I followed that book to the letter, and took my chances. You basically know how that turned out."

"Not really," Esteri said. "I'd think with your power, you'd be a master thief by now. Nothing could keep you out and no prison could keep you in."

"I thought so too," Tius said, "but it turns out that even in the underworld, most people don't want to do business with a monster, and it's hard to eat paintings and fancy jewelry you can't even show to a normal shopkeeper. I got by for a while, lifting coins from peoples' coffers rather than the good stuff, but eventually I burned all my bridges and had to make for a new city. Erikis found me shortly after that and brought me here, so I guess I got what I wanted, just not the way I thought I'd get it."

"I'm sorry," Esteri said. "You mentioned my mother... how old are you, Tius?"

"Thirty-four," Tius said. "Which probably sounds old, but I'm actually the second-youngest person in the village. Well, third-youngest, now that you're here."

"It's not that old," Esteri said. "I've had men your age try to court me." Such advances had never been welcome, and Esteri had made her displeasure at men twice her age thinking they could woo her known, but it had happened.

"So," Esteri said, "there haven't been any wars since then... who else is younger than you?"

"Avina." Tius replied, "She was born two years before I got here."

"That's an odd way to put it."

"Not really," Tius said. "The whole town was still pretty excited about it when I came. I remember it was a few months later that her third birthday rolled around. Everyone pulled together and made her all sorts of gifts, even baked a gigantic cake. Do you have any idea how hard it is for us to get flour up here? We basically have to trade for it, which means hauling each bag up the mountain on foot."

"You don't mean..." Esteri put the pieces together. She looked like a child of her parents, she had been born in the colony... could it really be possible? "Accursed can't have children... can they?"

"Most of the time, no," Tius said, "and from what I hear it took nearly fifty years for Gelvira and Frideger, but Erikis is fond of saying that in a lot of ways every one of us is unique, and it turned out that the two of them weren't quite incapable after all. So Avina was born, and as it turns out, born with our curse."

"That explains a lot," Esteri admitted, "though I have so many more questions. I should probably ask Avina herself, but do you think you could tell me some of what being born Accursed means?"

"You know almost as much as I do," Tius said. "She's way more powerful than most of us, and changes way more completely. She's also been growing up, and we aren't quite sure when or if she's going to stop getting older, getting more powerful, or both. Erikis might know and he might have told her, but if he does and did they're not sharing."

Part of Esteri wanted to pity Avina, who had never had the chance to be human, who didn't know if she would live forever or waste away and die in front of her friends and her family. Part of Esteri recalled Avina holding her down, and thought that the girl had not been dealt such a poor hand by fate.

Tius was silent.

"So," Esteri said, "about the bout... how would I actually beat you?"

"With a stick," Tius said. "I don't lose wrestling matches, though against Avina it's a draw."

"Sticks are an option?"

"Most of the time," Tius said. "I'm not sure why Radegond didn't bring them out."

That would have far fewer problems than pinning, Esteri reflected. She could fight properly without risking her modesty. And she had been doing so well, in yet another fight that she had no chance of winning, that she liked her odds if victory was possible.

"Well then," she said, "I want a rematch."

"Right now?"

"No," Esteri said, "but I'm going to have a fair fight at least once today, and when I do I'm going to win."

***

Radegond had won the debate, at least in terms of Esteri continuing to spar and attempt to decipher the nature of her power, this time with wooden staves, and the nature of the contest being to three touches.

Esteri was not very good at striking. Radegond constantly criticized her form, tried to instruct her on stance and swing, but Esteri did not have a warrior's background and didn't seem to take very well to the instruction. Jabbing at the air, or striking an object, her clumsiness was beyond evident, but that all seemed to change when she was pitted against another person. Shortly into any fight, her eyes would turn black and while her motions were still picked apart as clumsy, jerky, or inarticulate, she usually found her staff in the right place at the right time to block incoming blows, even ones she had not consciously seen coming.

Esteri herself would have chalked such prowess up to a very real desire to not get hit, but both Erikis and Radegond felt it was something more, some sort of sixth sense about danger, though neither of them could explain the more profound changes that had occurred in her sleep.

All the while, she began to get more used to her companions: Radegond was far less harsh than she appeared. It was not that she didn't get angry or frustrated, but she did seem to care deep down and never seemed quite as wrathful as her constant yelling would indicate. Hathus, on the other hand, Esteri did not think that there was anything underneath. He was irreverent and incapable of treating matters with gravity, even when Esteri tried to talk to them all about her plans for the trip to Lysama, plans that had a very real risk to all their lives. He would have made a fine jester, but as a traveling companion she would just have to learn to live with him.

Tius was quickly the favorite of those she would set out with, though she suspected she would have to get to know Gelvira, Frideger, and Erikis better before she could say that with confidence. Though he occasionally tripped over his words trying to maintain some veneer of formality and station, the mask of polite deference did nothing to really conceal an earnest kindness and interest in Esteri's personal well-being. To think someone like that could have once been a criminal was almost enough for Esteri to find herself rethinking Kalest's treatment of petty thieves. Almost.

And Avina... Avina still terrified Esteri, and though she admitted it was largely due to first impressions, that was not entirely the case. At times, Avina was genial and kind, with an honest vigor that suggested, while she was but one year Esteri's junior, the Accursed-born girl was far younger than the princess in many ways. At other times, Avina became cold, standoffish, and even dipped into behaviors Esteri might have called nasty had they lasted for more than a moment, a single dark look or spiteful word. Esteri could figure no pattern to whether Avina treated her as a friend or as a bitter enemy.

Somewhat after midday, though, a halt was called to the whole thing; a concession both to her and to Erikis, Esteri figured. After that, she was finally able to see more of the village. It was small and quaint, but very well built. On three sides, it was shielded more or less by mountains, and on the fourth approach, the least steep, tall trees hid most of their workmanship from prying eyes. This place was surely, by natural barriers, one of the most isolated in the world, despite there being a human town just at the foot of the mountain.

There were somewhere near forty small buildings, mostly with stone walls and clay-tiled roofs. Most were dwellings, but there were storehouses, a meeting hall, and a few workshops as well. The Accursed did not have much, but they did not need much, for it seemed that most of them were part-time hunters, and at other times would harvest nuts and fruits from wild groves they had seeded ages past. Indeed, the trees of the forest and the southern slope were all fruiting sorts, though they grew in something approximating nature's chaotic arrangement rather than the even rows of the foothill orchards near the palace.

There were two streams as well. The first, from which the Accursed drew their water, ran from what Tius said was an icy spring far higher up the mountain. It cascaded into the hollow in which the Accursed had built on the northern side of the plateau and there formed the border of their town before flowing down the lazy slope to the east. The other stream, which flowed down the south side, was used largely to wash away anything that needed to be removed from the village. Though they used most of what they made, there would always be waste where there was any living thing. The source of that stream, Avina had said with much delight, was a set of pools in a shallow cavern the Accursed had found, which at all times were pleasantly hot and in which the residents of the village did their bathing.

It must have taken an age to find such a site, Esteri reflected, guarded by mountains and presenting every natural resource or at least the opportunity to produce them, but then the Accursed had been in this world a very long time – perhaps since the days when Kalest was covered by the endless Birds' Wood – so they had had an age to find it and settle in it before the wars that had birthed most of the colony's residents ever began.

The Accursed were not entirely farmers and fighters. In the afternoon, Esteri made sure to meet their tailor, a man who had been an Indris quartermaster some five centuries before but had been volunteered for sacrifice as an Accursed when he was found to have his hands in the clothes of an officer's wife while they were still on the lady. He seemed ecstatic to sew for her, and while she had only wanted an outfit that fit her form right, was swiftly promised three or four for various occasions.

When the measurements were done, Esteri insisted on visiting their other industries, their forge and their kiln, the mason and the carpenter. Though for time being she needed nothing from any of them, most had already been alerted of her presence, as Erikis had told them a new home would soon need to be erected in the hollow.

Esteri sought out Erikis shortly thereafter. He listened patiently as she lambasted him for his presumptions, and then calmly pointed out it cost them nothing if she chose never to return – war was coming, and someone would likely inhabit the lot sooner rather than later.

After that, Esteri's time since she last slept in her own bed and had her needs attended by chambermaids and ladies-in-waiting began to wear on her. This was when Avina mentioned the source of the second stream, and suggested the two of them might feel somewhat better after visiting.

There was still something uncomfortable about being around Avina, but Esteri would have to endure the girl's presence for far longer, and the hot springs did sound like just what she needed.

Thus, Esteri readily agreed, and walked the path up the mountain. To have called the springs a cave, it seemed, was somewhat misleading: there were rock walls on three sides and a slight overhang covered the backmost pool of three, but the other two were open to the sky directly above. There were a few constructions at the pools, small rooms that Avina explained were for changing or drying off, and beside them pegs on which clothing could be hung, some of which were adorned with silk robes that would be adequate to conceal the body while resting in the water.

Soon enough, Esteri lowered herself into one of the pools and breathed a sigh of relief. She would stay at least a little while, until the aches her travel, unquiet sleep, and past day had left her with faded.

"So…" Avina said. "You know a lot about humans, right?"

Esteri nodded. "I'm not quite sure what you mean, but I was one until very recently."

"Yeah," Avina replied, "and a princess. Everyone here listens to Erikis because he knows everything about Accursed, so you had to learn a lot about your people, right?"

"I suppose."

Avina looked Esteri in the eyes. "Do you think they'll come up here?"

"Why would they?"

"Well," Avina said, "I can think of a few reasons. Like the stream... we wash things down the stream, and then it joins up with other streams and flows right past a human town at the foot of the mountain. I've heard they catch fish in the river, what if they catch something we threw away? They'd know somebody touched the water before them."

"Someone up one of the streams," Esteri said. "There's nothing to say that it's this one, or that there's anything strange about whoever's up here. And besides, this town has been here a long, long time from what I understand. If anyone was going to check up on it, someone would have generations ago. When you've endured here as long as you have, I can't imagine that changing unless something changes here, too."

But of course, Esteri realized, something had changed. The princess of Kalest had come among them, and with her father and the queen desiring her head, no less. How hard would it be to follow her tracks? She hadn't taken any effort to hide them, so for all she knew there was a huntsman or assassin climbing up the mountain while she blithely bathed herself in a hot spring pool.

"Something wrong?" Avina asked, "I didn't hurt you earlier, did I?"

"No," Esteri said, "I was just thinking about home – where I came from, that is."

"Do you miss it, then?"

Esteri leaned back, sinking a little lower into the water.

"Not as much as I thought I would," she said. "I miss the fine bed and the fine food and the fine clothes, and not having to fight in a stone ring until my whole body protests. I miss my brother, some of my servants, and the man my father used to be. But all the same... I can bear it. I've been part of this place for one day really, if even that, and already I'm comfortable here, in some ways."

Avina looked at Esteri strangely. "I think that's the hot water."

Esteri laughed. "I do admit that it's a fair bit better than the baths back home. More convenient too. Though I wouldn't say no to the lavender oils and soaps we had. All the same, I don't think it's just that. I've received a good deal of raw treatment here, but all of it has been very honest, and of honesty and decency the former is by far the rarer at court."

"So you like people beating you up?"

"No, but I do like people who don't lie to me, or coddle me when it's against my best interests."

"You must hate Tius, then," Avina said

"Ha! He has been walking on eggshells, hasn't he? But he's a decent sort, and I suppose I can enjoy a little coddling... but only a little."

A dark look flickered across Avina's face, but she smiled again before speaking.

"Well," she said, "that's neither here nor there. I hope you find your place here. After all, anybody might be able to fill in that new place but they're making it with you in mind."

"I hope so too," Esteri said. She remembered the idea of the huntsman climbing the mountain. However unlikely the exact scenario was, she couldn't let herself get too comfortable until her business in Kalest and Lysama had been finally resolved. It wasn't the time to be thinking what curtains she'd like or how she would earn her keep. Not only did every day she stayed endanger these people further, but each one that added onto her comfort and complacency made her want to risk her life in Lysama all the less.

"But," Esteri said, "that's not for me to decide. It's a dangerous world down there. Are you sure you're going when I must?"

"I'm not a child," Avina said harshly. "I'm sixteen. I'm a woman and I'm more powerful than anybody except maybe Erikis. I'm not staying cooped up here while my mom and my dad and my friends go down the mountain with you. I'm going to see the world out there, and I'm going to come back, and I'd like to see them try to stop me."

Having been on the receiving end of Avina's power, Esteri couldn't argue that it would probably take an army to do a thing to her.

"Well," Esteri said, "That's good. I'll be glad to have you along."

Esteri stood, and began to wring out her hair and prepare to leave. The comforts of the village had become far, far less comfortable since she slid into the hot spring.

CHAPTER VIII

Piru

King Piru stalked the halls of his palace, ever more frustrated. No reply from Indris, still. The Confederation was always slow to act on matters of state, since no one leader could really speak for all of it, but the situation was quickly becoming ridiculous. Should he order an invasion under the pretense that their silence was a tacit agreement to side with Lysama? Or did he have to wait for them to actually do something to wrong him, rather than wronging him by doing nothing?

He could also attempt to invade Lysama through the mountain passes, rather than taking the easy road through Indris, but the fortification along the border was such that even if it was possible, and Piru did not doubt that it was, the cost to take the passes and carve a road into the heart of Lysama that way would be so great that his army would never reach their capitol without a miracle.

There were always the Hyperboreans, his wife reminded him. They had been willing to help make his dreams a reality before, they could do it again. If the fortresses along the border fell to treachery, the armies of Kalest could enter Lysama untouched on the grounds of Esteri, and their numbers would be sufficient to stamp out the Lysaman resistance, especially if some of the enemy was caught unawares.

But last time, Hyperborean aid had, along with his own unthinking arrogance, cost Piru his daughter. What would be the price to subvert the border? Could he afford the inevitable toll, and for such a deed, could his people? Even in Ukko's time, Hyperborea had been mysterious and feared, their hands meddling in politics in every corner of the world, untrusted but indispensable. How could Piru be sure that Hyperborea meant to aid him, and was not setting him up for a grand failure, broken before Lysama? Could he be certain that Indris' silence was not on their advice?

He hoped so, because he trusted Delphina deeply, even with what her advice had wrought. He loved her almost as well as he had loved Aliisa, even if it had taken time to become accustomed to the fact, and she believed the Hyperboreans meant to help.

Thus, Piru stalked out of the palace and down into the mustering grounds, and the barracks where Ukko had housed himself and those soldiers who he was training. He could use some good news, and while the rate at which trainees were removed from the group was always somewhat alarming, the progress of those who were left was one of the few things Piru could count upon to raise his spirits.

And the loss rate wasn't all bad news, either. After all, Piru had assigned most of the washouts – other than one that had been court-marshaled – to General Sauli. It was on Ukko's suggestion. They'd learned as much as they could, and would help teach the line troops techniques for use against the unknown. In Ukko's estimation, those he sent away were not wash-outs, but graduates.

"Ukko," Piru said. "Good of you to see me once more on short notice."

"Ah," the ancient young man said, "I can always make time for royalty. I imagine you want another status report?"

"That I do."

"Well," Ukko said, "five trainees remain, and I expect that is as low as the number shall go. The two that departed – it was a hard choice to lose them, they were both very skilled, but I suspect that they would have died quite quickly away from a proper battle-line. One of them, Loviisa Heikki, has the potential to be a great commander, maybe a General some day.

I trust you to know who would be best to foster that."

"I see. And these five, who are they?"

"I'm glad you asked," Ukko said, "They're an interesting number. Maria Tuisku, for instance, a young lady who favors a massive hand-and-a-half sword. She earned her place among my squad through sheer determination. Her unwillingness to surrender under any circumstances alone would not have taken her the full way, but she can swallow the pride that serves her so well if ordered to. Launo Aaroni Vapaa, on the other hand"-

"A noble?"

"Exactly so, yet he is the model of humility. He could have easily had a commission, and yet he came to me, kneels before a man he does not know the rank of, accepts his training and learns from his mistakes."

"They're polar opposites," Piru noted. "I can hardly tell what you are looking for."

"I trust you will understand at least one of my choices – Seija Lahti. I think I may have mentioned her before."

Piru nodded.

"Such skill in one so young... in some ways, she handicaps herself by favoring the meteor hammer, a clumsy and un-wieldy weapon, and yet I think she could surpass me if she had the time. If she were merely very good, I would have taken Loviisa, but someone who is so superior in every aspect, effortless the top of her class or any other... I could not refuse her, even if there were some ways in which she is a marginal choice."

"Such a woman is a great asset for Kalest."

"They all are," Ukko said, "not just the ones I retained, as I ever endeavor to remind you. Remember, I began with the most devoted, and with but one or two exceptions, as you re-call, each one could be something far greater than any soldier of lesser faith, I am sure."

"That is three," Piru said. "The other two?"

"There is Taavi Ruusu," Ukko replied, "who so many times

I almost pruned from my rolls. A commoner who dreams that he would be awarded a knighthood for his valor; such a petty goal that he states so often, and so personal, but at his heart he wishes to perform a service worthy of knighting, and sees gaining that recognition only as a sign that he has done well."

"If he helps you bring my daughter back," Piru said, "I shall be sure to ennoble him... and the others of course. He would be worthy. The last?"

"Acacia Suominen," said Ukko, "Is a large part of the reason I selected who I did, though all had their own merits. Acacia does not excel at any one field, but her competence in each is very high. She is devoted and stubborn, and skilled in a measure not commonly seen outside those raised for warfare. And above it all she is kind, a gentle soul who will never be consumed by bloodlust nor tempted to act out of vengeance... and with all the others, she has formed such bonds, even with Seija, that when they fight together they will act as one with the strength of all and more, rather than each with his or her own strength alone."

"Fascinating." Piru said. He felt as though he might have heard something of the sort before, but now this was approaching strategy.

"That is my secret to the mission you have given me," Ukko said. "No one soldier, not even I, could stand against an Accursed abomination. A hundred men might prevail, but they would become eighty, then seventy, and so on. But six... six of us will guard each other, and aid each other. We will cut with combined skill, and we will not fall because we will not stand alone. The six of us will seek Esteri, while the others sent among the regular forces will harden the battle-line in a broader sense, as specialists within regular units."

"I think I understand," Piru said. "You shall spare unnecessary losses. It also strikes me that a group like yours... you might be able to move ahead of the army. Even enter enemy fastnesses with them unawares?"

"If you mean the border fortresses over which you have

so often fumed," Ukko said, "I doubt we could throw open the gates for your regulars. The arts of stealth, when applied against humans and not beasts of the forest, are arts in which I am afraid I know no more than any man."

"Of course," said Piru. "I meant perhaps, if they hold Esteri in a city, you might extract her before we lay siege, maybe even from the siege."

"Perhaps," Ukko said, "and if it comes to that, it would be safer for her than waiting until the rams at the gates do their work. I myself had considered the possibility."

Piru stood. "Thank you, Ukko," he said. "I have placed my daughter's life in your hands, pinned the hopes of my nation on your wisdom, and the more I hear of your endeavor the more certain I am that I will not be disappointed."

"It is our kingdom," Ukko said. "Though I have been so long removed from its people, Kalest is my home. I am descended from wanderers of the Birds' Wood, and have shed more blood in its soil in my long life than I have in my body. I will protect it, and bring my granddaughter of granddaughters back to her father's arms if there is anything left of her to save. I swear it."

***

Piru looked out from the window, over the palace gardens, the mustering grounds, the city below. His faith in Ukko was greater than ever, but his faith in his path was no firmer than before.

For Kalest. That was why he walked his path, he reminded himself. For the future. He had not sacrificed so much, lost so much, to earn nothing for Kalest in the end. That was what kept Piru going, held his resolve firm... the idea that he would not just have lost Esteri, that it would not just have been his own fault, but that it would have been for nothing.

He had to lead his armies to war, and he had to win. Then at least history might remember him as a good king.

Piru heard the door open behind him, and footsteps enter.

"Piru my love," Delphina said, "I have the solution to our problems."

Piru turned around, and saw the Hyperborean ambassador with her. Naturally, he thought.

"What is this solution, then?" Piru asked, though he did not really want to hear.

"The problem is Indris' silence, is it not?" Delphina asked. "And that we can do nothing against them until they have denied us?"

"It is so."

"Then," Delphina said, "if we had another reason for war with Indris? That would correct the issue. We could march tomorrow, if we had the reason."

Now that was something that might be worth hearing. War with Indris was the goal, it would enrich the people of Kalest and provide them a road into the heart of Lysama. As long as the cause was good enough to put the hearts of the soldiers and the people into it, Piru could accept it.

"Tell me," Piru said.

"If I may," the ambassador said, "what if your majesty had proof that Indris aimed to profit at Kalest's expense? That Indris had allied itself with Lysama internally, and delayed your majesty's actions for the purpose of allowing Lysama's armies to pass its borders? Would that be reason for your majesty to make a pre-emptive strike?"

"Is this true?" Piru asked. "Or do you intend to fabricate this proof?"

"Your majesty," the ambassador said, "Hyperborea has long been party to all treaties of all nations, and witness to their pacts, whether those agreements are made publicly known or not. If Indris and Lysama had between themselves a secret treaty, it would not be secret to us, would it?"

"And you claim," Piru said, "to betray such a secret to me in this hour, when we wait on the precipice of war?"

"Hyperborea has no territorial aims on the mainland," the ambassador said, "but we have never claimed neutrality in its politics."

It was true, but it was not an answer to his question. Perhaps the ambassador felt Piru did not need to know. Perhaps Delphina saw fit to keep from him whether or not he was helping to perpetrate another deception. That seemed likely – she knew his conscience pained him, but perhaps did not realize that it could become no worse, and he would rather not be ignorant of the truth of the matter.

"No," Piru said. "You claim to be friends and allies of Kalest. I do not doubt that your compatriots in Lysama and Indris claim that Hyperborea is a friend and ally of those nations as well, and when I come to the world with your revelations about a secret treaty, they will say Kalesti spies must have gained access to it."

"Then you would see the proof?" Delphina asked. "Our armies will march."

"First tell me, is it true?"

"Partially," the Ambassador admitted. "Lysama and Indris do have such a treaty, but Indris debates hotly whether or not they shall honor it. Their senators bicker – some hold honor highly, others fear Kalesti might or take offense to Lysama's provocation. It is an old agreement, some say. Kalest's demands are too much, say others. They will say Kalest presents the greater threat. They will say Lysama presents the more immediate threat. They will say that both will invade the war will be fought on Indris soil if they do not choose a side. They will say that they shall surely take the brunt of invasion and fall if they do choose a side. The wisest few hope Kalest will act before receiving an answer, and storm the border fortresses of Lysama."

With such considerations, Piru realized, Indris would never give an answer. If they broke their treaty, Lysama would avenge themselves upon Indris. If they did, they knew they had no standing army, and that Lysama would use what little force they had as a shield against Kalest. He was waiting in vain.

"Give me something I can show my generals," Piru said, "and something that I can tell the public. Indris must burn –

they must all believe it."

"King Kalest makes a wise choice," the Ambassador said. "We will provide the documents – indisputable proof – and anything else that your majesty requires, in exchange for this consideration: Hyperborea wishes free access that our scribes may make a copy of the Chronicle of Kalest."

That was an interesting price, but one that ultimately cost Kalest nothing. The Chronicle was Kalest's sacred book, and its secret history. There were versions, of course, that the public had – chapbooks and tomes that retold many of the stories of Kalest's founding, its people, its wars. Disconnected stories that wove together into a tapestry of glory, sang the praises of Kalest's gods and of its kings and queens. But the true chronicle was a series of many massive books, the oldest of which were faithful copies of even more ancient scrolls and inscriptions.

Every monarch of Kalest added his or her own reign to the Chronicle: an unbroken thread of Kalest's history from the days of the Birds' Wood to the modern era, the secret history that only those with royal blood could ever know. The chronicle told of Ukko, it told of saints and sinners alike in their own words, granting insight into the reigns and minds of both the most exalted and most reviled rulers the nation ever had.

To give such information to Hyperborea was a frightening prospect, but they had not demanded the original, and Piru wondered how much they already knew; they were a great kingdom when the woods were first tamed.

"Done," Piru said.

The ambassador bowed. "I shall have the documents by sunset, your majesty."

He left, and Piru was alone with Delphina.

"You see, my love," Delphina said, "this will all work out for us. A lovely little war, Indris burning to feed our forges, and then Lysama, at last. The Chronicle of Kalest? It shall soon be the world's chronicle, will it not?"

"Indeed," Piru said. "A good, strong land."

But hadn't Kalest already been good and strong? Were not those descended from the wanderers of the Birds' Wood already the hardiest and most noble of all people? But grander ambitions were already underway. They could not be stopped, not anymore.

"A kingdom worthy of our son," Delphina said. "He shall not regret what transpires in the coming months, nor will the people he someday rules, enriched as they will be by our efforts."

Tuoni... he was only eight. He did not understand what war meant, nor was he party to his parents' plans for his future. He only knew that his sister, whom he had dearly loved, was now lost to him, and he mourned her as though she were dead because the truth was too complicated for his young mind to handle.

"I should speak with him," Piru said. "I haven't made the time since this all began."

Piru turned to the door.

"I only hope," he said, "that your Hyperborean friends are as true to us as you believe."

***

Piru stood before his son's door, where his tutors said that he was, and knocked.

"Tuoni," he called. "It's your father. May I come in?"

"Oh!" Tuoni called back. "Sure, dad!"

Piru entered. His son's room was very sparse in decoration, the boy preferring spartan quarters. The things he had were fine, of course, the four-post bed with its silk velvet bedding neatly made, a dresser and table of rich oak, a grand and tall mirror. Tuoni was seated at the table and... examining alchemic glassware?

"What are you doing?" he asked, walking over to the table.

"Don't worry," Tuoni said. "I'm only doing what Doctor Onni said I could do."

Piru picked up a flask with a thick, red liquid in it. "Is this Blood of the God?" he asked. "I should have to speak to Doctor

Onni if he let you have this."

"Please!" Tuoni said. "I'm not going to do anything bad, I promise!"

"Alchemy is a dangerous art," Piru said. "You shouldn't be practicing it without supervision, and probably should not be practicing it all."

"But... I have to know what happened to Esteri," Tuoni said. "I want to help her!"

Piru sighed. Trust his son to move forward, heedless of the costs he might face along the path, heedless that he might fail and what that could do. In some ways, Tuoni was too much Piru's child for his own good.

"That," Piru said, "is a job for alchemists, not for princes. Let Doctor Onni and Doctor Markku work on finding a way to help Esteri. If there is a way, they'll find it."

Tuoni hugged his knees. "Esteri always helped me," he said. "All the time. Now I've got to do something for her."

Piru shook his head. "The best thing you can do for your sister is to be strong. If you get yourself hurt dabbling with Æther or Blood of the God on her account, how will she feel then? She'll want to see you better off than when she was taken away.

"Please," Piru said, "I'll let you read all you want about Alchemy, just promise me you won't work with its materials. Have Doctor Onni show you anything you want to see, as long as you don't touch it yourself. Promise me you won't?"

"I promise," Tuoni said.

"I'll be sending him by right away," Piru said, "to take this glassware back to the lab... but first, I did want to talk to you about something very important."

Tuoni nodded, listening intently to his father.

"Tuoni," Piru said, "I don't know if you've realized, but after what happened to Esteri, you will be king of Kalest some day. It will be your duty to protect and provide for its people, however many they are. All who live under Kalest's flag, you understand? It's a heavy burden, and as the Chronicle tells those of us bound by blood to the crown, no king nor queen has ever failed to be troubled by it in a dark hour."

"Dad?"

"I want you to promise me something else, Tuoni," Piru said. "I want you to promise me that when you are king, you will be a better one than I have been, Tuoni. I have made... made such difficult choices, weighing the needs of some of my people against the needs of others. I have made these choices in the hopes that you will not have to. That you will never need to sacrifice one life to better another. But the world is a harsh place sometimes, so," Piru sighed, "what I want you to promise me is that you won't just look at the end of things. Your father walks an unfortunate path to a better world, but to preserve that world, you must hold every part of it sacred."

"I don't know if I understand," Tuoni said, "but... I promise, I'll be the best king I can be."

"In some ways," Piru replied, "I hope that you never understand."

"Okay, dad," Tuoni said, though is tone indicated that he was still somehow uncertain. "Is... that what you wanted to say?"

Piru sighed deeply. Other things could wait at least until the Hyperborean ambassador came. Until then, he could at least be close to his son for a while. Perhaps... perhaps Ukko could do to meet another of his descendants. He was usually done with training by this hour, so it was worth a try.

"You know," Piru said, "if you don't mind leaving that Alchemy text be for a while, perhaps you could come with your old man. There's someone I'd like you to meet, if he is about. He is a very important man."

"Really? Who is he?"

"Well," Piru replied, "it's a bit hard to explain, so perhaps I shall let him. Could you come?"

"Sure," Tuoni said, jumping to his feet. "I'll come."

For the first time in perhaps a very long time, Piru smiled as he led the way back down to the barracks.

Piru might have made mistakes, he thought, but at least he could try to do right today.

CHAPTER IX

Tius

Tius stood in the morning light, ready for what was ahead. He had a backpack on his back, a sword at his hip, and a solid walking stick in his hand. Around him were the others ready for travel: Gelvira and Frideger standing close together, Avina near to them, Radegond, pacing moodily and then Esteri, waiting patiently.

Esteri was different than anyone Tius had ever met, and surprisingly enough, not what he had expected of a Princess either. Of course, she was beautiful, and she did have her haughty moments. However, most of them seemed to be in good humor, which was like many of the things she did. Her wit was cutting, but never too deep.

"Where is he?" Radegond growled. "It is not like Erikis to be late."

"It will be fine," Gelvira said. "It's not as though leaving a little earlier or later will matter in the end. We will get to Lysama when we get there."

"Discipline is important!" Radegond said. "Even for the most powerful of us! For the gods' sakes, our resident princess had the decency to appear when she was asked to appear."

Esteri cleared her throat. "And, as the point of this expedition, I would suggest you not be too hard on Erikis."

Esteri was smirking, and then Tius saw why. This was going to be good.

"Too hard?" Radegond demanded. "Perhaps in your tower with a hundred servants waiting on you hand and foot you can afford to be soft, princess!"

"Oh, really?" Esteri asked. "Then what do you intend to do?"

"If this were my army," Radegond declared, "he would have been flogged, and I or any other commander would come up with a creative punishment. He might salute squirrels in the yard, or be doused in rancid butter."

"Rancid butter?" Erikis asked, having walked the path from where Esteri spotted him approaching to right behind Radegond. "Interesting, but I thought you were against wasting supplies."

Radegond spun around. "You!"

"Please, Radegond," Erikis said, "spare me your tongue. I am quite aware I have delayed proceedings, but now there is no cause to delay them further."

"Fine," she said, then turned to Esteri. "I suppose you think that was funny? Well, enjoy it, because we have a long day ahead!"

Radegond began to march quickly down the hill. As the others followed, Erikis matched pace with Esteri.

"You know," he said, "I never thought I'd see someone get the better of Radegond like that."

"You enjoyed it?"

"Your majesty has a good sense of humor for royalty," Tius said with a smirk of his own.

"Well," Esteri replied, "you have excellent manners for a thief and an outlaw, so I suppose we are even."

Esteri laughed.

"You know"- she began, and then Avina appeared between the two of them.

"So!" Avina said, loudly and cheerfully. "We're finally headed off into the outside world, huh? What do you think it's going to be like, Tius?"

"Um, Avina..."

"I bet," Avina said, "that we see a lot of stuff we never would back home." She took Tius' hand and held it out in front of them "We're going south through Indris, right? Did you ever see the ocean, Tius? Dad says that on just the right day, you can't even tell where all that water ends and the sky begins, so the people who live down there call the sky the Sea of Clouds? Can you imagine it, something as big and open as the sky, and you could swim in it! It would be like we could all fly like Radegond."

"I don't think we're going that far south," Tius said, "maybe not even into what's technically Indris territory. Big caravans may not be able to get through the foothills, but we can."

"That's fine," Avina said, picking up the pace and bringing Tius along. "I'm sure there's plenty to see there, too, even if it is more mountains."

Tius shrugged. "I couldn't really say. It's not like I saw much of the world before."

"Well," Avina said, "we'll see it together."

Apparently, they were speaking loud enough for others to hear.

"This is not a sightseeing tour!" Radegond bellowed. "We have a very important and very dangerous mission, and you three children back there will take it seriously!"

"We'll still get to see some of this world," Avina said quietly. "She can't make us shut our eyes."

She had not released Tius' hand, and in fact was squeezing uncomfortably hard – even in her normal body, Avina was incredibly strong.

"Avina..." Tius stammered, shaking his hand

"Sorry," she said. "I was just wrapped up in the moment, you understand?"

"I do," Tius said, "but you still need to watch your strength. You could really hurt someone one of these days."

"I would never hurt you," Avina said

Tius remembered their practice bouts, and rubbed his smarting hand. She might not mean to, but Avina was more dangerous than she realized. Tius fell silent.

"So," Avina said, "why did you agree to come, anyway?"

Tius shrugged.

"Because I was asked," he said. "I didn't really think about it much. I guess Radegond is turning me into one of her jump-when-I-say-jump soldiers like she always threatened after all."

"That's it?" Avina asked.

"Well," Tius said, "did you really think about it?"

"No," Avina said. "Mom and dad were already going, and you were going, and I'm not scared of the world out there, as long as it stays out there when we come back."

"You like to remind everyone you're all grown up now," Tius said. "You could have stayed, if you didn't want to come."

"Just because I don't need my parents to look after me all the time doesn't mean I want to sit around and do nothing while you all head off into the world."

By then, they'd gotten off the good paths near town, and were hiking down the south face. Tius wasn't alone in focusing on his footing and continuing down the mountain in silence.

***

Before nightfall, they managed to reach the town at the base of the mountain. Tius had seen it before once or twice, and to him it was nothing particularly interesting. He had lived in one of the biggest cities in Kalest as a human, so the idea of a few hundred people wasn't frightfully many, even if he'd lived over a dozen years among under fifty.

Avina, though, couldn't contain her wonder, and after a moment's thought the reason was obvious: she, unlike the rest of them, had never seen so many people in one place, had never heard the hustle and bustle of even rural human life.

While her wonder and excitement had to be obvious to anyone who gave her much of a look, the mixture of what Tius could tell was joy on one side and fear on the other kept her constrained. She was doing well, overall, but not so well as to make a mistake out of carelessness.

Esteri, on the other hand, was clearly afraid and little else. With her hair hidden beneath a cloth and a hood that might have been suspicious on such a beautiful day, at least she wasn't immediately recognizable. They were still in Kalest, and would be for quite some time, after all. Tius didn't envy her: the most that any of the others had to do in order to avoid detection was nothing. Esteri actually had to hide.

And even with her head covered, her face was not. When Tius had lived in Kalest, new coins were minted with Esteri's mother on their face, among other designs. Would someone be able to compare a clipped copper to the real thing if they were unfortunate, or did she never sit for such a portrait?

Tius considered asking her, but since the thought had not occurred to him until they were among humans, he did not find an opportunity where he could be certain of not being overheard, nor could he think of a phrasing that wouldn't give them away if someone did hear it.

As late as it was, they made for the first inn they were directed towards. There, Erikis was in charge – among the other things he did for the community, he kept a stash of human coinage. Among each other, the Accursed mostly just did what was needed to keep the town together. With so few people and so little contact with the outside world, there was little they could pass among each other that would matter: there was only so much of anything to go around, and precious few luxuries.

But, now and again, they traded with the world outside the mountain. Erikis, or sometimes one of the others, would go down and barter some of their crafts for useful things they could not get themselves or had in too little quality, like good flour, foreign dyes, or cloths other than the goat wool they themselves husbanded.

At the same time, he and others accumulated a stash of coins from every nation for times of trouble, and this was one such time: The small group was actually carrying quite a lot of money, segregated into Kalesti and Lysaman coins, though most of it was from antique minting and might turn a few heads or be difficult to convince more cautious merchants to accept.

"Eight for a night," Erikis said, calling the landlord over.

"Hm," replied the landlord. "I can fit four to a room. Will you be wanting more than two?"

"Four, if you can spare them," Erikis replied. "What would the cost be?"

"Well, let me see.... Four rooms? That'll be... four bits a room... two double-eagles. Another'll get you all a hot supper if you'd like?"

The double-eagle was the smallest coin Kalest minted, and so was often split into halves, quarters, or eighths that were called bits. It was a pretty reasonable price, or Kalest had started putting more silver in them since the days when Tius lifted the little coins from fat merchants standing around market stalls.

"Will this suffice?" Erikis asked, placing a coin on the counter. The innkeeper picked it up and examined it.

"Kalevi IV?" he said. "It's a heavy coin, but I don't know it."

"It's an old mint," Erikis said, "and very pure silver. Certainly worth three double-eagles."

The landlord weighed the coin in his hand.

"Maybe," he said, "or it could be a hunk of lead. You might know, but the next person I pass it off to might not. I'll count these as one double-eagle each."

"I guarantee you any merchant with more wits than the mule that drags his cart will take it at a better value than that."

"May I?" one of the men at the bar asked. He was older than any of the Accursed looked but not truly old, and while he was richly dressed Tius reflected that he would not have tried to steal from the man, for he had a canny look about him.

"Certainly," Erikis said, and the landlord passed the coin over.

"Interesting," the rich man said. "It's been a long time since I've seen one of these." He weighed the coin in his hand and examined the edges. "But I have seen them before. I'll give you three double-eagles for it."

"My thanks, sir," Erikis said. "I am Erikis. I have more of its like, if you're interested."

"Larssi," the man replied to the introduction. "I'll gladly repeat the trade, but if I may ask… where does a group of young people like yourselves come by a wealth of such antique currency?"

Tius was very glad that Erikis was the one doing the talking. He would not have been able to come up with an answer himself, much less do so without arousing too many suspicions. More than just Larssi and the landlord were watching them, so the answer was very important.

"We come from a very small village," Erikis replied. "Coins enter and leave our possession only rarely."

"Really!" Larssi said. "I'd appreciate it if you told me where your village lies. It seems like you could use a peddler like myself passing through a little more often."

"You shall not find it," Erikis said, feigning sorrow. "We had a very bitter winter after an ill harvest. That is why we are setting out into the world, you see; only a few of the elders stayed behind in case the land should recover and we wanderers return."

"Well," Larssi replied, "if you're looking for a way to make your fortunes, then I suppose I have some good news for you. I've just come from Indris, and my time there leaves me little doubt that there shall soon be a war on the southern front. From what I've heard since crossing the border, it shall likely extend into Lysama too."

"You call that good news?" Esteri demanded, stepping forward.

"For some, young lady," Larssi said. "When a village burns, its land does not stop being good land, so if you are a farmer you might move in after the war is done. Of course, before then, it is likely that the armies of all involved nations will take any recruit willing to pledge to the cause. And for a merchant such as myself, war is very good for business. Even small conflicts can be turned to large profits; imagine what a full-scale invasion will do!"

Tius put a hand on Esteri's shoulder.

"Est," he said softly, calling her by the shortened name they deemed would likely be safe among the public, "calm down. It's not as though anyone enjoys the killing."

"Now there's a smart man," Larssi said. "Today's enemies can be tomorrow's customers. But what do I know? It's not like there's been a war like this in my time, so perhaps you should ask someone who was about when Arynias and Tyrvad clashed and Kalest intervened, though I don't know that you'll find any in a place like this."

"If we might resolve the matter of coinage…" Erikis said.

"Of course, of course," Larssi replied. They began to carefully spread coins on the counter and debate over their relative values, but soon enough the landlord was paid and the room keys were divided among the group: Erikis with his own, Gelvira and Frideger in another, and the five remaining separated along gender lines.

Tius, more weary than desirous of the thick stew that was being served, resolved to retire early.

***

Tius sat on the small cot, surveying the shabby room. It was larger than his bedroom at home, and it was probable that most of the things in it were newer than his, which had been made long before he came to the colony. Yet at the same time, it felt so much more weary, so much more worn down by their years.

Hathus sat on one of the other cots and yawned.

"Well, my young friend," he said, "after today's displays there can be no doubt. You, sir, have what I would like to call a plague of good fortunes."

"What are you talking about?" Tius asked. He wasn't exactly as tired as he had thought, but he was too weary to deal with double meanings and convoluted banter as Hathus loved to spin.

"Why, could it be you haven't noticed?" he asked. "On one side you have, as you seemingly always have, cute little Avina practically begging to be yours. But now! Now, young man, you also have the fiery, womanly Esteri waiting for your embrace. Were your choice not so painful, I would envy you and demand to know how you had managed to get yourself in such a position. As it is, I cower at your doom."

Tius picked up the sagging down pillow from his cot and halfheartedly tossed it at Hathus. "I've heard more than enough of this," he sighed.

"You don't believe me?" Hathus asked. "Remember, I have more years than you've been alive on you, and quite a sum more experience with the matter besides, but young people never do listen to their elders do they?" Hathus smirked. "Just remember that one is probably inclined to taking the lead herself and certainly unaccustomed to receiving 'no' as an answer, while the other is quite capable of squashing you into jelly."

Tius could see that Hathus wasn't about to let the topic go. It amused him after the first denial, and that meant Tius' reaction was part of the fun. Well, what happened if he played along?

"So," Tius said, "what would you do?"

"Me?" Hathus asked. "Well, I am an old man whose fancy remains faint stirrings of memory even as winter melts into spring, but if I were in your position, I should either make my decision right away and hope to survive letting down the other lady, or delay it as long as possible, until you can ignore one or the other no longer because she has thrown herself upon you in some moment of powerful passion, or one finds some other handsome youngster who will return her affection, leaving you with the other but always wondering what would have happened had you chosen the other way around."

Tius sighed. "Really?"

"Well," Hathus said, "I expect if you try to follow that advice, you will fumble blindly with your own feelings until you stumble into an answer, and whether the exotic, royal beauty or the slender maiden you have known so many years is your decision, find your arms ripped from their sockets by the other. In other words, about what I expect might happen had I said nothing at all."

Tius rolled his eyes. "Thanks, then," he said. "I'm rather attached to my arms, so forgive me if I don't provide the amusing sight you're looking for."

There was a knock at the door.

"Tius?" Avina called. "Are you there?"

"Yes," he called. "Come in."

Avina entered the room, closing the door behind her.

"Should I head downstairs?" Hathus asked.

"No," Tius said, then looked to Avina. "What's on your mind?" he asked.

"Oh," she said, eyes darting to Hathus and then back to Tius, "I just wanted to talk a little about this town, that's all. Can I sit?"

"Sure," Tius said. Avina sat down next to him.

"Is this like your old home?" Avina asked.

"What do you mean? The room?"

"Maybe, but really the town."

"Well," Tius began, but then there was a knock at the door.

"Hello," Esteri called. "May I come in?"

"Of course," Tius replied. What could Esteri want? She tried the handle, but apparently Avina had brushed the latch shut when she entered. Tius stood and walked over to the door, and Hathus did the same.

"Well," Hathus said, "that's my cue to see what they're serving at this hour. Have fun."

"What do you..." Tius began to ask. "Never mind."

Hathus trotted out of the room, and Esteri slid inside, quickly scanning the room and its occupants.

"Forgive me for interrupting," she said, her voice anything but apologetic, "but I felt like I had to talk to someone."

"What about?" Tius asked, taking a seat on one of the unused cots. Esteri seated herself next to him.

"It's about that man, the merchant from downstairs."

"I remember," Tius said. Avina had moved herself to the cot across from them, and Tius suddenly felt quite confined. He reminded himself that Hathus would enjoy seeing his discomfort, and that there was probably a much better reason for this.

"Well," Esteri said, "I don't think I trust him. Any man who thinks he can make a tidy profit out of war has his priorities in the wrong place, and the way he looked me... I fear he might have an inkling of who I am."

"He knew a lot about coins," Tius said. "Do they put your face on any these days?"

Esteri thought for a moment, then nodded. "I sat for an official portrait for that sort of thing last year. I think they started striking coins with that image in the fall... the big silver ones, with the two trees on the back."

"Well," Tius said, "keep yourself covered up as long as we're here, and hopefully he'll think the idea's too preposterous to follow up on."

"And if he doesn't?" Esteri asked. "If he guesses? I may be stronger now, but I'm still no fighter."

"Then," Tius said, "you should probably stick close to Radegond. She's the most skilled fighter among us, she sleeps with one eye open and has a few more in the back of her head – not literally, mind."

Esteri looked away. "You're sure? It seems sometimes like Radegond would be all too happy to have me gone, this must be such a bother."

"Don't worry," Tius said. "She may yell a lot, but she's really not that angry, and she'd certainly never botch what she considers her mission."

"I'd just feel safer with someone else around, you understand?"

"Well," Tius said, "you're rooming with Avina, too." He looked up to Avina. "If that creep tries anything, I don't think anyone could blame you if you went all-out on him."

"All right," Esteri said. She seemed sad, or perhaps still nervous?

"If it's any peace of mind," Tius offered as she stood up, "I could stay up outside your door tonight. We're all here to keep you safe, after all."

"It's all right, really," Esteri said. Tius stood, and walked her to the door.

She placed her hand on the handle, then turned and kissed Tius on the cheek.

"You're a good man," Esteri said. "Thank you."

Esteri left the room, closing the door behind her.

Was that normal? Tius lifted a hand to his cheek. He hadn't been around humans for a long time, and never around nobles. It was likely just the parting that was in fashion, as he'd heard Indris folk would sometimes give a kiss on each cheek as greeting.

"I'm sorry about that," Tius said, turning back to Avina. "You were saying?"

"Nothing important," Avina said grumpily.

"You don't want to talk anymore?" Tius asked. He could at least guess that might be related to Esteri. The two girls sometimes got along swimmingly and seemed to be the best of friends, but at other times each seemed quite bitter the other existed, particularly Avina. She had been in one of those moods the whole day.

Avina looked at the floor, but made no motion to leave, so Tius sat down next to her.

"Well," Avina said, "if you'd like to tell me about your old home, I'd like to listen. Maybe we could get some wine, too."

"If there's anything my old life taught me," Tius said with a laugh, "it's that wine is expensive. If they have any here, you don't want it or Erikis wouldn't let us have it."

"Hm," Avina said, leaning on Tius a little. "If you say so. How is this place different than where you grew up?"

"This place is a lot smaller," Tius said. "In fact, it's probably closer in size to our village than the city. I couldn't tell you much more about differences, since we haven't really seen a whole lot of this place."

"And the city?"

"It was hard," Tius said. "With so many people, nobody can really care about everybody, and some just don't have anyone to care about them at all."

"That sounds awful," Avina said. "Well, you're not alone anymore, Tius."

"I know," Tius said. "Things got a lot better for me after Erikis found me. But, it's not that bad for everyone. There are just people who slip through the cracks."

Avina sighed. "You know, Tius, sometimes I wonder about you."

"What's that supposed to mean?"

"Nothing," Avina replied with a broad smile. "Since we're going to be going through Kalest, do you think you could tell me about it?"

"Well," Tius said, "it's not like I know what things are like nowadays."

"Please?"

Tius thought about it for a moment. He might only know Kalest as it was when Avina was an infant, more or less, but some things he couldn't imagine changing, like how the state made sure everyone learned some of the great stories of Kalest; the Birds' Wood and the Founding, the Times of Survival, the Captivity and the Liberation, the reigns of Kalest's greatest kings and queens.

These were things anyone Kalesti would know, tales that shaped them as much as did the stories and the rules of the Gods, and Avina probably didn't know either of them: neither of her parents had ever been Kalesti.

"If you don't mind hearing some old stories, there's a lot you could learn about Kalest."

"Sure!" Avina said.

She listened close, leaning up against Tius as the night wore on and no doubt she grew very tired and Hathus finally returned, at which point she quietly excused herself.

"No bruises," Hathus commented. "I'm surprised. I would have thought her highness would have slapped you until you were black and blue."

"Actually," Tius said, too ready to sleep to realize he was throwing fuel on the fire, "she gave me a kiss on the cheek when she left."

"You poor sucker," Hathus said. "Good night, and good luck. You're going to need it."

***

The next day, they left the town and started tracking south by southwest at Radegond's instruction. The border was close to the west, but the mountains were nearly impassible, and surely patrolled. A group traveling across them would almost certainly be accosted by soldiers from one side or another, and Esteri found out, long before they could ever reach Lysama's capitol, particularly if it was Kalesti troops that caught them.

Tius was not alone in worrying about their route: they would be passing dangerously near to Indris, which would seem to be a warfront. If they were unlucky, they could be walking into the mouth of hell itself. Radegond assured the rest that they would be fine: a war in Indris would have its front farther south than their path across the foothills.

The days went by, one after the other, and slowly began to fade into each other, they developed their own pattern. Hathus never gave up heckling Tius about Avina and Esteri, at least when neither of the women were within earshot, which was rarely: one or the other generally sought him out for company during the day, sometimes both. When they weren't, they seemed to spend time with each other or with Avina's parents. Since Hathus had a habit of making an ass of himself, it seemed natural enough: neither Radegond nor Erikis made any efforts to be approachable.

Somehow, impossibly, they made it to the foothills in the

south without incident. The crossing was hard, hard enough that Tius understood why the hills were not fortified in the same way as the mountain passes. The rugged land was full of thorn bushes and broken rocks, and would be thoroughly impossible to march over, or even ride horses across.

Still, on foot and not needing to maintain formation, it was only mildly miserable, and a good deal of that was because Radegond was forcing them to move at double pace to somehow counteract the ruggedness of the land, walking their path from dawn until hours after nightfall.

It was dark when they crested the last ridge into Lysaman territory. As they bedded down for the last time in those damnable hills, Tius found himself restless. Wandering the edges of camp, Gelvira found him.

"Having trouble sleeping?" she asked.

It would have been strange for anyone looking at the two of them, but Tius regarded her as something of an aunt.

"A bit," Tius admitted.

"Has my daughter been giving you a hard time?" Gelvira asked.

"What?"

"Oh," Gelvira said, "I just know she can be a handful. Now more than ever really, since she's such a mature woman who doesn't have to listen to her mother anymore."

"No," Tius sighed, "Avina's actually been rather... tolerable, I guess."

"Well then," Gelvira said, "any idea what the problem might be?"

"I guess I'm just worried," Tius said, "about what might happen when we get down there. This trip has been entirely too uneventful so far."

"Well," Gelvira said, "the reason why the seven of us are here with the princess is because we can handle what the world can throw at us."

"It's not that I don't trust Erikis' judgment," Tius said.

"It's that you want to be sure the princess is safe?"

Tius nodded.

"Well," Gelvira said, "that's only natural. Esteri has made quite the impression... on all of us, really. She's very strong at heart, but all the determination in the world and all the thorns of Kalest's Rose won't save her – that's what you're afraid of, am I right?"

"Are you sure you can't read minds?" Tius asked. "Because I'm not."

Gelvira laughed. "I'm almost a hundred years old," she said, "and half decent with people if I do say so myself. Experience counts for quite a lot."

"When you care to use it," Tius said.

"Oh? Let me guess this one, too – Hathus has been himself quite loudly. Did I guess somewhere close?"

"It's nothing," Tius said. "He just wants to see me squirm."

"Well then," Gelvira said, "don't let him. He'll give up soon enough. He doesn't have very much patience, you know."

That was sound advice if Tius had ever heard it, but it was hard to follow. Hathus' constant needling had planted the seed in his mind, and now he wondered just how much truth there was to it. He and Avina had a long past, and their relationship had always been changing, from the days when he could pick her up and carry her on his shoulders to pleasant banter in long evenings, sparring partners, friends. Would it change even further? Had it changed without his noticing? And as for Esteri, Tius never would have thought a woman like her would speak so much as a kind word to him, much less seek out his companionship. He could have been just as mistaken about her intentions.

No matter how Tius tried to ignore it, the question nagged at him.

Well, he'd try to not let it show. It was all nonsense, probably. Probably, it would be forgotten as soon as Hathus found some new amusement.

But stranger things had happened.

CHAPTER X

Ukko

Ukko stood before his trainees. No, he stood before his friends. For the most part they were exhausted, beaten, and out of breath, because while had weeded out the very weak, and those who couldn't form a cohesive team, he had only sharpened their skills a little, and there was much they could learn before setting out for the front. But, for the most part, they were smiling as well

"One more go?" Maria asked, looking to Acacia.

"I think we can get it this time. Sir?"

Ukko smiled himself, and nodded. "One more go, but really you've done well enough. You're only trying to beat your own time."

"You got through it faster," Acacia pointed out, "and on your own. I saw it and I don't know how you managed."

"If you insist," Ukko said, "though there's more to a day's training than this, especially today's.

Acacia looked to the others. "We can call it quits, or we can go on," she said. "I'd like one last chance at the course, but it's your choice. Are you with me?"

Taavi and Launo voiced their agreement quickly, and Seija, clearly uninterested, acquiesced all the same.

They were stronger than they realized, and when they got through the mess of obstacles, Ukko applauded them.

"You've all done very well," he said, "though you're slowing down now, rather than speeding up."

"Well," Maria said, "we'll have another go tomorrow then."

"Actually," Ukko said, "I don't think that will be happening."

All his trainees looked at him with various emotions on their faces, mostly confusion but annoyance from Maria and mild interest only from Seija.

"During one of your later runs," Ukko said, "a messenger came from the King. Based on the progress of the army, he wants us to move out tomorrow. We will be on deployment, and quite far away from this little obstacle course."

"Really?" Taavi asked. "We have a mission?"

"A very important mission," Ukko said. "We are going to rescue the Princess of Kalest from her captors, and on the way we are going to put down any great abominations we come across."

Ukko sighed.

"I can see you don't think you're ready for that," he said, "and frankly, no one ever is ready to kill, whether it's a monster or another person. But I have faith in us, that when we are on the field of battle we will not hesitate, will not waver. We are more valuable to each other than all the skill we might gain in our lives, and that is why there will be a change of protocol when we leave the training grounds. From tomorrow on, I am no longer to be your teacher or your commanding officer. As his majesty speaks to me, I shall still impart his orders, but… if you can, I would have you treat me as one of your own, my words and opinions when they are my own to be weighed and considered as you would any other."

Ukko was, in some ways, making a calculated move. They would have a long enough journey to the border, even short-cutting the fighting in Indris to arrive ahead of the ground force, and if the five of them could trust him as a comrade by the time they saw battle, both he and they would be far more likely to make out with their skins intact.

But, on the other hand, Ukko badly wanted it to be possible. His years on end in the ancient forest felt like a dream now; the numberless days of hunting and wandering and resting in that old, stone lair were hazy. These days, spent with his five young trainees... they made him feel more alive than he had in a long time. He had been called to defend Kalest before, but each time it was as a specter of the nation's might, riding into battle as a champion and vanishing without saying a word to any soldier. These days... they were like the ones he could clearly remember, meeting with kings and queens and their children in the deep wood, or even more than that, like the days when he had been a mortal man.

It was a good feeling.

"Well," Acacia said, "if that's how you feel, and if we're really done for the day, then we should start now."

"Excuse me?"

"I think she means that you should come with us," Launo fielded. "We often visit a certain tavern after hours. They have good meat for dinner more often than not and decent drink."

"It'll be fun," Acacia offered. "Taavi's uncle runs the place, too."

Ukko smiled. Of course, he needed to report to Piru some time in the evening, but it was not urgent. He could make time for his friends.

"It sounds lovely," Ukko said. "I shall come."

Even Seija gave a slight smirk.

"Well," Acacia said, "we'll have to make an exceptional night of it if we won't be back here for a while."

***

Hours later, they walked, or at least mostly walked given Launo's stumbling, out of the tavern.

"You know," Acacia said, "it seems like you do know how to have a good time, once you get into it."

"It's not that," Ukko replied. "I'd simply forgotten."

Ukko had thought long and hard, even before his first drink, about how much he would tell his new friends. He had decided that they at least deserved to know the results of his story, even if not the circumstances that lead to it.

"Forgotten?" Acacia asked. "Is that what being a commander does to you?"

Ukko looked around. The streets were quiet – it was just the six of them walking.

"I believe," he said, "that to this day I have not been totally truthful with you. I have avoided telling a lie, but at the same time I have allowed you to believe a falsehood. I would like to rectify that, if you would listen."

The five young people muttered assent.

"You likely guessed at one truth," he said. "That I am older than I appear to be, if only because I look scarcely your senior and was put in the position I was in."

"I'd just thought you were a friend of the King," Taavi admitted. "Not that there's anything wrong with that, or he'd put you in charge just for that, but... well, it made sense."

"The truth is," Ukko said, "and if any of you think this to be the alcohol talking either to you or to me I shall be glad to confirm it in the morning, that I have been alive for over a thousand years... though remembering now what it is like to be among other humans, I am not so sure that I have really lived as many."

"What do you mean?" Acacia asked.

"It means," Seija said, smugly superior, "that Ukko here is Accursed. Am I right?"

"Half," he said. "I am... unique, as far as I have ever heard. I was given a dose of the same potion that makes them as they are without knowing it, and found as years wore on that I was standing still. In all other respects than that, I am as I was the day I drank it."

"Hm," Seija growled. "Well, that's strange." She seemed to be considering carefully what it meant for her.

"I'm not sure what to say," Acacia muttered.

"I can't tell you," Ukko said. "I can only say that I felt you all deserved the truth. I may have to put my life in your hands, or you put your lives in my hands. It is something too important for me to keep such secrets."

Ukko closed his eyes. "If any of you feel like you can't go into battle with me knowing that, you are free to leave, or request that I not accompany you. It is better if we fight without doubt than that we fight with greater numbers, though the loss of any one of you I fear would be a dire blow."

A moment later, one of the lot embraced him, then a heartbeat later another. Ukko opened his eyes in time to see Launo add his arms to the rest of them. Seija was the only one not part of it, at least until Acacia reached out with one arm, grabbed her by the wrist, and pulled her forward, at which point the stoic woman at least made some small show of affection. Even more showed on her face, a warm and honest smile that, while faint, was so rarely given.

"Thank you," Ukko said, tears filling his eyes. "I... I am so proud to have known you all."

"Just remember," Acacia said, "you're one of us now. And we're going to stick together to the end."

Ukko's heart swelled to be surrounded by such people. Acacia... Maria... Launo... Taavi... Seija. Was the world full of more people like them? Ukko hoped that it was. No matter how prone humans were to repeating their mistakes, if there were a few of them who were as good as these, humanity might just be in better straits.

"I will remember," he said. "I promise."

Seija stepped back.

"We've got a long day ahead of us," she said. "We should probably get some rest tonight."

"I've got to admit," Maria said, "this is going to take some getting used to. But on the plus side, it means one of us has a lot of experience cutting open the Accursed monsters, so that's a win as far as I'm concerned."

The hug broke up slowly, and the lot of them began to walk back towards the barracks again. Ukko reflected that he would not sleep for a while longer, but he knew he would be fine.

***

In the morning, the six of Ukko's company, including himself, were given swift horses – a dozen, so that they could ride hard through the day ahead, switching mounts when one tired. They had much ground to make up – Indris' armies were crumbling before Kalest's forces. No doubt they would soon be overrun, and quicker than Lysama could likely predict.

Ukko had to get ahead of that line. If the fighting reached wherever Esteri was being held, she might be killed in the conflict or executed by the enemy to prevent her rescue, and if Lysama was preparing an Accursed army it would be best to begin the conflict with them far away from other people.

They had ridden for three days, and while each was less comfortable being farther from the well-paved roads around the capitol, each had been a day of higher spirits as they found the rhythm that suited them and those not familiar with horses became used to the saddle.

Acacia rode up next to Ukko. Her control of her steed was still unsteady, but far better than it had been.

"Do you mind if I ask something?" she said

"Not at all," Ukko replied. His pride stung a tiny bit to admit it, but she had the same effect on him that she did on all their other compatriots; Ukko could not help but smile a little.

"Before... before you found out you weren't aging, what sort of person were you?" She shook her head "That's not quite right. Who were you before? Hm..."

"I think I understand the question," Ukko said. "I am proud to say I was a Knight of Kalest, born to hold a sword, which my times were unkind enough to demand I wield often to protect my Queen."

"And the world, in that age... what was it like?"

"Oddly," Ukko said, "not so different than it is now. I wonder somewhat at how little some things have changed. Did civilization reach its pinnacle before even my time, or is there something holding us back?"

Ukko looked to Acacia. Her expression turned very grim

thinking about the matter.

"It is nothing to worry about," he assured her. "People do live longer lives now than they once did. I have studied history more recent than myself since returning to the company of humans, and find that plagues grow scarcer and less devastating with each generation. That is a good thought, isn't it?"

Ukko projected optimism, but was not himself so sure. He had advised Piru of the futility of conquest, of how history repeated itself time and time again, and each captivity of one nation by another was followed by a liberation and the restoration of ancient borders. But why did it have to be so? Some of the histories talked about great visionaries, not only in politics but in the sciences. Yet medicine lurched forward only slowly, and in every other field nothing came of these geniuses for long.

Ukko had his own theories as to why, but he would not speak them in polite company.

"May I ask you something as well?" Launo said, riding up to the other side of Ukko.

"Certainly."

"There are legends," he said, "of a knight who has arisen from the mists when Kalest has been in great need of aid. It has occurred to me that there might be some truth to it."

"That," said Ukko, "I could not tell you for certain. I have ridden to battle since my exile from common life a few times, when the king or queen of Kalest saw a need to call on me, but I am not terribly familiar with the legends so I cannot say if they were my exploits or not."

Ukko suspected that some were. He had often used poor visibility, such as mist or fog, to turn the tables on invaders, cutting down their commanders in honorable combat and leaving the rabble disorganized, only to retreat out of sight before Kalest's army knew more of its benefactor than his silhouette.

"Well," said Launo, "that's answer enough. It is good to know that there is one fellow knight who does honor to the title."

"What do you mean?" Acacia asked.

"Meaning no offense to you or anyone else in this company," Launo said, "but I had expected at the calling to be surrounded by men and women of my own station. That I am among largely common folk – again, no offense meant – is a sad commentary on how seriously some people take their oaths and honors."

"And why should that offend us?" Maria called from behind. "We stepped up where spoiled brats stepped out, and so did you. They're the ones who would take offense, and they should. It's their own fault."

"It might not be so grim," replied Ukko. "For every blooded knight that takes the field, Kalest employs scores of common soldiers. It might just be that you were the only one swift enough to arrive on time."

"It's like me," Acacia said. "I'm sure there were a lot more people from the city coming, but when the king asked for people for a dangerous, important job, there were just too many of us jumping at the chance."

Launo nodded. "That could be," he said, "but it's those who came when called who understand what it means to be devoted." He looked over his shoulder. "Isn't that right, sir Taavi?"

Everyone had their little games, and one among Ukko's friends was addressing Taavi as though he were already a knight sometimes, in part because he always shied away from the accolade he so deeply wanted.

"I don't know that much," Taavi said. "I just want to help."

"That's the point," said Acacia. "Doing good."

"And never giving up!" added Maria. Naturally, she would inject a little of herself into the matter.

"It is the core of honor," Launo said, "as I am certain the King is aware."

Seija, who had been riding far from the rest to get a better field of vision on the countryside, came riding back towards the rest.

"There's a reservist camp just over that ridge," she called, pointing it out. "Should we check in?"

"I think so," Ukko said, turning that direction. "Three days is long enough, and they've likely been in contact with the front."

***

Ukko went to the commander of the camp alone, displayed his rank and privilege to information, and asked if there was any news.

"Not as such," the man said, "but… there was one thing you might want to follow up on if you get the chance, for all that it's worth."

"And that is?"

"We had a merchant who came through try to collect the bounty for information about Her Highness, the Princess."

"Tell me," Ukko said. The commander's tone had been dismissive, but men the commander's age, who had seen a good deal of the world but not enough, often overlooked or called impossible the most important things they could hear.

"He said he saw a woman he took to be the Rose traveling in the company of seven others. They used only antique Kalesti coins, which he said meant they were not from Kalest, and on speaking with a particularly drunken member of the company later that night, he learned that the lot of them were set on a path into the heart of Lysama."

"Interesting," Ukko said. That meant that until very recently, if this report was to be believed, Esteri was unharmed, and on Kalesti soil. Even by foot, with the woman struggling, a band more dedicated to the trek could have made it to Lysama long before. Perhaps it was a case of mistaken identity, or perhaps there was something more to the tale.

"Do you have a full report?" Ukko asked. "Or failing that, is the merchant still here that I might question him?"

"I had a man take down descriptions of this party," he replied, "and give him the few coins for an unverified lead. Even if it's the only one I know about, it's not a whole lot and doesn't make a lot of sense, does it? The Lysamans took her, and that's that. Hardly need a bounty for information at all."

That was somewhat worrying, Ukko realized. Piru had seemed sure Lysama was to blame, and that his daughter would be in Lysama by now. Well, the latter part was only good sense, given the former, and the former itself a natural assumption. Still, if he had no doubt, he would not have offered coin for confirmation.

"May I see this report?"

"Sure thing," the commander replied, and started searching through papers until he found a few loose pages and handed them to Ukko.

Ukko read the descriptions of seven men and women who claimed to be from a village that had fallen upon hard times, who carried century-old coin and were largely furtive in their ways. He saw, as the merchant had, holes in their story – one leader said that they were looking for any place to make some minor fortune, but another man when somewhat tipsy insisted that Lysama was their destination. What Ukko saw, though, that the one who had given the description had not seemed to think worth noting, was that he judged the lot of them to be of the younger generation: only one woman past thirty in the band.

As with the rest of the report, it might have been nothing: a young woman with a face not unlike Esteri's who covered her hair in public, traveling with friends and compatriots. For fortune, perhaps, or maybe to Lysama – drink drew out stupidity as often as it did truth. But on the other hand, there was a clear pecking order related, and this band supposedly from one small and isolated village consisted of men and women with backgrounds in several nations.

Ukko had to consider the possibility that the kidnappers or traveling companions Esteri was with were, themselves, Accursed, and in that he did not relish the idea of fighting seven at once.

"Thank you," Ukko said, returning the papers. "That was very informative."

"Really?"

Ukko shrugged, "It's unverifiable, of course, until someone actually does find her highness. If it's false, it's worthless, but if it's true it gives me a few ideas of what we might be up against."

"And what would that be?"

Ukko shook his head. "It won't help to say," he replied, "and on the chance I'm wrong I'd rather not say."

"Well," the commander said, "I suppose that's your privilege. But... you think there's a chance she's still alive?"

"If I say there is?"

"Then," said the commander, "I'm sure the men and women of Kalest's army will leave no stone unturned in the search."

"And if there is not?"

"Then Lysama will burn for taking her," the commander said. He motioned to the entrance of the tent "Out there are the most devout citizens of Kalest. Many were poor, even starving, but Kalesti are strong. The crown saved their lives, and now they will give those lives back if they have to. The recruits... many of them are no older than Her Majesty. They saw that beautiful child as children. They celebrated yearly as she grew. Each and every one – they loved her. And the older men? They remember her mother, who fed the poor and more helped them to help themselves."

"Then," Ukko said, "whether for justice or for revenge, they shall fight their best. It is my firm belief that Esteri is alive, and that we shall bring her back to Kalest, but perhaps I merely hope."

**

The ride continued after that. Though Ukko and his band drove on with purpose, it was easy to forget that these were soldiers of Kalest. They chatted and joked with each other, and despite his rank and his age, Ukko was not left out, nor held reverent, nor spared from their japes at times.

That was good, Ukko thought, for when they approached the Lysaman border, they would have to leave their identity as soldiers behind. The forward camps reported that refugees of Indris were pouring into Lysama in front of Kalest's armies. This seemed for the best – the army enjoyed the idea, expecting that the extra numbers would tax Lysama's resources rather than adding to its fighting forces. For Ukko, though, it meant an easy stream of people to hide amongst.

Near the border, Ukko threw another log onto their fire.

"It's time to leave our allegiance behind," he said. "Tomorrow, we'll cross the front. Kalesti colors won't be safe."

"We barely have any," Seija said. "It's not like that's a big deal."

"No," Ukko replied, "but it's still good to remember."

Taavi looked wistfully off into the night ahead of them. Launo focused on the fire, steeling himself. Maria polished her massive sword, admiring its edge, and Acacia... Acacia looked Ukko's way and smiled.

Faintly, Ukko remembered what felt like another life, his first life. He remembered fighting a battle at the central pass, the lifeline for Lysama's armies that marched across Kalesti soil. Then, he had been mortal and young. He saw his commander, one of the great and venerable generals of Kalest, fall. He bellowed his challenge to Lysama's commander, their champion, and man to man claimed his enemy's head. He remembered how the Lysaman armies broke at the sight and he remembered how, when he rode back to what was Kalest's capitol in those years in triumph, he had seen a smile much like Acacia's that was meant for him.

"You know," she said after a moment, "people are still going to ask where we came from, how we came by our arms. We should make sure we have a good story."

"Well," Ukko said, "we might be sellswords, or even Kalesti deserters if pressed. Have you a preference?"

"I'd rather not be known as a deserter," Launo said, "even in jest."

"Well," said Acacia, "we could go with something more fanciful. We could say we're hunters of monsters. Slayers know no borders."

"Really?" Ukko asked. "I had not heard of this practice."

"Well," Acacia said, "there aren't a lot of them. Some people say the last of them stopped hunting when the Accursed roaming the wilds after the last great wars grew too thin in number to warrant them. But, these are dark times, and there should be Slayers again soon enough."

"I like it," Maria said.

"It's a good thought," Ukko said. "It spares our honor and gives us cause to walk unobstructed through these foreign lands. Does that seem a fair decision?"

Taavi and Launo assented and Seija made clear she did not care one way or another.

"In some ways," said Ukko, "it is even true to our purpose. Since our company has no name or number yet, let us be the Slayers."

"To the Slayers!" Acacia cheered, lifting her water skin in imitation of a toast, and all the others echoed.

Ukko hoped that they would not be needed to fulfill the task their name entailed, but at the same time, he remembered the report of Esteri potentially traveling with seven Accursed and thought it likely. He looked at his friends, at the other Slayers, and thought they could handle the danger.

CHAPTER XI

Avina

Lysama wasn't that different than Kalest, Avina thought. Though the buildings looked quite different and the towns were laid out in strange patterns, the people looked more or less the same, and had only faintly different accents than the Kalesti did. These were the ancient enemies, the nations at each others' throats?

There were some differences, she realized. The Lysamans seemed to live more apart from each other. They were a quieter folk, and their streets filled with the susurrus of dozens of private conversations rather than the roar of Kalesti markets they had passed through before.

Moreover, where the Kalesti had the schoolhouse, the courthouse, and the manor of a lord mayor looming over any center larger than a village, in Lysama the grandest of all structures was invariably the church, with its high bell-tower and dedication to the Sun God Tharias. The Kalesti did pray, and the larger towns they passed through had churches, but they were small, wooden places with dedications to the whole pantheon or to Malakas, God of the Hunt.

Perhaps Tius could explain better. He'd been Kalesti, and while her father was Lysaman, her father didn't like to talk about his past. Tius, though, was in the company of the princess.

Esteri vexed Avina like nothing else. She was very nice, charming even, and she could get the best of Radegond or even Erikis with her wit, something Avina appreciated. Really, they should have been good friends. But she was trying to steal Tius away, Avina was almost sure, and that was something that she couldn't let stand.

Most of the time.

Sometimes, she thought that Esteri didn't really have anyone else close to her own age to talk to; Tius and Avina herself were the only ones who were close. If Avina hated her, and kept her and Tius apart, Esteri would have nobody, and that was hard for Avina let stand, too.

So most of the time, Avina tried to make sure she was there too, to be friends with the princess and also to ensure that Esteri got the message about Tius. Sometimes, though, when Avina felt small or she noticed a conversation that had already begun, she didn't have the heart to intrude right away. This was one of those days.

Erikis might also be able to explain things to her, Avina reflected. Erikis may not have been Kalesti or Lysaman, but he seemed to know everything, and he was always very patient with her.

Erikis was speaking intently to a local man, who himself seemed quite frightened, but as Avina watched Erikis thanked the man and turned back towards the company.

"What was that about?" Avina asked

"Oh," Erikis said, "it appears they've discovered a Blood of the God wellspring in the fields, and many here see it as a bad omen."

"Blood of the God?" Avina asked, forgetting for a moment the questions she had wanted to ask. "What's that?"

"Ah," Erikis said, "an alchemical reagent that, as you might have gathered, wells up from the ground in some places. It's thick and red and possesses many strange properties. Owing its color and consistency, there's a folk belief that wellsprings form where drops of the proper blood of a slain god, the Fallen One, rained upon the earth when he was slain. It's a ridiculous notion, seeing how new wellsprings are found all the time, but as you may have noticed, Lysama takes tales of the gods very

"I feel like I've heard of it before," Avina said. There was something there, on the edge of her mind.

"Maybe in passing," Erikis admitted. "It's the chief component of the potion that makes people Accursed, along with mineral water, various herbal extracts and oils, and indigo Æther."

"Oh!" Avina said, "That makes sense, I guess." She remembered her former query. "Hey, Erikis… do you know why Kalesti and Lysamans don't get along?"

"It's a long and complicated story," Erikis said, "though at this point a portion of it is that they both lust for revenge over some slight the other has given them in the past. Why do you ask?"

"Well," Avina said, "they look really similar. At least, they look more like each other than either like Indris folk or Aryniasians."

"Looks are not everything," Erikis replied. "I think the biggest issue is right over there." He pointed at the church.

"The church?" Avina asked.

"Lysamans see Kalesti as godless heathens," he replied, "and in turn, the Kalesti see Lysamans as closed-minded zealots."

"Who's right?"

Erikis shook his head. "The world doesn't work that way. But even with Lysama's last crusade long out of living memory, both sides remember things that happened then."

There was a shout from the right of them.

"Kalesti dogs!" a young man yelled.

"Heretics!" shouted another.

Erikis sighed. "Case in point."

Avina looked to what was happening. Four or five young men of the town had surrounded Esteri and Tius. One had shoved Esteri to the ground, and Tius was trying to help her up.

"You dare treat a lady so?" Esteri shrieked as she stood.

"They make no ladies in Kalest," one of the men sneered, "only whores and sinners who don't know how to honor Tharias."

"Wait for the guards to come," Erikis told Avina. "If they are not entirely corrupt, they will break up this squabble peacefully."

"And if they don't?" Avina demanded.

"There are ways to handle this without your talents," he said. "I will try to stall them from doing anything too stupid."

"What did you call me?" Esteri said, seething with rage.

"Something," said Erikis, loudly walking forward, "that is better off not repeated." He turned to one of the young men, who seemed to be the ringleader of the lot.

"What seems to be the problem, friend?"

"This wench"- he began

"Wench?" Esteri shrieked. "Mind your tongue or I'll break your teeth in."

Avina saw that Tius was holding Esteri – no, holding her back. His arm about her waist, his hand at her elbow... he was gripping tighter than was friendly.

"Please, my good man," Erikis said. "If you could tell me the nature of the offense I shall ensure there is no repetition. These people are known to me, but your lands and ways are not known to them."

"She profaned Tharias," the man declared, "in the shadow of his own temple, no less!"

"I stepped on the worthless little idol that had already fallen to the ground," Esteri yelled. "It was an honest mistake!"

"You trod upon the symbol of the Sun God!" the Lysaman rebutted. "It's only right you should receive the same treatment."

"If I may," Erikis said, "I think she knows to be more aware of where she puts her feet." He glanced over to the side of the road, and Avina followed his gaze to a market stall. "Was the icon in question one of your wares, perhaps? I can compensate you for it, if you feel it ruined for its purpose."

"It isn't ruined," the man said, softening somewhat at Erikis, "but it makes my blood boil to see a Kalesti whore treat the world the gods lend us as though she owns it."

"I understand," Erikis said, "but I would be very grateful if you would allow the matter to drop this time. I do not think that anyone here wants trouble with the authorities, and they are sure to be on their way after that commotion."

"Fine," he said, and nodded to the other young men. "Hey, Kalesti!" he called at Tius. "Keep your bitch on a short leash, you hear me?"

The young men snickered at the two of them.

"Bet he paid for her," one said.

"I wouldn't give two bits," laughed another

"You hear me?" the leader repeated. "Or are you just as stupid as she is?"

Tius looked up at the man. Avina got the impression that he hadn't really been paying attention until the end. He had been looking at Esteri the whole time before, now he was looking at the Lysaman. Avina had never seen Tius with that look in his eye before.

"I heard what you said," Tius said between gritted teeth.

"Good. Now you and her get out of my sight and go do whatever sins and sacrileges you Kalesti are fond of far away from good folk!"

Tius let go of Esteri.

Immediately, Esteri stepped forward and threw a punch at the lead Lysaman. Before he even realized she was moving, she connected, and from the sound of it, it was a clean hit to the left front of his face. As he stumbled back, spitting out blood from what was probably a cut lip and broken tooth, Avina smiled. Had she been in Esteri's place, she would have done no different.

The other four Lysamans fell on Tius and Esteri quickly after. Tius swept his leg at them, knocking two flat, but rather than following up while they were on the ground, moved to help Esteri. she had kicked one of the Lysamans that had been menacing her between their legs, and he was writhing on the ground in pain, but the other had grabbed her from behind and was trying to force her arms behind her back.

More joined in on the fighting – far more than Avina had hoped. Radegond also jumped forward, trying to extract Esteri and Tius. For his part, Tius was doing as well as Avina would have expected, knocking the Lysamans flat without hurting them too much. Still, there were a lot of them, and more of them were focused on Esteri.

A shrill whistle sounded, and three men on horseback approached. As they did, a Lysaman man, older than the ones that had started the fight, grabbed Esteri by the hair and pulled. She screamed, hit him in the gut, and stumbled back, her scarf coming undone and falling away.

A lot of the men stopped fighting right then, vanishing into the crowd as the riders approached, blowing their whistles. Did they recognize her? Was that a bad thing?

Esteri, Tius, Radegond, and even Erikis were surrounded, the three horsemen riding in a circle about them as another trio approached. At least two of the three had swords drawn, no less.

This was going to get very ugly, Avina thought. She darted into the center – if needs be she could throw a horse and rider through the nearest wall, she was pretty sure.

This wouldn't even be a hard fight, she reflected as her parents ran in as well. They outnumbered the armed men, and every Accursed was worth at least a couple armed soldiers. Avina herself was worth an army. She was worth this whole town, and she'd stomp them flat if she had to.

"Hear me!" Esteri called. "I am Esteri Piritta Metsaa Kalest! I have entered Lysaman territory in the hopes of gaining an audience with your king. I have traveled in secret for my own reasons, which I will not utter here. Here today I have received very rough treatment from your citizenry, which I am willing to forget if those of you with better sense shall aid me in seeking my audience."

"They're spies!" a woman shrieked from the assembling crowd. "Kalesti spies! They should be hanged!"

Avina watched as Esteri picked out one of the riders, the one with his weapon still sheathed, and spoke to him.

"I promise nothing," she said, "because no path is guaranteed success, but if you listen to her, what hope I bring to save your kingdom dies with me."

"This is above me," the one she spoke to said to his companions. "Somebody get the captain while we deal with the rabble."

One rode off, the rest closed in. Avina tensed, preparing herself to throw a horse.

"These people are under my protection!" Esteri called, more calm and even than she had been, "They are my traveling companions and loyal to myself and my quest and no other power. I will not be separated from them and will have your heads if they come to harm."

Silence followed. Tension. There were hundreds of Lysamans, coming out of their holes and quiet, private mutterings to form a great crowd surrounding the scene. Avina had no doubt she could handle that many, if things turned sour. Only a few had weapons... but Avina realized she wasn't alone. Tius could be hurt if he didn't see an attack coming, so could Radegond or Avina's own mother. Even Hathus, who had slunk into the circle at some point, wasn't immune to swords and arrows like Avina, her father, or Erikis more or less seemed to be.

Avina planned the attack in her head. If she tossed one of the lot, she could probably take another three, or call it two to be safe, on the other side of the circle out of the fight. Until the one who rode off came back with reinforcements, that left two soldiers, one next to her and one farther away. The one next to her was dead meat, the other one would get a chance to react. How much damage could he do? He might strike for her father or Erikis, and that would be it for him, but he could also hit her mother, or Tius, or Esteri, even Radegond or Hathus. If he got very lucky, he could kill any one of them.

Avina wasn't going to take that chance unless she had to.

A rider in gilded armor and a full helm approached, flanked by a banner man and the one who had left to get the 'captain.' The rider approached.

"So," a woman's voice echoed from beneath the steel helm, "the Princess of Kalest graces us with her presence. My men tell me you say you're here to save our land, but from where I'm standing it looks an awful lot like you're the one who has brought down your father's wrath and endangered it in the first place."

"If I meant to bring Lysama to ruin," Esteri said, "I would not be within its borders. There are a thousand places within Kalest I might have been secreted away if I was to simply be kept out of the public light for a time on pretense of assassination or kidnapping."

"I must admit," the captain said, "you are very bold to start a fight on foreign soil, say you will forgive the offense, claim to offer salvation for a nation, and then threaten to claim the heads of its soldiers should they displease you."

"I start no fights and threaten nothing, though I do finish fights and swear a good deal."

The captain made a 'hmph' worthy of Radegond's greatest frustration.

"So," Esteri said, "will you conduct me and my compatriots onward? I had hoped to not have to deliver on my oaths."

The captain laughed. "Bolder and bolder! You are unarmed and unarmored, girl. Anyone with her wits about her would be begging for mercy, not dictating terms."

Esteri narrowed her eyes.

"I ask you again," she said, "and in clearer terms. Peace or death. Choose wisely."

"And yet no doubt I'd be hanged myself if I skewered you," the captain said, "by the Kalesti for regicide or my superiors for the temerity alone. I suppose I must choose peace, though you and your company will come with me to the barracks and hear the terms I offer."

"That is acceptable," Esteri said. "Lead the way."

Avina was impressed. She had been sure the captain was going to start a fight or force Esteri to, and yet Esteri had called the bluff Avina had not even noticed was there. All the same, she was itching for conflict, and itching to change, and couldn't help being somewhat annoyed when she did not get the chance at either.

***

They were brought to a squat, stone building, and led inside. The Lysaman horsemen dismounted, and the captain removed her helm, revealing a woman a little older than Radegond looked with brown hair, brown eyes, and a hard visage.

Avina waited patiently, still fearing and hoping at the same time that she would have to unleash her power.

"My terms will be simple, Princess of Kalest," the captain said, "so I will tell them to you straight away. Since your signet ring proves you are who you say you are, we will take you to the King, who will see you if he wishes it. But when we take you, your hands will be bound and you will go before him as a prisoner and not a dignitary."

Avina furrowed her brow. That made little sense, but it would not be a problem. Avina was sure she could break any bonds they could apply, and was pretty certain that Tius could slip them and Hathus fight through it. That would be enough to free the rest.

"Looking to enrich your own glory, captain?" Esteri asked. "What happens if I refuse?"

"Then," the captain replied, "I throw you in my jail with your friends, safe and sound. It's another way out of our little dilemma."

"And when my father's armies reached this place," Esteri said, "we would likely die for your pride. But you have agreed to help me, however selfishly, so I shall agree to your terms." She held out her wrists together. "Go ahead, clap me in irons."

Avina saw that Esteri was smiling, and couldn't help but smirking herself. Had it been Avina's choice, she likely would have attacked several times over, the timing had just not been right, but Esteri... she did not think that the only reason that Esteri was smiling was that she knew they could be free any time they wanted to. The princess probably had some plan for when they got to the capital, and it would likely not end very well for the captain.

"I'll do that soon enough," the captain said. "For now I must make ready for our journey. Be aware there is only one exit. Do not use it and do not touch anything."

The captain left the room with the eight of them in it.

"Sorry," Tius whispered to Avina. "I know you're probably cross with me for this."

Avina thought about it. Of course there were a few things about how the day played out that made her upset, even upset with Tius, but if he meant failing to restrain Esteri, that wasn't one of them. Most of them, Avina couldn't bring herself to tell him.

"What?" she whispered back.

"I could have stopped this whole mess," he said. "The princess likely would have been quite upset if I had, but at least we wouldn't be here."

"Why are you apologizing to me?"

"Well," Tius said, "Hathus wouldn't care, Erikis and Radegond will be lecturing me enough later, and your parents would probably tell me to talk to you anyway."

"No," Avina said, "why aren't you apologizing to Esteri? You should have let her go earlier. Those idiots deserved to be beaten into the ground."

"Remind me," Tius said, "to not take your advice when violence is on the table."

Avina smiled. "That's part of my charm, isn't it?"

"Something like that," Tius whispered, and Avina couldn't help but giggle.

"Something amusing back there?" Esteri asked.

"Not much," Avina said. "What's your plan, anyway?"

"To go to Lysama's capitol, tell them of the treachery approaching, and if I can find a way, to avert the war."

"No," Avina said, "I mean for the captain lady."

"That depends on just how embarrassing she makes the trek," Esteri said. "If I'm forced to lower my face to a bowl of gruel on the road, or must endure being paraded through the streets in chains, it will end very poorly for her."

"We could just break out," Avina said. "Once we're on the road. I'm sure we'll get the opportunity. They don't know what we can do."

"I'm sure we could," Esteri said, "but I doubt the king of Lysama will listen to me if my cause is stained with the blood of his servants, and that's very likely what would happen."

"He'll listen if you're in chains?"

"The chance is better," Esteri said.

"Well," Avina said, "how well do you know this king?"

"Essentially," Esteri said, "by reputation alone, though I think I was introduced when he visited Kalest's court for my father's wedding with Delphina. He is a weak man whose crown weighs him down and bows his head, but by all description he is a good man who would not wish suffering onto any peoples. My only worry is that his advisors might be less favorable. They're bound to have a lot of influence, and I don't know who they are."

Avina nodded, but she didn't like the sound of it. If the king wasn't in charge, they'd be in the hands of whoever was, and as far as Avina knew, weak people didn't tend to stay in charge. Of course, Avina admitted she knew very little about kings. Maybe they were a special case.

The captain returned not long after, with several other armored guards.

"Bind their hands," she ordered, and the others began placing thin, steel manacles on the seven Accursed other than the Princess.

"As for you," the Captain said, pacing to in front of Esteri, "these will ensure you remember your place within Lysama's borders."

She lifted a heavier set of manacles and a large, iron collar from her pack.

Avina smiled as they put the cuffs on her. The captain had no idea what she was getting into.

CHAPTER XII

Esteri

Esteri stewed bitterly on her situation. The journey to the capitol, she reflected, had not been the most miserable that she could imagine. Captain Jean and her soldiers had, away from other folk, treated her and her friends with at least decency, if not respect. When camped in the wilderness their hands were unbound so they could feed themselves and rest in some comfort, though while they marched they were kept moving by their bonds: Esteri's friends in a long train, rope connecting the manacles at their wrists, and Esteri herself dragged along with a chain attached to the collar at her neck. It was galling, an offense to her pride that was unforgivable, but not intolerable and some of the soldiers were even kind when their captain wasn't looking.

The entrance into the city, however, was another thing altogether. Captain Jean rode at a pace comfortable enough for Esteri follow walking, which was good because she rode holding her helm under one arm, reins in one hand, and Esteri's leash in the other. She trotted up the high road, occasionally giving Esteri some extra slack so that she could wave at gawking crowds, who did not seem to know what to make of the spectacle.

As well they shouldn't, Esteri thought. Jean rode like she was at the head of a triumphal parade, but for all the commons of Lysama knew, she might have been the one to bring war to their borders. Perhaps some thought that since she was not skulking or shying away this development was a cause for celebration, but others had more level heads.

At the very least, Esteri promised herself, the captain would have no cause to celebrate.

The march did one thing – by the time they reached the palace, the king and what Esteri judged to be several of his guards and a few of his chief advisors were waiting at the top of the steps. Esteri was marched forward, and forced to her knees before him.

King Baudouin Emmanuel Deschamps Lysama, or Baudouin V, looked older and wearier than Esteri had expected. It was hard to believe he was younger than her own father, for his hair was thoroughly grey and while he might not have been bent by age, he stood hunched in on himself, as though shielding his body from the world.

"Lysama greets you." Baudouin said, shakily as though uncertain of his words.

"I thank you, King Lysama, for this chance to speak," Esteri said. "These are dark days for our kingdoms, but I hope that they can be made somewhat brighter now."

"What has brought you here, princess Kalest?" he asked.

"Why," Esteri said, "as you can plainly see, it is Captain Jean of Arenfort who has brought me here. I ask you to be merciful in dealing with her. Perhaps she did not realize how unseemly it would be for me to come before you not only dressed as a peasant but covered in dirt from the trail, as filthy and unwashed as a beggar and bruised from the passage besides. It is true that she has dragged royalty by the leash like you would an unruly dog, riding upon her steed as I walked beside, heedless that the contrivance could break my neck if I slipped and fell and was dragged along by it. It is also true that she insisted on giving me and my loyal traveling companions this treatment or else she would have cast me into her dungeons heedless of the danger that could pose to your nation."

Esteri could not keep a faint smile from her face as she observed King Baudouin's horrified expression.

"But," she said, "as the grand parade of me and my companions through your fair city attests, I am quite certain that she has done what she has done in the hopes of gaining your favor or the favor of the people of Lysama, and for such ambitions and aspirations there are certain rewards."

That was a great difference between Lysama and Kalest, one that Esteri had long known but never understood – the Lysamans, at most times, vowed to hold humility above any other virtue save piety. They abhorred boasting, where Kalesti only felt it wrong if a man could not live up to his words.

"I see," the king muttered. "Yes, the rewards of such actions are very plain. Guards, release Princess Kalest and those who travel with her from her bonds, and see that her escorts are well cared for within the Hold."

Now that was more than Esteri had expected, though not more than she felt Jean deserved – as the Lysamans reacted to the pronouncement, she did not doubt that the Hold meant the dungeons.

Jean did not protest as she was lead away, but her stare was locked beyond the horizon, looking through the scene around her to the ruin of her ambitions. It served her right.

Esteri stood, though she motioned for the others to remain kneeling and hoped they understood.

"King Lysama," she said, "it was not just rude conduct that brought me to you. I meant to come with words of warning, but with the situation in Indris I suppose it is no news that King Kalest, my father, intends war upon you."

"Yes," Baudouin said, "yes... over your own vanishing. We can now return you to your father, and will have peace. That is why you have come, is it not? Whoever stole you from your place, it is they who will be punished, and Lysama will offer them no safe haven from Kalesti law."

"I am afraid, King Lysama," Esteri said, "that my news is much more dire. My return to Kalest would not save your people, for I was not stolen from Kalest. I was poisoned, and it is a miracle of the gods that I am alive to tell you that the one who would have me dead, and Lysama blamed, now sits on

Kalest's throne."

The Lysamans recoiled with gasps of horror, and Esteri could not meet their eyes, she gazed at the ground, heart heavy as lead in her chest. She could still blame Delphina, her stepmother, but even if she did, her father had known, and had turned a blind eye. Saying as much or worse dredged up the pain she felt after leaving in her slip and jewels that night. It was no easier to accept but no less true than it had been then.

"Then what good are you?"

Esteri looked up at the speaker, a Hyperborean man in formal robes. His badge of office marked him as the chief ambassador.

"If Kalest shall have war with Lysama no matter your fate, then you can do nothing to help your gracious host. Oh lord of Lysama, allow Hyperborea to take custody of the girl. We are neutral ground, and not a soul could blame you for passing Princess Kalest to us to exonerate your nation."

"Hold your tongue!" a man in impressive cloth-of-gold raiment demanded. "Even heathen royals have the Divine Right. Princess Kalest should go where it pleases her."

"My good Archbishop," the Hyperborean replied, "I only offer the safest and most honorable road for Her Highness."

"And," the Archbishop replied, "you would drag her along it like that loathsome woman. Your majesty, have I not said a thousand times that these godless serpents should be banished from your presence?"

"Such slanders!" the ambassador exclaimed. "But, your majesty, I forgive the harsh tongue of your holy man. He speaks from his heart and not his mind. We both want the best for Lysama."

"Your majesty," Esteri said, "I did not come here to tell you what you already knew. I will tell my tale freely to the folk of Arynias and Tyrvad, who no doubt hold Lysama in the wrong now, and who might intervene against my father. But wherever I shall go from this day, I and my companions are hungry, weary, and dirty. I beseech you, grant us at least one night of hospitality beneath your roof."

To this, the ambassador and the Archbishop quickly agreed, and not a voice from the rest of the assembled crowd was raised against it. Slowly, carefully, the king declared that it would be so, and the gates of the palace were made open to Esteri and the others.

Esteri lead the way in. She was in Lysama, and still alive, but what was she going to do now?

***

Esteri took the next few hours enjoying the basic aspects of the life to which she was accustomed: she bathed with fine soaps, perfumed herself with scented oils, and dressed in fresh clothes that were brought for her, a sea-blue dress of silk velvet with a bodice of cloth-of-gold. Likely it was an old thing of Lysama's queen, but it suited Esteri even if it was not so well-fitted as her traveling clothes. A servant brought her a lunch on a silver platter – a sampling of aged cheeses, fresh berries, a few strips of salted lamb and an elegant glass of vintage red wine with a beautiful fragrance.

The hospitality was almost good enough for her to relax inside as well as out, and she reclined upon the softly cushioned couch and tried to remind herself that the worst was probably over. The world would hear her story, and not even Kalest could hope to stand against their combined might, especially if any of her father's armies turned upon their king at the affront revealed. General Katri or General Anselm well might.

Yet somehow, the thought hurt her even more. Her father would likely be torn off his throne if he did not know when to back down, and even if he did, she could still never go back home. Her family, what was left of it, was dead to her or her to them. Even Tuoni... if she lived long enough, she would vanish back up the mountain with the other accursed, and not return to be his big sister again.

There was a knock on the door.

"Who is it?" Esteri called.

"Just me," Gelvira replied.

"Come in."

Gelvira entered. She had cleaned herself up and been given new clothes as well, in her case a heavy dress of green and pale peach that Esteri guessed had been gifted to Lysama by Gelvira's native Arynias, for both its style and its weight were suited to that cold land.

Esteri had not talked with Gelvira as much as she wished, she realized. It was true that if Esteri lived, she would have a very long time to swap stories, but that was no excuse to ignore her.

Gelvira smiled. "It's a more pleasant lot here than you expected, isn't it?"

"I had hoped," Esteri said.

"You know," Gelvira said, "I was a noble lady myself once. Not a princess or anything fancy, but my family had land and money and some fine things to our name."

"Really?" Esteri asked. "What happened?"

"Well," Gelvira said, "I think nothing to the rest of them. But I was born with the bleeding sickness, and nothing else was helping keep me away from Teriana's waiting arms."

Teriana was the goddess of the dead. Most folks regarded her as a darker figure, feared and respected, but the people of Arynias loved her and worshipped her above all the other gods, for she ruled the eternal country in their view, and did so with motherly benevolence.

All the same, Gelvira or at least her family had chosen a life as Accursed over death. The two of them, Esteri realized, were probably far more similar than she had thought.

"It must have been a hard choice."

"Not really," Gelvira said. "Oh, I struggled with the idea for weeks, keeping that potion on my bedside, but when I sliced my hand open eating a piece of fruit with a knife and just bled and bled until I felt faint, I knew I wanted to live more than I was ready to die."

Esteri nodded sagely. "When was that?"

"Oh," Gelvira said, "about eighty years ago now. But that's

not why I came here."

"Do we need a reason?" Esteri asked. "I used to talk with the serving girls – no offense, I just didn't have any other play-mates – and I've missed the chance to chatter with nothing hanging over my head."

Gelvira gave Esteri a warm smile. "We can chat, just the two of us girls, any time. But right now?" She sighed. "The fact that I was landed means that I know a thing or two about the intrigues of court, and can make a guess about what's going on with the king here."

"And that is?" Esteri asked.

"Well," she said, "he's a good man, but I don't think his decisions are his own. You ought to be around him sometimes if you can, or people without your best interests in mind will be dictating what happens."

Esteri thought about the Hyperborean ambassador. He had seemed intent on her being taken to Hyperborea. Given how cozy her stepmother was with her countrymen, Esteri did not trust their island for a moment.

"Should I go now, then?"

"Well," Gelvira said, "you don't have to. Especially with a weak man making them, decisions of state are not finalized lightly nor quickly."

"But, of course, that means my voice needs to be heard louder and longer."

Gelvira shrugged. "Even so."

Esteri embraced Gelvira quickly. "Perhaps this evening, when his majesty is done listening to advisors, we'll catch up?"

"If you're not too busy," Gelvira said

"Why would I be busy?"

"Oh," she replied, "I thought you might run into Tius, if my daughter doesn't first."

Esteri laughed. "I might check in on him. Really, on every-one. But we'll have some time. Thank you."

"I'll be around," Gelvira said. "I hope you'll have a little fun sometime today."

***

Esteri had been directed back and forth to the king, yet nowhere she had been sent had she been able to find him. She was on the trail, she felt, and many said the king had just left. The last, the archbishop, had mentioned he was in the company of the Hyperborean ambassador and that Esteri had just missed them.

Esteri asked after the servants in the halls, and heard that they were walking to the Overlook, a quiet wing of the palace the King enjoyed where the windows opened out onto the city spreading below.

Once in the Overlook wing, Esteri had no one to ask – the halls were empty and silent. She checked each door, looking for the king and the Hyperboreans. Finally, she discovered them, in a broad ballroom. Esteri entered on the upper balcony, and they were on the floor below.

"You see, your majesty," the ambassador said, "the Kalesti will not be stopped. Tyrvad and Arynias see more profit in Lysama's own fall. But Hyperborea understands. We offer you an escape from your fate."

Esteri wanted to shout, but some fear deep within her kept her silent, listening to their voices echoing through the hall.

"I do not understand," the king said, then turned to one of the other Hyperboreans. "Ulfr, was it?" he asked, and the man nodded. "Could she really be Accursed?"

"Assuredly," the man Esteri presumed to be Ulfr replied, "and there are bound to be many more in Kalest's armies. If they are willing to go far enough, even if she were telling the truth, Kalest would still triumph against human forces."

"What can I do?" King Baudouin asked. "How can I save my people?"

"Hrafn," the Ambassador said, "come forward."

Another one of the other Hyperboreans approached, raising a flask.

"Most nations do not understand the Accursed the way

that Hyperborea does," Hrafn said. "The potion, brewed properly, has effects that vary depending on the drinker, most especially on the drinker's mind."

Esteri felt sick, and backed away from the railing. She closed her eyes, and found the image of a great, black monster beneath the lids. She forced her eyes open again. The nameless fear still kept her from calling out.

"In this way," Hrafn said, "the nature of an Accursed is based on the nature of a human. One who desires a weapon shall be granted foul claws or acid spittle. One who fears death might seal wounds in an instant. One who is monstrous, or perversely who fears becoming a monster so much that the image dwells on his mind, shall degenerate into one. But we who are of Hyperborea have learned from records of times the potion has been misbrewed how to change this, and obtain reliable results."

Hrafn held up the flask. "This potion was brewed with a distillation of Blood of the God instead of the unrefined form, and red Æther as well as indigo. Whoever drinks of it shall become the most powerful Accursed ever to walk this earth. It will hardly be a curse."

"You offer this to me?" Baudouin asked. "Will it really save Lysama?"

"Perhaps." Hrafn said, "if the mind in that body is truly dedicated to Lysama. Who can be trusted with such power? Why, certainly, a man who could sweep away invading armies could topple a king as easily."

"Indeed," said the Ambassador. "While Ulfr will remove one problem from your house, if this potion was given to a man who proved treacherous once empowered, even Hyperborea's aid would not protect your highness from harm."

"Kingship is a heavy burden," Ulfr said. "No one knows this better than you, lord of all lands in the grace of the sun. No one can understand what it means to live a life devoted to your nation except yourself. You must choose wisely."

"Your underlings think you weak," the Ambassador said.

"They believe that they control you. The archbishop, the generals, the lords... they all see you as a puppet, dancing on their strings. They say you do not have the strength nor the vision to protect Lysama. If they had the option, they would dethrone you."

"I..." Baudouin gasped. "I believe I understand. Yes, I am weak, I have always been weak, Tharias aid me."

Esteri wanted to scream, but her voice died in her throat. Her vision was strange – the shadows were converging where the Hyperboreans surrounded poor king Baudouin.

"All we offer is power," Hrafn said. "If you wield it, your name will go down in history for it."

"The power... the power to protect my kingdom."

He reached out slowly, unsteadily.

"The mightiest ever to live," the Ambassador said.

"Blessed by divine blood," Hrafn added.

"A weapon of holy judgment," declared Ulfr.

Baudouin seized the potion, and Esteri ran.

***

Esteri hurried through the halls. Something terrible had happened, was happening, was still going to happen. But who could she tell? What could she do? She should have challenged them there, but if the 'problem' Ulfr was to remove from the house of the king meant her, she likely wouldn't have had a chance.

"Princess Kalest!" a servant called. "Princess Kalest, wait!"

Esteri stopped.

The servant boy caught his breath. "There are visitors calling for you, Princess Kalest. A young Kalesti man and several friends of his."

Tius was the Kalesti man, she wagered, and more of her friends besides... perhaps together, they could figure out what to do.

"Very well," Esteri said. "Lead me to him."

The servant brought Esteri to a small antechamber and showed her in. The people inside were unknown to her.

"What?" she said as the door closed behind her. "Who are you all?"

A tall, youthful man with long brown hair bowed before her.

"We call ourselves the Slayers," he said, "Though that is not our purpose here. My name is Ukko."

Slayers… something about that, the way Ukko said it, rang a bell. For that matter, the name Ukko was somehow familiar, like something she had once heard or read.

"I'm so glad to finally meet you, your majesty!" one of the others, a young woman with black hair braided on either side of her head declared. "Really, it's an honor."

Ukko smiled. "We've come to bring you home, Esteri."

"Home?" Esteri asked. "No… No, I'm not going back. Not until this awful war is done, and even then," something within her prompted her to speak, "even then I cannot really go home."

"I understand," Ukko said. "The curse you have must be hard to bear, but if this talk is any indication, you have kept your humanity. Your father will be so happy."

"My father tried to have me poisoned!" Esteri shouted. "He will kill me if I go back."

"That's…" Ukko seemed shaken. "No, I have seen in his eyes the sorrow when he speaks of losing you, the grief that tears his soul. Your father loves you, Esteri. Please, come back with us."

"We're the Slayers!" another woman, this one with bob-cut blonde hair, declared. "We can protect you, and we won't ever give up!"

Slayers, Esteri now remembered, men and women who pursued the most monstrous of Accursed, the ones that plagued the countryside killing at will, and laid them low. Sometimes a profession, sometimes an order, they rose up after wars left countless living weapons orphaned and disappeared when their quarry was gone.

"If that is what you are," Esteri said, "and if you have any loyalty to me as Princess of Kalest, I have dire news."

"What is that?" Ukko asked.

"I have seen the Hyperborean ambassador to this land and its king. The Hyperboreans... they convinced him to take a form of the Accursed potion altered to make him, in their words, the strongest to have ever been created. Perhaps he could keep his mind and human form, but in my heart of hearts, in the pit of my soul, I know that he will soon become a monster to ravage these lands."

"If that is true"- Ukko began, but he was cut off by a mighty crash that shook the palace.

"Whatever he's become," the blonde woman declared, "if he's threatening you, we'll cut him down to size."

"Esteri," Ukko said, "I do not know what happened to bring you here, but I do know I shall do my best to bring your trials to an end. I will return here when we have dealt with what the king has become. Then we will take you home."

The Slayers stood, those that were seated, and placed hands on their weapons.

"Be safe, Princess," Ukko said, and led them out of the room.

Esteri left as well. She would find her friends, gather her things, and be gone before Ukko and his Slayers returned to the castle of Lysama. Deep inside, she wanted to believe him, that what she had heard her father and stepmother saying was the product of a fevered mind, recovering from the poison that had ravaged her body and her transformation into an Accursed being. But at the same time she would not, could not believe this strange man's words over the evidence of her own senses. She had to keep going.

Esteri rounded a corner, and then she froze.

She did not know why she froze, she just did. She tried to force her legs to run, but they would not move. Her body shifted her weight quite independent of any of her thoughts, standing still and peacefully while her mind tried desperately to run or scream. What was happening?

"I am so very fortunate," Ulfr said, behind her, "that Hrafn had a second Talisman of Command."

Esteri turned around, unable to stop herself from moving like a puppet on strings. Ulfr stood before her, holding a small medallion on a chain, its center swirling with some crimson fluid.

"In some ways, you know," he said, "it is very limited. Control over a single Accursed, and how I must focus my will in order to make you do anything! And that at the cost of gold alloyed with violet Æther and divine heart-blood. But it shall all be worthwhile."

Ulfr paced around her. He pressed himself against her back and whispered in her ear.

"But so much control!" he hissed. "And so fine. Perhaps I can make you speak, perhaps not. I could make you moan." His free hand coiled around her, reaching up and cupping her breast as he held her close and helpless. "But I need no Talisman for that. We have a very long journey to Hyperborea, and I can think of so many pleasant ways to spend it."

Ulfr let go, and Esteri began walking forward.

"We had best get going."

CHAPTER XIII

Acacia

Acacia emerged onto the front steps of the castle. From one of the side wings, overlooking the city, there was a cloud of dust hanging in the air. It failed to conceal the source of the damage, at which Acacia stared in numb awe.

"Is that King Lysama?" Taavi asked, somehow able to find his voice when the rest of the Slayers were rendered mute with horror.

The thing that strode from the shattered side of the palace, that now meandered down into the city below, was shaped much like a human, though nothing else about it was like an ordinary person. Its skin was pitch black, though glowing crimson veins spread along its limbs, raiding out from a pulsing mass above its heart that dripped bloody fluid. It was a block or so into the city, buildings coming up to its shoulders at best, and behind it was a wake of burning rubble where it had passed.

The former monarch, if that was what he was, gazed lazily from side to side as he waded through his city. When, momentarily, he looked their way, Acacia saw his face – it had a look of a bare skull, charcoal black and crowned with a tangle of horns, burning tears falling from those empty sockets.

"Whether it is or it isn't," Ukko said, "we have a clear duty to bring it down."

"Do we?" Seija asked. "I'm not going to argue with fighting that monster if you insist, but Kalesti troops are miles away, and it's walking away from the palace and the princess. We could let Lysama count the cost."

"We didn't decide to go forth as Slayers for no good reason," Acacia said. "I don't know if we can win, but I think we have to try. If it gets the upper hand, the last of us standing can run and get the princess out."

"Like hell I'm going to run!" Maria said. "Kalesti don't run from monsters."

"If you are the last," Ukko said, "remember that making sure Her Majesty lives is more important than making sure a monster dies. There will be other monsters."

The question was, of course, how they were going to fight it. They could barely reach its ankles! Perhaps they could topple it that way, and reach something vital when it fell, but Acacia didn't like the idea of being anywhere near its feet.

The creature stopped a moment, then delivered a brutal kick to some noble's manor on the high streets it stalked.

"Though perhaps," Ukko said, "not ones so big."

"I don't know what this means," Launo said, "but… I think there's a man riding on its shoulder."

Acacia strained to see and indeed, there was a figure up beside that massive head.

"That settles it," Acacia said. "We've got to get up to its level somehow. We won't reach that man up there, friend or foe, if we just hack at its legs."

Acacia began to hurry down the royal road as she talked, the others following behind her.

"The manors in the high streets are too far apart!" she called, "If we confront it there, we'll only get one chance before it topples the building we're all on. We've got to lure it somewhere else, where we can get from rooftop to rooftop."

"That shouldn't be difficult," Ukko said. "It's headed more or less for the cathedral. It looked like just beyond that, there were plenty of buildings."

"Those are the slums!" Launo shouted. "Those structures will probably collapse at a stiff breeze."

"It's our best chance," Acacia said. "If this is anything like

Kalest, those buildings are stronger than they look... and all the people will be working somewhere else in the city right now. They'll be more or less empty."

Acacia gritted her teeth and hoped she was right, that anyone left would flee. There was no time to force an evacuation.

Running, even at a pace where they could still talk, Acacia and the other Slayers had pulled comfortably ahead of the abomination. The Cathedral of Tharias loomed above them... nobles on one side, commons on the other. If they were lucky, the alleys on the south side of the church would be too small for the thing.

Acacia, in the lead, pushed open the doors, only to find the pews full of frightened people, multitudes that had no doubt seen the monster that used to be their king. Had they not seen what way it was moving?

"Everyone needs to get out of here!" Acacia shouted. "Run now! Get away from this side of town as fast as you can!"

A few of the praying masses looked up at Acacia, tears staining their horrified faces, but none of them moved.

"It's coming this way!" Acacia yelled. "You have to run!"

Ukko stepped in front of Acacia. "Is there a priest here who leads this flock?" he demanded. "Time is very short."

An elderly man in ornate golden-yellow robes stood tall, and approached, the crowd making way for his passage.

"I lead this congregation. Why do you ask, Kalesti?"

"No doubt you have seen the monster coming down from the palace," Ukko said, "Unless it turns away very sharply, it shall soon be upon this very building. You need to get your people safely out of its path."

"These walls are ancient and solid, and blessed in the name of Tharias," the priest said, voice quivering, "If they do not stop this monster from consuming us, what will?"

"We will," Ukko said. "We mean to fight that creature from Tharias' roof, where we can look into its eyes as we cut it down. And if your church does not hold, we will retreat south."

"What good is a sword against such a creature?"

"Please, your holiness," Ukko said, calmly. "Trust in the resourcefulness of humans and the safety of distance before the strength of stone. Prayer and blessings will be on our side either way."

The priest nodded gravely.

"I will see the people out as quickly as I can," he said. "They will listen to me. Please, the stairs are up ahead."

Acacia didn't wait any longer, but hurried forward, not listening to the priest address the crowd to get them moving.

The ancient stonework of the cathedral felt very solid: the walls were quite thick to be built so high. Perhaps they would at least slow the creature down... but how long could she keep her footing on a building under siege?

Up above, the wind blew from the palace to the north, carrying with it the scent of cinder. Smoke rose in the swath of the approaching Accursed abomination, no doubt set in the rubble and splinters of rich men's manors by Baudouin's blazing tears. Those empty sockets gazed fixedly at the cathedral, at her, char-black teeth forming a hideous grin, horns arrayed in the mockery of a many-pointed royal crown. Acacia met that gaze, and felt her knees weaken. Could she really stand before something like that? In her left hand, she held one of her swords, but her grip was unsteady, ready to let it clatter to the tiles of the roof and slide to the streets below, as useless as she was bound to be.

A hand took hers. Another clapped her on the shoulder. She looked to her right and there was Maria, linking one hand with her and another with Launo. The hand on her left shoulder belonged to Ukko, and beyond him were Taavi and Seija. They were all terrified, she realized, somewhere deep inside. Even Maria and Seija no doubt felt fear like she did, because they would all be helpless alone. But, they wouldn't be alone. That was the whole point of the Slayers.

Acacia tightened her grip on her sword.

"Are you ready?" she asked.

Each of her friends replied in turn. Seija looked down her nose at the danger walking towards them, Taavi nodded and said he would have to be. On the other side, Launo proclaimed it was his duty, Maria that she was born ready. Ukko himself, distantly, said he had waited for such a battle.

"Well then," Acacia said, "let's not disappoint."

They stepped away from each other and drew their weapons.

The beast and its rider approached the cathedral, and stopped at the edge of the Cathedral.

The man upon the monster's shoulder, which was roughly at level with the lower slope of the roof, was a Hyperborean with silvery-white hair and golden eyes.

"Who are you to stand in the path of Baudouin of Lysama?" he demanded.

"Apparently," Ukko said, "important enough for him to stop. I imagine from that you control that unfortunate soul."

"Piru of Kalest's immortal, I'd wager," the Hyperborean said. "My, my, I would have thought you'd be giving my associate a difficult time about Princess Kalest. Since you're here, that makes him unopposed. It is quite fortuitous."

"What?" Ukko demanded. "If you meddlers harm Esteri, your island isolation will not save you."

"Bold words," the Hyperborean said, "to stare death in the face and threaten an impossible war for reasons you do not even begin to understand."

Baudouin began to lift his arms.

"I think we understand enough." Ukko declared. "We will release Baudouin from his torment, and then we will return Esteri to her land, no matter what your pawns would do to stop us."

"Very well," the Hyperborean said, gesturing dramatically, "then I, Hrafn of Hyperborea, shall be known as he who"-

Seija bolted forward, down the tiled roof. She stopped just short of the edge and swung her meteor hammer in a horizontal arc. The heavy head moved blindingly fast, clearly too fast for Hrafn to realize what was coming, and slammed into the side of his head. The force of the blow knocked him against Baudouin's jaw and obliterated his skull, blood and gore spattering the side of the giant former king's fleshless face. Hrafn's body toppled from its perch into the streets below and Seija jerked back her weapon's chain, recovering it for another strike

For a moment, everything was silent. Then Baudouin opened his mouth.

A high-pitched shriek issued forth, as well as a rush of wind as hot as a furnace and reeking of fetor and burning flesh. Seija ran back up the roof before Baudouin slapped a claw down right where she had stood. Shards of tile flew in all directions and a moment later a section of the wall gave way, leaving a gaping hole in the structure but failing to cause the rest of the area to crumble.

"I think you got its attention," Launo said.

Acacia looked behind her. The tall tenements of the slums were close enough to the edge of the church roof, but only along the back side, away from the bell tower.

"All right," Acacia said, positioning herself so that their escape was directly behind her. "How do we kill him?"

Baudouin began to press his body against the wall of the church. The structure shook and high above them the bell rang in the tower, but for the moment at least it held.

"He still has a human shape," Ukko replied. "That means he should have most of his human weaknesses – his neck and head or his heart. The problem is cutting deep enough."

Baudouin screamed again, and shoved forward with a surge of strength. The wall on his side of the church crumbled and Baudouin advanced, crushing into the structure, grinding away feet of stone at a time before him.

"Can he understand us?" Taavi gasped. "King Baudouin! Can you hear me?"

Baudouin didn't seem to register Taavi's speech. He continued his progress into the church, grasping the bell tower and pulling upon it. The stones of the tower began to crack.

Seija redoubled her attack. Her meteor hammer gave her a better reach than any of the rest of them could pretend to, but her slams, swings, and whips, though swift and accurate, did no more than chip a single tooth.

"Get back!" Ukko shouted. The tower was beginning to fall. Seija listened, and barely escaped before the stone came crashing down. The arch of the roof buckled, and Baudouin shrugged off the rain of lighter debris and stepped into the gap. The church was failing quickly, but Acacia looked for an angle she could use to attack it. That skull seemed hard, and the horns protected it... but the back of Baudouin's neck, or the blazing veins on the sides near where Hrafn had stood... she only had to get around.

Ukko, Launo, Taavi, and Seija were retreating towards the tenements. Acacia looked to her side. Maria, massive blade drawn, also looked ready to attempt an attack here.

No, Acacia realized. If she was going to get a chance to strike, Baudouin needed to have his attention elsewhere.

"We've got to fall back," Acacia said. "Out there, we could get out from in front of him."

"Got it!" Maria said, "I'll cover us."

Acacia ran, gaining speed as she went down the steepled roof, and finally vaulted over the small gap to the flat roof of the tenement. She hit the roof with a roll before springing back to her feet. Maria jumped over a moment later, and none too soon, for the Cathedral, no doubt the sturdiest building anywhere in the city, was crumbling now not only under the assault of the monster that king Baudouin had become, but also under its own weight. Too much damage had been done. The near wall crumbled, stones striking the walls of the tenement and filling the alley they had just jumped over with rubble.

"Fan out!" Acacia shouted. "He'll have to focus on one of us, and the rest can get around him!"

Acacia went left, jumping from the roof they started on to

another. Baudouin smashed into the first tenement. Unlike the cathedral, it took little effort for him to make it collapse in on itself. Slamming his shoulder into the structure shattered the building and barely slowed him down as he continued forward, pursuing Ukko. Did he know that Ukko led them, or was he simply the most directly forward?

The swath of destruction as Baudouin began to wade through the buildings as though they were deep water was mercifully narrow. Maria was on the same side as Acacia herself, with Seija, Taavi, and Launo opposite. They ran, leaping the gaps between buildings where Lysaman architecture overhung the streets, keeping pace behind Baudouin and his path of dust and cinders.

As they came close to Baudouin, just behind his shoulders on either side, Ukko stopped running, and turned to face the great abomination. Baudouin stopped advancing as well. He lifted his right arm to strike at Ukko. That was Acacia's signal. She gripped her swords backwards, ran to the edge of the building, and leapt.

A second later, she landed on Baudouin's left shoulder, driving her blades deep into his flesh. The muscle was as soft as she expected, yielding to the point of her sword but firm enough to support her weight. She tried to get her footing, but the giant was turning quickly, making it nearly impossible to do anything but hang on.

The strike that was meant for Ukko stopped, but now Baudouin was reaching across himself. Reaching for her. Acacia looked up to see the great, dark hand approaching, and then stop again.

"Hey!" Taavi shouted. "Over here, you big lug!"

Around Baudouin's head, Acacia caught a glimpse of the boy, hurling a stone at the monster's face. Was he actually hoping to hurt such a creature that way?

No, she realized, he was distracting Baudouin. He was giving her time. As long as the abomination kept rounding on whatever offended him most recently, they had a chance.

Baudouin swung, and his left side heaved upwards. Acacia found her feet, and for a moment approaching the monster's neck meant running downhill. As he shifted his weight back to normal, having crushed half a building beneath his fist, Acacia rammed her blades into the side of his throat and held on for dear life. Hot blood, glowing faintly crimson, poured over her hands. It stung, but like too-warm stew and not boiling water. She gritted her teeth and did her best to bear it.

Baudouin roared up at the sky, a blazing surge of cinders falling from his hideously empty eye sockets. He had noticed that, that much was certain.

Acacia's friends were shouting, throwing stones, and in Seija's case striking at Baudouin. She knew that if he didn't take the bait, she was as good as dead. She swung her weight around, trying to reach his back where hopefully he would have a hard time reaching. Blood continued to gush from the wound – were Baudouin human, the strike would have threatened or even taken his life, but Acacia couldn't be sure that the same rules applied to such an impossibly massive Accursed.

Baudouin lowered his head and surged forward, ramming his crown of horns into the building Ukko stood upon. For a moment, he stopped there, and Acacia took her chance. She pulled her blades free of his throat and dashed to the back of Baudouin's neck. With all her might, she drove both swords up to the hilt into the base of his skull. The strike was sudden enough, but she felt her swords scrape against bone and deflect to either side of the spine. Baudouin stood tall again, and Acacia was hanging from him, helpless.

For a moment, Acacia struggled. If she could find a foothold, she could pull one blade free and try again, a little higher or lower to slide between the vertebrae. Her hands ached, and while she gripped the hilts as tight as she could Acacia felt her fingers going numb. If she had to keep supporting her own weight by her hands, she wouldn't last much longer. She had to make her next strike count.

Then she felt his hand close around her.

By any standards, Baudouin was impossibly strong. He effortlessly picked her up off the back of his neck. Acacia kept her grip on one of her swords, while the other was left embedded. Instead of simply squashing her, he brought his hand around and held her in front of his face, upside-down and so tight that she could barely breathe.

If there was any humanity left in the former king, it only showed in the vague curiosity his unchanging face seemed to regard the small thing that had caused him such pain. His hot, carrion breath washed over her, the stink filling Acacia's mouth as she gasped for air, nearly certain that she was about to die but struggling to live all the same.

Her hands were free. At least she had that much, and in one she still held her sword. She craned her neck to look down. She wasn't that far over an intact roof – if she stabbed one of his fingers, Baudouin might drop her. If she landed on her head, or missed the roof, or if he decided to squeeze harder or fling her away instead of dropping her, she was done, but if everything happened just right, she might live a moment more, and she didn't trust in the monster having mercy on her for much longer.

Acacia looked back up. She took as deep a breath as she could manage, grasped her remaining blade with both hands, and struck.

Baudouin released her with a howl, and Acacia fell. In the instant of her drop, she did not manage to see where she was going. Before she could even really think about trying to twist herself around, though her reflexes had already started to do so, her fall ended. The hard impact with the roof, though, never came, as Ukko caught her in his arms.

He fell to one knee from the force of her landing, only to spring back up and sprint away from the edge as Baudouin's hand crashed down on the structure. In the far half he deposited her on her feet and deftly picked up his sword from where he must have dropped it.

"What happened?" he shouted, loudly that all might hear.

"I hit bone!" Acacia shouted back, hoping the others were close enough to hear. "We need to strike higher or lower. One of my swords is still in there; we can use it as a marker!"

"I'll break right through if I have to!" Maria shouted, a building away. "Just get me an opening!"

Easier said than done. Acacia, beside Ukko, fled to the next building in the line. The slums were large, but not arbitrarily so. They were running out of space before the walls. Acacia turned inward, hoping the path of destruction would soon be brought to an end.

As she turned, leading Baudouin in a broad arc, she realized that Maria, standing more or less still as the three on the outside struggled to keep up, would soon be cut off, but also behind Baudouin. If Acacia and Ukko stood their ground then, it would be Maria's best chance, but if she didn't manage to take advantage of it she was out of the fighting.

Seija, clearly enough, saw it as well, and joined Acacia and Ukko in their path. They made another jump, then a sharp turn. Baudouin followed, and the three of then turned to fight.

Somehow, Baudouin's awful visage held no further terror for Acacia. That leering skull, those tears of flame, they had frightened her as much as they ever could. In that moment, Acacia smiled.

She glanced to either side of her. Ukko and Seija were facing the titanic beast with the same smile. At least, Acacia thought, she was in good company. She met Baudouin's gaze

"You should have squashed me when you had the chance!" Acacia shouted. "Now bring that ugly skull of yours a little closer."

For a moment, Baudouin hesitated, and then he lunged forward. His hands smashed into either side of the building, and as Acacia and her friends ran to the far end, his head smashed down where they had been, horns shattering their footing. As Acacia turned back towards him, she saw Maria make her move, leaping onto the monster's spine and then driving her massive sword deep into it to keep from falling.

Baudouin lurched. Maria's strike was far too low to kill him, but her attack must have found home, for his legs trembled, and slowly he sunk to his knees, his head grinding through each floor in the building beneath them.

"We have to finish it!" Ukko shouted. "There's no telling how long he'll stay down!"

Ukko leapt down, onto Baudouin's slowly descending horns, and Acacia and Seija followed. To their left, Taavi and Launo were making their way down an awning and across to Baudouin's right shoulder

Acacia found her footing on the sinking horn and made her way forward, across the back of the skull to where it met the flesh of the neck and her blade was planted firmly in the bleeding mass. There, Taavi with his sword and shield and Launo with his warhammer met them.

Taavi was the first to strike, going to his knee and burying his sword into Baudouin's flesh.

"I can't drive it deep enough!" he called. "Launo, help me!"

Ukko, for his part, attacked the nape of the neck, hacking away flesh to expose the spine below, while Acacia reclaimed her sword to attempt another strike.

Acacia didn't know what strike finally did it, whether it was her own stabbing at the base of the skull, Seija behind her swinging her meteor hammer into the head, Launo and Taavi hammering in the latter's sword or Ukko at the nape of the neck. It may even have been Maria's strike, or the loss of blood from all of them together. But, whatever the reason for it, Baudouin let out a hissing groan and sank down towards the ground once more. His body warmed, and the Slayers fled from it, into the rubble all around, convening at once beside his ruined head. His glowing veins did not fade like the blood that had been shed, but brightened steadily. The heat increased, and finally the skin peeled away, the veins bursting into flames.

There, the six of them stood, watching Baudouin, the lamentable king of Lysama, burn from the inside out, down to his black bones. Only as the flames began to spread to the rubble did they turn away, confident at last in the stillness of his blazing body.

"We need to get back to the palace," Ukko said.

CHAPTER XIV

Tius

Tius looked at himself in the mirror. The fancy noble's clothes he had been given to look presentable in the court were awkward, somewhat ill-fitted to him and certainly unfamiliar. In all his life, Tius had never had formal cuffs, much less emerald-studded cufflinks. He sighed at his reflection, trying to decide if he looked anything other than ridiculous. Perhaps he should have used some of his traveling clothes? He was Esteri's bodyguard, not her peer; he would be better with something plain and functional and a sword at his hip.

Tius picked up the sheathed sword. Like most things made by the Accursed it was simple, functional, and built to last, not to impress the gentry of the land. The worn scabbard and battered hilt would be sure to draw attention if he took it. For that matter, was he even allowed to be armed in the presence of a king? Tius didn't know, and didn't want to make the wrong decision.

Then Tius heard a mighty crash in the distance. No, not really the distance... it was close enough to at least be on the palace grounds, which meant that Esteri was now in danger. He hung the sword from his belt as quickly as he could and bolted out into the halls.

Finding Esteri was going to be difficult, Tius realized, unless he was fortunate. They had all seen the room she had been accorded for her stay. If she was there... Tius broke into a run, frantic to find Esteri. Coming to the right door, he nearly burst through, but tried the handle instead. The door opened freely, and Tius stepped inside.

"Gelvira!" he called, seeing Avina's mother pacing worriedly. "Where's Esteri?"

"I don't know," Gelvira said. "I'd guess she's wherever the king is."

"We need to find her," Tius said. "That noise was too close for comfort."

"Well," Gelvira said, "you can try, but I'll stay here, in case she comes back. We'd hardly want to pass by each other, would we?"

Tius sighed. It was hard to stay frantic, talking to Gelvira.

"What do you think that was?" he asked.

"I don't know that either," Gelvira said, "but I'd agree it couldn't have been good. Go, find the princess. I'll bring the others back here if I can."

Tius left the room. This was a problem – Esteri could be anywhere. But, he realized, she wasn't exactly hard to spot.

Tius stopped one scurrying servant, then another, asking after Esteri, Princess Kalest, or the woman with the blood-red hair, whatever it took for them to confirm they hadn't seen her, until finally one frightened girl spoke to him.

"I saw her," the lady said, "walking from the east wing to the overlook with some Hyperborean walking behind. She looked distraught."

"Where is the overlook?"

"You shouldn't go there!" the girl said. "That's where the monster came from!"

Monster? Was that monster what caused the terrible noise, or did the girl just hear the same echoes and assume they had a living source?

"If that's the case," he said, "Princess Kalest shouldn't be there either. Please, tell me where it is."

The girl quickly stammered out directions, and Tius was off.

The overlook was empty, but despite the lack of anyone to help, it was not that hard to guess where Esteri's trail might have led. From any of the windows, it was not hard to see that a grand ballroom, cityscape spreading out below it, had been nearly destroyed, roof collapsed and walls strewn across the grounds. From those windows, Tius also caught a glimpse of the monster – a great black thing taller than buildings, walking down into the city.

If Esteri had gotten into trouble, Tius wagered she would be where the damage was, and he made for the ruined ballroom.

Tius entered on the lower floor, and sure enough, Esteri was there. Standing beside her was a Hyperborean man, wearing an expression of smug satisfaction. Esteri herself looked horrified, but she was not looking at the damage – her tear-filled eyes darted around while the rest of her held perfectly still.

"Esteri!" Tius called.

The Hyperborean turned.

"My, my," he said, "your friends are faster than I had anticipated. But you must know, it is no matter. I wonder, should I let you see his doom or not?"

Tius drew his sword.

"I don't know who you are"- Tius began, but the Hyperborean cut him off.

"I am Ulfr," he declared, "the ever-hungering wolf. Unless you want to be devoured, I suggest you flee."

"And let you hurt Esteri?" Tius asked. "Not a chance."

Ulfr smiled. "I was hoping you might say something so predictably noble."

Ulfr drew steel himself, a short, double edged sword. At the same time Esteri started to move, turning about with unnatural stiffness.

"I wonder," Ulfr said, "just how well you will be able to fight."

At that, Esteri rushed forward. Her face was still transfixed with fear, and her movements awkward and sudden. What was going on?

Tius blinked, leaping as smoke up to the remnants of the

upper floor. Esteri stopped, and Ulfr turned to face Tius.

"An interesting trick," Ulfr said. "You might provide some sport after all."

Tius watched Ulfr closely. He held his sword at the ready in one hand, but in the other he clutched something shining and golden. He gestured with that hand, and Esteri danced upon his puppet strings, shambling quickly but unsteadily towards the surviving stairs.

That, Tius decided, was Ulfr's more important weapon. He did not know how the Hyperborean was controlling Esteri, but he did know that he couldn't fight back against her, which left him at a disadvantage if Ulfr decided to keep her close.

Tius waited until Esteri had nearly reached the top of the stairs, and then blinked down to the floor below, materializing near Ulfr. Tius took a swing with his sword, but Ulfr was fast, blocking and attempting his own cut in two fluid moves. The man may have declared himself the wolf, but he moved more like a snake.

"Pathetic," Ulfr said. He made a slash so quick that it was nearly invisible, and a gash appeared on Tius' arm. "Do try to keep up."

Tius tried to force himself to focus on Ulfr. The man was fast, that was true, but Avina was faster. Radegond too, probably. Tius had kept up with them, he could handle Ulfr. All the same, Tius was forced on the defensive, parrying a barrage of swift cuts and jabs.

Tius managed a glance at Ulfr's off-hand. The thing he carried was some sort of amulet or talisman, gold around a red orb that seemed to swirl as though it were fluid. Faintly, between strikes, Tius tried to remember if he knew anything about Hyperborean ways and alchemy. Erikis had talked about it enough for Tius to recognize something unnatural when he saw it, and its purpose was painfully clear.

He had to get it out of Ulfr's hand.

Tius blinked, using his power instead of taking a simple step. He could feel his warping begin, but heedless of it Tius blinked again, to Ulfr's other side. The Hyperborean was still at pace with him, turning to match Tius' magical darting to and fro, but he was not fast enough to keep up and keep striking.

Tius gritted his teeth, at least when they existed. He needed an opening. He needed more speed. Even training with Avina, he hadn't pushed his blinks nearly this close together, turning to smoke instantaneously on regaining his human body. He darted from side to side, back and forward and through Ulfr. His motions grew erratic, not solely in an attempt to baffle his foe, but because Tius himself was not taking the time to think of his destination.

Finally, he caught a momentary glimpse of something to his liking. He was over Ulfr's left shoulder, and Ulfr had turned his head to the right instead, no doubt following some spiraling wisp of smoke. With only one chance at the opening, Tius struck, bringing his sword down on Ulfr's wrist. It hit resistance for a moment, but then the bone parted or shattered before his strike, and the blade passed clean through.

Ulfr screamed and stumbled back. Esteri, at the base of the stairs, screamed as well, and fell to her knees, clutching her head. Tius gripped his blade with both hands. He looked down his nose, now long as the muzzle of a beast, towards his thinned and elongated fingers, directly at Ulfr. Tius was taller now, the changes to his legs having added nearly a foot to his height and no doubt, he thought idly, having ruined his fancy clothes.

"I'll skin you, wolf," he growled in a voice distorted beyond recognition as his own, "like any hunter would your kind."

At that, Ulfr ran. Tius blinked into his path, but Ulfr was too canny, and had already diverted himself over the edge of the ruined ballroom and down into the grounds below.

For a moment, Tius thought of the best way to pursue him, but then he remembered Esteri.

"Princess," he said, turning back to her, "are you hurt?"

"Only my pride," she said, looking pointedly away from

Tius, "which is better than you can say."

"It will pass," Tius assured her, though he had never gone so far. He was, for the most part, certain he could go back, but there had to be some doubt.

"I mean your arm," she said. "I saw him hit you."

"It's nothing," Tius said. It was a lie – he could feel the ache, and the blood soaking the cloth against his skin. It wouldn't threaten his life, but at the same time he could hardly ignore it.

"We need to find the others," Tius said, his voice slowly sliding towards normal as his muzzle faded into a human face. "Gelvira said that she would bring them to your room, but I don't think we will stay safe in the palace for long."

"There you are right," Esteri said. "I fear it won't be safe anywhere anymore."

"We will protect you," Tius said. "I promise."

"All the same," Esteri said, "we can't really leave here until you're back into a human shape."

She still hadn't looked at him since the fight had ended, but Tius realized that might be natural enough. He probably wouldn't want to look at himself either.

"I can't," Tius said, "but you can. It's probably more important that you get out of here"-

"No," Esteri said firmly. "I'm not going to leave a man behind because he saved me. And... well, forgive me if I'm not entirely comfortable with the idea of going out there on my own. There were other Hyperboreans, at least two."

"What happened?" Tius asked.

"I saw King Baudouin," Esteri said, "in this room. The Hyperboreans were talking to him, circling around like vultures, telling him that he needed some new power to have a chance to save his people. The poor man... they brought out a potion, and offered it to him, the worst curse imaginable and they called it salvation. That's him, out in the city. When I closed my eyes, I could see it, a crowned skeleton, weeping tears of flame for what he had lost."

Esteri stood, and walked over to Ulfr's severed hand, extracting the amulet from it.

"From what Ulfr said," Esteri said, "one of the other two has another of these awful things. They're controlling him, forcing a king to trample his own kingdom into the earth."

Esteri sighed.

"Pitiful man," Esteri said. "He wanted to do good all the way to the end, he just didn't know how."

Tius looked out at the city, at the horned giant carving a swath of destruction through its structures and its people. He wondered what the endgame was, but accepted that he might never understand the trials of kings and courts that birthed that monster.

"The warp is fading fast," Tius said. His hands looked almost human, and he was back at his normal height, though his legs ached.

Esteri looked up at him, tears filling her beautiful blue eyes.

"You're right," she said. "We... we should be able to go soon."

She made no move, kneeling on the precipice, looking out over Lysama's capitol. It had been a beautiful day out when they were paraded through those streets in the morning. The sun was shining, only a few wisps of cloud in the azure sky, but now smoke and screams were rising to meet them.

"Are you going to be all right?" Tius asked.

Esteri shook her head.

"I don't know what's worse," Esteri said, "all the things that have happened, or the feeling that I knew before they did and still couldn't stop them."

"You can't know what the future holds," Tius said. He thought about trying to take her hand, but his were still a little unnaturally gaunt, the veins blackened.

"But what if I can?" Esteri asked. "In fights, what happens to my eyes, how I start to move. It's like I can predict what you or Avina or anyone is going to do. My eyes go black and before you even swing, I'm ready to block."

"That's one thing," Tius said. "This" he gestured at the missing wall, "is something else altogether."

"And another thing... the first morning after arriving in your village, Radegond woke me from what I could only remember as a horrible nightmare, only I was warped farther than when I fight. I have to wonder if that nightmare isn't coming true, if I couldn't have known had I just remembered."

"Esteri..."

"And that's the last piece of the puzzle," she said. "The potion. Have you ever wondered why one person becomes a monster, and another doesn't? Why you can do what you do but Hathus slings fire?"

"I hadn't actually thought about it," Tius admitted. "I assumed it was random chance, maybe part of the potion. A drop more of this, a residue of that in the flask, you know?"

"One of the Hyperboreans told Baudouin it depends on what kind of person you are, and what you're thinking when you take the potion. Gelvira was bleeding out from a cut, and now she can make her skin like stone. Hathus... he volunteered to be a weapon for Kalest, so he summons destructive fire. What were you thinking, Tius?"

"I was thinking," he said, "how I could be a master thief."

"And you got just what you might have needed to become one," Esteri replied. "And me? I was afraid of dying, but more even than that, I was mad at myself for not having seen the poison coming... and remembering how my mother wanted me to be a wise queen some day. It makes sense... it could have been a lie, what that man said, but it just fits so well."

"Even if you can see the future," Tius said, "it doesn't change the past. Maybe Erikis could help you learn how to control this power, how to prevent a repetition of this tragedy, but you couldn't stop them here. You tried your best; I know you must have, that you'd never do anything less. If you failed after doing as much, the blame doesn't rest on your shoulders."

"We should get going," she said. "You look presentable

enough, other than the ruined clothes, though…"

She reached up, and tore his sleeve where he had been cut, then tied the wreckage around the wound.

"I'm no doctor," she said, "but it's probably better than no bandage at all. It's not too tight?"

"It's fine," Tius replied, rubbing the wound as though to hold what little blood he was losing in.

Tius stood, and offered his good hand to help the princess rise. She took it, and when she stood embraced him.

"Thank you," she said, barely louder than a whisper but full of feeling. Tius returned her embrace, silent for a moment.

"We…" Esteri muttered. "We should move on."

Tius nodded, and they headed back for the heart of the palace.

***

Tius opened the door to Esteri's room, hoping Gelvira at least had returned to it. Instead, he saw that all his friends were there, along with their things. Even Tius' own pack had been recovered, and was sitting on a table.

"Esteri!" Radegond shouted. "Where the hell have you been? And Tius – is that blood? You both got into a fight and let yourself get hit? Clearly I didn't give you a hard enough regimen."

Gelvira smiled. "We're all glad you're both alive and well," she said. "Really."

"I got the upper hand in the end," Tius said. "That's what matters."

"Please listen to me," Esteri said. "We need to get out of the palace, probably out of Lysama as well."

"Why?" Erikis asked. "What happened?"

"Quite a lot." Esteri said. "First, Baudouin has been turned into a monster. The city burns beneath his heel even now. Hyperborea is to blame – they turned him into that thing, and one of their men tried to kidnap me, and said he meant to take me back to that land. I don't know exactly why."

"There is more than that?" Frideger asked. "I'll be needing

some hard spirits after this, I can tell."

"Before the Hyperborean found me," Esteri said, "I met with a group of Kalesti soldiers lead by a man named Ukko. They were here to take me back to my father. I can't let that happen."

"Where are they now?" Radegond demanded. "How much time do we have?"

"They went out to fight Baudouin," Esteri replied, "but if they have any sense, they'll have turned around. They could be in the palace looking for me now."

"Let them come," Avina said. "I'll tear them in half."

"Nobody is tearing anybody in half," Esteri replied, "not if they don't attack first, at least. In any case, all I can do is run now. Baudouin is gone, Hyperborea seeks me, my father has found me. I wouldn't begrudge anyone for not wanting to follow my path any longer. You've done what you set out to do, to bring me here. No one has a duty to follow me any farther."

Tius looked over the room. Even Gelvira and Frideger, normally prone to kind smiles or mock-drunken wisdom, wore grave and sober expressions. They had to consider the offer, he realized. Avina's parents didn't want to speak for each other or for her, Radegond could accept completing a mission, Hathus had only come along for his own amusement. And Erikis? Erikis was as ever a mystery. Did he know what the Hyperboreans wanted with Esteri or with Baudouin? Did he care?

Someone had to speak up first.

"I'll stay with you," Tius said. "Wherever you mean to go from here, I will follow you if you would have me along."

"I'm coming too," Avina said. "Just because I haven't gotten to fight anything yet."

Her parents stepped forward silently, side by side with each other. After that, Hathus was the next, laughing and declaring that he'd come along. At that point, Radegond folded her arms across her chest.

"You've got a lot to learn about warfare," she said, "and I'll be damned if I let you run off without getting an earful of it from me."

After that, Erikis smiled.

"Well," he said, "it seems like our company has quite easily made up its mind, and I must admit I am curious about what these Hyperboreans intend."

Esteri breathed a sigh of relief, and Tius was inclined to do the same. While he would have followed Esteri alone, he was barely able to hold off one more or less ordinary swordsman. How would he fare against a more fearsome foe?

"All I really know is what I said," Esteri told Erikis. "They are responsible for turning Baudouin into a monster, and they meant to take me to their lands for their own ends."

"Ransom?" Radegond asked.

"I doubt it," Esteri said. "It wouldn't make sense."

"I have a few ideas," Erikis said. "Did you have a course in mind from here?"

Esteri shook her head.

"Then," Erikis said, "I have a suggestion. We should head north, to Tyrvad. The people there know magics alien to the rest of the world, and have little love for Hyperborea's meddlesome embassies. It will not be perfectly safe, as their dislike for the Accursed is greater than other lands, but then if Hyperborea has its eyes set on you, nowhere in this world is safe."

"We might as well head north," Esteri said. "At the very least, I would not trust any road that would take us closer to Indris and my father's armies."

"That's well and good," Frideger said. "You change into your traveling clothes, I'll see if they didn't leave you a bottle or two of something for the road. Best get drunk and get out before someone gets the bright idea to start giving out the blame for Baudouin."

Tius smiled, for unlike Esteri he knew Frideger's drunkenness was largely in jest, and the man had a good point in any case. No one else knew the Hyperboreans were responsible.

They might even suspect Esteri.

Esteri slipped off into an adjoining room with her pack, and shortly emerged in traveling clothes, hair covered and pack slung over her shoulder.

"Well," she said, "I suppose I'm as ready as I'll ever be."

She closed her eyes and lifted her head some.

"Esteri?" Erikis asked.

"I don't see anything," she replied. "Perhaps we'll not face any disasters along the way? Or do I just not know how to do it?"

"Esteri," Erikis said, far more harshly than Tius ever would have expected from him, "what exactly did you mean by that?"

"I will explain," Esteri said, "but when we have time. For now, we have to move."

The eight of them left the room. Largely decked in grubby traveling clothes, packs on their backs, they must have been a suspicious lot. But heads did not turn for them, the nobles and servants too busy panicking over the doom that had come to their king and their city. The eight Accursed left by the north, away from that hell, and onto the expansive grounds of the palace.

It was no castle, meant to hold against an army – they needed only leap a small stone wall, scarcely higher than they were tall, in order to escape into unclaimed land beyond.

The palace had been built in the hills, and the land kept rising for a time after they left. At the highest point, before they began a descent into a deep green valley on the other side, Tius looked back at Lysama.

Smoke rose from the city, and the sun shone blood red through black clouds as it sank lower in the sky. How many homes burned? How many lives were lost? Did Baudouin still rampage at Hyperborean command, or had some heroism ended his reign and reign of terror alike?

Whatever the answers, they were behind. He hoped that the people lived, hoped they would be able to rebuild and that their unfortunate king now rested at last, but he could do nothing to help that along.

Tius looked away from the burning city, down into the green valley his friends were making their way into. That was ahead of him. He had put things closer to his heart behind him before, he would put Lysama out of mind.

Tius did not sleep easy that night, tormented by dreams of fire and wolves and the screams of the dying.

CHAPTER XV

Delphina

Delphina sat in the somber reading room. This was a place, she thought, more dangerous than the battlefield. This was where queens and ambassadors gambled with the fates of nations and the lives of their citizens. The battlefield was just where the contests in quiet chambers played out for everyone else to see.

Quite frankly, Delphina did not care one shaved bit for any Kalesti down on the street. Not personally, at least. Piru cared, and Delphina kept their interests in mind knowing her husband was aligned with them. She did care a great deal, though, about Kalest. It was the homeland of her father and her husband, the land her mother had chosen, and the land to which Delphina owed any loyalty she had. Of course, she would not let her companions in the chamber know either of these things for certain.

"Tell me again," Delphina said, small and useless strands of lightning arcing between her fingers in a theatrical show of arcane displeasure, "how your masterful agents failed so utterly."

"You misunderstand, queen of all this side of the sea," one of the three ambassadors replied. "Our operations in Lysama were not a failure."

"You failed to break Lysama's armies," Delphina said coldly, "and you failed to keep my miserable stepdaughter in your custody. In what way did you not fail me and your masters?"

"Oh your radiance," the most ranked of the ambassadors, whose name Delphina recalled as Ormr, said, "it is a qualified success we admit. But Baudouin of Lysama is dead"-

"When he should be alive," Delphina replied, "and flattening the defenses of his former land."

"He is out of power. His son is dead. His child niece is hiding in some dark hole, and will lose her head if she lifts it above the ground before your majesty says otherwise. Lysama knows not who to turn to for its rulership, and with the success of Kalesti heroes who slew Baudouin, there are some who wish to turn to your husband for arbitration."

"And?"

"Your most glorious of majesties, it means that Lysama's armies may stand, but in disarray – they will not stand against Kalest."

"That is acceptable, I suppose," Delphina said, dropping the little spell she'd thought to offer intimidation with, "but your failure to capture or kill Esteri is not. I see no qualified success there, only miserable excuses from that loathsome worm, Ulfr of the severed hand."

It pleased Delphina to mock their efforts, pleased her more to mock their failures, and pleased her most to mock Ulfr. The instant dislike she had taken to the man had not been improved by the lack of results he had delivered since coming to Kalest on such heavy recommendations from Ormr.

"Were time not of grave import," Ormr said, "we would return Ulfr to you, to do with what you pleased. But we have few souls with even the requisite training for his mission, and none close enough to take over the hunt. It is regrettable, but we must allow him an opportunity to redeem his failure, rather than punishing it in whatever manner Delphina the Magnificent deems fitting."

"So you admit he failed?" Delphina pressed.

"Ulfr, yes, but Hundr who sat at the right hand of Baudouin may have granted us a new option for obtaining our aims. We may not have need of the wretched girl who so offends you by living after all."

"Do tell," Delphina said

"Hundr was privileged to witness the arrival of her companions into the house of the king of Lysama. Hundr is of the second generation, and blessed with the sight of power as are the first generation of the elder council. There are two who travel with the girl who could stand for her, perhaps even with a better likelihood of success. Perhaps even dead."

"Then we can return to our original covenant," Delphina said. "Esteri will be dead before I hold your side of the matter fulfilled."

"It shall be as you require," one of Ormr's assistants promised.

"And there is one more thing that I shall require," Delphina said. This, she had been waiting on for some time, looking for an opening to extract one further concession from Hyperborea. Their failures had given it to her, and offering mercy came with the unspoken right to demand some form of payment.

"Whatever you name," Ormr said, "if it is ours to provide to she who outshines sun and moon, we shall make it so."

"I am of the blood," Delphina said. She knew that no matter how innocent she framed this request, it was very dangerous. Everything hinged upon it, so she had to be sure to establish her right to extract it. "In the eighth generation, as your own pedigrees record my mother as being of the seventh. And, it is my will that has provided you the means to your glorious ends. I and my family shall share in the glory that is to come, this we have already agreed upon. But when the time comes, and the Council convenes to claim the birthright of Hyperborea, which should now be very soon, I require a place of honor to be mine, and to be present in it at the hour of ascendancy."

"It is a trifling thing," Ormr said. "I have no doubt the Elder Council should allow it, and indulge you in claiming whatever place you desire to be your own."

"I want your assurance, Ormr," Delphina said, "that it will be made clear to the Elder Council that these are my terms, and I expect their agreement in respect of our long relationship. After all, Ukko seeks the same party your Ulfr does, and we have already seen what occurs when their interests clash with yours."

"Of course," Ormr replied. "I swear it will be so."

Ormr stood, and led his minions out of the room.

Delphina sank back into the velvet chair, smiling. That had gone perfectly. As long as the Hyperboreans managed their side, Delphina's ultimate victory would be assured.

Her only regret was that she would not get to see Esteri die, but when she closed her eyes she could remember the girl's mother. The Ruby of Kalest laying in state, a nation mourning, and Delphina finally free to pursue what she had always desired. How she had loved Piru, from the day they met! But he had never seen her, not really, not while Aliisa was alive. And two years after she was in the cold ground, Delphina and Piru were married.

The official story, what any doctor could tell, was that she fell suddenly ill, her body giving out all at once with no cause to be seen. Even Markku, clever as he was, ruled it a wasting sickness, and all the alchemy of all the doctors could not cure it; they had not used the cursed potion then. In reality, it was a cocktail of poisons, Hyperborean hands, and Delphina's promise to render Kalest open to them once she was queen that had finally killed Aliisa. Only one part of her remained, and that part, Esteri, was damned on Delphina's word as well. Hopefully, the wretched girl wanted to live enough that in the end she'd understand some part of how Delphina felt, what it meant to have the only thing that matters stolen from you.

Of course, Esteri would not be able to suffer the indignity for a decade as Delphina did, but Dephina was comfortable with that much; she wanted the girl dead more than she wanted her to suffer.

Reminiscing over past and future victories, Delphina

found, was ever so slightly bitter-sweet. Remembering how Aliisa had died reminded Delphina that the woman had lived. Thinking on Esteri's impending doom reminded her that the girl was still alive and Ukko was still on her trail.

She rose from her seat, and made a graceful exit from the room for no one to see. The present was what mattered, and in the present Delphina had everything she really wanted. She was determined to enjoy it.

***

Delphina stood beside her son, smiling. The boy had taken an interest in alchemy, likely to do with his half-sister's fate, but as far as Delphina was concerned, it wasn't an unhealthy hobby as long as he didn't play with any of the dangerous reagents. As such, she had decided to try to indulge his interest as best she could. The queen of Kalest knew nothing about Alchemy, but she had learned a little of how to cook from her own mother, who had often had to handle her own food on the road as an agent of Hyperborea, and they said that Alchemy began in the kitchen.

"It's all about proportions," Delphina said, looking to the chef for a nod. As much as she at least knew what a few things were here rather than in the laboratory, she was not exactly familiar – flour on a silken dress was hardly presentable, "You have to have the right amount of butter, sugar, and flour or it won't come out very well. Quite a lot like alchemy, isn't it? And you can actually sample the results here."

Tuoni smiled. "I like that part," he said. "I'm glad you're here, mom."

Delphina knelt down and hugged her son. "And I'm glad I still have you," she said.

Tuoni poured in the next measure of flour and began to stir. It wasn't fitting work for a prince, but Delphina could not deny him, much as she had never been able to train him out of the love for his half sister that had left them here.

"Will they catch the poisoner soon?" Tuoni asked.

"Of course, dear," Delphina said. "Our forces are already in

Lysama. I've even heard the king of Lysama has fallen. Only just for what he's done, isn't it?"

"No," Tuoni said, "I mean the one that poured the poison in the water. I... I was looking for Doctor Markku and talked to Auntie – General Katri. She said I should be careful until they catch the poisoner."

"I... No, honey, they haven't found Lysama's hand here yet," Delphina said. That had always been a slight flaw in the plan – not one that was really worthwhile to solve up to this point. A devious enough assassin easily could have fled the country, and that was what everyone would assume. However, if suspicion about making a capture had reached her son, clever as he was, what did the adults around them think? "You said General Katri told you to be careful?"

Tuoni nodded.

"That's right," he said. Delphina's darling little boy looked back at the pan full of thick, golden dough. "I think it's ready to go in the oven. What next?"

"Well," Delphina said, "why don't you ask Chef Lyyski here to show you how to..." She tried to think of something simple. "Make a sauce perhaps? Mommy needs to see to the kingdom."

Delphina hurriedly showed herself out of the kitchens. How much did anyone – Katri perhaps – suspect? She dusted off her dress, waves of magic wind lifting dust and flour away and leaving the cloth and her hands alike pristine, and determined that she would find out, taking aside the first servant she found and demanding that general Katri be summoned to a particular antechamber. Delphina would have answers. Then she could decide what had to be done. Katri had always been quick on the uptake, which is why she had been one of Delphina's favorites, not to mention a favorite of the court as a whole, until now, but she was forceful and opinionated, perhaps enough to outweigh the value of her wits.

It took several minutes, but Katri arrived in formal uniform, a jeweled rapier at her hip. She bowed before her queen.

"Katri," Delphina said, addressing the general by her given

name and dispensing with heavy formalities, "I hear you have been speaking to my son of late."

"Yes, your majesty," Katri said, " most recently yesterday evening. His highness is a fine and respectful young man. Your majesty has much cause to be proud of him."

"Thank you for your assessment," Delphina said coldly, "but I think I know my own son. He has a kind heart."

Delphina paused to let Katri speak, but did not intend to allow the general to get much of a word in edgewise.

"You must be proud"-

"Kind." Delphina said, "but also fragile. The loss of his half-sister has already pained him greatly. Did you know, Katri, that he has taken a great interest in alchemy after learning what became of her? It is a noble profession, but it is not healthy for a boy his age. And now you frighten him with tales of a poisoner lurking our halls? I fear my baby will not be able to eat or drink."

"I am sorry, your majesty," Katri said. "I did not intend to cause the child undue distress. But I do not think what I said is merely some tale."

"No?" Delphina said. "This manor employs only true Kalesti. No soul within the castle would harm us. It was clearly a Lysaman agent to have delivered the poison."

"Even if that is true," Katri said, "the crown has made no great investigation, nor closed whatever route the assassin made use of to gain entrance to your halls. Your majesty, I have used my idleness here away from the front to make as much of an investigation as I have been able to do. I have found no traitor, nor have I found the route by which any agent might have entered our fastness, reach the kitchens, poison a pitcher of water that was sure to be delivered to the royal table, and escape unnoticed. I fear that all your majesties may be in grave danger."

"And you choose to speak to my son of this?"

"I mean to speak with your husband, his majesty," Katri said, "but I have hoped to find more evidence, or at least a plan of action. I trust your majesties to be taking precautions, but I also know that sometimes children do not realize the reason for the things we do, and when I saw him in the halls alone, I thought it prudent."

Delphina breathed a sigh of relief. Katri was very smart, and very perceptive, but all the same she was fixated on the story given to the public. She was searching for Lysamans, and she would never find any.

"Thank you, loyal Katri," Delphina said. "I shall be sure to let my husband know of your efforts, though I hear you may be needed on the front some time soon. Certainly, the search will continue in your absence, though I am not sure we shall ever find the precise weakness Lysama's agent used, seeing as we have found none so far."

"That is exactly the matter," Katri said. "I have begun to fear something, deep in my heart, that may mean the danger here is greater than we might have imagined. I have no proof, but the news of recent days has fortified my suspicions."

Delphina narrowed her gaze. "What suspicions are those?"

"Your majesty, I believe ambassador Ormr may have been involved in the poisoning."

"That is a very dire accusation, and you have already said you have no proof."

"No proof, that is true," Katri said, "but Hyperborea has hands in every nation. They are neutral – mercenary. They have no love for nor loyalty to Kalest. If the price was right, is there any doubt they might betray us? Especially, I have heard disturbing rumors about the Lysaman front, that an Accursed monstrosity the likes of which has never been seen appeared in their capitol. In every war, alchemists experiment with that damnable potion, but Hyperborea... they seem to understand it better than anyone. Lysama must have paid dearly for that creature, even if it ran out of their control. I doubt they could have created the thing I have heard tell of on their own."

Delphina stepped close, eyes darting to Katri's jeweled sword. It was the only weapon in the room, and Delphina could reach it. If she struck down the general, it would silence her. She could call the guard, and claim Katri had tried to kill her. She could claim that Katri had been behind the poisoning of her stepdaughter, had been bought by Lysama long ago.

But then what would happen? Katri was well respected, and not just by Delphina herself. It would be hard to make the rest of the military, especially the officers under her command, believe that Katri had been a traitor. Someone would investigate the story, and there would be far more holes than in the tale that Katri herself was busily dismantling.

Delphina took a breath, and let it out. She could get Katri out of the capitol, at least, far away from any facts of Esteri's poisoning. She could take her cavalry to the front with all speed. She was even a good candidate to manage the occupation forces – the woman had an even hand, a heavy respect for law and order, and a problematically analytical mind.

"Thank you, Katri," Delphina said. "It's an interesting theory, one which I will certainly keep in mind before dining with the ambassador. But all the same, no doubt being here when our armies fight in the south of Lysama has put a great strain on your mind. I will speak to my husband, both to see your theory investigated and your forces deployed to the front, where they truly belong. You may go."

Katri gave a formal bow, and left the room. Delphina, alone, considered her next move. There was more to this than just Katri. She would have to produce some proof of the crown's safety – an executed serving girl with Lysaman gold in her purse, perhaps. Then Tuoni could sleep easily, and Delphina herself a little sounder.

***

Delphina entered her husband's chamber. The door had been locked, but she had the key.

"What is the matter, dear?" she asked. She knew Piru – he had never opened himself to too many souls, but all the same, for him to shy away from the public light, it meant that there was a darkness hanging over him.

Piru, sitting at his writing desk, halfheartedly indicated a small scroll.

"A message?" Delphina asked, walking over to him. "Let me see that."

It was from Ukko, relating in so many words what Delphina's Hyperborean contacts had essentially already told her. Baudouin of Lysama was dead, after being transformed into a gigantic monster that ravaged his capitol. Ukko's story revealed that he knew the Hyperboreans were behind the events, but since he did not know why, he had not made that fact known to the people of Lysama. At least the immortal had a savvy enough head for politics to accept that.

There was more, though: he told of an encounter between he and his band and the princess. While Delphina was quite relieved that he had not managed to secure her, the fact that he had gotten close enough to do so had Baudouin's fate not interceded was worrying. In that section, he said how Esteri seemed to still be lucid, intelligent, and good of heart – essentially redeemable, in Ukko's estimation, but that she seemed to be suffering from some paranoid delusion that her father meant her harm.

"She knows," Delphina said. "That is what troubles you? We both knew this was a possibility, and we both know what has to be done about it, don't we? Recall Ukko, tell him there is some task more important to the nation than this search. You can contact him, can you not?"

Piru shook his head. "I will not do that," he said. "Ukko will not be shaken by her words, that is what is important."

"Esteri will not come back!" Delphina snapped. "I am sorry, but that should be clear. If your daughter was ever to return, it would have happened there in Lysama. Continuing to hope to bring her peacefully home is a fool's errand, more even than simply when we knew she had turned herself into a monster."

"Please," Piru said. "To come this far I have done my own flesh and blood a grave dishonor – and her mother too, rest her soul – if I am to leave a good legacy, be a good king, I must at least try to mend that wrong, whether or not the world should ever know of it."

"You have a kingdom to think of," Delphina said, "and not only that, you still have a family here. You have me and Tuoni – do we not matter to you? The hours you spend grieving your daughter you could spend with your son. What is lost is lost, do not throw more of your life away in vain attempts to reclaim it."

"You have said as much before," Piru said, "and you are right as you were about moving on after Aliisa... but I will not recall Ukko. They are six, his band. Whatever heroics they have done, they will not turn the tide in battles of thousands – those he appointed to the regulars serve that end. They and a quiet hour can serve to still the voice of my conscience that haunts me so bitterly. If they do not succeed, and return empty-handed, I will not have lost much. If they manage to bring Esteri home... well, I do not know what I will do then. It will be a hard road, maybe as hard as burying her, though the reasons will be different."

Delphina thought carefully, "If I may," she said, "I think I can help. Hyperborea has other agents in the region, and I could convince them to spare some resources to aid Ukko, particularly if he needs to go beyond Lysama for this. I would need only a small thing from you."

"And that is?"

"A letter," Delphina said, "one that gives its bearer authority to speak with your voice. Otherwise Ukko is unlikely to trust any Hyperborean, after what happened with Baudouin. The man is clearly a fighter worthy of his legends, but he does not know the modern world. Having one of our allies to guide him could be very valuable."

Of course, it was not as though she would have to bargain with Ormr. In fact, such a token was likely to be able to earn her some concession or other, favors to be paid back later, assurances of her place when the time came. And, if successfully employed, it would bring Esteri to her end.

"I can do that," Piru said, "but I would have you tell Ormr that I do not appreciate his methods, and would expect his agent to offer guidance to my ends only. Baudouin's fate is... I can accept it, but I think I liked the Hyperboreans better when they were on no one's side, in some ways."

"I will," Delphina said, "but I'd like you to do something in return."

"And that is?"

"Come out of your room," Delphina said. "It is a lovely afternoon, and our son has been putting his interests in alchemy to better use under Lyyski's direction in the kitchens. Enjoy some time with us, sample the things he's made, and try to smile some when you do. I cannot remember if you even have since Esteri left. War is hard on a king, but that doesn't mean you can't enjoy a little life."

Piru stood, put his arms around Delphina, and kissed her on the lips.

"There... there is nothing I would sooner do. I am sorry to have provided so little light in our days for so long."

Delphina smiled and blushed a bit. "Write the letter," she said, "then meet me and Tuoni in the feasthall. I'll find him, and our family will have at least a little cause for mirth."

CHAPTER XVI

Esteri

Esteri looked over the hills. The rolling, green hills of Lysama had faded into a scraggly yellow-brown over the previous day, and the mountains in the northern distance loomed tall with white caps. The lowlands ahead were rough country, rocky ground with tufts of small grass, not at all like the fields and forests of Kalest.

"Do you think we're in Tyrvad's territory?" she asked Erikis.

"I would guess we are," he replied, "but we will not know until we find some sort of settlement. We had best keep moving."

Erikis had driven them northward at a grueling pace in the days since they fled the palace of Lysama. Before, he had been calm and composed, and a font of occasional wisdom. But from that day, he had gained a grim determination, and taken the command of their company, displacing Radegond from her position as the driving force behind them.

"The castle is far behind us." Esteri protested, frustrated at his stern commands. "We are far from Lysama's law and far from recognition. Why press ahead?"

"I will make matters clear when I must," he said.

"And I will not accept that!" Esteri shouted. "What's the hurry? Lysama has fallen, our quest has failed. I want to tell the world but that doesn't mean you should be pressing us on!"

"You must trust my judgment, young princess."

"No," Esteri said.

Erikis turned about. "Excuse me?"

"I said no."

"Yes, but why?"

"Look around you," Esteri said. "We're tired and hungry, bone-weary from days of such abuse. Everyone but you and Avina is flagging, and still you insist we keep moving, keep up the pace. I for one am not going to go another step until I hear a reason why."

"You are very young," Erikis said, "and it shows. What would do if I refused? Stand on that stone until hunger and thirst consumed you? Abandon your professed duty to the world?"

"I am rather expecting you to talk." Esteri replied. She glared hard at Erikis.

"Very well," he said with a sigh. "Spare me the stubbornness of youth. There is more reason to go to Tyrvad than simple safety from the Hyperboreans."

"Good," Esteri said, folding her arms across her chest. "Now tell me what that is."

"Long ago," Erikis said, "a great and terrible power dwelled in Hyperborea – God to some, demon to others. According to legend, it was the Ancestor Gods of Tyrvad that defeated that power. Now, what you call a god might vary, but the tale is more or less true. I should know. I was there."

Esteri waited, hoping that Erikis would explain on his own what relevance this tale had to the modern day.

"Baudouin," he said, "was no ordinary Accursed. It did seem to be a variant of the potion that created him, but there were threads of power in his being that were very familiar. Even too familiar, I might say. I believe that the Hyperboreans have dredged up some remnant of that ancient power, and that they may resurrect it sometime soon. Before that happens, the Ancestor Gods must awaken. They can assuredly put down Hyperborea's demon god once more."

"I see," Esteri said.

"I do believe that this is relevant to your own mission," Erikis said. "It is likely that Hyperborea is allied in a formal sense with your father and stepmother. After all, your stepmother is of their race. And why curse Baudouin so rather than experimenting in the dark, far from civilization, unless they meant to damage Lysama for Kalest's conquest? They may betray Kalest, but until they do their aims align. Dealing a blow to one also means harming the other, and no matter how well-trained Kalest's armies, they could not stand against the power Hyperborea would wield."

"So," Esteri said, "you want to prevent Hyperborea from resurrecting this power, or at least from getting to use it if they do, before we work on stopping my father's aggression."

"Which, of course, may already be a moot point," Erikis reminded her. "Lysama is so weak that if he stops there, any campaign against him would be punitive at best."

"I can accept that," Esteri said, "but why didn't you tell us before?"

"I did not wish to frighten you," Erikis said. "You have not seen all the things that I have seen – not even you, Radegond. Without my perspective, this new mission might be quite terrifying."

"Are you kidding?" Avina asked. "This is amazing! We're going to see a battle of gods! You've seen one before, right? What was it like?"

Erikis chuckled. "Well," he said, "I don't know how much I can really say, but I can try."

"All the same," Esteri said, "the Ancestor gods have waited a very long time. Could we find a place to camp, and rest our weary limbs for one day, before taking a somewhat more comfortable pace?"

Erikis sighed, "I suppose that would be acceptable," he said. "Have you seen any good sites, Radegond?"

Radegond nodded. "Over the next ridge, there's a stream. It's not much, but it means fresh water, and enough foliage we might find something wild to eat rather than depleting our rations with the rest. We can make it before sunset if we hurry."

"There you have it," Erikis said. "Is that acceptable to you?"

Esteri nodded. "Very much so," she said. "Lead the way."

The group began walking again. Esteri slid to the rear of the pack, and shortly after, Tius followed.

"Thank you," he said.

"Excuse me?"

"You weren't the only one thinking those questions," Tius replied. "Avina and Radegond are tough as nails, and I think Radegond can cheat. I mean, does she even feel an ache in her wings if she puts them away? I don't know. But me and Hathus, and Avina's parents... we couldn't keep it up any better than you."

"Well then," Esteri said, "I don't see what I need to be thanked for. Someone would have said it eventually."

"I'm not so sure," Tius said. "I mean, I toyed with the thought, but I don't know if I'd have ever called Erikis out like that."

Esteri chuckled slightly, "We learn we may be caught between warring gods, and you're more concerned I earned us a day's reprieve?"

"Well," Tius said, "I've got a lot of experience paying no mind to what people above me do. Other than your mother, I don't think there was a single noble who ever said a word or lifted a finger that reached the world of a thief. The way I see it, the gods probably don't even notice us. We're like ants, or grains of sand."

Esteri wanted to protest, but she knew it was more or less true – what lords and kings did was mostly the concern of lords and kings, the common folk just paid their taxes and kept their heads down unless it came to war.

"Well," Esteri said, finally finding some way to argue, "I suppose that's one way of looking at it. All things considered, I'm surprised you came along with me. After all, I'm a noble myself."

Tius turned his head away from Esteri. "I made my choice,"

he said, "and I don't regret it."

"Even when your feet ache, leagues from home in a strange country?"

"Even now," he said. "I'd rather be here, with everything that entails, than safe and comfortable at home."

Esteri couldn't help but smile, though she did not understand why.

"Well," she said, "I'm very glad for that. If not for you... I don't know what would have become of me by now."

Esteri remembered Ulfr's threats. Of course, she might have died before then, even on the mountain where the Accursed lived, but the idea of remaining in that man's clutches was too horrible to contemplate or to forget.

"Anyone else would have done the same," Tius said. "I was just in the right place at the right time."

"So you say," Esteri said, "but you don't sound like you really believe it." She circled around him just a little, and though he tried to turn his head farther, it wasn't enough. "You're blushing, Tius."

"It's nothing, really."

"Oh, all right then. At the next chance, when we must tell the world about my father and Hyperborea, I shall be sure to include how gallantly you rescued me from their clutches, refusing to turn your back on your princess no matter what they offered, fighting with no concern for your own health or safety. It will be a very grand tale."

"Please, stop."

"Why should I?" Esteri asked. "It's true."

"I don't need praise or accolades," Tius said, uncomfortably. "I did what I did and I'd do it again, but... well once a thief, always a thief. I don't do well in the public light."

Esteri guessed that wasn't the whole truth, but decided that he deserved a reprieve from any needling.

"If that's how you feel," she said, "I won't drag you into it. But if you run in after me, you're on your own there."

It was then Esteri noticed how far they had fallen behind.

"We'd better keep pace," she said, "or Radegond will be yelling for an hour straight." She turned to face forward and began taking long, deliberate strides, focusing on her pace and footing rather than the protests her legs were making.

***

That night, Esteri found herself sitting at the edge of the firelight, gazing out into the darkness. She had turned away at first because she found herself at a lull – Gelvira and Frideger were talking quietly with one another, Avina was chatting loudly with Tius and Hathus, Radegond was off hunting and Erikis... Esteri had no particular desire to approach him.

Once she had started to look off into that darkness, she found she could not really look away. Esteri knew that there was nothing out there, that Baudouin's blackened form would not suddenly emerge from the shadows, nor Ulfr slink from them to steal her away, at least not with her friends so close. But for every terror that her mind banished, it invented a new one that she could not so easily put away, no matter how unreal, and she could not turn her back on them.

In a way, the darkness seemed to take on a dimension of its own. Esteri tried to pick out shapes in it, warnings of new horrors yet to come, but they remained elusive, out of reach.

A hand touched Esteri's shoulder.

"Something troubling you?" Gelvira asked.

"Some things," Esteri said, not sure where to begin

"Well," Gelvira said, sitting down next to her, "why don't you tell me about a few of them? I can't guarantee that I'll be able to help, but I can try."

Esteri thought. There was so much she could say, but she decided to pick the most sickening first. She reached into her pocket and retrieved the amulet Ulfr had carried, the golden disc with the swirling red orb in its center.

"This is part of it," Esteri said.

"What is that?" Gelvira asked.

"When... when the Hyperborean found me, he used this thing to control my body. I couldn't move, couldn't scream, couldn't speak. I had to do exactly as he wanted me to do, and if I'd been there any longer," she shuddered, "well, I don't want to think about what would have happened to me. I'm not sure if death would have been the most of my worries. I was so helpless! I can't wash that feeling away, the feeling of being able to do nothing, forced to watch as someone else controlled my body to suit his needs."

"I may not know about this thing," Gelvira said. "Erikis might, so I'll show it to him if you'd like."

Esteri looked at it, then back. "I might... later."

"But," Gelvira said, "I think I might know a thing or two about being helpless. I'll tell you a story, and maybe that will help."

Esteri nodded silently. She wasn't sure how a story could help her get over that horrible feeling, the crippling certainty that she would be at that monster's mercy, but she was more than glad to hear it. At least it might take her mind off the past.

"You see, when I was mortal, there were many things I could not do for myself. I had servants of my family household that waited on my every need, mind you, and I'm sure that there are people who would call my life then a sort of paradise. But, that's not what I wanted. I wanted to be like everyone else. I wanted to get out of my bed, where I spent most of my days, and go riding out in the hills I could see from my window. I wanted to ride a horse more than anything, but not only was I a young lady, I had the bleeding sickness that made everyone treat me as though I was fragile as glass."

"What happened?"

"Well," Gelvira said, "one day I decided that enough was enough, marched down to the stables, and demanded that the stable boy saddle me a horse or I would tell my father his blood would cure my affliction. I never would have done such a thing, of course, but he didn't know that and did know my father would do anything to keep me alive. So, he saddled me a horse, and helped me climb astride it, and I rode."

"Somehow," Esteri said, "I don't think that's the end of the story."

"More or less," Gelvira replied. "I fell off just outside the stables and was bedridden more than usual for weeks, with my whole left side black with bruises. It almost killed me, in fact. If that stableboy hadn't dragged me back inside, and yelled at the top of his lungs until someone heard him and sent for the doctors to see to me, I would have died."

"So what's the lesson to take from that?" Esteri asked bitterly. "That I should just accept my limitations?"

"No," Gelvira said. "At least, not exactly. Sometimes, any one of us could be helpless. But all the same, should the worst happen, there are plenty of people out there who will help us, and then some day we'll help them right back. I think the stable boy ended up my father's bannerman once I explained the whole matter. So what you should take away isn't that you were helpless, it was that you were helped."

"It was just luck that Tius got there," Esteri said

"Luck," Gelvira replied, "and his plain determination. I doubt he'll admit it any time soon, but I do think he cares for you. My daughter is very, very jealous of that."

"Should she be?" Esteri asked. It was a stupid question. She ought to have been the one to answer it.

"I don't know," Gelvira said. "I think of Tius almost like he was my own son, but I have to admit I don't really know what he's thinking all the time. I also don't think Avina really knows what she wants, but that's neither here nor there."

Esteri was glad for the darkness, as she was sure she was blushing quite brightly red. Gelvira was frustratingly direct when it came to some subjects.

"So," Gelvira asked, "was there something else on your mind?"

Esteri looked back at the darkness for a moment.

"There was one other thing," she said.

"And that is?"

"I... I think I have the power to see the future. It's how I

move so fast in spars when my eyes turn black, why I sometimes just know to say or not say something, maybe even how
I found your village so quickly. I saw Baudouin's monstrous
form when I closed my eyes, before he drank the potion. If
only I could control this sight, I might have been able to save
him."

"Hm," Gelvira said, "but you don't know how to practice
future sight, the real good stuff and not the stuff that's yours in
combat, is that right?"

"About that," Esteri said, "what good are visions if I don't
know the rules, or how to get them when there's still time?"

"Well," Gelvira said, "from my experience, the easiest way
to learn how to use a power is just to try to do it. When I
was just starting out, my skin would harden if something hit
me, but now?" She held up a hand. Bands around her forearm
turned stony and then back again. "I can call it pretty pre-
cisely. Maybe your visions are the same way. I'll tell you what
– why don't you look into my future?"

Esteri nodded. "I'll try," she said. She thought about it for a
moment, and then sat cross-legged, facing Gelvira. She rested
her elbows on her knees and held out her hands, palm up.

"Okay," she said, "give me your hands."

Gelvira placed her hands in Esteri's. Esteri closed her eyes,
and tried to focus.

For a moment, there was nothing and then, everything.

It was evening, in some rocky land. She stood, facing... the
Slayers. They were there, standing opposite. Ukko said something, then his head whipped to his right, and then, discon-
tinuity hit.

Esteri jerked herself back, breathing heavily, drenched in
sweat, afraid.

"My eyes..." she said. "How are my eyes?"

"Black as night," Gelvira replied, "and there's more besides
that."

"Gelvira I... I don't know, but I think we're going to get into
a fight with those Kalesti I met in Lysama, the ones who were

trying to take me home."

"Is that so?"

"I was seeing it from your eyes, so I don't know exactly what happened. It was all so sudden, I"-

Esteri hugged Gelvira.

"I want you to leave us," Esteri said. "I think I may have seen your death, and I'm not going to have anyone die on my account. I don't want that."

"Now, dear," Gelvira said, "take it easy. I'm rather hard to kill."

"Don't just say that!" Esteri cried. "I can't take it! I don't want you, or anyone to die!"

"And if I leave," Gelvira said, "who's to say someone else won't fall in my place?"

"Gelvira..."

"You'd be fewer against the same foes," Gelvira said, "so if I die in our future together, in our future apart, is it my daughter? Or my husband? Or Tius?"

"What if it's no one?" Esteri asked. "Shouldn't you take that chance, and go home?"

Gelvira sighed. "Of all of us, Radegond and I are the ones that aren't quite so afraid of death. It's funny, actually, because it's for very different reasons. She's never been afraid, and wrote herself off as dead when she drank the potion. And me? I was petrified of dying, every day of my life, and every day since that fear was taken away from me has been a blessing, something I wouldn't have had otherwise."

"You can't be comfortable with death," Esteri said. "You have a family to live for, and your friends."

"I'd rather not die," Gelvira said, "but everyone does sooner or later. Often quite a lot later for us Accursed, since we only die violent deaths, but later all the same. When my time comes, I only hope I can look it in the eye, and accept that I've had all the days with Frideger and Avina and all my friends, and smile."

"If it comes like I saw it," Esteri said, voice trembling, "it will be something out of sight."

"Now," Gelvira said, "I'm sure you can tell me all about what you did see, so when the time comes I can know when to protect myself. But how about we look for a happier future? Maybe you can predict something in specific. How about your love life, dear?"

"If you'll forgive me," Esteri said, "I would rather leave that a mystery."

Gelvira smiled. "Well, I suppose it would be more fun that way. I just thought that perhaps looking for something other than pain or death would do you some good."

"It would," Esteri said, "but if I look into my own future, I could see anything. Even something I don't want to." She wasn't sure what would be worse, learning that she would be dead, learning that she would end up in Ulfr's clutches, or finding herself more directly in the throes of passion with someone she cared for.

"Maybe," Esteri said, "do you have any dice?"

Gelvira nodded. "Hathus does."

"We could play a gambling game," Esteri said. "It doesn't matter what for, but maybe it should be something so it feels important. I'll try to predict how the dice will fall."

"That sounds like a plan," Gelvira said. "I have just one amendment."

"And that is?"

Gelvira grinned.

"We clean out Hathus if you can."

Esteri smirked back, feeling just a little better.

"All right," she said. "I can live with that."

***

Esteri could not rest easy on the day she had demanded. Her vision of Gelvira haunted her. If the Slayers caught them, would it be because she had demanded they rest their feet rather than carrying on as Erikis had wanted? If she died, would it be Esteri's fault? She had told Gelvira everything she could about the encounter, every detail she had seen, and hoped that it would give Gelvira the chance to escape such a fate.

Oddly, Gelvira herself seemed more comfortable spending the one day idle. Most of Esteri's companions did – they were happy to rest, comfortable beside the stream. They did not share her restlessness, and why should they? They had not shared her vision.

Other than Esteri herself, Avina did seem a little uncomfortable starting around mid-day. Esteri watched her, and hoped that she would invent some solution to this idleness that threatened to consume them.

And, after not too long, Avina did.

"You know what I want?" she said. "I want to have meat for dinner. I want venison, or roast boar, or whatever else is out there. We've got a camp, we should go on a hunt, some of us."

Radegond sighed. "I suppose you expect me to scout out the prey. I would rather not, quite frankly. Her highness won us a day of rest, and this is how I shall take mine."

"I'll go," Esteri offered. Of course, she knew nothing of how to hunt any animal, not what animals would exist in this hard country, but it would be something she could do to keep her mind off the future that she dared not look at but could not forget.

Avina frowned.

"No offense," she said, "but I'd like to actually catch something."

"And I can help," Esteri offered quickly. "I'll be sure to lead us to where game is, as long as I look for it."

Esteri pleaded with her eyes, desperately hoping that Avina would make no further protest against Esteri's help in this matter.

"What?" Avina asked, then shook her head. "Never mind. Your black-eye instincts, right? I guess you can come along," she turned to the rest of the crowd and raised her voice, "since nobody else seems to care!"

The rest of the group didn't stir, though Tius did look a little hurt.

"Here," Radegond said, walking over to her gear and lifting up her spear. "Unlike Avina, you need a weapon."

She tossed the spear over, and Esteri caught it.

"Thank you," she said. Avina was already marching across the stream.

"Come on," Avina said. "I want to be able to bring something back before nightfall."

Esteri hurried to catch up.

"Right," Esteri said when they were out of earshot of the camp, "where should we go?"

"You tell me," Avina said. "You're the one with the freakish instincts."

"Oh... right, what should I be looking for?"

"Bacon," Avina replied. "If there's a boar or a pig around here, you find it and I'll kill it."

Esteri nodded, and tried to turn her mind to the food. She started to lead the way, turning subtly north-east. She didn't know if she could really sense anything, or if it was just less steeply uphill, but it felt like the right way to go.

After the first ridge, they entered a sparse forest of tall, dark pines, a bed of brown needles carpeting the sunny paths between their narrow trunks. In that landscape, Avina spoke.

"So," she said, "when this is all over, what are you going to do?"

Esteri thought about it. For a moment, she was tempted to try to look into her own future, a mad voice telling her that she would be happier knowing. She shut it down and shook her head.

"I don't know," Esteri replied.

"What do you mean you don't know?" Avina asked. "What do you want to do?"

"It's not that simple," Esteri said. "I'm royalty. That doesn't just come with fancy clothes and good food, with silver and gold. It comes with a duty. My father always said that it would be my place to maintain a strong Kalest, a nation that could stand the test of time. My mother... she was fond of saying that I had to look after the kingdom's present too, and all its people. That's what I was born to do."

"I think I get it," Avina said. "When your dad dies or gets thrown into prison or something, you're queen of Kalest, right? And since he went all crazy and tried to kill you, that means this isn't done until you're queen. And then you're queen forever."

Esteri shook her head.

"I still hope my father can be saved, but even if he can't, I don't know if I can take up that duty," she said. "I don't think the people would accept an Accursed queen. If I try to take up the mantle, it would be civil war."

Avina shrugged. "What choice do they have? You're the princess and they've got to deal with it."

"They could side behind my brother," Esteri said. "I love him dearly, but I don't know if he could refuse if the lords of the land started championing his cause against mine."

"Whatever," Avina said. "If the people of Kalest are stupid enough to do that, they don't deserve a nice queen."

Esteri raised an eyebrow. "What did you say?"

"Nothing important," Avina growled. "Anyway, I was just curious if you were going to come back up the mountain or not."

"Your village is a lovely place," Esteri said. "I can't deny I'd probably enjoy life there. A simple life. I just don't know if my conscience will let me seclude myself up there, or if I'll even be able to go back once the world knows who I am. I wouldn't want to lead danger to your home."

"Bah," Avina said. "Bring them on."

"I'm surprised," Esteri said, "I wouldn't think you'd want me there."

"Who said I did?" Avina replied. "I mean maybe it would be nice to have somebody who's not about a hundred years older than me to talk to, but that doesn't mean it has to be you."

Esteri smiled. "Somehow, I thought you might feel that way."

They were silent for a moment, but before too long, Avina spoke again.

"So, I heard you were working on trying to see the future better."

"Did you?"

"Well," Avina said, "Hathus was kind of loud when he found out why he was losing everything at dice."

Esteri laughed. "I suppose he was. But he was a better sport about it than I would have expected."

"What did you win, anyway?"

"Let's see," Esteri said, reaching into her pockets and pulling out the contents. "This is my half of the take, your mom took the other half because it was her idea. I've got... Four double eagles, a bit, one of those fat Lysaman silver coins, the weird-shaped Tyrvad gold, and a harmonica."

"He gambled his harmonica?" Avina said with a gasp. "No wonder he was mad!"

"I'll probably give it back," Esteri said. "It wasn't a fair game, after all."

Esteri thought that she should probably give the coin back too, except for the fact that the Accursed had little enough use for them that it wasn't a big loss, whoever carried the money. It was actually a decent value, she reflected. The Kalesti coins weren't worth that much, and the Lysaman coin, though heavy, was likely adulterated with lead. But Tyrvad gold was decently respected for its purity and the face value of the coin was high to begin with, even if its form made it seem more like a charm or other piece of jewelry than currency. She pocketed the coins again.

"You've got to make him work for it," Avina said. "You can't just hand it back."

"Why?" Esteri asked, "Is that some sort of rule?"

"No," Avina said. "It would be missing a great opportunity. Why do you think mom wanted to mess with him to begin with?"

"Well then," Esteri said, looking at the harmonica, "I'm

sure I'll think of something."

Avina smiled, and the two of them walked quietly for a moment. When Tius wasn't nearby, Avina could be a rather pleasant individual.

It was perhaps two hours after setting out that they began another ascent, and as they crested the hill, emerged from the forest. A stony field of pale grass spread before them, and on it was civilization. Or, at least, what passed for civilization in Tyrvad – great halls of massive timbers, houses with roofs like the hulls of ships, and over it all a great, long crimson banner with the golden dragon passant of Tyrvad stretched with serpentine coils along its length, fluttering proudly in the wind.

"Well," Avina said with a sigh, "there goes our hope for a hunt."

"Maybe," Esteri said, "but I'll bet they have a butcher. And I still have my winnings."

"So what you're saying is..."

"There's not just civilization there. There's probably bacon."

CHAPTER XVII

Ukko

The Slayers rode quietly into the Tyrvad town. Here, north of the border, they did not have the favor of the locals that they had unwillingly enjoyed in Lysama, nor could they invoke King Piru's favor as they had in Kalest itself. Here, they were strangers.

The days since the fall of Baudouin had been strange, even for Ukko. He had lived so much of his life away from the company of other humans that being thrust into their midst was, in its own way, an alien experience.

In that battle, every one of the Slayers had faced death, and they had escaped it by hairsbreadths. All of Ukko's companions had been changed by the experience. Some more than others, and all in different ways, but it was a trial they were going to have to face. The most marked changes had been Launo and Maria: he had gained something of a sense of humor, while she had lost hers, now devoted to the quest above all else. Ukko hoped that they would both be more themselves given time, even if Launo's changes made him more personable. Taavi was also badly affected; the bright-eyed boy had seen one of the worse horrors this world had provided, and often stared into the distance, Baudouin's monstrous visage no doubt looming over the horizon.

On the other end were Seija and Acacia. It was hard to notice, sometimes, how they were different now than they had been, for they retained the natures that were close to their hearts. Seija, however, who had been closed-mouthed out of a smug superiority, now wore less arrogance and more grim determination. Acacia, though still effervescent, now sometimes seemed to speak furtively of life and the future when she was not watching her words.

Acacia... Ukko told himself that all the Slayers were his friends and comrades, that though he had relieved himself of any command with more weight than first among equals, he would not and could not play favorites. Most of the time, when Ukko dreamed, it was dreams of a dark forest, whether the one he had spent so long within the confines of or the great Bird's Wood of which that forest was but a paltry remnant. Sometimes, he saw a world that was long lost, saw the son no one could know was his, the broad fields and towering trees of Kalest of old, the shining halls of its castle that he had strode through as the greatest of Kalest's knights and champion of its queen. Rarely, though, his present life intruded, and then it always began with Acacia.

Ukko tried to push such thoughts away. He was far too old for them, and attempting to follow a kidnapped princess through a foreign country was certainly not the time.

Once in the bounds of the town, the Slayers dismounted, and lead their horses the rest of the way. Tyrvad was at least somewhat more familiar to Ukko than Lysama had been – it was a rough country, and the ways of its people were old when Ukko was young. How long since their ancestors had sailed far and wide, and still their timber halls had roofs like inverted ships? Ah, but Kalest itself had been little different in Ukko's time, and he remembered the wooden and thatched-roofed feast halls and palisades that only slowly had been replaced with stone when the vestiges of the Bird's Wood faded away and men began to quarry the rock underneath.

In such a town as this, there was no inn, and so it fell to Ukko to speak to the head-man of the village and request with greatest humility lodging for his Slayers and news of the recent passage of any other bands of strangers.

The headman was very genial, and more so when Ukko

introduced his Kalesti band as Slayers. The old, grey-bearded chief had laughed and treated all the strangers in his presence like they were old friends, and offered them the right to rest in the great hall with a roaring fire, if only they would share some good story of their hunts past to the assembly there in the evening.

To this, Ukko quickly agreed, for while he could have told some tale of his youth or his days emerging from the wood to defend Kalest, the six of them had just come from the greatest battle against the most terrible Accursed he had ever faced, and any one of them could regale a ready crowd with the story.

The Headman, then, told Ukko that there had been another band of strangers to pass through the town not three days past, and on foot, that it had been eight strong young men and women of many countries. No doubt, Ukko thought, this was Esteri and the Accursed who shared her road or forced her along theirs, but he did not share this with the headman, for there was no need to alarm him over a thing that had already happened and hurt his people not at all.

After that conversation, for the headman's eccentricities and joviality caused it to wear on, the sun was low enough that Ukko and the other Slayers were admitted to the Great Hall and given their seats of honor in which they might rest themselves before the night's festivities. Owing the season and the town's position both in Tyrvad and in a shallow depression, the sun set very quickly after, though not so swift that it did not seem that the news had spread to the whole town. Fires were set in the fire-pits dug into the dirt floor, and the scents of a great feast being cooked drifted in on the wind. No doubt some weekly festival had here been co-opted, for in towns like this communal feasts were common things.

Soon enough, the hall was full, and as its inhabitants waited for their food and drink, they demanded their tale. To this, Taavi stepped forward. Most times, he was reserved, but he was familiar with long nights among strangers, and his lips became looser in the presence of alcohol, whether or not he had any himself. Further, while Taavi would never admit it himself, he had some poetry in his heart.

He began very weakly, describing in a shaking voice how they had come to Lysama castle, and how the castle shook. Then, his eyes fixed far away, and he raised his voice to tell the hall what Baudouin had looked like and, omitting Hrafn from the tale, how they had faced the former king upon the roof of the cathedral and the tops of the tenements beyond. He recited as though the words flowed through him nearly every cut that had been delivered to Baudouin, of Acacia's fearless assault and Maria's great leap to at last lay the creature low.

When Baudouin fell, the assembled hall cheered.

"A fine tale!" the headman cheered. "And had not whispers of it already come north to us, I may not have believed it. To think, a monster that could tower over Lysama's heights! It is an honor to host those who could defeat such a creature."

Ukko and Seija did not try however halfheartedly to deny the honor. Seija, Ukko assumed, because she felt it was deserved and Ukko himself because he knew that the people of Tyrvad, at least in his time and he presumed still nowadays, loved boasting so long as it was true.

After that, food and drink were deemed ready and brought out. Trenchers were filled with meaty, thick stew and masses of potatoes, all steaming hot. At the head man's direction, cup-bearers brought out large horns banded with silver, filled them with a strong, sweet mead and presented them to the honored guests of the village. Ukko drank sparingly, owing both the potency of the drink and his need, as he felt it, to ensure with further, lesser tales that they remained in the good graces of the crowd and their hosts.

Ukko needn't have worried, for he was not alone in playing the good guest. Launo knew the great stories of Kalest better even than Ukko, who had lived some of them, and while they were not personal stories they were tales that were less known to these people than they were at home, and quite pleased those who listened to him, while Taavi was himself better versed in folk tales the likes of which made the rounds of taverns at home.

As the evening wore on, Seija boasted at to some provocation that she could drink as much as any man, to which the crowd went wild, electing a champion and cheering both on as they downed horn after horn of the mead and finally both failed to finish the same one, Seija dropping half the measure when it slipped from her fingers, but her opponent having to be escorted out to vomit. Of course, Ukko suspected that Seija had drunk quite a bit less before starting.

Acacia, who must not have realized the potency of the mead, faded early on, and rested herself against Ukko, leaning her weight on his shoulder and speaking only occasionally for the most of the night, though there remained lucidity to her words, and other than an apparent torpor she did not show any other signs of drunkenness. Quite in contrast to her peers, Maria remained largely sober and largely quiet, which later on astounded the men and women of Tyrvad in some ways more than the stories and contests.

It was deep into the night when the hall began to empty, slowly at first and then faster, more leaving until it was only those who had been part of setting and maintaining the feast that night – the cup-bearers and servers who Ukko gathered only filled such roles one monthly feast out of three, and the village head man who remained, aside from the Slayers themselves. The tables were slid out of the way, to the sides of the hall, and rolled mats of furs brought out to give the guests a good place to rest, arranged around two of the fire-pits, which were left burning.

"A fine night, fine night," the head man said. "You lot have the spirit for it. We've not had a gathering like that since the solstice."

"Well," Ukko said, "perhaps your people were merely ready for another revel, though I am amazed you were able to organize it so swiftly."

The head man laughed. "It was a feast day anyway!" he declared. "Though all things considered it was right to re-dedicate the matter in honor of your victory."

"We mean to leave in the morning," Ukko said. "I trust that shall not be considered a breach of your hospitality?"

"No," the head man said, "not at all. Though if some of your company are not fit to travel until later in the morning, that is fine as well."

With that, Ukko thanked the head man again, and he also left the hall. The Slayers were alone, and quickly began to retreat to the beds of furs. Ukko laid himself down, and turned his head to look into the fire. A moment later, another body laid down beside him. He turned his head.

"Acacia?" he said quietly to her.

"Hm?"

How to speak to her? How to object?

"There... are six places." Ukko managed.

Acacia blinked, then shook her head. "Do you mind?"

Now there was a question with no answer. What could he say? What would even be the truth?

"I thought you might be more comfortable."

"I'm sorry," Acacia said. "I don't want to bother you."

She sat up, and Ukko did as well

"I just... Well, you said I wasn't supposed to think of you as a commander or anything... and... I guess I don't really know what I'm saying. Maybe it's the mead."

"It was very strong." Ukko said, "and I don't doubt you'll realize just how much tomorrow. Until then, well..." Ukko thought. Was there really great harm? Acacia always kept close to him, and she was young, had not left a life behind, buried beneath a thousand years of history in the crumbling halls of what had in those days been the great castle of Kalest and now stood only as mossy ruins. "You should rest wherever you feel most comfortable. I just thought you mightn't have noticed me."

Acacia laid back down.

"All right, then," she said. "Good night, Ukko."

Ukko turned back to the fire, and drew his cloak close about himself.

"Good night," he whispered.

***

It would be merciful, Ukko thought, if they did not catch up to the princess the day after the revel. Taavi, Launo, and to a lesser extent Acacia and Seija were not in the best of states, and if the Accursed surrounding Esteri forced a fight, they would have to be at least as capable and coordinated as they were against Baudouin. The former king had been bigger and mightier than any other Accursed that Ukko had ever heard tell of, true, but he was also stupid and outnumbered.

Of course, unless Esteri's band was traveling very slowly indeed, it would be difficult to close the gap in a single day, even on horseback when their quarry was on foot. Owing, perhaps, to their collective discomfort, the day was passed largely in silence until they made camp for the evening.

"So," Maria asked, "when we find the Princess... what if she still won't come along, and not because she's being forced to go?"

"Easy," Seija said. "We do whatever we have to. That's the mission, right, get her highness back to Kalest."

"It is," Ukko said, "but there is more than that to consider, I think."

In truth, it was a problem Ukko grappled with, and did not have a good solution to. If the band that surrounded Esteri was comprised of her enemies, of course the Slayers would do their duty in every sense, and cut down their opponents, whatever it took. But Ukko didn't know what had transpired in the palace after they departed to fight Baudouin, and it was possible, considering the girl's apparent dread of her father, that she had left willingly in this company.

In that case, what could he do? He had not lived a thousand years to believe that everyone who suffered from the curse needed to be put down, nor could his companions believe as much – after all, they knew Esteri's condition. If he accepted that the princess could be saved, he had to accept that those who traveled with her might be, essentially, blameless of any crime. Hopefully, they could be convinced to listen to reason.

And it gnawed at Ukko, not knowing with certainty who had poisoned Esteri, his descendant. It was not on Baudouin's orders, that much was clear. It could still have been someone within Lysama, for it had become clear in the days since his death that Baudouin had been a weak man and held his country together largely as a figurehead, but what did they have to gain? Why Esteri?

If Lysama was not culpable, it might have been Arynias, but then what did Arynias stand to gain? They had not, so far as any news had reached Ukko, attempted an invasion of Kalest while the majority of Kalest's armies were away in Indris and Lysama, nor had Tyrvad, though it would have been quite against that nation's character. There was Hyperborea, of course, but they were inscrutable in their motives as they always had been.

In short, it was becoming frighteningly possible that while Esteri could not have been correct about her father's part in the matter, that the poison had come from within Kalest – Kalest, after all, had profited from the war that followed. Ukko could not say such to Piru without potentially starting a blind hunt for treason, so he kept his opinion to himself. But, perhaps, he would remain in the world when his task was done, if only long enough to discover the truth of the matter.

"Ukko?" Acacia said, looking up at him.

"What is it?"

"Why do you think Hyperborea did that to Baudouin?"

It was a question that Ukko had thought before, that they'd probably all thought before, but no on had put words to.

"You're asking that now?" Seija said.

"Well," Acacia replied, "I was thinking about it more, after Taavi cut it out of the story. We know it happened, and we know that with their hands everywhere, it's probably not a good idea to spread it about too much, but it happened the same day Esteri arrived at the palace, and that is our business."

"I don't know," Ukko admitted. "It's troubling, to say the least. It's not unheard of for the Hyperboreans to whisper in the ear of a king, advice that serves their own ends and not the interests of their hosts, but this went far beyond most of what I'd heard of them."

That, Ukko saw, troubled his companions greatly, and why should it not? If the ancient game that Hyperborea played with the rest of the world had changed its rules, who could know what would next suffer for it?

"Of course," he said, "that means that it's quite possible Hrafn was acting on his own, hoping to gain power or glory by Baudouin's removal from the throne and subsequent enslavement to Hrafn's will."

Acacia and Taavi seemed to breathe sighs of relief, ready to accept that possibility, but none of the others seemed quite convinced that such a thing was a sufficient explanation. Ukko couldn't blame them; he had not quite managed to convince himself, even if he preferred it to be true.

***

The second day out, the Slayers were able to pick up their pace. Esteri's company had left something of a trail, and they were upon it. If they hurried, they might catch up by the time the sun set, perhaps even before.

Any hope of reaching Esteri in good light was dashed when the trail took them along the shores of a lake with towers of rock beside, rolling slopes covered in the debris of rockfalls past, shattered stones ranging from boulders to gravel. Unable to keep the horses at a good pace through such terrain without risking them falling, Ukko accepted that they would have to push onward into the darkness rather than making camp when the sun first touched the horizon. Above all else, he wanted to be done with this matter.

It was late in the evening when the Slayers rounded one of the spires, and spotted the light of a campfire not far away. They dismounted there, and tied their horses to the outcropping, before approaching on foot.

The party around the fire was lit well, and blinded to their approach, affording Ukko an opportunity to take note of them. Of the eight they had been told passed through the Tyrvad town, the same eight as had been brought before king Baudouin, as the merchant had seen in Kalest, two were missing: the tall, severe woman and the young, slight girl were nowhere to be seen. That might be good – if they were far enough away and matters came to a fight, it would be six of the Slayers against a mere five Accursed, rather than seven.

Finally, Ukko stepped close enough, into the light, and called out.

"Princess Esteri," he called.

All six figures who had been around the fire stood. Ukko quickly took their stock – an Aryniasian woman with bob-cut black hair was the closest to the Slayers. Beside her, a Lysaman man with a bit of a pot belly and a small beard. Farther back was Esteri, and a Kalesti man who stepped carefully in front of her. Another Kalesti man was somewhat away from the rest, and deepest in the far side was a Hyperborean looking quite unconcerned, unlike all the rest.

"I must ask, your majesty," Ukko said, "that you now come with me."

"Oh?" the Aryniasian woman asked, taking another two steps towards Ukko. "And I suppose you'll take her home, safe and sound? Have you ever thought that maybe home isn't the safest place for her?"

"Gelvira!" Esteri called. "This is it, please"-

"I know what I'm doing," Gelvira replied. She looked back at Ukko.

"So what are you really here for?" she asked.

"We come, yes, to return princess Esteri to the safety of her home. I know what she must have told you, for she said as much to me in Lysama, but believe me when I say she must be mistaken about her father. I will help to uncover the truth of the matter if she would only come with me. Please, step aside."

"Her highness isn't going anywhere against her will," Gelvira replied, "and as her friend I am not just going to step down so you can change that."

At that instant, there was a flash of motion, and a sound like shattering stone, like breaking bone. Seija had struck, much like she had against Hrafn, but Gelvira had moved with uncanny speed, as though she expected the attack, and had raised her arm in the way. That arm, though, was a bloody ruin – Seija's weapon had wrapped around it before impacting, and the strike had been particularly devastating, carving a crater through flesh and bone and leaving it attached only by a narrow band of skin and muscle.

A blast of fire followed, Seija tumbling back as it crashed against the rocks where she had stood, yanking her meteor hammer back as she did.

"Enough!" bellowed Ukko. This was already a disaster – he should have reprimanded Seija for attacking out of parley before, but it had not seemed quite so awful a deed them. Gelvira was screaming, crying in pain, but somehow it seemed that both sides had heard him, though the Lysaman man and the Kalesti who had stood between the Slayers and Esteri had rushed to Gelvira's side

"Esteri," Ukko called, "is it truly your wish to travel with these people?"

"Yes," she said. She was far enough from any of them, and the Slayers had the upper hand. If she wanted to run, she could have run then.

"Then tend to your wounded," Ukko said. "I do not pretend to understand why you choose this road, and it will be my duty to attempt to move you from it, but I would do so with honor. Seija!"

She turned to face him, rage in her eyes.

"Go back to the horses," he demanded. "We are withdrawing, and you will be the first."

For a moment, Seija hesitated, and Ukko regretted for the

first time that he had given up the rank he had over the other Slayers, for while they had still to this point respected his word as though his orders held greater weight than their own thoughts, he could not force obedience.

But, after a tense moment, Seija darted to the back field, and then walked away from the scene. The others, wordlessly, followed after her one by one, until only Ukko remained, standing between his own friends and soldiers, and the friends of Esteri that he seemed bound to clash with.

"I am sorry," he said, quietly hoping the Slayers did not hear. "Unless you have some miraculous power of healing among your number, she will lose that arm, and you will lose her if you try to save it."

"Who are you, Ukko?" Esteri asked. She too had approached, and was kneeling next to Gelvira. "What are you?"

"I am a man who would bring you home to your father's arms," Ukko replied, "and who would not if he thought there was any danger for you, any malice towards you in that man's heart. Believe me when I say I did not want to see anyone hurt over this matter."

"You have a poor choice of company, then."

He could rein in Seija, he told himself. He had worried he might have to when he selected her, but her skill was so great that he could not refuse her while there remained any hope to draw out the goodness inside her, while he thought Acacia or Taavi could temper her. His choice now had a real cost, and Ukko knew that he and Gelvira, not Seija, would be the ones to have to live with that.

"You should have met them at a better time," Ukko replied sadly. "Please, Esteri... I beg you to reconsider."

"And if I don't?"

"Then," Ukko said, "what can I do? My king's command and my princess's will are opposed. I must heed both, but cannot."

"Pretend you couldn't find me," Esteri said. "The world is very big."

"I cannot do that," Ukko said, "but I can give you time before I come again. Hide your trail well."

Ukko himself turned and stalked off into the darkness.

By the time Ukko reached where they had tied the horses, the rest of the Slayers were already waiting.

"You should have let us fight," Seija said. "We would have won, it was six against four."

"And we would have killed Esteri's companions where words might have sufficed instead. Now the path shall be a good deal harder."

"There's something else," Taavi said. "You saw him, right, the Hyperborean?"

Ukko nodded. "I did."

"Have you ever heard of a Hyperborean Accursed before?"

Ukko had to admit that he had not. Even if they never entered a proper war, there had been enough time that there should have been a story or two, especially when anything to do with Hyperborea entering the public light quickly became legend, and tales were invented where truth was only suspected.

"I wonder what his game is," Acacia said, "if her majesty is really safe while he's around."

Ukko mounted his horse. "Perhaps we shall find out," he said, "but not tonight. Even if there is danger from that man, we struck another quite unjustly. We must give them time to tend to her... or to grieve. And Seija? I hope you understand that you are expected to never repeat such a performance."

Seija refused to meet Ukko's eyes, which he supposed was as close as he would get to an admission of guilt from her.

"We should find a good place to camp," Ukko said. "We will be there for some time."

CHAPTER XVIII

Tius

Tius looked over Gelvira. She was still awake, which amazed Tius. She had lost a lot of blood, as well as her arm above the elbow. The wreckage of her lower arm had to be cut away, the stump seared with flames while strips of cloth, the remnants of Tius' damaged noble clothes, were tied tightly around it, the combined effect keeping her from losing any more blood.

Avina and Radegond had returned from their hunt just a little while after the encounter, and it took all that Tius, Esteri, Erikis, and Frideger together could do in order to keep Avina from running off after them, and in the end only staying by her mother's side while her life hung by a thread managed to restrain Avina.

Tius couldn't say that he didn't understand how she felt. Gelvira may not have been Tius' mother, but she had been more of one to him than his own, and it was agonizing to watch her lay there, not certain if she would pull through or not. Part of him wanted revenge as much as Avina did.

"My mom's going to be all right?" Avina asked Erikis quietly.

"She will live," Erikis replied. "That much we can be thankful for."

Tius breathed a sigh of relief. Erikis had never indicated that he had been a doctor in any life, but you didn't reach his age without knowing a thing or two about what people could live through.

"I still say we should take revenge," Avina said. "They hurt my mom. We need to make sure they don't hurt anyone else."

Esteri looked away from the scene. Did she know those people?

"When Gelvira is well enough to walk," Erikis said, "we will have to move onward. We don't have the time to hunt competent soldiers fast enough to catch up with us."

"Let me and Radegond go tonight!" Avina protested, "If they light a fire, we'll see it, and I can take what, six lousy soldiers?"

"Hm," Erikis said, "maybe you can. If you managed to surprise them away from their arms you could kill at least one, but these are the people Esteri said went out to fight Baudouin that day. Even down one or two of their number, I don't think you should be too sure of your victory."

"Then come with us," Avina said. "You've never even showed off your full power, and you're at least as good as me."

"The day may come when you see what I am capable of," Erikis said, "but you had best hope it does not."

Avina stamped her foot. "And what's that supposed to mean?"

"If I was going to explain myself plainly," Erikis said, "I would have done so from the first."

Avina turned her back to him, sulking. She had every right to be upset, but Tius himself could think of a few reasons Erikis might be uncomfortable with unleashing himself. Plenty of Accursed could hurt themselves if they overused their powers, and what counted as overuse was different from person to person, and then there were some who stopped being able to tell the difference between friend and foe, even if they returned to their human minds later.

"Avina," Tius ventured, hoping that saying what he knew to be true for the third time would finally make an impression, "remember, they're not really all our enemies. The one woman, the one who did that... I think it horrified the others, at least her boss."

"Seija," Avina growled, having picked up the name. "If I got a crack at her, I could live with that."

"And," Tius said, "their boss said he'd have to keep coming for Esteri, so you don't have to race after them tonight to get the chance."

"I know," Avina growled, "but they'll be expecting it then. Why should I give them a better chance than they gave my mom?"

"Because you're a better person than that!" Tius said. "You've talked about all the things that are awful in humans before, and yeah, I said we have that down in us too, but do you, personally, want to be that?"

"Fine," Avina said, "but I don't have to like it."

She sat down.

Tius had another cause for relief. Assuming Avina meant it, he didn't have to worry about her getting herself killed. Of course, she had said as much twice before, so he couldn't be certain it would stand. At least, Tius hoped, her repeated if temporary acceptance of reason meant that she didn't feel able to go off on her own.

And, as offended or grieving as they were, no one else was ready for blood. Esteri and Erikis, and Tius had to admit he was part of that number, knew that such a response would probably get someone killed who shouldn't be, which might even include Seija, despite what she had done. Radegond didn't think it was sound strategy, and Frideger... Tius had never seen the man so serious or so full of sorrow. He had barely spoken, even to his daughter, and Tius guessed he would not leave his wife's side.

Hathus, of course, was a bit of a wildcard. If the thought amused him at the moment, he could take off at Avina's side. Tius hoped his friend had a better head on his shoulders than that, but it wasn't something that Tius wanted to leave to such a guess.

Tius took a few steps, and knelt down next to Frideger and Gelvira.

"Hey," Gelvira said weakly.

"Hey," Tius replied, forcing a smile. "Have you been hearing all this?"

"Some," Gelvira said. She looked to Frideger. "Our girl's got quite the hot head, doesn't she? You'll have to make sure she doesn't do anything too stupid."

"You're going to be around to help me," Frideger said, desperate.

"Of course, dear," Gelvira said, "but... not right away. So you're going to have to handle our little handful. Tius, I know you have the princess to worry about, but if you could keep an eye out for Avina too, it would help."

"Of course I can," Tius replied, "but what do you mean, not right away?"

"I mean," Gelvira said, "I'll be going back to the village. It's not that far, as the crow flies, and I'll just be a burden if I keep traveling with you."

"Then we should all go back," Frideger said. "You and me and Avina."

Gelvira shook her head. "You've an important task, now as much as ever, and beyond even that our daughter needs to see the world. She can't be kept at home forever, though I do hope she'll always come back. And I'll be moving so slowly until I figure out how I'm balanced now, not to mention I won't be much good in a fight without my right arm. I didn't make this decision without thinking about it."

Frideger nodded sadly.

"I'm sure we'll all be back home soon enough," Tius said. "All we have to do is wake up a bunch of slumbering gods and save the world. How hard could it possibly be?"

Gelvira smiled, almost laughed despite the pain she was still clearly in.

"Sometimes I could almost forget you aren't my own son," she said. "That sounds like something Frideger would say. Doesn't it dear?"

"Maybe," Frideger admitted. "Well, yes."

"Sometimes I do too," Tius said with a sigh. "After all, I know the two of you better."

Tius had never known his father, could hardly remember his mother as he'd last seen her when he had only ten years behind him. As far as he was concerned, blood or no, his friends in the Accursed village were his family.

"So," Gelvira said, "I hope nobody minds if I close my eyes for a while. It's been a long day."

"Don't worry," Frideger said. "We'll be here for you when you wake."

Gelvira rested her head back a little farther and closed her eyes. Tius felt a twinge of fear inside, but he trusted she would open them again.

**

By the next morning, Gelvira largely had her color back, and the seared, tied-off stump had largely scabbed over. Most Accursed healed faster and more completely than humans, and Gelvira was mercifully no different. Though she would never get her arm back, it was clear that she would recover as much as she could quite quickly.

They re-bound her wound, removing the tourniquet and tearing the remnants of the clothing used to make it into passable bandages and tied them all around the ragged end to protect it to the elements. Gelvira made her intent to depart known to the whole of the band, and not a soul long objected. They sorted out their things at the camp site, and set aside portions of dried food, water, and money for her to hopefully have an easy journey, assuming her packs were not too heavy.

Frideger and Hathus both nearly insisted on going with Gelvira. After all, if something befell her while she was traveling alone, it would be far more dangerous than two traveling together. But to both of them, she said roughly the same things, that she would be fine, and that their talents would be needed deeper into Tyrvad. Tius nearly offered his own assistance, but suspected he would receive the same answer.

For the first half of the day, Gelvira insisted on light activity: sitting up, taking her breakfast unassisted despite the newness of her injury, pacing briefly around the camp. Her strides became longer and more sure in the second half of the day, and she took up a walking stick in her hand to steady her balance. By evening, she felt well enough to go, but given both the hour and her condition, Frideger was able to insist she stay another night.

But, in the morning of the second day, Gelvira made ready to leave. She said her goodbyes to her family and her friends, and gave a particularly vehement and loud thanks to Esteri, who shrunk from such attention. It was pointed enough, and the princess' reaction strange enough, that Tius thought to inquire.

"What's that about?" he asked, after Gelvira pressed her thanks again.

Esteri winced.

"Her highness," Gelvira said, "had a vision of that night. Except in her vision, I had no idea what was coming, and the blow took my head."

"What?" Avina shrieked. "You knew, mom? You knew and you still stepped up?"

"If not me," Gelvira said, "it could have been any of us, and they might not have gotten off as lightly as I did. We should all be thankful it happened this way."

"But you got hurt," Avina protested. "You could have been killed!"

"I know, dear," Gelvira said. "It wasn't a choice I made lightly, but when the time came... it was the only one I could make."

"I don't understand."

Gelvira smiled sadly.

"And I hope you never have to," she said.

Gelvira looked up towards the sun.

"Look at the time," she said. "I should get going, or we'll be stuck another day, and who knows how much grace we really have?" She looked up at all the rest of them. "Take care of yourselves," she said. "Come home soon."

And with that, she left.

When Gelvira was out of sight, over the hill, Tius looked back at the others. Their faces were ashen, but at least some seemed to be recovering their composure. Frideger, of course, seemed to find no peace in this parting. Esteri as well was shaken, trembling, and looking into the northern distance.

"We should get on the road ourselves," Erikis said. "The path to the place of the Ancestor Gods will become harder the further we go into Tyrvad. If we keep a good pace, we could reach the valley gate within a week."

Of course, Tius had no idea what that meant. He assumed that this 'valley gate' was somehow an important landmark. He would ask about that later. For now, as they began their march to the north, he was more concerned with Esteri.

"What's the matter?" Tius asked.

"Are you asking if I've had another vision of doom?" Esteri asked. "Because I haven't. And now I don't know whether or not to wish I had."

"Whoa," Tius said, "that's not what I meant. But I guess that's what's bothering you?"

Esteri nodded.

"Why?" Tius asked.

"I don't know how many times I've seen the future now," Esteri said, "but every time... it's been nothing but pain, and terror, and death. After I first had that vision, I thought I might be able to stop. Shut it away, stop seeing such terrible things. When Gelvira wouldn't leave, I thought it was doomed to happen, and all I could do was know that pain was coming. The reality is... more complicated than that."

"And better," Tius said. "Now you know you can change the future. If you don't like what you see, you can make it different."

"That's just it," Esteri said. "Now I want to look. Now I want to know, but it's still so terrifying. I feel like I'll be happier if I don't know, but can I even conscience that? Every time something bad happens, I'll wonder if I couldn't have stopped it... but I can't stop everything, can I? I can feel it driving me mad already."

"No offense," Tius said, "but that's spoken like a true queen."

Esteri flinched. Tius hadn't been secretive about his distaste, at times, for the nobility in the past.

"And I mean true," he said. "Someone who's trying to be what the nobles who talk and talk and never do anything for their people are supposed to aspire to... and now I'm starting to see why most of them don't bother. You've only got the seven of us now to worry about, and it's still too much. It would be too much for anyone."

"So what should I do?" Esteri asked. "Grow a thicker skin? Turn a blind eye to the fact that you're putting yourself into danger for my sake? I... I don't know if I could forgive myself if you died."

Tius looked away for a moment. Really, he didn't know the answer. The morality of changing the future wasn't exactly something that it had occurred to him to worry about, nor the practicality of it.

"Pace yourself," he offered. "You may have a great gift, but you're still only human. I'm not going to say you aren't right to think of using this power for good, but you can't let it tear you apart. I don't know if that makes sense"-

"No," Esteri said, "it does, though it's not an easy choice."

"Well," Tius offered, "how does it work?"

Esteri seemed to think. "It helps if my eyes are closed at first," she said. "Though that didn't stop the visions of Baudouin, that was going to happen very soon and I was very close, and I don't think I warped then."

Tius offered his hand. "If you want to try," he said, "I'll try to make sure you don't trip over anything."

Esteri placed her hand in his. "Thank you," she said. "I'm going to try to see... should I try something safer?"

"Like what?"

"Well," Esteri said, "so far, except for dreams I haven't remembered, all my visions have been about something close at hand. So if I don't try to focus on something else I guess it would be about you."

Tius smiled. "And do you think I'm safe?"

"No one in this company is," Esteri said. "I... I feel like maybe I could try to look into my family's future, my father or my half-brother. I know them, and we share blood."

"To be fair," Tius said, "that doesn't seem like a good idea, if there are things you don't want to see."

"I'll try for my brother," Esteri said. "Tuoni is safe back in Kalest, and he should have a long life ahead of him. I don't know why anyone would hurt him."

"Sweet kid?" Tius asked.

Esteri nodded.

"I wish you could meet him," she said. "He's nothing like his mother at all."

Esteri closed her eyes.

"I'm trusting you," she said, an edge of humor in her voice for the first time since that night. "If I fall and break my neck, it's your fault."

"I won't let you down," Tius said, grinning from ear to ear.

Esteri closed her eyes, and the two of them walked close together for some time. Minutes passed, and while Tius couldn't really protest, he wondered if it always took that long.

Then, Esteri started very suddenly. She jumped, and her feet slipped out from under her on the loose stone. Tius held her hand tightly and quickly caught her, free arm around her back. As he tried to help her find her footing, he noticed that her eyes were jet-black... and her cheeks were bright red.

"I saw something I shouldn't have," she said, voice small.

"What was it?" Tius asked. "How far off?"

"Nothing bad," she stammered. "No... I just didn't want to see that."

"What?"

"Ah... where to start?" Esteri murmured, now solidly on

her feet again and keeping pace. "Well, before that I saw my brother crowned. I guess that will probably happen soon, though it's possible the podium was simply very large – I was seeing through his eyes, you see."

"And then?"

"I saw... well..." Esteri looked away. "I didn't mean to! It's not like I have any control over what the future shows me when I look!"

"What is it?" Tius asked frantically. "You still haven't said."

"I saw..." She groaned in frustration. "Well, I'll recognize my brother's future wife when I meet her." Her voice grew quiet. "At least, I'll recognize her if she isn't wearing anything."

"Oh," Tius said gravely, feeling himself blush a bit in sympathy. "Ah... I can see why you might not want to see that."

Esteri sighed. "Well, it does tell me that Tuoni's basically safe unless I manage to do something that changes it. And assuming these visions always work the same way. He's eight years old, and only just, so he's a long, long way from marrying anybody."

"Not that long," Tius ventured.

"It's a long time!" Esteri snapped. "He's my little brother. Little. He's not marrying anybody any time soon."

"If you say so," Tius said. "How about you? Had your parents arranged something for you?"

"No," Esteri said, vehemently. "I was given the freedom to choose from among any suitors, though of course my father could refuse to bless the union if he didn't approve, and that would be the end of that."

"Then did you have anyone in mind?"

Tius wished he had kept his mouth shut almost as soon as he had said it. What could have possessed him to ask such a question? Even he knew it was impertinent, and he would not be surprised if Esteri decided to strike him for it.

Instead, she smiled.

"No," she said again. "Not that I didn't have enough suitors, but I wasn't even inclined to consider the matter seriously. I gave them very little thought and even less of my time, if any. I suppose I thought I would know what was right when I met it; someone loyal and brave, kind and gentle but fierce and strong, and handsome of course. A rare combination, I'm sure, but then I have my choice."

Tius gave a weak laugh. "I can see how that might be hard to find."

"Perhaps not as hard as all that," Esteri said, "but it's very hard to be sure where a man's heart lies."

An indescribable fear was building in Tius, and he searched for a way to very quickly change the topic of conversation.

"So," he said, "was there any other future you wanted to try to see?"

"Not right now," Esteri said. "I think my sight is honor-bound to surprise me unpleasantly whenever I employ it. But thank you."

"It's no problem," Tius said, and lowered his head to watch his footing, and picked up the pace to keep up with Erikis.

***

That night, Tius sat down next to Avina. She had spoken very little since her mother left back towards the south

"Hey," he said. "You holding up alright?"

"I'm fine." Avina replied, sullenly staring at a bit of dried meat in her hands as she hugged her knees to her chest.

"Come on, Avvy," Tius said, calling her by the childish name she wouldn't admit she liked. "I know you better than that."

Avina looked down, and a gust of the icy wind that never quite seemed to stay still in Tyrvad blew across them, blowing strands of her long, raven-black hair across her face.

"I'm not afraid," she said, solidly. "I won't be afraid."

"I never said anything about that."

"I know," Avina said, "but it's still true. I'm not going to be afraid."

"Of course not," Tius said, trying to smile. "Why should

you be? You're better than any of us, except Erikis. I bet you could handle this all on your own."

Avina looked towards Tius.

"Not that I couldn't," she said, "but I don't want you or Esteri or anybody to go all the same. You're not going to leave now, are you?"

"Of course not," Tius said. "You can count on that. But what does that have to do with being afraid?"

"Well," Avina said, "there are those people out there, the ones that hurt my mom. And there's where we're going, and the fact that we're supposed to wake up some ancient gods to kill another ancient god and I don't even understand..." She shook her head. "Another girl could be really, really scared right now, but I'm not. I'm not going to be. Nothing's going to scare me."

"Of course not," Tius told her, though he was quite certain that she was feeling very afraid. Not of those Kalesti, maybe, but of something. Maybe the thought of danger finally caught up with her. Of course, he wasn't going to call her on it. If she ever admitted to being afraid, he'd tell her to be strong, so she was a step ahead.

"How about you?" Avina asked.

"Oh," Tius said, "I have to admit I'm a little worried about these things, but afraid? It's hard to say. Frankly, most of the really, really scary stuff is over my head. I've lived as a thief and a hunter, I don't know a thing about kings or gods. So I guess it still doesn't seem quite real."

"Even after Lysama? After... that night?"

"In some ways," Tius admitted, "I know what happened and it's terrible, but just the idea... that a kingdom fell while we watched, that your mom was hurt like that. It's too much. It doesn't make sense to me. I'd say it was like I think I'm going to wake up except that I know it's all real. I understand it. But I don't feel it."

Tius shook his head. That wasn't quite right. It wasn't that the gravity of the matter didn't hit him. It was subtler than that, like Tius simply couldn't conceive of things getting any worse. He wasn't afraid, but he thought he ought to be.

"That's no good," he admitted. "I don't really know how to explain it."

"Well," Avina said, "If you're scared you can just stay near me, alright?"

"Hey," he protested. "I'm supposed to be the one who says that."

"Well you can't grow to thrice your height and punch through stone. I can."

Tius shrugged. Avina was right; whether she was frightened or not, she didn't really need his protection, and he had his hands full with Esteri anyway. He was sure the princess could hold her own in an honest fight, but so far no such challenge had presented itself.

Avina, for her part, looked a little more comfortable. She stretched her legs out and leaned back against Tius rather than hunching over herself, tilting her head back to look up at him.

"If it's bothering you," she said with a smirk, "I can pretend to be weak and helpless."

Tius didn't know whether to take her seriously or not.

"No thanks," he said. "If you can take care of yourself, and I know you can, that means I've got one less thing to worry about."

Avina frowned.

"Well, don't stop coming over just because I don't need to be protected or anything."

Tius laughed

"Don't worry," he said, "I won't."

Avina's eyes darted around the camp, and she sat up straight.

"I think you should go look after the princess right now, though," she said. "She doesn't look like she's doing so well, and my mom's not here to chat with her anymore."

Tius looked around himself. Esteri was at the edge of the

firelight, looking into the darkness. It couldn't hurt to say hello.

"All right," Tius said. "I'll be back over some other time."

CHAPTER XIX

Ulfr

Ulfr rode proudly for the wilderness, hunting either of his quarries. They were not difficult to follow, when they encountered populations, particularly not the band that had killed Baudouin the monster. They were hailed as heroes – never mind that nearly a hundred people were killed by the monster king himself, and half of the city burned down in his wake. It was less damage than Hrafn had hoped for, but the idiot had lost his head somewhere in the mess.

Ulfr read once again the papers that the hawk had brought him. Such delightful creatures, even if crude and continental, for when dealing with such provincial fools a way to deliver physical documents to the wilderness was quite necessary. And the papers! A blanket statement from the King of Kalest, giving whoever held them the authority to speak with the king's voice. It was more than Ulfr could have ever hoped for, and he was already dreaming of ways to use it.

He would, of course, complete his mission, to either take the princess alive to Hyperborea or else bear back alive or dead one of the other two: a girl with long, black hair or a man who seemed himself Hyperborean. Particularly the latter of those two, Ormr had written, and without a Talisman of Command – Hrafn's having never been recovered – Ulfr saw no reason to prefer another victim.

In considering the bounty of the future that unfolded before him, however, he also had to think on the past. His stump ached, and far away from Hyperborea he could get no suitable replacement for his severed left hand. The ones responsible for that would pay, Ulfr would be sure. The boy would be food for crows, and the princess... she would join him eventually, Ulfr supposed.

All Ulfr had to do was bring these 'Slayers' into line. They were Kalesti, and so they would likely kowtow to their King's wishes, but the man who lead them now was very old and very strange, in his own way – gifted by the potion but not Accursed, or so Hundr had guessed. It was possible that Ukko would resist, and then Ulfr would have to be very careful. He might dispose of the immortal, yes, as even such a man had to sleep some time, but Ormr considered the aberration very valuable, and would give Ulfr hell if he did dispose of the man. He might even keep Ulfr on the continent for years more, trapped in the backwaters, rustic and stinking, that such barbaric lands had to provide.

The journey had not been without amusement. Though Ulfr had to go hooded and cloaked to hide his race and therefore allegiance, the guise of a wandering merchant had its allure. He had sold a young woman hemlock and told her it was a love potion she ought to give to the man she desired. It was a pity he had to leave before he saw the inevitable conclusion. In Tyrvad, the locals had less and were not so easily fooled, but their pride made it easy to incite them into contests they could not win, and the coins and baubles Ulfr claimed as tokens of victory in rigged games would serve him in good stead.

That is why you work alone, he remembered Ormr telling him after he had described some similar pastimes. Ulfr did not care that his countrymen could not abide his presence for long. They called him a sociopath, but all the same they admitted a sociopath was what they needed. The Elder Council played its game, moving kings across the world like pawns upon a board. How many lives had they ended over the years to satisfy their amusement? Ulfr simply took a more personal, more gratifying approach.

Not that the continental folk were any better, of course. Ulfr remembered Delphina and her husband, dreaming of conquest, a world in their clutches. That man had sold his own daughter for war, and any man put in his position, with his power, Ulfr was sure would do the same without a second thought.

The Council and their chosen ambassadors recognized Ulfr's skill, and allowed him his entertainment so long as it did not come back to them, and Ulfr was content. Really, he only wanted to return home because of his hand. Once that was fixed, he would gladly remain their agent among such a numerous, gullible people for as long as they desired.

On the second day out of the Tyrvad town, Ulfr found who he was looking for – the so-called Slayers, camped upon the shore of a still lake. Camped in the middle of the day, no less. What indolence was this? Well, if they were fools it would be that much easier to assert his control.

"Hail!" Ulfr called as he approached.

As Ulfr rode up, the Kalesti folk faced him. A few of them placed hands on their weapons. Had they seen Hrafn? If they knew too much to be useful, Ormr could not blame Ulfr, whatever he did with them.

"Hail," one of them, whom Ulfr guessed to be Ukko, said darkly.

"It is high time I found you," Ulfr said, dismounting and taking the papers again in his hand. "You are Ukko, are you not?"

"Who asks?"

"I am Ulfr," he declared. "I come on behalf of Ambassador Ormr and through him the King of Kalest."

"Forgive me," Ukko said, "if I feel this claim quite extraordinary and in need of some sure proof."

He was listening, Ulfr realized, however reticent he was to do so. Ulfr took out the letter and held it out, unfolded, the seal pressed to the bottom and the signature upon it as unmistakable as the language granting its holder authority was plain.

"Here you see it," Ulfr declared.

Ukko stepped close enough to read.

"It is by my order and for the good of Kalest that the bearer of this should speak with authority second only to my own, and receive respect and obedience in line with what I myself would be granted. King Piru Rekorius Metsaa Kalest."

A darker look came over Ukko, which the ancient man was trying his hardest to suppress. Ulfr could guess he doubted the authenticity, or how Ulfr had come by the vague document, and was searching the paper and his own insufficient mind for a way to escape those words.

He could not find any. Ulfr had control.

"I see," Ukko said. "What brings you to these wilds?"

"The same thing as you," Ulfr said. "The trail of her majesty, the Princess of Kalest, and those who travel with her. I will direct the hunt now. There are facts you have not known. In order to triumph in our aims, you will do what I say." He gave a smirking glance to one of the women, the one with bob-cut blonde hair, grey eyes, and a sword no doubt too big for her to heft. "Anything I say."

"Careful," said another of the women, with icy blue eyes and a tight, brown braid. "You won't say very much if your head ends up separated from your body."

Ulfr snarled.

"You dare threaten me, wench?" he snapped, "Remind me what the penalty for treason is in Kalest!"

"Seija!" one of the men, a scared-looking boy with brown hair and green eyes, exclaimed.

"Relax," Seija said, "I'm not threatening anyone. I'm harmless. I just thought I ought to remind you that this is a very dangerous land, especially for foreigners like us. Anything could happen."

"I see," said Ulfr, eyeing Seija carefully. He had been told very little about the group other than Ukko. He thought vaguely that the blonde woman was called Maria and was decently sure that the man who had not spoken – the one with black hair, a shield in one hand, and a war-hammer at his hip – was named Launo and was a noble, but beyond that he didn't really know their capabilities or inclinations.

"Well, you had best watch your tongue. There may be commanders and lords less forgiving than I am of such inarticulate statements."

"Ambassador Ulfr," Ukko said firmly, interrupting the interchange, though struggling with the title of address

"Master," Ulfr corrected. "Or Agent, if it pleases you better."

"Agent Ulfr," Ukko said. "I would know how your presence and command changes our mission."

"A very good question. Some of the persons surrounding her majesty are now persons of interest. They are wanted, dead or alive, and will be returned to Hyperborea. One of the two would suffice – there is a man who himself appears Hyperborean, and a young-seeming girl with long, black hair. Additionally, there is a third whom it is the king's will should be killed, a Kalesti boy who leaps through space as smoke and shadow."

Ukko seemed to consider this.

"I do not doubt nor refuse your orders," Ukko said, "but I would know the reason for them. What interest does Hyperborea have in these three?"

"That is not for me to say," Ulfr replied. Hyperborea's schemes were not shared outside its blood. The awakening of the Fallen One, into a state controlled by the Elder Council, would bring Hyperborea power undreamed of, a might far greater than what they currently wielded over the continent. They might retain some of these worthless people as slaves, but the time for manipulation from the shadows would be over. If it worked correctly, of course. The council's schemes changed so rapidly he could scarcely believe they would actually resurrect that old thing. "But Hyperborea and Kalest are bound by treaty. Our aims in this are one."

"So you say," Ukko replied. To Ulfr, it was not the most promising of answers, and the angry stares of the rest of his supposed Slayers reinforced that. Likely, there would come a point where Ulfr would have to abandon them, separate them, or bleed them off, particularly if the Accursed did not manage to kill any of them.

"Indeed. Now, our hunt awaits us, so prepare to return to the road. You have clearly been slothful enough to not already be upon the road by this hour, and my command shall not tolerate it."

***

That night, Ulfr concealed himself in his blankets, and waited for the treachery he suspected, wide awake but hiding the fact. Sure enough, the Slayers began to leave the camp one by one, walking a bit away where he could not hear or see them, awake or otherwise. Ulfr crept up, silent as the dead, and observed them from the shadows.

"I don't like this," Ukko said, "but at the same time, we have no grounds upon which to consider it illegitimate."

"How about Hrafn?" the girl with black pig-tails said. "After that, I think we've got good reason not to trust this Ulfr fellow."

"Indeed," Ukko replied, "but there is a difference between not trusting the man and considering the documents he provided to be fake."

"The king could be in danger," Seija said, "especially if they're real. Especially after what happened to Baudouin."

"I'd hope," Launo said, "that his majesty is not so dull nor so desperate as to fall prey to the treachery the princess told us claimed King Lysama."

Interesting. They even knew Hrafn's name, though clearly they had not been told of Ulfr's own presence at Baudouin's transformation. How much had the idiot told them before he had been killed? And more importantly, had they claimed his Talisman of Command? If they had it, that would make Ulfr's job much easier and more enjoyable, either establishing control over Esteri or simply forcing her friends to kill each other. Perhaps he could even do both.

"It's still possible Hrafn was working alone as well," Maria said, "not likely, but possible."

Good girl, Ulfr thought. Sow the seeds of doubt so that he would not have to later. And at least Hrafn had not given away their endgame even if he had offered up his name and his life in the end. These Slayers could still be salvaged, if they did not turn upon him now.

"As long as we can bring her majesty home safe," the brown-haired boy said timidly, "we'll be okay, right?"

"Yeah," Seija replied, "unless that's not their plan. He could turn on us the minute we get those three he wants dead, dead, and then kill her too. The one in Lysama was controlling Baudouin somehow. I'm worried he might be able to control us."

That was unfortunate. If they had the talisman, they didn't recognize its significance, which really was a shame. If Ulfr managed to recover one or both of them, he might be forgiven at least somewhat for losing his in the first place. The talismans were not easy to come by, having to be made with some flesh cut directly from the Body of the God.

"Are you afraid, Seija?" the boy asked, shocked.

"Hell no," she replied. "I'm just not stupid and not interested in hurting any of you if I end up dancing like a marionette on some creep's strings."

The thought was quite appealing, and made Ulfr wish that there was a way open to him to control the bodies of the living as the Talisman afforded a way to control the bodies of the Accursed. If there was, the wench would be his first target. She was the one who had dared to threaten his head. He'd make her take her own, but only after he was sure she understood just how utterly she was a puppet.

"It's a reasonable worry," Ukko said. "I had heard of Hyperboreans being able to lead the Accursed, but we know too little to be sure their skill stops there. If any one of us were turned against the others, it would be a hard fight. I do not doubt we could keep the real enemy in mind, but depending on the control..." He shook his head, "It is probably best not to think about such things. For right now, let us think of what we know."

Ukko paced back and forth in front of his troops.

"We know that it was Hyperborean interference that turned King Baudouin into a monster. We know that a strange Hyperborean travels with Esteri and her Accursed allies, allies that Esteri seems to care for, claims to be traveling with willingly. We saw them act, and it was too natural and uncoordinated for me to believe that the Hyperborean controls them, though when dealing with their magic it is impossible to know. And we know that Ulfr has come to us with a writ from King Piru, granting him great authority. We know as well he wants Esteri's Hyperborean dead. That means that of the men of that nation, they are of at least two factions. We do not know which one Hrafn was on, or if he was on another, but in the absence of any evidence, it would seem as likely as not that he was aligned against Ulfr, or Ulfr against him."

"We need to be careful," Maria said. "By the same token, it's as likely as not that the two of them are on the same side. Seija is right. The king should be warned about this."

Now there was interference that Ulfr did not need. King Piru was currently an ally of Hyperborea, but Ormr had seemed concerned about Delphina's handling of the man. She was, he said, perhaps too loyal to him, and not enough his master. If Piru was given good cause, he could turn against Hyperborea, and Delphina might not help. Of course, how much would that matter? All the same, Ulfr would not have it on his own head.

"I agree," Launo said. "One of us could leave, and go back to Kalest."

"And what if Ulfr turns against the rest?" the pigtail girl asked.

"If that's a problem, Acacia," Launo said, "then I'm not sure how having six of us instead of five would help."

"Still," Acacia said, "whoever stays is in danger. If we all keep on until we know Ulfr's intentions, we're all taking the same risk. If one of us leaves, that person is safe, more or less, but the rest of us will be in graver danger. Who'd be the one to go? I... I couldn't."

"It's a fair point," Ukko said. "If we really do have anything to worry about, sending one of our number back to Kalest near guarantees a confrontation. We might all scatter, and return to Kalest by different roads, but then if Ulfr's orders are legitimate, we would all be deserters, and given the heritage of her majesty the Queen, there is a good chance the crown has chosen to utilize Hyperboreans, even if it presents a danger."

Amazingly, thought Ulfr, he had the right of it more or less.

"So," Seija growled, "we do nothing?"

"For now," Ukko declared, "we try to ascertain truth or lie for ourselves. We remain vigilant. We keep watch two at a time. I will take the middle watch with whoever else would accept it."

"I will," said Acacia.

"You want last watch with me, Taavi?" Seija asked, and the boy nodded energetically.

"Well," Maria said to Launo, "I guess that leaves first for the two of us."

Ulfr thought this was both good and bad. On one side, with them not taking watch alone, he would have much more trouble preventing an alarm if he decided he had to start slitting throats. On the other side, knowing when each would sleep and wake afforded Ulfr the chance to spy selectively on his disloyal and untrusting new underlings, and two at a time meant that they might talk, and he could discern further who he might be able to sway and turn against the rest.

At this, Ulfr slunk back to his place. They would no doubt discuss a few more bits of logistics, and that gave him the time to make it appear that he had never moved. The time would come when he would reveal he knew of their debated treachery, but that was not tonight. As much as he hated to admit it even in the least, he still needed the fools for some time. When that miserable boy came to lie in a pool of his own blood, watching with his last waking moments as his precious princess received her own torments – then he would be rid of Ukko and return whichever prize was convenient in triumph to Hyperborea.

CHAPTER XX

Esteri

For the third time, Esteri dreamed of the Cursed Land. She stood upon a plate of steel with bars that reached her waist, looking out from a great height over its expanse. The sky was a mass of black clouds through which filtered bloody red light, and the land below was no more inviting. Here and there she saw fields and woods, grey and dead. There were towers as well, that glimmered crimson in that hideous light, stretching up to the sky like the steel swords of incomprehensible titans.

The platform upon which Esteri stood raced forward upon a road of steel suspended in the sky. It passed over the dead lands, passed through the high and imposing towers of the land, approaching the grand castle that, on its mountaintop, sat astride the land. It was far away, but she was moving very quickly, and grasped the railing to steady herself.

As she flew towards the castle, that awesome structure that loomed so terribly in the distance, she came to gain a sense of its scale. It was far vaster than the greatest castle of Kalest, so massive that if its rooms and halls were similarly scaled, no doubt Baudouin in his monstrous form could stride through them as the knights of Kalest strode through her palace.

And, as though a legion of that terrible giant did inhabit the place, it radiated a nameless dread. There was something there, Esteri felt, something so terrible that she would turn her face away and hide from its presence, hide from its gaze. It held so much fear for her that she wished in her mind, wished in whispers, and finally screamed that she would go the other way.

The platform did not obey. It followed its sky-road ever onward, towards the heart of the ruined land, towards that nameless fear in its domed castle of giants. Finally it slowed, stopped, halting near the gates of the castle. Esteri opened a latch, and the bars swung away. Despite her fear, she stepped onto the solid stone of the castle, marched forward to its cyclopean doors.

Those doors were as a great maw, the stony walls that might have been adorned with tapestries or portraits, flanked with suits of armor at attention, instead roiled with faces and limbs, moaned in torment. Esteri lifted her face to the rib-cage-arched ceiling, and a rain of warm blood fell lightly upon her. She lifted her sword – a sword she had never seen before, elegant and beautiful, with silver grip and azure blade – and pointed it forward, returning to her inexorable progress into the heart of all the horror.

Doors opened before Esteri, the creak of their hinges the whimper of souls in agony. She gazed into the great forum, and for a split second, Esteri saw. For a split second, she understood. Then she awakened.

***

Esteri woke up in terror, in a cold sweat. Tius was looking over her to her left, Avina to her right. Both had frightened expressions on their faces, or perhaps awe-cowed.

Esteri remembered she was having a nightmare. She remembered a sky of black and crimson that she had dreamed of before. She remembered steel swords and raining blood, and she had dreamed that before too. She remembered the sword, its beauty stark against the evils that surrounded it, and that was new. She could not remember anything else.

"Are you alright?" Tius asked.

"I'm fine," Esteri said. "It was just a nightmare."

"Not just," Avina replied. "You're pretty badly warped, like three nights ago."

"Like the first morning in the village," Radegond said. "And just our luck. If my scouting is anything to go by, we shall be reaching a small city sometime this morning. We should hope you are cleared up by then."

Esteri reached up and touched her face. Her skin felt strange, leathery, and she had been told that it was a dusky shade with blackened veins. Her fingers, dull as their sensation was, moved up her forehead, and found a small horn sprouting from it, though not long after her initial touch that disintegrated back into nothingness again. She pulled her hand away from her face, and watched as, slowly and painstakingly, the crackling lines of darkness receded from her wrists, towards her talon-like fingertips, and she wondered how she had not immediately noticed.

"It's always gone down quickly before," Esteri said. "I don't see why today would be any different."

"Well," Radegond said, "do you remember anything about your nightmare this time? Right now we don't know a damn thing about them"

"I remember," Esteri said hesitantly, "blood. A rain of blood. Swords that cut the clouds. I think I was walking, maybe running? I remember a sword too. It was silver and blue, and beautiful somehow."

"Interesting," Erikis said.

How was it interesting? To Esteri, the idea that such a nightmare could be prophetic was terrifying. If such a sight had, in her dreams alone, managed to horrify her as much as she felt it had, then what would become of her when such a dark dream turned into reality?

"I don't really find it interesting," Esteri said. "It was a dream... Even a dream of the future will have parts that are just a dream, I hope. If the skies really will rain blood, I'm not sure what good any of us can do."

"There have been many sages," Erikis said, "who find ordinary dreams to be prophetic, and they insist that dreams have a code of symbolism. I do not personally know any of the theories about it, and I seem to remember them disagreeing, but it is quite possible that if you have a vision while asleep, it will not be literal. You say you see swords tearing the sky, making it bleed? It could simply be war, which we already know your father perpetrates. You see an azure sword? The banners of Arynias are blue and silver. Perhaps if Kalest is to be brought to heel, Arynias must be part of the fight. Or perhaps they shall be doing the invading."

Esteri considered it. She didn't think that sounded right, that there was something she was forgetting that would make the disjointed, horrifying images make sense. But, at the same time, Esteri wanted to believe what Erikis was telling her. She had every desire to have her visions be anything other than literally true.

"It's possible," she said, trying to convince herself of the fact.

"There, you see," Erikis said. "For the time being, you can forget about the swords and the spears. Your body is already well on its way to forgetting."

"That's good," Esteri said. She looked around. Tius was still fixed on her. Back in Lysama, she couldn't even look at him when he was badly warped, and it stung somewhat to know that he didn't flinch looking upon her twisted visage. "Thank you all. We should probably start moving. I can keep my eyes closed if we get to the town before that fades."

Esteri stood. Dry rations were passed about for breakfast, and water skins as well. Radegond wasn't wrong about how close the city was, or in that it was a city of at least some description, for they entered the outlying fields well before noon, though well after Esteri's warp had disappeared.

The city, such as it was, was built upon a hill, rising upwards as they entered. Unlike the earlier town, it was walled with high walls of stone, at least twenty feet high. More of the construction was stone than in any of the other Tyrvad settlements they had passed through. The crimson and gold dragon banners of Tyrvad flew over most of the larger buildings, a particularly magnificent pennant fluttering in the wind above the small keep that stood upon the top of the hill.

If the architecture was more like that of familiar Kalest, the people were as well. In the smaller towns of Tyrvad, the folk had been as warm as their land was cold, which Erikis said was a necessity for living in such harsh conditions, for no one would survive long without help from other folk. In the city, however, they kept to themselves more or less like Kalesti did. Erikis, taking the lead within the walls, said that this was good as well, for few travelers came this deep into Tyrvad, and he would not like to have their business questioned.

"Why?" Esteri asked. "Aren't we doing something good for them and for everyone?"

"That may be," Erikis replied, "but they are a superstitious folk, as are most mortals, and will not take kindly to our like interfering with their gods. In fact, we are nearly relying on that fact. The last time I was in Tyrvad, the way was not guarded by any living soul, though I must admit I still could not pass it."

"You still haven't told us," Esteri reminded him, "exactly what we will be doing."

"Well," Erikis said, looking around to ensure no locals were close enough to hear what we said, "their dwelling place is ringed by mountains, and one pass, built into a gateway scarcely wide enough for two men to walk abreast, is the only way in or out of the sacred place. The gateway, I am loathe to say, is sealed over with Old Magic."

"How do you expect us to do this, then?" Esteri demanded. "Have we been on a fool's errand here while who knows what befalls the south?"

"I examined that gate for days," Erikis said, "and I think that the key to open it shall be need. Your need, in specific, shall throw open the passage."

"Why me?"

"Because," Erikis said, "you are the one who best understands the danger shadowing the world. Even I, who know better the threat upon the northern island, do not know the world that needs the aid of its gods so well as do you."

"I don't understand."

"It reacts to thought," Erikis said, "so think long and hard about what needs to be done."

"I might be more sure of myself, then," Esteri offered, "if you told us more about the days of old."

"Of course," Erikis said. "Somewhere private? If we aren't going to move onward today, then at the inn."

"Oh no you don't," Radegond said. "We're resupplying and heading out the other end. You can chat in a field."

***

As they left the town, Erikis began to speak, remarkably without any further prompting. Esteri was sure that she would have to rip the story out of him by force, based on how evasive he had been in the past, but it seemed that with their goal now coming ever closer, he was eager to finally share what he knew.

"The story begins many years ago," Erikis said, "so many that I must admit I have lost count, for against such a number the snow of winter, the thaw of spring, the turning of leaves are as swift as the rise and fall of the sun... And who has not one time or another forgotten what the day is?

"In any case, in those days only the far north, what are now Tyrvad, Hyperborea, and parts of Arynias, were civilized lands. Those were the days of gods and demons, or at least what might be called either one. Most of the deities now worshipped have no relation to what walked the earth in those days, though some perhaps are conflated memories of them – but, ah, I'm getting off topic.

"One of the Gods of those days was a very mighty creature. He could change his size and his shape, and sometimes walked the world in the shape of a man, and sometimes stood astride it as a giant without even the barest resemblance to human shape. As a man, he loved many mortal women, and his children became quite numerous, owing that they were themselves immortal, and their children quite long lived.

"But that old god was not a friend of all humans. The men of Tyrvad, who you likely now see as backwards, were then the strongest and wisest people, and many among them wielded magic. For generations the children of the God and sorcerer-chiefs of Tyrvad warred with one another at the god's behest, but though the blood of countless soaked the fields, neither side could achieve the obliteration of the other. Eventually, the children of the god grew sick of the endless fighting, and in dire secrecy spoke with the greatest mages of Tyrvad to bring an end to their conflict."

"Mages?" Esteri asked. "But... there's no such thing, is there?"

"In those days," Erikis said, "magic was somewhat like alchemy is today. I couldn't say why all the old sorcery has been forgotten or lost, but suffice to say none now live who practice it, nor have they for millennia. In any case, suffice to say that the children of the God betrayed their father. They gave a group of the greatest sorcerers of Tyrvad an opportunity to strike against him, and granted them the knowledge of the Blood of the God so they could bless their weapons to strike him down. The great one fell to this treachery."

"Blood of the God," Esteri said. "I know that substance. It's the main component of the Potion!"

"Indeed," Erikis said. "I had long wondered just how those wellsprings came to be, seeing as that unlike in the old folk tales, the God died in a single space, and no bits of flesh were flung across the world."

"You said it was some sort of mineral slush!" Esteri protested. "Now you're telling me it's actual blood?"

"In a word," Erikis said, "yes. I am sorry to have lied before, but it is a long explanation, and benefits nothing. It is easier to accept the alchemist's version of the story, or was until Lysama."

"What does that mean for us?" Esteri asked, hugging herself. She had drunk the blood of an ancient demon god! Somehow, that was much worse than simply an alchemical reagent.

"Nothing," Erikis replied, "which is why I did not burden you with the knowledge. Now, as I said I had wondered, but Baudouin's fate revealed to me that the Hyperboreans must still have the body of the God, and that it must still be in a very intact state, possibly even alive save that it lacks any mind or will, for no mere blood could have created such a powerful being."

"And you think they're going to wake it back up?" Esteri asked. "After they killed it?"

"Given Hyperborea's games over the years," Erikis said, "now that I know they have the body, I think they're probably trying to find a way to control it. Put one of their own in charge. They might even succeed, if they had the right offering. I suspect that they meant to use you alive."

"Ulfr did say that Hyperborea was where he was taking me…"

"Indeed. And while I do not know why they felt you would be a fitting component, I can guess that you are not the only one who would work, and that they might not need a live catalyst if they got their hands on the right one."

"So, the Ancestor Gods, where do they figure into it?"

"They are the very sorcerers," Erikis said, "who slew the God those ages ago. After their victory, they knew they had a power that had never before been attained, and might never again. They turned themselves to stone, sleeping until the day their countrymen might need their aid once more. I believe that one or two of them have been roused in ages past, but never all at once."

At that, Avina butted in. "Think they'll be happy to see us?" she asked. "You must have known at least some of them, right? They'll sure be surprised that you're around."

"Well," Erikis said, "I doubt they would recognize me. As for being happy to see us…"

Esteri let the talk fade into the background. She focused on what she needed. The Ancestor Gods, whatever they were, had put down a war-mongering tyrant once. They could do it again, and that was exactly what they needed. Ulfr, at least, had been out to awaken this old god of Hyperborea's, had done what he had done to her for that end, though she doubted the worse threats were part of it. She couldn't let men like him get a power that would let them rule the world. She had to pass through. She had to awaken the gods.

The mountains loomed ever closer, and Esteri thought that she should reach them tomorrow, or the day after at least. Once they were there... then perhaps she could rest, and let someone else take part of the burden. She hoped that would be so, but somehow she felt it would not be so simple

***

That night, in the dark, Frideger approached Esteri. She looked up at him in surprise, for he had talked quite a lot, but never really to her.

"Your highness."

"What is it?" Esteri asked. His dark eyes were intent, and his face that until Gelvira's injury had always held a smile now frowning and severe, showing around his eyes his great age.

"Drink?" he asked, offering her a flask. "I've got a few words to say you might need it for."

Esteri accepted the flask and took a sip of the potent Tyrvad mead inside.

"All right," Esteri said.

"Do you trust him?" Frideger asked.

"Who?" Esteri replied, and then she thought about it. She trusted Tius with her life and that was plain to see, and Hathus had done nothing to merit any distrust. "Erikis?"

"Aye," Frideger said. "He's the one I mean."

"I think I do," Esteri said hesitantly. "He's very old and very wise. He knows things because he was part of their history."

"Hm," Frideger, "that's true, but still I don't know."

"Please," Esteri said, "tell me why."

"I've known Erikis for over three and a half centuries," Frideger said, "and of all the folk I've known he's one of two who saw right through me, the giddy drunk, and knew I understood. He treated me like an intelligent man, trusted me with hard truths, and I trusted him right back. But ever since Lysama, that old man has changed, and I don't like it."

"I noticed." Esteri said, "but he's still been forthcoming enough."

"Really?" Frideger asked. "So many lives of men I've been around him, and only now he tells this story of the old days, about a monster god that we're all bound to by blood. Only now does he claim knowledge so ancient, only now does he speak of magic. I had thought he was forthcoming before, honest and true, a good friend and a wise guide. Now I don't know how much of his guidance was a pack of lies, or where the truth is incomplete."

"And you're worried," Esteri said, "that it might not be done with? That what we're seeing now might not be the whole truth, either?"

"Aye," Frideger said, pulling out a second flask and sipping from it. "You've got about the right of it."

"Well," Esteri said, "what's the worst that could happen? How would him keeping the full truth from us change our mission?"

"That I don't know," Frideger replied. "The Tyrvad... they've had their Ancestor Gods a long, long time. I don't doubt that they're real, or that they're probably good folk who I'd like to share a flask with any day. But how about that door that you need to need to get through? Do you think he'd tell you the full story, if it might make you doubt?"

"No," Esteri admitted, "but all the same, can we risk Hyperborea getting this old god under their control? If we can't refuse what Erikis asks, we'll have to keep moving forward. I'm sorry, but I don't know how much of a choice we've been left."

"Very clever, isn't that?"

"What?"

"Even if you don't trust him, you still have to help him. I knew a man or two who used words like that back when I was a mortal. It's why I drink – that, and I'm a mighty fine brewer with a tongue for all the finer liquors our world has to offer – but I started because of what it does to words. Keeps them from twisting, turning into knives and cages, like they're wont to do, shed meanings like a snake shedding its skin."

"I'm, betting you didn't exactly choose to take the Potion," Esteri said.

"No," Frideger admitted, "but I couldn't refuse it either. It was a very clever set of words, you see."

Esteri nodded sagely, and took another sip of the mead. Part of her wanted to know more – desperately and powerfully wanted to know all she could about Erikis and Frideger. But ever since she had found her sight with Gelvira, she had been torn between that desire for knowledge and the fear that it might bring her only sorrow.

"I'm sorry," he said. "It's not as though he meant for any of us to get hurt. It's not like I don't keep things from Avina, telling myself I'll tell her all about them when she grows older, and becomes a little wiser. Who knows, maybe that's all Erikis is doing, giving simple answers to hard questions, waiting for the day when we're as old and wise as he is, or just need to know. All the same, I've polished off most of my stash, and I still can't make the worries go away."

Esteri handed the flask back. "You need this more than I do," she said.

He took it back with a nod.

"All the same," Esteri said, "why are you telling me this?"

"Two reasons," Frideger said. "The first is because you're the youngest of us, bar my own daughter, who practically knows Erikis as her own uncle. You're not set in our ways. The second, was that I was going to ask you to look into my future."

Esteri recoiled slightly. She could do it, of course, but what would she see? Of course, if she saw disaster, then maybe she could help prevent it. On the other hand, she had to think there were dangers to meddling with the future. What was the worst that could happen, indeed? How was she to know she would not trade bad for worse? Still, if he asked it of her, she told herself, she would do it. Esteri held out her hands.

"All right," she said.

"I said I was going to," Frideger replied, "but you've reminded me the mess we're in. That man in Lysama, who was going to take you away to Hyperborea. That's a devil we know, and even if there's one we don't know around here, we've still got to fight him, and damned if there isn't but one way to do that. So if you see a happy end to your quest, there will have been no point, and if you see a bad one, what the devil do we do? Unless I can answer you that much, I won't put the burden on your shoulders. I'm sorry."

Esteri withdrew her hands. As much as she was ashamed of the fact, being released from having to turn her eyes to the future brought Esteri some much needed relief. It seemed to come on its own more than enough, even if not so clearly as when she called it.

"It's all right," she said, and swallowing her discomfort added that if he ever changed his mind, she would be willing to do a reading.

Frideger took a great swig from one of his flasks, and walked away.

***

Two days later, they came to the Door in the Mountains. It was a strange thing, a simple thing, a place where the mountains formed a sheer cliff, a flat wall of stone that rose high into the air, and at its base a double door seemingly etched into the rock. Radegond had flown up, but reported she was unable to fly over the peaks, though she could see the other side and said that the sheer cliff that defied her flight was no thicker than a castle wall, beyond which there was a long pass and some flat lands inside the mountains.

Esteri placed her hands on the door, and she felt it. She felt the magic she had doubted even existed coursing through her, felt it challenging her thoughts and her nature. Felt its very presence sapping her strength. It was questioning her, and she was wanting.

Esteri forced herself to focus. She had to see the Ancestor Gods. She had to warn them of the danger that was coming to the world. Once they were awake, they could decide if she had done right or done wrong, but it was their place to rebuke her, not the place of a door!

Still it resisted. She could almost feel it budge, but she was so weak... was it actually hurting her somehow? She didn't think that it was, she thought it was just taking all her strength to challenge it, but she couldn't be sure.

Esteri put away those thoughts. She thought of her father, the memories of her mother, the cruelty of Delphina. She thought about poor Baudoiun, about Gelvira who had paid so dearly, and nearly with her life for this quest. She thought about her brother, and the future that he needed to have.

The doors gave way, swinging easily open. Esteri's arms were leaden-heavy, and her head and eyelids were the same. It was like when she had ascended the mountain upon which the Accursed lived after walking who knew how many days. She was so tired.

Esteri sank to her knees and closed her eyes. She felt hands upon her, heard voices, and smiled. Her friends were here, and they could take care of her, but for now she needed to sleep.

CHAPTER XXI

Avina

"She has simply fainted," Erikis declared. "I suspect she will be fine in a few hours, if not sooner."

Avina watched as Tius carefully picked up the princess in his arms. She looked away. She told herself that she should be happy for him, and for the most part, she was. Avina was far less jealous than she had expected. She supposed that if she had to lose Tius to anyone, Esteri was the one she'd choose. The princess had proved herself to be everything Avina had not expected – loyal, brave, and kind. That did not mean, though, that Avina didn't feel some sting, didn't still love Tius herself even if she was content with friendly banter.

Avina decided to put her displeasure behind her, literally, and strode first through the door. On the other side, the path widened, but not too much – there were still high walls on either side, focusing her vision down towards where the pass ended and the land on the other side of the mountain wall would unfold before them.'

"Avina," Erikis called from behind her. "A moment, please."

Avina stopped, but she didn't look back. She didn't have to look back, she told herself. She was a strong girl who wasn't afraid of anything, who couldn't be hurt. She wasn't afraid of some statues, that was for sure.

"Avina."

It was her father's voice behind her, and she softened a little.

"I'm okay," she said, "but the sooner we get going forward,

the sooner we can go home and see mom, right?"

"That's no reason to run off," he said.

"I wasn't running off," Avina protested. "I was just getting a head start."

Her father hugged her. "It's all right," he said. "They've waited untold years, they can wait another few minutes for us all to face it together."

Avina turned around.

"Okay," she said, "but because I want you to be there, not because you told me to stop."

Frideger laughed. "Of course, of course. That's always the way, isn't it?"

By then Erikis, Radegond, and Hathus had caught up, and Tius with the princess in his arms was slowly making his way behind them.

"I think we can start moving again now," Avina said. Her father looked behind them, nodded, patted her on the back, and let her go onward.

In the lead, Avina set a quick pace. Hopefully not too quick, but her greater stamina than any of the others was somewhat made up for by her shorter legs. She could shift, of course. There would be no one on the wrong side of the door in the mountain, not until they got to the Ancestor Gods.

Avina stifled the urge. She didn't want to run away from everyone else, she wanted to lead them.

Soon enough, Radegond had pushed her way up alongside Avina.

"You know how to lead a march?" Radegond asked gruffly.

"Tius still has to carry the princess," Avina said. "I could go faster, but I don't want to."

"That's not what I asked," Radegond said. "If you want to lead, you're going to have to know how to keep a steady pace, and a rhythm."

"It's not hard," Avina protested.

"Marching is important!" Radegond shot back. "And you've started skipping three times. Here, watch me – even steps!

You can't speed up and slow down at random, that's not the way it works!"

Avina smiled as she tried to mimic Radegond. That was, after all, Radegond's way of trying to be nice.

By evening, Esteri had come to, though she was still weak. The plains in the heart of the mountains were dry, the grass tall. In the distance, a solitary structure loomed, its domed roof visible for what must have been miles in every direction owing to the shape of the terrain, for Avina guessed it to be of modest size, much smaller than the Lysaman castle.

That, Erikis said, was the resting place of the Ancestor Gods.

Avina had always liked Erikis' stories. He hadn't been around as much as her parents or Tius when she was little, and Avina didn't think he'd ever told the same one twice, so she didn't know them as well, but he was very good at the telling.

"So," Avina asked, "how many Ancestor Gods are there?"

"Twenty," Erikis said, "as best as I can tell. Twenty survived conflict with the god they killed, and twenty names are revered by the men of Tyrvad, though I do not know if all of them chose to be turned to stone."

"What do you know about them?"

"Well," Erikis said, "they are human, in the end. They are flawed as humans are, and whatever their struggles, however effective their attempts to avoid the fact have been, they are mortal. They will die."

"I mean," Avina said, "as people, what are they like?"

"Ah," Erikis replied. "Warriors. I suppose you might call them brave from that, or foresighted in preserving themselves for the future need, but they might have been better served by passing on their skills and weapons to others, so on that score I find them average."

Avina paused a moment. There was a bitterness in Erikis' voice that she had seldom, if ever, heard.

"You don't seem to like them very much," she said, "but you think they can win?"

"I know they can," Erikis replied. "They did it before, after all. But what a human is capable of and what a human does are sometimes very different."

Avina nodded. It seemed strange that they would be going to these lengths to awaken humans, if they were so fallible, but Avina supposed that whatever they were, they were the best shot anyone had.

"We'll reach their resting place tomorrow," Erikis said. "I hope you'll understand a little better once we're there."

"I can't understand what you don't tell me, Erikis," Avina said.

"There are some things for which words are ill suited," Erikis replied. "I wish to know, though, what you feel about this."

"If it's all we can do," Avina said, "it's what we have to do." She thought very carefully about her words, her place in the world. She knew about Accursed and a bit about humans, but how much did she know about gods? Was there anything she could say, anything she could do?

"If Hyperborea raises their god," she said, "our village won't be safe. So we have to stop that if we're going to be able to go home."

Erikis nodded carefully.

"It might not be that terrible," he said. "It's hard to admit, with the Princess here, but you might not have too much a stake in it."

Avina looked away.

"Esteri is my friend," she said. "Despite everything, I want her to be happy too, and that guy who tried to take her away, those people who turned Baudouin into a monster, they'll ruin everything."

"I couldn't agree more," Erikis. "Though they are my kin, they have long since abandoned any hope of redemption.

Avina nodded silently, unsure what she could say, and so content to say nothing

*

It was late the next day when they reached the resting place of the Ancestor gods. It was a grand building, but ultimately smaller than Avina had expected. The domed structure stood atop a small hill, square pillars of solid stone holding up a rune-etched pediment. Thick walls and smallish double doors led inside to the rotunda. There were, in total, about twenty statues, as Erikis had said. Three, two men and a woman, stood in the center of the room. The rest were in alcoves along the far wall.

Faint light filtered in from many high slits in the construction, and the sunset shafts illuminated faint dust in the air. Avina felt, more than she had passing through the churches of Lysama, that this was a holy place, that there was the presence of something else. She guessed it was the spirits of the Ancestor gods, waiting to live again.

Esteri was inspecting one of the ones along the walls, while Erikis walked up to the trio in the center, Avina hanging back, near the unadorned wall.

"How do we wake them?" Esteri asked. "Is it like the door."

"To be frank," Erikis said.

Pain struck Avina, and noise, shattering stone, metal clashing against it. She screamed, and grasped at the pain. It was a spear, its silver haft extending from Avina's left shoulder, head buried firmly in the rock wall behind her.

If she were a human, Avina reflected, that would would almost certainly be fatal in the long run. But Avina wasn't human. She had never been human, and human rules did not apply to her. If she just transformed, her wounds would disappear, and stay vanished when she returned to her human-like body. All she had to do was get the spear out first – if she didn't, the wound might not heal – she had no idea if it worked both ways. And even if it did function both directions, when she grew in size the spear might cut through to her heart if it was still there.

"We don't."

Through the haze of pain and fear, Avina could see Erikis, or what used to be Erikis. His form flowed, shifting with ripples of black and crimson. He stood tall amidst the rubble of the three central Ancestor gods, his face the only part of him that seemed untouched, smiling serenely from out a sinuous but massive form.

What was going on?

"Erikis!" Avina's father demanded. "What have you done?"

He was full of rage, stalking towards the center.

"Old friend," Erikis said, with half a laugh, brandishing claws like swords, "I haven't been entirely honest with you."

Erikis leapt, arcing high through the air, landing beside one of the other Ancestor Gods. Deliberately, he reached up to the man's stern, bearded face, glowering down from upon his pedestal. Erikis wrapped his claws around the stony form.

"These fools," he said. "These imbecilic, worthless mortals were given the power to kill a god! It was a power they never should have wielded – none of their misbegotten kind. How it has burned for ages to know that I am a shadow of my former self, to think my body and all my power with it had rotted into dust, lost forever thanks to the callous deeds of those who would see but a hundred years, if that, and the treachery of my own blood, they Hyperboreans! How I stewed, and hated, and dreamed of the day I thought would be impossible."

Erikis squeezed. The statue crashed, then crumbled in his grasp, its head smashing into several pieces, accusing eyes staring blankly in separate directions.

"But now I know my dreams can become reality. And this time no mortal with a sword and a dream of glory will stand before me!"

Avina reached her hands up to the haft of the spear. She had to pull it out! She tugged at it, but the tip was lodged firmly into the wall, and without anything to really brace against, even Avina's considerable strength was insufficient to pull it free.

"You!" Frideger shouted. "You're this... this demon god? Is anything you've ever told us true?"

"Quite a lot, actually," Erikis said, stalking on massive legs towards the next statue. "And I'm terribly sorry for your daughter's state, but you see, in my current state she might actually be a threat to me, and I can't have that in my moment of triumph."

Frideger stepped in front of Erikis.

"She's not the only one who won't let you kill these people."

"Now, now," Erikis said, "step aside."

The lanky abomination struck Avina's father, and he flew back several feet and fell to his knees, gasping for breath. It was a blow that would have killed even another Accursed outright, but her father could heal from almost anything. They didn't exactly know his limits, but a crushed chest was inside them.

Erikis walked up to the next Ancestor God. A blast of fire from Hathus washed over him, but it seemed that his form didn't burn like normal flesh. His hair smoldered, and he gave the statue a cruel blow, shattering its torso

"I..." Frideger gasped. "You..."

"Lie down, old man," Erikis said. "When I am done here, I will reclaim my body from my traitorous children, and then perhaps I can do you a good turn, if you play nicely."

There was a dark flash, and Tius appeared next to Frideger.

"Get back!" Frideger yelled. "He'll kill you!"

"You really think you know a lot about me?" Erikis said. "I don't want to kill any of you. Just don't get in my way."

Avina wrung her hands around the spear, desperately attempting to get some grip on it, free it somehow the wall. She could feel her body getting weaker, the blood soaking her shirt and flowing slowly downward.

"You hurt my family!" her father shouted. "You threatened my friends!"

Erikis again tossed him back, shattering another statue. How many of the Ancestor Gods were left? How many were rubble?

Frideger stood and moved to defend the next one.

"This world will feel my vengeance," Erikis snarled, even his face slowly stretching, fading from humanity. His legs and arms were spindly, but his hunched back had grown massive and bulbous. Avina tried to force her back against the rock face, push the soles of her feet against it. She pulled with all her might and for once felt the shaft move, however slightly. A new surge of blood oozed from the opened wound, and Avina realized that if she did this too poorly, she could very well kill herself before removing the spear. If she stayed still, she could wait for help...

There was another crash, another flash of shadow. Tius appeared in front of Avina.

"You're going to be okay," he told her, placing his hands on hers. "You need this out, right?"

Avina looked up again. Hathus, Radegond, and Frideger were fighting with Erikis, Esteri was sprawled on the ground, clawing at stone wreckage and fighting to catch her breath. As she watched, Erikis grabbed one of Radegond's wings and tore it free of her back. It wouldn't hurt Radegond for long, but it would take her out of the fight. With Hathus' flames ineffective... Avina needed to get into the fight sooner rather than later.

"Pull," she told Tius. "Come on, pull!"

He strained against the spear. Avina felt it flex inside the wound, and gasped in pain.

On the other side of the room, there were two, perhaps three of the Ancestor Gods left standing, and her father, bruised and bloodied, standing against Erikis. He picked up an axe with a shimmering azure blade, one of the weapons that the broken Ancestor Gods had carried.

Tius stopped pulling.

"Are you okay?" he asked.

"I have a spear in me!" Avina managed to gasp, her voice weak. "Come on, pull."

"I... I don't know how to manage safely."

"You dare?" Erikis roared, voice distorted by his continuing transmutation.

"I do," Frideger replied, hefting the axe, "if this is what it takes"

"Who told you of those ancient days?" Erikis demanded. "Put that weapon aside, and I can guarantee your safety when the world drowns in the blood of those who have wronged me."

Frideger swung, striking one of Erikis'... Avina guessed the writhing tendrils on either side of his form used to be his arms.

"Pull now," she whimpered.

"Okay," Tius said. "Together with me. On three. One."

Erikis roared, shrieked in agony.

"Two."

Erikis surged forward. Half a dozen limbs struck at Frideger. Tendrils ran through him, and Avina did her best to not scream or cry out for her father.

"Three!" Tius shouted, and Avina pulled together with him. The spear tore free of the wall, free of her flesh. And she slumped to the ground. So much blood... but now, she was free.

Avina's body roiled, wound vanishing as her clothes melded together into her monstrous shape. She roared a challenge to the sky, to Erikis, and looked...

Only to see Erikis lift her father high, and as her father swung the axe again, wrenched the limbs that impaled him away in every direction. Blood and viscera rained down on the field, and Avina stood, horror-stricken.

There wasn't a body left for him to regenerate.

Erikis turned to face her, and smiled, the gash that was once his mouth turning up at the ends.

"It really is unfortunate," he croaked, "that it had to end this way."

Avina screamed, and surged forward. She was faster than anything! She was stronger than anything! She would make him pay!

She collided with the opposite wall, and spun around to find Erikis standing again in her path. She rushed him again, but once more somehow missed the mark.

"Really," he said, "if I'd realized how clumsy you were, I could have done this all with you free and clear."

Avina let out an incoherent roar, and this time pounced towards his location. Despite his ungainly shape and great bulk, Erikis was surprisingly nimble.

"Better," he said, "but I've no desire for a hard fight, and my task here is done."

Stiff membranes spread from his back, two pairs, glistening and wet. He tensed – was he going to fly with those? Avina wasn't about to let him. She could jump...

"Bury what you can," he said, "then come after me if you must. But if you do, you will die."

Erikis leapt upward, and Avina after him. For a moment, she caught his tail, or possibly the extended mass of his legs, but then he slipped up and away, crashing through the ceiling above, into the fading twilight.

Avina fell back to earth, amidst the wreckage of her friends and family and the ruin of their hope. Her strength left her, and she shrank back into her normal form, her tattered clothes appearing around her tiny, fragile body.

Amidst the blood and horror, she wept.

CHAPTER XXII

Erikis

Erikis alighted on a mountaintop in the night air, feeling for once in untold years alive. Not that he was, mind. Erikis was still a fragment of his former self, a slip of soul and flesh, barely held together by divine magic, flung away from his great bulk when mortals had strived to slay him. He had lost count of the time he had been existing in the pathetic, reduced state, of the years since he had realized he would not regenerate his true self no matter how much time he was given.

Slowly, he pulled his form back under control. Curse Frideger's stubbornness – killing the man was not something that Erikis had wanted to do, though it did not bother him, but the time he had spent fighting in such an unbridled manner had pushed him towards the edge. Had he called on much more power, he might have started to degenerate.

That was one of the dangers that Erikis had discovered shortly after his death. He had many shadows of his former power, but he needed to come closer to his true form the more he wanted to use, and the mass of flesh he had poured his soul into could not, on its own, support life. If he went too far, he risked dying a second death, just as surely as if his human form was destroyed. What he would become in that state, Erikis did not want to find out.

And, soon enough, he would not have to. The 'Ancestor Gods' would not rise to oppose him, and no one else knew the significance of their weapons. Even if the little band he had been forced to betray picked them up rather than leaving them interred with rocky fragments, they would not be able to wield such weapons against him.

The only thing about that which worried Erikis was Esteri's dream. A bleeding sky, impaled with blades; this seemed like something Erikis would do when he regained his body, and she had seen herself wielding one of their loathsome weapons. Perhaps he should have killed her when he had the chance, but it was too late to worry about that.

His body, clad in the tatters of his traveling clothes (for Avina was the only one of his blood he had ever met who could transform objects with her, though they largely seemed to just vanish when she became her greater self), reflected now something mostly human. The tips of his fingers were hardened and sharp and scraped the ground, and broad membranous wings that were the focal point of flight magic stretched from his hunched back, but the rest of him was in shape--heart, lungs, muscles and organs that he had been too long mimicking rather than actually having.

It would have to do. The balance between power and life was precarious, and he had pushed farther than perhaps he should have in order to ensure his victory there.

Now that such a thing was achieved, Erikis set his mind to his next goal: understanding the game his ungrateful children were playing on the continent. For millennia, they had fostered wars, stifled growth, and Erikis had been content with that. Bloodshed pleased him, and he had thought that the Accursed might one day birth their doom. He had been grooming Avina for that post, but she was no longer needed.

The question was, how clever was his blood? If they were good, it was possible only their most trusted agents would know. Ulfr, wherever he was, had to know where he intended to take Esteri, at least. Other than that, anyone on the continent could be ignorant.

Granted, Ulfr would not have been able to ask alone. Someone had to know where he was coming from, that he would pass and how. He needed supplies and a connection to his masters, which meant that someone had to be able to find him.

Erikis stretched his wings. Massive, mighty wings they were, that could carry him far indeed. He could make it back to Lysama in a few days, but disliked though they were, his descendants could be found in Tyrvad as well, and the capitol of that land was closer still. The night was young. He might be able to make it there before dawn.

***

Erikis arrived still hours before dawn, the night dead and dark. The moon was low in the sky and a bare crescent, and no one looked high into the sky to witness his approach against the faint light of the stars.

The great hall of Tyrvad was not the same as the castles of Kalest or Lysama. Instead of building upwards, for the most part, it was a sprawling set of structures each only a single story high. Now where, in all this would they keep the Hyperborean ambassador? Certainly, not too close to the heart, but at the same time they could not quarter him or her too far away.

Erikis decided to take the direct route. He glided over the grounds until he spotted a guard on patrol. Just one, and isolated from the likely sight of any others.

Erikis dropped out of the sky onto the woman, the claws of one of his hands digging into her flesh while the other wrapped around her mouth to stifle any scream. She fell easily, and Erikis knelt upon her, pinning the woman to the ground.

"I will ask you one question," Erikis said. "If you do not answer it plainly with the first words out of your mouth, you will die, and I will be gone before any of your compatriots can come into sight."

The woman did not seem afraid. Troubling, but if she cried out it would be cut short.

"My question: Where do your quarter the Hyperborean ambassador?"

Erikis released the hand over her mouth.

"The western tower," she said. Erikis had seem such a structure, three floors high though in total height not as great as the peaked roof of the central structure. "On the top floor."

Erikis replaced his hand over her mouth, and then snapped her neck. He dragged the woman's body into some bushes where she likely would not be spotted for some time yet. It was her misfortune that killing her silently was easier and more sure than trying to knock her out or bind and gag her.

Erikis leapt back into the sky, and flew to the west. He landed lightly upon the roof of the tower, and considered for a moment that the guardswoman might have lied to him. The tower could very well be the main barracks for the guard, or a sealed, dusty wing. It looked too small for the former, though, and if it was the latter Erikis would simply have to track down someone else to ask his question to.

Erikis stood tall, and then dove through the roof, into the room below. Amidst the shattered wood , he spied the bed, and swiftly grasped the figure on it. A Hyperborean man, to be sure, and therefore likely the ambassador.

"Well met," Erikis said with a grin.

"You..." the ambassador gasped. "What are you?"

"That is not your concern," Erikis said. "I have questions for you, and you will answer them."

Erikis let the man's situation sink in.

"The first question is this... Your people hold a divine corpse. Where?"

"I don't know..." the man stammered. "Don't know what you're talking about.

"Unfortunate," Erikis said. He did not think he was being lied to, but he could not be totally certain. "My second question: Do you know the agent called Ulfr?"

The man nodded. At least Erikis was getting somewhere.

"Good," Erikis said. "Now, if you will, where is Ulfr now?"

"I don't exactly..."

Erikis pierced the man's shoulder with a talon.

"Explain."

The man grunted in pain and tried to take deep breaths. Erikis allowed it. He wanted his answers more than he wanted to watch the miserable man suffer.

"I was told... that he leads a group of Kalesti."

"Kalesti?"

"Soldiers," the Ambassador said, "who had been under the command of a man of impossible skill. Ulfr was to take control of them. I was to ensure he was well supplied if necessary, so he is probably in Tyrvad."

The ambassador couldn't have known how useful that information was, of course. The self-proclaimed Slayers no doubt, and they would be on Esteri's trail, just a little behind. That was good news, but there were still some questions left unanswered.

"Now," Erikis said, "you don't happen to know any details about his mission?"

"No..." the Ambassador muttered. There was a loud knock on the door.

"Send them away," Erikis said.

"I am fine," the Ambassador called. "Leave me be!"

"Sorry, sir," the voice replied, and then footsteps led away.

"Good boy," Erikis said, a grin spreading far too wide across his face.

"I know nothing more about Ulfr," the ambassador said, "so please, let me be."

"I have a final question or two for you," Erikis said, "and then I will decide what to do with you, do you understand?"

The ambassador nodded.

"Who gave you the orders regarding Ulfr?"

"Ormr," he replied, "Ambassador to Kalest."

"And why?"

"It is part of an agreement," the ambassador said, "with Queen Delphina of Kalest. I know no more than that."

Erikis spared no time tearing out the man's throat. As he watched the miserable whelp die, a feeling came over him. He had some time, he thought. Not enough to rest, but there were moments before dawn, and in his reduced form he had some mortal needs. He raised his hand to his mouth and began to feed.

***

Erikis left the capitol before dawn came, and rested at the nearest high peak, out of sight of the ground. When he rested, he dreamed for the first time in an age.

It was not, exactly, like a mortal dream. More, it was a continuation of his thought as he slept in that high place.

The dream was of the days of old. Erikis stood in his hall, great and resplendent, his concubines lounging on the velvet cushions about him. Some of his children opened the grand doors of his palace, and let the Tyrvad delegation in. Erikis, as he was then, did not think much of them. He did not notice their azure-hued weapons, enchanted with his own divine power.

Not until they had already cut him.

Erikis had existed for eons already in those days. He was not older than humanity, as was sometimes purported, but he had a memory of days that no folk remembered in their histories. Out of all that time however, it was then that for the first time, Erikis felt pain.

The battle had been brutal, but its outcome had been decided in that first stroke. No matter how Erikis reshaped his body and his soul, he could not shake that wound, nor any of the other wounds that followed. They cut, and they hewed, and so Erikis hid himself in a deep heart, and played at death, and when they cut his body and made to lay fire against it, and had slain his vast majority, he sloughed away, and should have died but for the potency of what he poured into that fragment.

The fragment was now the whole of his body, this thing that fit so easily into a human skin and could not live if it was allowed to be too much itself, this thing that he had, existing in a state farther from its nature, become all too accustomed to. It should not have been needful for Erikis to hide and, indeed, it would not be for longer. Once he regained his flesh, which he had so long believed destroyed and dispersed, he might regain his old power, and wreak vengeance upon those who had wronged him, and establish his lordship over those he ought to rule.

But the idea of his old enemies nagged at him, and he thought of the ones who killed the giant born of his heart's blood, and those with mortal weapons. The Ancestor Gods of Tyrvad were shattered into ruin, but their arms he could not so easily destroy. He did not fear those who had become part of him, nor even Avina who knew not that she was more his child than that of her parents, but he did fear those with the skill and the will to do what the Ancestors of Tyrvad's great houses had done so long ago.

And if he discovered them, he might also discover Ulfr, and with him the location of his body.

They had beaten Baudouin, that was true, but Baudouin had been a dumb brute with far too much power, and Erikis was wise and clever. He could take Ulfr, or he could slay them all, and the latter had become a quite appealing idea.

CHAPTER XXIII

Tius

Tius knelt and put a stone on the cairn they had raised for Frideger. He did not know if the stone itself was the remains of something else, but he did know that, his respects paid to the man who had been so good and so fatherly to him for so many years, it might be better to concern himself about the living.

Avina was trying to be strong. He had seen her, just after Erikis had gotten away, but since then she had dried her tears, and choked back the sorrow in her voice, though if she had said so much as ten words Tius would be amazed. He knew she had to be in more pain than any of them: they'd all respected Frideger, and liked him. They'd all trusted Erikis, and been stung by his betrayal. But Avina had idolized Erikis, and Frideger was her father. As much as Tius wanted to offer some sympathy, he suspected he couldn't even really grasp what she was going through, set alone in the world in such a way.

No, Tius reminded himself, looking around, not alone. He would be there to do what little he could for her, and Esteri as well. Ragegond and Hathus in their own ways... they'd all pitch in, they'd all try to help her in her grief, however keenly they felt some shadow of it themselves.

But they'd all been working on the cairn, and now sat exhausted about it. The stones were raised over what remained of Frideger, and now? All were silent. Radegond stared into the sky, while Hathus gazed at his feet and Esteri sorrowfully upon the grave. Avina was away from the rest, looking out over the field, curled in against herself, back towards the rest.

Tius walked over to her, and as he came close he saw why she was turned away – her eyes were red, and her cheeks stained with fresher tears than the ones she had shed within the great chamber.

Tius tried to not focus on that sign.

"Avina…"

"I'm fine," she said.

Well, that at least was something. Tius tried to think, whether he ought to humor her, ot admit he saw through her claim.

"Well," he said, deciding on the former route, "what do you think we'll do now?"

"I don't know," Avina replied. "Go home? Give mom the news? What else can we do?"

"You really think that's a good idea?"

"I don't know!" Avina answered. "I just… I want to get back at Erikis, but he's gone. I wanted to help with this mess, but now we've got no way to. I wanted… I wanted to see what the world was like, and it's not a good place."

Tius frowned bitterly. "Yeah… I see what you mean."

After a brief silence, Avina spoke again.

"What would you do?"

Tius thought about it. In many ways, Avina was right about things. They had reached what was supposed to be the end of their journey twice now, and they didn't know where to go, or what to do. The Ancestor Gods of Tyrvad were rubble, Baudouin was dead, and Lysama looked likely to bow to the suzerainty of Kalest, as Esteri had put it. They had failed utterly.

And yet, Tius did not want to give up, could not simply say that they should all go home, tell Avina she'd never see justice done.

"I think we've got to try for something better," Tius said. "We can't just… just let this happen. Whatever Erikis is planning, whatever game the Hyperboreans are playing, it won't just leave us at home like the world has in the past. I know I'm not the old wise guy, but I'm sure nothing like this has ever happened before."

"I can't..." Avina muttered.

"Can't?"

"I can't lose anyone else," she muttered, now struggling to contain yet more tears. "I can't take it! How do humans handle it, when everybody they know is always going to die?"

"We're pretty tough," Tius said, "humans and Accursed alike. It hurts, I know, but"-

"But nothing!" Avina shouted, and then her voice went quiet again. "If anything happens to you or Esteri... Radegond or Hathus... I don't know what I'd do."

"Tear whoever was responsible in half?" Tius ventured.

"Except I couldn't... couldn't fight when it mattered."

Tius winced. Comforting someone in a time of need was not something he knew how to do, forcing him to rely on uncertain instincts. He put an arm around Avina's shoulder.

"We'll do better," he said. "We'll make this as right."

"We can't"-

"At least," he said, "we'll make it so your father won't have died in vain. I promise."

"No," Avina said. "If you're going to promise me something, promise me that I won't have to bury you too. If things look too tough, you get out, just keep yourself alive. That's what matters, that's what mom would want, what dad would have wanted."

Tius looked away.

"Please," Avina said. "Promise me."

"Avina..."

Tius wondered if she realized what she was asking. If he was in mortal danger, that meant everyone else they both cared about was too. Tius didn't want to promise her anything if he didn't mean to keep his word, and he had learned in Lysama that if he had to, he'd stick his neck out without even really realizing it.

She looked at him, full of a despairing sorrow that Tius had never seen cross her visage before.

"You're not going to, are you?"

"I... I don't know what will happen," Tius said. "I want to be around for you, I want to be able to give you my word, but I don't want to have to break it if it's the line between sticking it out and fighting so me and Ragegond, or Hathus, or Esteri both live, or running away just to save myself."

Avina looked down again.

"I understand," she said, the fire having gone out of her.

"It's not... Avina, I can't tell you for sure I'll make it. But I can promise I'll do my best. I know all of us will."

Avina looked away.

"Just... I'm fine, okay?"

Like that she was turned in on herself, shutting the world – and Tius – out again.

It was cruel, he thought, to leave matters like this, but it would have been crueler to pacify her now only to break her trust.

Perhaps truth was the best path to take. In any case, it was the one Tius had chosen so far.

"You know I care about you," Tius said quietly.

"Don't," Avina said.

"Avina, I"-

"Don't lie to me," Avina said, cutting Tius off with her curt, morose command. "I know you think I'm just a little kid. I know... know that it's Esteri you really care about. Never mind you've known her fewer weeks than I've known you years. Never mind that she'll probably break your heart."

Avina sniffled.

"I don't blame you. You... you can't control these things. I know I can't, or I would have by now, changed things one way or the other. But... don't lie, and say it's not true. It won't make me feel any better."

"I know," Tius said. Dimly, he registered the shock that Hathus had been right in all his teasing, but what was in front of him was far more important. "But Avina... there's more than one way to care about someone. You... Yeah, I'll admit, I can't shake the image of the bright little kid I could carry on my shoulders, even if you are grown up now, but that's not what I was trying to say. I mean..."

Tius sighed.

"I never really had a family when I was human," he said, "You know that. But when I came to the colony... your mom and dad took me in like I was their own son, treated me like no one else ever had. They let me into their home and their lives, which included you. I don't... I don't really know what it would be like to have a sister, but I'd have to guess it would be something like this."

Tius shook his head. Half of him wanted to restrain his thoughts, to stop talking, but he decided to let it go, not think back on what he was said, or ahead to what he was saying, and just speak.

"You're the closest thing to a family I've ever had. You are my family, and I'll always love you for that. You probably remember what the elders"--mostly Erikis, but Tius wasn't about to speak that monster's name--"say. Passion comes and goes. A lot of humans can't hold onto it for forty or sixty years, much less for a hundred. Or a thousand. But in a thousand years, you'll still be my family, and I'll still love you just the same. And... I can't give my word to someone I love if I don't know I'm going to be able to keep it. But please, Avina, trust me when I say that there's nothing I'd rather be able to do than be able to spend a day with you when we've lost count of the ages between then and now."

For a moment, Avina simply stared at him, eyes wide, lips parted, face filled with wonderment, though for better worse Tius guessed even she did not yet know. Then, with great suddenness, Avina flung her arms around Tius, and began to sob into his shoulder.

What have I done? Tius thought, I've told the whole truth, and now...

"Thank you," Avina whispered. "Thank you so much."

Tius held her, saying nothing for a moment lest her disturb

her thoughts.

"I... I never would have thought. That matters so much more!"

Tius found himself smiling faintly. As her tears faded away, he dared speak softly.

"Are you going to be alright?" he asked.

Avina sat back up straight, and managed to force a smile.

"I think so," she said, and then after a pause, "I'm sorry if I've acted badly. I didn't..."

"It's okay," Tius said. "There's been a lot weighing on you. Now more than ever."

Avina nodded, then looked around. Relief crossed her face when she noticed, as Tius had a moment before, that there had probably been no one within easy earshot for their conversation.

"You should probably worry about Esteri, too," she said quietly, "She hasn't been to war any more than we have. Hathus and Radegond... I guess this isn't really new for them."

Tius gave Avina one more quick hug, which she returned.

"I'll check on her," he said. "How about you start planning with Radegond?"

Avina nodded, and trotted off. Tius hoped that her mind might be, at least for a moment, off the burden of her loss, but there was no spring in her weary step, nor did her shoulders fail to slump when no doubt she returned to the morose facts of reality.

***

Tius found Esteri in the ruined chamber, amidst the shadows and dust of the shattered gods. She stood there, beneath the broken dome, turning one of the azure-bladed swords over in her hands.

Tius stepped forward hesitantly, and Esteri turned around.

"Oh," she said. "Tius. It's you."

Her voice was flat, and she didn't meet his eyes

Tius approached slowly, quietly. He looked down, the princess' ill mood as plainly evident as its cause.

"Yeah..." he said. "It's me."

A moment passed, Tius thinking how stupid he had to seem, how stupid he was for trying to approach her without an idea of what to say.

"I... um... wanted to check on you," he admitted.

"Thank you," she replied, voice hollow. "That was very kind of you."

"Esteri..." Tius started to talk, but cut himself off. Once today, speaking his mind had been a good idea, and he wasn't sure he wanted to push his luck.

"Do what you want," she said quietly when it became clear that Tius would not continue.

"And," Tius asked, "what will you do?"

There was a long silence. Esteri was focused intently on the blade in her hands, seemingly closed off to the rest of the world.

"The power to kill a god," she said. "That's what he said." Her hand closed around the hilt of the azure sword. "We're going to need that if half of what Erikis said is true."

"You want to go after him?" Tius asked.

"Of course!" Esteri shouted, looking up at him, actually seeing him for once. "Don't you?"

"I do," Tius said, "but this doesn't have to be your fight."

"He made it my fight," she replied. "He lead us here. He used me. I will not simply be used! I may never become Queen of Kalest, but that doesn't mean I'll forget what my father taught me. About justice. About vengeance. About power."

And then, as though she suddenly realized what she said, she looked away, dour rather than angry again.

Tius ventured to step closer. He saw the worry on her face, and tried to read the words she mouthed silently.

"Your father?" he asked, guessing her words.

Slowly, Esteri nodded.

"There's what I know," she said, "and then a lot I don't understand. I could hide from him forever, but at the same time, I can't. I couldn't live my life that way, never knowing who had the truth, me or Ukko. I've wondered, since the meeting with him where Gelvira... where that happened. Did I imagine my father's voice? Those damning words? I don't think I could, but all the same... I have to know. But Erikis comes first."

Tius nodded. "If there's anything I can do for you..."

"What?" Esteri asked.

Tius hesitated, and Esteri bitterly looked away.

"I..." he said. "I'll follow with you as long as you need me."

"I don't need anyone. I shouldn't. I thought I did and look where that's gotten everyone."

"As long as you want me."

And it was Esteri's turn to pause. Her shoulders slumped slightly, and some of the tension seemed to leave her.

"Tell me," she said, "what do you think makes for the poorer ruler – one who cares too much for her people and loses for fear of risking them, or one who cares too little and achieves perhaps great things at terrible prices?"

"I'd say you're not my ruler," Tius replied. "You're my friend. I want to help you because... because of that, because it's the right thing to do, not because you command me, not because I owe anyone fealty. Any of the rest of us – Avina or Radegond or anyone – they'll be the same. So don't worry about what we do like the choices are all on your head. We make our own decisions, it's just if we would decide to abandon you we'd have done it in Lysama. But we wouldn't."

Esteri closed her eyes, and took a deep breath.

"That," she said, "is going to take some getting used to."

"Really?" Tius asked, scratching his head. "It just seems... normal to me. No offense."

"None taken. I just... if I said jump, someone would jump. Always. Which meant I was responsible, because they'd even jump off a cliff."

"Do you miss it?" Tius asked.

Esteri smiled. "You know," she said, "I really don't."

And then after a moment in which she looked up and away

in thought, she spoke again.

"Alright," she admitted, "perhaps just a little."

After a moment, she looked back at the blade in her hands, and her momentarily lightened mood soured once again, though Tius hoped she was on the mend as much as any of them could be.

"So," she said, "we have a plan. Kill Erikis, then get some answers from my father... try to stop him from doing anything else like the invasion of Lysama, whether for my supposed sake or with me an an excuse. I won't sit idly by."

It was more a series of goals, Tius thought, but goals he could agree with.

"Do you think," he offered, "your sight could help?"

Esteri looked away from him for a moment.

"I've thought about it," she said. "The future can be changed, I know that now, but I still don't have the best control over what I see."

She sighed.

"But that's just an excuse, isn't it? I'm afraid, afraid I'll see something terrible and not know what to do to make it any better. And that's foolish, if I don't see anything at all that doesn't stop it from happening, it just means I'm as ignorant as I was when I downed a cup full of poison."

Esteri set the blade aside and sat down. "What I wouldn't have given to know, however awful it would be to just watch myself die. I could have avoided it, and now that I have that power, have I been using it? Have I been saving lives?"

"You saved Gelvira," Tius noted. "We've been over this before."

"I did," Esteri said, "which is why I'm such a fool for having not looked even more. I could have prevented all of this."

Tius shook his head.

"We don't know that," he said, "and you can't let yourself get obsessed with trying to see everything about the future. You said as much yourself."

"Was I right to?" Esteri asked, looking up. "If... if I master this"-

"It's hard to explain," Tius said, "but I know a story that might."

Esteri patted the ground beside her, and Tius seated himself.

"Before I came to the Colony, the way I heard it told, there was a man there named Kolur. He was a bandit leader of some sort, though honestly it sounds like he was some sort of village head-man too. He was given the potion as punishment for crimes and a chance at redemption, fighting in some war or other. He became an Accursed like you or me, rather than a beast, a fate that claimed about half his people. Of the other half, he was the only survivor by the end of the war. Accursed fought on the front lines. We're stronger than normal people, but there's only so much that we can take. And Kolur, he never learned during the war what he could do. Only after he escaped in the wake of no one knowing what to do with him when the war was over, and he found his way to the colony, did he learn that he could heal people. Close wounds, cure diseases, and so on.

"Once he learned, he worked at it all the time. It wasn't long before others noticed that his warping was... worse than most. It wasn't quite as obvious as mine, but it was like he paid in his own blood for everything he mended. But he kept at it, trying to fix everyone, all the time. He even traveled beyond the Colony, the mysterious doctor with the miracle cure. He couldn't sit by when he thought he could help people, but in the end? As I heard it, and you can ask her for more details, Radegond was traveling with him in the lowlands, one spring when there was a plague among humans. No matter what she said, he wouldn't stop and leave matters to real alchemists. Eventually, he died, just keeled over trying to set some kid's broken leg with his power when he didn't have any more to give.

"The point is, if he hadn't tried to take on all the world's woes he'd still be around, helping people. He might still be around offering his miracles in a hundred years. Or a thousand. But instead he worked himself to death thinking only about what was happening right now."

Esteri looked away.

"Look," Tius said, "just... don't drive yourself crazy. If you think you can help, you can try, but if you spend all your time looking at the future rather than at life unfolding, you'll never reach that future."

After a long hesitation, Esteri spoke.

"I understand," she said. "All the same, I can try right now."

Esteri took a deep breath, then slowly exhaled.

"Would you like me to leave you to it?" Tius asked.

"No," Esteri said quickly. She waited a moment, then spoke again. "I... I don't know how this is going to go. I could hurt myself, by warping or otherwise. I'd like you here to keep that from happening."

"I'll do my best."

"Just make sure I don't fall over and crack my head if something goes wrong," she said.

For a moment, there was nothing.

"Well?" she asked, glancing to his hand. Carefully, hesitatingly, Tius put his arm around her shoulders. Esteri let out a heavy sigh.

"That will do," she said. "I'm going to try... to see the future. Do what you must to snap me out of it if anything looks... troubling."

And with that, Esteri closed her eyes, leaving Tius to silently consider his position. First Hathus and now Avina seemed to be convinced they knew where Tius' heart was on the matter, and Tius himself couldn't deny that something stirred when he looked at the princess. But if it was so obvious to everyone else, why was it so hard for Tius himself to sort the matter out, to determine what he wanted to do, what he could do?

She was beautiful, though Tius found that not the greatest of her virtues, not when she had her wit to her name. And there was longing when Tius looked at her, a sad and wistful desire. When had that begun? Not at first, certainly. By the catastrophe at Lysama? Tius didn't know for certain. And why that feeling, that reminded him of his days as a thief, and the happy-sorrow of seeing a family at play?

Because you see what you can't have, a voice within Tius replied. That's what longing really means, isn't it? The thief who fancies a princess, but status is something a man can't steal.

And then the thought entered Tius' mind that it might not be so utterly fanciful. Here they sat, Tius with an arm around her shoulders, Esteri's head now resting faintly on his shoulder. If anyone saw the scene outside its state they would probably guess the two young lovers. And they were both Accursed, without a station in the lives of mortals. And it wasn't just Tius the others had been so sure of...

He swallowed hard. Those thoughts didn't have that distant ache but the present dread of not being sure what to do. Tius hadn't dated since making a fool of himself in front of Silja Nurminen when he was twelve!

Just be yourself, he told himself, if you have a chance that's been good enough so far.

And maybe ask Hathus for advice, if he could get a straight answer out of the man, but for now there was the enviable task of keeping Esteri safe as she attempted to glean some hint of things to come.

Moments later, Esteri jumped. Her eyes snapped open, stark black at first but slowly beginning to clear.

"I know," she said. "I know where Erikis will be soon."

"Then let's get everybody together," Tius said.

"There's just one problem," Esteri said. "I saw... Ukko will be there, too. If we want to face Erikis, we won't be alone."

Tius nodded. "Who knows?" he offered. "Maybe we'll be on the same side this time."

CHAPTER XXIV

Acacia

The rugged scrubland that dominated Tyrvad, brown and yellow as it was, was all around them, and as Acacia awakened to her surroundings she found herself wishing idly that she was back home, with water and trees and houses all around.

She would not have traded the friends she'd met for anything in the world. Even Seija was not as taciturn as she liked to appear. And for their mission? It had started the stuff of stories, their aim to battle monsters and rescue kidnapped royalty. Once Ulfr had arrived, though, it all seemed to sour somewhat. They never talked, too much menace and too many secrets. Acacia was sure that the Hyperborean was up to something, but like Ukko and the others she could see no real way to oppose him. Not without proof that his letter from the king was forged, which wasn't forthcoming in distant Tyrvad.

She looked forward at the high mountains they would need to pass on Esteri's trail, and felt sick when Ulfr had them set camp at the mouth of an open door in the mountain

The silence was too much at last. When night had fallen, she found Ukko sitting away from the rest, most of whom were dozing, watching the dark as he had taken to doing, and sat by him.

Ukko looked up at her.

"Hm?"

"I... wanted to talk a moment. If you don't mind..."

"Of course," Ukko replied. He glanced over his shoulder, pointedly at Ulfr, who was asleep. "Do you mean country matters?"

Their code for trying to communicate on the sly about the Hyperborean.

"No," Acacia replied. "It's just been too quiet of late thanks to those country matters."

"Alright," Ukko said, wWhat about?"

Acacia was used to making small talk, but not with someone like Ukko nor somewhere like where they were, but she tried anyway. She'd go crazy otherwise.

"I was wondering... about when you were young. How the world was then."

"Ah," Ukko said, "not as different as I wish it were. The borders were more or less the same, though Indris then was a kingdom, not some strange confederation. The people were neither less noble, nor more than those of this age. They grumbled about the youth, as they do now, but it hasn't really changed. I suppose steel was new, then – in my grandfather's time we only had iron and bronze, and the rank and file still mostly carried the same in mine, with steel reserved for those with rank. I wonder at that, sometimes."

"Wonder why?" Acacia asked.

"I've lost proper count of the years," Ukko replied, "though I'm sure they could be figured with a little work. But in all that time, how has fared the world, and our science in it? Steel was the last great discovery to reshape how men live their lives and fight their wars. We did discover it, so clearly the world is not unalterable, but all the same, is there nothing more? Is this the pinnacle of life? Part of me wishes to believe that we can do better, but another would know why we haven't."

"I never really thought about that," Acacia admitted.

Ukko smiled. "And you are no worse off for it. Forgive my musings – you wanted to know about life back then?"

"If it's not too much trouble," Acacia replied, "I'd like to hear something about your life."

"Ah," Ukko said. "I remember, when I was about your age, a bit younger really, I got into a fight with my older brother.

In retrospect it was a petty thing – he had ridden down my dog on his horse. An accident, I'm sure, but he wouldn't even apologize for it. So, before he was to train, I soaked the padding in his gauntlets with glue. It took hours of prying to get them off his hands, and days before you couldn't find some blotch of cloth still stuck on. Our parents were furious, and made me apologize, grudgingly as I did. To my wonder, my brother then apologized for what happened to Bosse. After that, I really said I was sorry, and the two of us at least were back on speaking terms."

"You know," Acacia said, "I never took you for a prankster."

Ukko shrugged. "I suppose I was before going to war. After that I took to unconventional tactics, but had to be the model of a Kalesti warrior at home, for the most part."

"In other words, you only pulled anything when you knew you wouldn't be caught."

Ukko laughed, then shook his head. "Oh, I made only one indiscretion," he said, "and I still haven't decided if I was rewarded or punished for it."

"The potion?"

"That would be my consequence, yes."

One thing Acacia had been around Ukko long enough to learn was that the man never lied, but he could bandy technicalities forever if it didn't please him to tell the straight truth. She could surmise that his indiscretion wasn't the potion itself, but somehow led there? She knew better than to ask after it.

"And what of yourself?" Ukko asked.

"Oh," Acacia said, "I'm nothing special."

"Look at where you are," Ukko said, waving a hand out to the night expanse of Tyrvad. "You're a soldier of Kalest, deep in a foreign land, on a secret mission for your king to do with monsters, magic, and conspiracy. That's the stuff of legends."

"I'd think it would make anything else I've done seem a little uninteresting."

"Well," Ukko said, "I might like to know where you came

from before running into me."

Acacia suppressed a laugh, remembering her less than stellar introduction, then took a breath.

"What's there to say?" she asked.

"For one," Ukko replied, "I've never heard you speak of your parents."

Acacia shrugged. "They're dead," she replied. "Years ago. Plague. It happens. But I was old enough to at least pretend to work, and I've always had tons of friends so it's not like I was out on the street or anything awful that could have happened. And I miss them, but they wouldn't want me to cry about it. I don't, mostly."

"I'm sure they'd be proud."

"How about your parents?"

Ukko sighed. "The needs of court were many... as were my siblings. Older brother, younger brother, and two little sisters. So I can't say my parents and I were close, as family goes. But all the same my mother cared for me, and my father taught me of honor and swordsmanship. I shall always remember them well, and hope to do them proud."

"I think I understand," Acacia said.

"Is that why you were so eager to join the army, perhaps?"

"Oh, no!" Acacia replied. "My parents didn't much care for the idea of me soldiering. They didn't want their precious daughter getting killed on foreign soil. I don't mean to, though, I just..." She shook her head. "Taavi wants to be a hero, I just wanted to do something that would mean more than odd jobs at market. Do king and country proud. I didn't think it would be quite so personally, of course."

"Do you regret it?" Ukko asked.

Acacia answered in an instant. "Not on your life. Do you?"

"After all these years," Ukko replied, "I'd be lying if I said I'd never considered what might have followed had I chosen a different road, but I do not regret it."

"I've been meaning to ask," Acacia said after a brief pause, "was there any..."

Ukko was gazing up into the night sky, jaw clenched, one hand on the hilt of his sword. Acacia reached for her blades as well, and looked up.

After a moment, she saw a shape flicker in front of stars. She couldn't track it well, but she could see what Ukko no doubt saw: it was far too big to be a bird.

Motion! Acacia caught sight of the thing again. There was no doubt it had come about. It was circling.

"Get the others up," Ukko said, quietly, as he stood. "I don't know what that is but I don't like its looks."

Acacia hurried back, and quickly roused Seija, Taavi, Launo, and Maria. She didn't care if Ulfr slept through the matter or not.

"Ugh," Maria groaned, struggling to her feet, sword in hand. "What's the emergency?"

Acacia looked upwards, and pointed. "There," she said.

Maria looked. "Well I'll be," she said, "it's coming straight in alright."

"Straight..." Acacia reflected. She turned her eyes back to the skies and recognized the dive for what it was. She ducked and rolled out of the way as a massive, fleshy thing streaked above her, towards Ukko.

Ukko, at least, was faster, and by the time Acacia had her bearings, he had sidestepped and given the monster some dire wound, his sword glittering crimson in the moonlight.

That sight also afforded Acacia a clear view of the monstrosity. It was a hulking thing, bulbous, with thin wings of stretched skin and tendrils like tree roots, unwieldy hands with massive, sword-like talons... but that face! The face that stared towards her in the firelight was all too human, with a man's eyes, patches of blond hair, and a smile that looked for all the world as though someone had stretched a human mask over a much larger head.

Accursed, she thought, and decidedly not like the Princess or her friends.

The creature laughed.

"My," it said, voice breathy with a gurgle behind it, "how dearly the little flies want to bite. Bite off more than they can chew."

Ukko backed towards the rest of them as the thing advanced, lumbering forward.

"Do they know when they look death in the eyes? Do they bow in prostration before a god?"

"We do not fear you," Ukko declared.

"Then it is ignorant," the creature hissed, stumbling forward. "They will know fear before they die."

It took another lurch forward, and Ukko shouted his command.

"Ground it!" he cried. Acacia rushed forward, and saw the others doing likewise, moving to surround the creature. Seija struck first, her meteor hammer sailing through the air to sweep the creature's wing. But the monster reacted in a flash, tendrils lashing out. One struck Acacia at the waist, and almost coiled around her before she dropped to avoid it. That thing was fast!

Acacia rolled away and got her feet back under her in time to see the beast surge at Ukko in a flurry of saber claws, lightning fast but not quite fast enough to pass Ukko's guard. It had grabbed Launo with a tentacle, and Taavi and Maria were on their backs. Seija still stood, but she struggled to pull her meteor hammer from its grasp, a feeler coiled around the length. She dug her heels into the earth and seemed to be losing ground.

"You think you can resist?" the creature crooned. "You think your pathetic, human spirit won't fail even before your flesh does? You know nothing!"

Acacia circled behind the thing. She held her blades carefully, maneuvering towards its blind spot. As she did, the beast whirled on her and surged, and it was all Acacia could do to back off in the face of its advance. In the motion, Seija, unwilling to release her weapon to the enemy, was pulled from her feet and slung around, knocking Ukko flat before it finally released its grip on the meteor hammer. The monster reared up, and Acacia feared what would follow, but then flopped backwards. Acacia saw Maria dodge to the side, and as it turned away from her noted a gash on its back... a gash that was slowly closing.

"You think you wound me? You believe you can inflict pain upon a god?"

"You aren't any god," Maria spat. "You're just an overstuffed mushroom!"

"How to repay such insults? Shall I flay you slowly, or eat you alive and screaming when I've done with the rest?"

Seija struck. Her meteor hammer smashed into the stretched wing, shattering bone and rending flesh, until half its length was torn off the rest of the membrane by weight.

That severed patch sizzled and transmuted, becoming a blob of bloody, gray-red tissue that might have weighed as much as the half a wing.

The beast turned on her and barreled forward. Acacia darted in, ducking one lashing tendril and dodging to the side of another before burying her blades into the soft flesh of the monster's body. As she struck, a tendril hammered her from behind, slamming her into its body, stunning her for a second, and driving her swords in up to the hilt.

Acacia didn't see what happened next, but she felt the creature lurch. Better than she had fared against Baudouin, Acacia held her swords tight, and twisted them to carve a massive gash in the monster's flank as it pulled away. When she could see the battle again, the thing had hoisted Launo by his ankle and was cutting at him with one claw as it forced Ukko back with the other. Launo, for his part, was holding his own remarkably well for being dangled upside down, but had taken at least one gash to his side that Acacia could only hope was no more than a flesh wound.

Acacia redoubled her own efforts, advancing slowly, using her blades to cut and parry alike. She could be kept away from the main body, but as long as none of the tentacles got the better of her, she was better off. Taavi, to her left, seemed to have the same idea, advancing shield-first. Maria, however, seemed to have other ideas.

"Or are you the god of things that cut like warm butter?" she shouted as she made a leaping strike that severed the tendril holding Launo. The knight landed hard and stayed sprawled on the ground at least a moment while the severed part once again sizzled and reduced to a chunk of half-rotted gore.

"Insolent whore!" the creature shouted. "Still thy tongue!"

It lashed out with one claw, and Maria brought her massive blade up to parry. The impact drove her back.

"You're one to talk, ugly," she grunted.

Acacia had made her way inside the guard. This time, instead of aiming to stab for some vital organ deep in the mass, she began to make swift cuts, hoping to sever something and keep its counter-attacks off her. For a moment, she seemed to have the hang of it, but then a massive blob of flesh surged and slammed into her, knocking her back.

Acacia found footing quickly enough to see the monster roiling, changing. Its wings had become bladed appendages of bone, and it had sprouted thick, powerful legs. Its body, though still bulbous and hunched, elongated, putting its engorged head, mouth now drooling over sharp teeth, at the end of a long and flexible neck, still with that warped mockery of a human face. Many tendrils still dangled from it, though the three or four largest had become something of a tail.

Acacia looked up at the creature and could no longer tell if they had hurt it at all. The steaming piles of rotted monster-flesh were still strewn about the battlefield, but was there really any less of it now than there was before? It honestly seemed to have grown.

"Kill it, you idiots!" Ulfr shouted, apparently having been roused somewhere in the prior fighting. "Isn't that what you're supposed to be good for?"

Not even Maria made a retort. They had the monster surrounded, and however it had grown, they had bested larger before. But though they coordinated their attacks, coming at it from every angle, the thing was now more agile than ever. Attempt after attempt was repulsed, and Acacia and the others forced to fall back or suffer whatever it would do to them. Ulfr continued shouting, rather than helping the battle, demanding more aggression.

Acacia was on the defensive. She'd strike at the head of the beast if she could, but for now she had to do her best to avoid her own death.

As the fighting continued, she realized she was losing ground, less and less able to perform any sort of counter attack, more and more on the back foot. Her eyes darted left and right and she saw Launo, hurt and struggling, Maria having to battle at the edge of her reach. She glanced, and saw Seija attempt a bold strike. For a moment it seemed like she might actually earn their first clean hit against the monstrosity's new form, but then the bony appendage that had once been a wing lashed out, and severed the meteor hammer's cord mid swing, the head sailing off over the beast and Seija left to stumble and fall with the sudden loss of balancing weight.

The creature turned to her, putting Acacia to its back. She tried to advance as best she could, but for her trouble its tails battered her, sending her sprawling yet again.

Acacia heard a shout, and saw Taavi running forward. He was at its right shoulder, menaced more by its claw and wing-blade than the tendrils that vexed Acacia. Leading with his shield, he charged at it, but where he should have fallen back or dodged the countering swipe, he just kept going, slamming into its bulk and stabbing it with his sword, but taking a deep slash across his back from the wing-blade for his trouble.

The creature turned its head. It struck at Taavi with both paws, tearing away his shield and crumpling it like it was a dry leaf. Still Taavi fought back, cutting as best he could, driving forward rather than withdrawing with at least his life.

And in a moment, Acacia saw what he was doing... he had

the creature's full attention.

Acacia looked at what awaited her, focusing on the back that was turned her way. A flash of memory came to her, and she ran forward, leaping over the tails and using her momentum to propel herself up its stooped back, until she came to the mound of its hunch, which is when she threw herself ahead, swords first. She drove her blades between its wings, and the creature lurched downward. Acacia held on for dear life, fearing its strikes less than what might happen if she was thrown to the ground. Thus, she saw when its head dipped, and Maria and Ukko rushed in from opposite to take their swings at the beast's exposed neck. Maria struck first, and cleaved a deep gash into its neck. The beast reared back, and Acacia, hoping she was more than useless atop it, threw her weight forward. Its bulk lurched down again, its neck low, and Ukko's strike bit into the monster where Maria had wounded it, and parted its head entirely from its body.

The body toppled over onto its side, and Acacia tried to throw herself free, ripping her blades from its back. She fell onto one of the bony wings, and felt something sharp slash near her hip. She rolled away, not entirely of her own volition, as the wing flailed upwards, raking across her side and tossing her a bit to finally come to rest with an agonizing impact on a rock.

The pain blinded Acacia for a moment, and she struggled to not scream, and to get her feet under her. She clutched her side, hand grasping through tattered clothing to find three long scratches and that one, deeper gash at her hip, blood oozing over her belt.

She heard a gurgling voice speak.

"But I... I am eternal..."

Her vision cleared enough that she thought she made out what followed, Maria stabbing her grand sword through the severed head and into the earth below.

For once, she didn't have anything witty to say. The body of the beast was still, and slowly losing distinction, melting into a gangled mass of indistinct flesh.

Slowly, Acacia limped over. Launo advanced as well, dropping his hammer and shield as he held his right arm to his body. Seija struggled up, at first crawling, but while Acacia had set her feet towards the head, unable to think of anything more, she could see Seija making her way for Taavi.

"Taavi?" Seija called dropping to her knees again beside him. "Taavi!"

Acacia wiped her eyes and tried to see. There was so much blood, the entire world too red and dark to tell where any of it had come from, but Taavi... she could tell he'd lost an arm. How much more was impossible to say.

Seija cradled his form as Ukko approached. She looked up at him, looking like the vulnerable youth Acacia never thought she'd see her friend as.

Ukko knelt beside him, and after a second lowered and shook his head.

"He's gone," Ukko said, choking back a sob of his own.

As Acacia arrived at the scene, she saw for herself – his right arm was gone, as was a large chunk of his right chest, and most of his gut. He was still, his breath already ended, blood cooling.

Seija looked up at the rest of them.

Ukko gritted his teeth, preparing to speak.

"He..." Seija said. "He gave himself up for... for us."

Ukko managed to restrain his own voice when answering. "His sacrifice will not be forgotten."

Seija lifted herself, and though Acacia could see that it pained her, held out Taavi to Ukko.

"Take care of him," she said. "I..."

She stumbled upwards, back to her feet, then over to where the severed head lay. She ripped Maria's sword from the ground, and kicked the ball of flesh over to the rest of them.

The face had become more human than ever – even fully human, and Acacia recognized it as the Hyperborean man who had been with Esteri.

At least, she recognized it for the split second before Seija brought Maria's sword down on the visage, spattering blood and cleaving it open. She struck again, and again, seemingly determined to grind the head of the beast to paste.

"Cease that at once, you cretin!" Ulfr demanded. Seija paused a moment, and turned towards him, and Acacia thanked her lucky stars she couldn't see Seija's face, because whatever her expression had been, it silenced Ulfr at once and made him jump back, away from Seija.

Seija went back to her work, the wet noise of her strikes continuing until it was replaced with Seija's own heavy panting, and she slumped to her knees, the sword left in the unrecognizable pile of gore that had been the target of her aggression. With Seija exhausted and utterly spent on the ground, Ulfr approached again.

"You louts made quite a mess," he hissed. "Of all the things I had thought to have to report to your king, incompetence was not"-

"One of our number is dead," Ukko said, cutting the Hyperborean off, "a braver soldier than whom you could not ask for. You, on the other hand, did not see fit to raise your hand against our enemy at all. Have a little respect, or get out of my sight."

Ulfr sneered, but held his tongue for a moment, pacing towards what used to be the body of the beast.

"All the same," he said, "you managed to not utterly fail to gain us an unexpected windfall."

He removed a palm-sized metal box from his belt pouch, and a wand of similar make. He touched the wand to the sizzling corpse, rolling the tip across its bloody surface until the box emitted an eerie note and a red glow.

Ulfr grinned.

"Prepare a sledge. This corpse must be transported to Hyperborea at once."

"First," Ukko said through clenched teeth, "we will bury our dead and see to our wounded. Then, if we are able, one of us will return to the nearest town by horse to get you a cart, and"-

"Your mission is to obey me!" Ulfr snapped. "Or have you forgotten?"

"Our concern is first and foremost for Princess Esteri," Ukko replied, "who you have said must come through that mountain door. As best as we can, we must be prepared for her. You can accept that, or you can test King Piru's faith in my word against yours all you please."

Ulfr said nothing, but stalked back to his bedding.

After that, Acacia, Launo, and Seija's hurts were all seen to. It would be some time for any of them to recover wholly, but they sutured Acacia's wound, and splinted Launo's broken arm, and wrapped Seija's chest to help her broken ribs, and then lesser hurts were seen to, as well as could be done.

By dawn, the body was shrunken and still, a horrible amalgam of human features in a featureless blob. The head was still ruined, unchanged from when Seija ceased her assault upon it, but there were times Acacia could swear the mass that used to be a face was looking at her, mocking her.

In the light, they set about the grim task of laying Taavi to rest. The ground was hard, the work bitter, and Ulfr ever eager to have them shroud the body somewhere and be done with it, but Acacia felt she had failed him enough already. She wouldn't fail to honor him. None of them would.

CHAPTER XXV

Esteri

In Esteri's opinion, it had taken far too long to head back to the Door in the Mountain. She had seen them at its mouth – Ukko and Erikis – but she feared that the moment would pass, and with the vision in the past she couldn't say if the appointed time was day or night, nor how Ukko nor Erikis would fare. She feared that Erikis would strike some bargain with Ukko, granting lies for service.

Radegond lead the way as they entered the narrow pass to the open door of the mountain, but Esteri followed close on her heels. About when she could see the door ahead of them, the rocks on either side looming very tall indeed, she heard a shout from the far end. Radegond gritted her teeth.

"Well," she said, "someone's seen us. You might want to stay back, in case we have to weather an ambush."

"If there's an ambush," Esteri countered, "better me than someone who can't see it coming."

Radegond gave an appreciative nod, and said no more of it. Esteri saw a shadow enter the frame of the door and wait. When she got closer, she thought she recognized the outline well enough.

"Lord Ukko!" she called.

"Hail, Princess." he replied, and Esteri moved ahead past Radegond, who stepped aside to allow it. The others kept pace behind her.

The view past Ukko, what little Esteri could see of it, was a matter of wonder. There was a cart there, and in its back a shrouded mass. Esteri could see two of the 'Slayers' there as well, the black-haired woman who had seemed friendly and the one who had hurt Gelvira, both sitting on the back of the cart, looking haggard. Then, into view stepped Ulfr.

"Now!" the Hyperborean shouted.

No one budged.

"Strike now!" he demanded.

"Forgive our current company," Ukko said. "He appears to have forgotten the main drive of our mission, which is your return, safe and whole, to Kalest."

"Disobedient wretch!" Ulfr shouted. "The king will know of your insubordination!"

"You see now," Esteri said, "what company my father keeps?"

"I must admit," Ukko said, "I have a mind to discuss the appointment with his majesty when next we have the opportunity."

That seemed to shut Ulfr up. He went to the cart and began barking orders at some of the others regarding that.

"If you will forgive me saying," Ukko said, "your number seems... diminished since our last, unfortunate meeting."

"It is," Esteri replied, "and not entirely by your own."

Ukko gave a grave nod.

"One of them, the Hyperborean who was with you..."

"What about Erikis?" Esteri demanded, sharply.

Ukko motioned towards the cart, and they peeled back the cover, revealing the corner of a bloody mass, and a ruined head with strings of blond hair.

"We believe he attacked our number in the night," Ukko replied as the cover was lower again. "Though under the circumstances..."

Esteri's vision came to her mind. She thought she remembered blood.

"He betrayed us," Esteri said quickly. No doubt Ukko thought Erikis had been on the same side of, if not her, than at least the same side as Radegond and the others. "As your

Hyperborean no doubt intends to betray you. What are you doing with the body?"

"That is not your business!" Ulfr shouted.

"It is... his business," Ukko said through gritted teeth, "in which we aid him by your father's orders."

"My father is not in his right mind," Esteri repeated.

Ukko looked away. "So you have said before."

Esteri gritted her teeth. She glanced past Ukko to Ulfr. Why had they loaded the remains of Erikis onto a cart? The man had declared himself to be a god... however much or little of what he told them was true, she certainly didn't want Ulfr to get his way.

"Stand aside," Esteri said. "We don't have a quarrel with you, only with Ulfr."

"You hear!" Ulfr shouted. "Strike! They would strike me, your king's voice in this land!"

"Please," Esteri said, "if you truly wish to do what is right, you'll help us bring that man to justice, or at least permit it."

"I would know his crimes," Ukko replied.

"Your crime will be treason if you do not protect me!" Ulfr shouted.

"For one, he was one of three Hyperboreans who made Baudouin what he became. And directly after we spoke in Lysama, he tried to kidnap me, a fate from which I was only spared by the vigilance of my friends."

"Lies!" Ulfr shouted. "She is insane, Accursed! You cannot trust her words!"

Esteri found her hand in her pocket. Her fingers clasped around a cold bit of metal, and she retrieved the talisman – the one Ulfr had used to control her. She held the thing up by its chain.

"Ask him to explain this."

Ukko took one look at it. "No doubt of Hyperborean make," he said. She watched as Ulfr backed up to the cart, the two of Ukko's number who were on their feet facing him.

"He tried to use it to control me, like a puppet."

"Like Baudouin," the brown-haired woman – Seija, Esteri recalled – said, struggling to her feet from her place in the cart. The blonde woman held her massive sword upraised, waiting for orders.

Ukko stepped aside. "We are at your service, majesty."

The blonde woman charged, but Ulfr stepped inside her reach and struck. She fell backwards after that, clutching her gut. The girl with black braids started to stumble to her feet but before she could, Ulfr leaped up at her, heaving her from the cart to the ground before clambering over the remains of Erikis into the driver's seat. Esteri rushed out of the door, and Radegond and the others were behind her. Radegond sprouted her wings, taking to the sky, while Hathus stepped forward, and launched a ball of fire at the cart. But it was already moving, and the flames only seemed to startle the shaggy ox, sending it rushing quickly forward. Esteri didn't run far – only Radegond had a chance to catch the stampeding ox and the villain riding the cart it pulled. Esteri watched as Radegond dove, and then a bright spark shot up from the cart, and burst with a bang when it struck her wing. Radegond flapped madly, but descended quickly, landing hard on one side of a hill as the cart bounded over it, and out of sight.

By then, Ukko had gotten the reins of a horse, and seemed prepared to give pursuit.

"Wait," Esteri called.

Ukko hesitated.

"You might catch him," Esteri said, "but you'd be alone. How much magic does he have left?"

"... We know not," Ukko said, "but I would trust myself against it."

Esteri's eyes darted to Seija, then back to Ukko.

"You seem more than reasonable," Esteri said. "We can try to hunt him here, or we can actually discern what's going on, before anything untoward happens."

Esteri followed Ukko's gaze as he looked over the others – Tius and Avina, in particular, near the mouth of the Door in the Mountain.

"Very well," he said, and stood down. Esteri looked, and Radegond was walking back towards them, seeming to be in no dire situation. Tius had a hand on Avina's shoulder, and the girl was glaring daggers at Seija, the reason for which was of course no secret. That woman, for her part, was ashen-faced, and Esteri noticed how her chest was bandaged and her breaths seemed shallow. Indeed, all of Ukko's band save the man himself seemed to be in sorry states. The blonde woman, Maria as Esteri would learn, remained sitting and muttered once or twice that it was just a flesh wound while introductions were made. Launo, a noble whose family Esteri had a dim recognition of, had his arm in a sling, while the friendly girl, Acacia, had bloody bandages on her flank.

Briefly, Esteri learned what had transpired since their encounter earlier in Tyrvad, how Ulfr had arrived with her father's writ and how they had been assailed by Erikis, and she was shown the fresh grave of one of their number, Taavi. Esteri in turn told her story, somewhat backwards she realized, beginning with their doings on the other side of the Door in the Mountain and Erikis' betrayal there, how Gelvira had fared, and then, at prompting, her tale of the events that had brought her to Lysama in the first place.

And that telling seemed to shake Ukko to the core, his gaze to the distance.

"Even hearing it from your lips," Ukko said, "and knowing you are in your right mind, it is hard to believe your father capable of such a treachery. Even now I believe he could not have deceived me in his grief at your loss, but I must admit that it could be a measure – a great measure – of regret."

Esteri nodded sadly. "I wish I could trust that I could go home," she said, "but I can't. Even if my father regrets what happened, even if he'd take me back, even though I'd like nothing more than to be a family again... there's still the queen to contend with."

"I did not have the pleasure, or displeasure as the case may be," Ukko said, "to spend much time in Queen Delphina's company. What little I did told me that she is shrewd, secretive, and absolutely has her husband's ear in all matters. I fear there is no graceful resolution to this."

Esteri looked up at Ukko.

"This seems terribly personal to you," she said.

Ukko nodded.

"Who are you, really?" Esteri asked. "You are no loyal young lord of the court, of that much I'm certain."

Ukko sighed. "I am a very old man, by the count of years. I have been away from my kin and country for a long time, in self-imposed exile since days when it truly seemed necessary to keep the peace."

"You mean," Esteri said, "you're one of the Accursed yourself."

"According to the best guesses of alchemist-kings past," Ukko said, "not exactly. Something about the flow of Æther in me being between Accursed and Human, I don't pretend to truly understand the technical details. I am, it seems, unaging thanks to a similar infusion to the one that changed you. Since my first lifetime, I have served the kings and queens of Kalest in times of need, spending the long years of peace to hone my skills beyond what I might have gained in a single lifetime."

"The Knight of the Mist," Esteri said. "I... read about you in the Chronicle."

Ukko smiled slightly. "It seems that story is particularly popular. The True Chronicle?"

Esteri shook her head. "I was trying to read that in order," she said. "I'd gotten to the reign of Queen Astrid the First. Well, I was about to start her section, at least. Is that before your time, or did none before write on you?"

Ukko laughed, a small and bitter thing.

"I'm sorry?"

"Likely mere pages from knowing what I would tell you," he said. "I trust all present company to take this to their graves."

Ukko's band quickly assented. Esteri swore to, and the rest of her friends followed suit.

"I first met Astrid when we were young. Too young to be concerned with politics, old enough to need someone to talk to while the council was in session. And when she was crowned so tragically early, I took the field out of a more personal loyalty than what I owed Kalest. I made of myself a great distinction, and she and I... we were headstrong and thought the world would bend to our wishes, especially when common men called me a hero." Ukko shook his head. "But the lords of the land threatened civil war, or revolt – not over me, but the remedy was that she would marry a respected one of their number. He was a good man, and very understanding. I think he knew even before Astrid was pregnant with our child. Certainly, at least one of her chambermaids did, and tried to do something about it. I'm still not sure why she thought to use some warped dilution of the cursed potion rather than ordinary poison. But the three of us – a queen, her king, and her consort – we deceived the world that the future heir was a legitimate child. Few beyond the royal family have ever known the truth. In some years, I realized that my son was growing up and my love was growing older while I was standing still. The truth of my condition was recovered from she who had done it, and to help preserve appearances I slipped into my self-imposed exile."

Esteri felt her jaw slack

"I am the ancestor both of you and your father," Ukko said. "It pains me in a way I have never known to have my descendants so bitterly at odds."

"I..." Esteri said. "Forgive me, this is more than I know how to take."

"I wish that this had been an easier introduction," Ukko said, "as I might wish the road forward were a clearer one."

"Grandfather," Esteri said, hesitatingly offering the honorific, "in my state, I can see what will happen, what may happen. But what I do not see is what I should do. I fear what

Ulfr's endgame may be, but I don't know whether we ought to pursue him, or if we would be better served challenging Queen Delphina... and my father if needs be."

"You wish my advice?" Ukko said.

"I do," Esteri replied.

"I would say you should return to the known world," Ukko said. "Where we stand now, I am not sure we can hope to unwind this web that Hyperborea has spun."

"Then Ulfr gets away?" Esteri asked.

Ukko closed his eyes.

"For now," he said. "If we slay him, what then? We are left with a monster's moldering corpse and no concept of what is or isn't safe to do with it. Oh, no doubt we could haul it back, perhaps bury it with the Ancestor Gods, but for all we know that could play very acceptably to the aims of Ulfr's masters. If, on the other hand, we make the deception known..."

"We might," Esteri said, "strip them of an important ally somewhere. At least we'd catch the notice of the rest of the continent. Who's with me?"

And the reply came, a chorus of all present, saying together and apart, "I am!"

CHAPTER XXVI

Ulfr

Ulfr fumbled with reloading the flare gun in the constantly jostling cart. It would have been hard enough to do with two hands, but with one it was nearly impossible. All the same Ulfr thanked his luck, and more than that his quick wit, for using that bit of Hyperborean 'magic' to put the others off pursuit, and that was the most important part. Never mind that Esteri still lived, never mind that Ukko and his band, chewed up as they were, were turned against their masters. In any other situation such an avalanche of failures would have doomed Ulfr to an ignominious demotion, but with the consolation prize in the back of the cart? That would see him hailed a hero, and granted the honors he was due. That was worth everything he had lost, everything he had suffered, and everything that had been botched through no fault of Ulfr's own.

Eventually, he got the flare gun loaded. Frequently, he looked behind himself for signs of pursuit. Ukko's band had horses, even if they may have scattered, and Ulfr was not foolish enough to assume that his cart was faster than a rider, as few of those as there might be left able to follow.

No pursuit came in the first day, nor as Ulfr pushed on, driving the ox in a steady pace through the night. He let it rest the next day, and when it was set well enough to walking caught some rest himself. No pursuit came. By dusk, Ulfr thought it safe enough to stop for the night. He hadn't started with that much of a lead; if they were going to pursue him, they would have caught up already.

There, in the fading twilight, he inspected the thing in the back of the cart. The head was largely unchanged, what was left of it. The mass of flesh that was the body seemed almost as though it was breathing, heaving slowly in and out. Ulfr himself was too late a generation to have the Sight, but even he could tell what he was looking at – the immortal part of a dead god. He contented himself that it wouldn't be getting up on its own any time soon, covered it well, and rested.

The next day, Ulfr made a decision. He might have headed for Tyrvad's capitol and gotten aid from the ambassador there, an armed escort to the coast, and a call ahead to be sure that he wouldn't have to wait for the pickup of his cargo, but the ambassador might attempt to claim the glory for himself, and that was something Ulfr could ill afford. He would make his own way to the western coast, near the Lysama-Tyrvad border, where Hyperborean ships often passed. It was a path that would take at least a week, more likely ten days were he not willing to set a grueling pace, and he would have to avoid towns in order to avoid questions about the mass of undying flesh that he carried. The closer Ulfr got to his goal, the more he drove himself forward. He shorted himself on sleep, shorted himself on food, and drove his ox as hard as he could without risking the beast's death, as that would be an inconvenience that Ulfr did not need. Yet he did not feel the grueling pace nor his grumbling stomach. There was glory to be won.

At last, his road met its end, by the shore of the sea, and after three days of waiting there, in which the ox was made to serve for meals, his flare gun found its employ, alerting a passing ship that an agent of Hyperborea demanded their aid.

They sent a landing boat to shore at first, and hailed him. Simple fishers, but that was enough for Ulfr's needs.

"Hail," their leader called.

"You!" he demanded. "I need to contact the Elder Council."

"Our ship has a radio," he said, "but we don't have a direct line..."

"I'll get one," Ulfr snarled. "Let me aboard."

And, cowed, his countrymen did. Ulfr stepped onto the deck and muscled his way at once to the small cabin with the radio, only bothering to growl demands for directions. Being surrounded by the works of Hyperborea was a mixed feeling. On one hand, he had so much fun with the backwards people of the continent, but on the other, no hawk could match the convenience of Hyperborean science.

"Dispatch," he barked into the receiver. "Dispatch!"

"This is dispatch," the operator replied, crackling with static. "To whom do we speak? Over."

"This is Ulfr – agent of the Elder Council, assigned to mainland operations. Call code forty-three-twenty-six. Four three two six. Requesting immediate contact with my proper superiors."

There was silence on the other side.

"Over," Ulfr growled.

"Understood, sir," the Dispatch said. "Confirmed four-three-two-six. We'll patch you through straight away. Dispatch out."

There was static again, and then another voice, curt and female.

"Report, Agent," the voice demanded. "Over."

"Svanna," Ulfr laughed. "Is that you, down to manning the radios?"

"Cut the crap," Svanna or whoever it was said. "You called in a forty-three-twenty-six, so this had better be good. Over."

"I have it," Ulfr said.

There was a long pause before Svanna filled in the 'over' for herself.

"Speak plainly you little freak," she replied. So it was Svanna. "If you're prank messaging a four-three-two-six I promise the council will have your head. Over."

"I have the Godhead," Ulfr replied. "It's seething in the back of a cart, would you like me to leave it there to rot a little more, or would you have our superiors make my return of our prize to its proper place possible?"

There was a pause, then the reply.

"Where are you? Over."

"I hailed a fishing boat," Ulfr replied. "Currently in some miserable little cove off Tyrvad. Worry not, the cart is still in sight."

"Wait there. Over."

Ulfr waited. As much as he enjoyed riling her, it might have been something of a misfortune to have gotten Svana on the other side, because she made no secret of hating him even more than most anyone he had worked with.

Several minutes passed, then the radio crackled to life again.

"You will be commandeering that vessel," Svana declared. "Have the captain contact Dispatch if there is any disagreement. Preparations will be made for your landing. Over and out."

Ulfr smiled and started doing what was most natural to him – giving orders to people who didn't want to take them.

***

The crew of the ship was miserable company, and the accommodations even worse. Things didn't get much better on the second day when the blood that oozed from Ulfr's load tainted their catch, causing the fish they had caught to become a rank spoil. Ulfr assured them with every non-binding promise he could make that they would be compensated for the trouble, and then gleefully suggested the layabouts work on doing something about the stench while Ulfr, of course, took some much desired rest and relaxation. They called him a sorry cuss and worse, but could do nothing. When they reached Hyperborean shores, the ship was escorted to a special dock, but there Ulfr would be disappointed. Where he had wished a grand triumph up to the royal palace where the Elder Council conducted their schemes and wove their arcana, the ship was boarded in quiet. First came soldiers, and on seeing them Ulfr stilled his indignation at the quiet greeting, for they wore the formal white-and-gold uniforms of honor guard and quickly ushered the whole of the crew on shore and out of earshot. And indeed one of the Elder Council boarded after.

Ulfr couldn't fail to recognize her. Even though the woman dressed down, eschewing the normal formal dress in which councilors could do little more than shamble, she had her badge of office and ornate mantle. And even if that were not in place, Ulfr would not have mistaken her for a common trollop, for like all of the First Generation she had an aura of majesty and grace that precluded her being some younger sister of Delphina of Kalest like she might have appeared to be at a glance.

And this, Ulfr thought, in a rare moment of introspection, was someone he could not afford to offend. Even the youngest of the First Generation were millennia old and wielded powers far beyond those of mortals, never mind their political authority.

She stomped up to the bloated remains of the Godhead, had the tarp torn away, and inspected the thing, pacing around it in slow circles, taking in the full sight and no doubt more.

"Impressive," she said at last.

"I only"-

"Not you," she replied. "This. Impressive of it to have hidden for all those years... impressive that it still clings to existence with its intellect destroyed, rather than collapsing into so much rotten meat at your gross manhandling."

"It was not I!" Ulfr protested. "The Kalesti slew it, hacked and slashed long after it was subdued, senseless brutes. I told them"-

"Silence."

Ulfr's protests stopped cold.

"Do you know who I am?" she asked, not even looking at Ulfr. Without giving him a chance to respond, she continued, "I am Saga, properly Councilor Saga, head of covert affairs. I normally take a hands-off approach of course, delegating to people like Njall which is one reason why we have not before met in person, but that doesn't mean I don't know what goes on in my branch. I read every report and file generated regarding exploits on the continent, which includes your mission reports and personnel files."

Ulfr swallowed.

"Njall had some very colorful things to say about you," Saga declared, "as did Ambassador Ormr. The less said about Colonel Svanna's remarkably out of character breach of professionalism in regards to your brief partnership, the better. Psychological analysis reports both sociopathy and narcissism, which until this year was narrowly counterbalanced by a track record of success in dealing with continental situations. Do you understand?"

"... No," Ulfr admitted. He was furious, but also totally lost, unsure what any of this had to do with his much more recent and much greater victory.

"In these current events, there has been very much the reverse trend – a string of failures you believe will be erased by this, admittedly unexpectedly great, windfall. Were you hoping for a parade? Really, I had half a mind to eliminate you in order to preserve secrecy until the Day of Ascendance was prepared. You may yet be rewarded for taking advantage of your good fortune, but first I must ask you one question. I expect you know the penalty if you answer falsely. Is your mark, the cursed princess of Kalest, dead?"

"... No."

Saga sighed. "Then before you are awarded the pension and regenerative treatment you are due, I will expect you to mitigate your mistake. I have transit arranged for the queen of Kalest to be shepherded here in respect for her fanciful demands for a place of honor at the Ascendance. You will be going to Kalest as well."

"I?" Ulfr asked. "A chaperon? Or do you mean her demise?"

"You won't be coming here with her." Saga signaled for

one of her guards, who opened a briefcase for her. From it, she withdrew several folders, leather folios in the style that Hyperborea showed off to the continent, and handed them to Ulfr. "After she has gone, if you don't receive a stop signal indicating her good behavior on her visit by its appointed time, you will deliver this evidence to the King of Kalest. Familiarize yourself with its contents, and you and Ormr will have the task of directing the king appropriately. Either way, when the situation is resolved, you may return with the envoys that ferry her."

Ulfr gritted his teeth. It sounded like a terribly dull mission, even if the ends would be amusing, but his stump itched fiercely.

"I would conduct the mission better if I had two hands," Ulfr said.

"And reveal to those not of the blood at Kalest's court that our magic can regrow lost limbs?" Saga replied. "I think not. You will go as you are. That is not a request."

Saga marched off, back the way she had come, and signaled to her troops, who began to shepherd Ulfr his own direction, leaving him wondering how his victory had gone so sour.

CHAPTER XXVII

Delphina

Delphina remembered what her mother had taught her about Hyperborean magic. There were, she said, two kinds of magic. The first was simply a matter of knowledge. It would seem like magic, but only because of a thousand years or more of murdered luminaries, stolen inventions, and burned libraries keeping the people of the continent without the benefit of discovery. What exactly that first magic, Hyperborean technology, entailed, her mother would not or could not say beyond some fanciful facts of taming lightning, speaking across miles in an instant, or sailing ships against the wind and tide. Things to keep in mind, but not things Delphina could try to copy while young and headstrong.

The second sort of magic was the art arcane. The Elder Council were naturals at it, as were some in the second or third generations, but it was something that anyone – at least anyone of the blood – could learn. There were those who thought it just another science, but the way that the Art altered the physical world and its practitioners interacted with energies beyond mortal ken set it apart. There were no tools, no instruments except for will and blood and rituals to focus both to the proper end. Few younger than the fourth or fifth generation bothered attempting to learn its ways, but Delphina's mother had been a prodigy, and she'd taught Delphina everything she knew.

It had been, Delphina reflected, not a particularly useful skill. The appropriate charms warded off wrinkles or blemishes of the skin, while others could grant a greater and more imposing presence in the minds of those who laid eyes upon her, or as she seldom used, have the opposite effect to allow one to walk largely unnoticed where she wished. That was as much of an inroad as arcana made into Delphina's daily life, cosmetics and parlor tricks. Larger rituals, ones she had studied intently, came with costs that Delphina wasn't willing to pay and didn't have the Hyperborean tools to shortcut. And their results, while wondrous and impossible things, were seldom applicable to a mortal. Delphina had been put even more off attempting anything that might have been over her head when her mother died in an arcane 'accident' that she had never proved was a Hyperborean assassination, nor openly admitted she thought as much of. But Delphina had still studied, kept her wits sharp as her mother had insisted she do. And Hyperboreans didn't care about vanity charms or other small magic, so let them think that was as much as Delphina practiced.

Her mother had not just given Delphina a general education in the framework of Arcana., but had also instructed her in the specifics of the Ascendance. It was a ritual that had been prepared for generations, and was in some ways the deepest secret of Hyperborea. Since bringing the matter up to Ormr, Delphina had made doubly sure of her food tasters and slept with one eye open, but she was of the blood, and had the right to know the promise. She hoped that was all they believed she knew or less, that there was simply some glory to be had. She had been careful to not speak in technical terms.

What she knew was that the Hyperboreans of the first generation – the Elder Council – were the sons and daughters of a god. It was a being of great and wild power that once walked the earth in innumerable guises, and in some took human women for its mates. The children of those unions were immortal, barring accidents, and had powers that other peoples did not. The Godhead spirited its consorts and children from their native lands to Hyperborea, the seat of its power, to dwell in what splendors it created. The sons and daughters of the god had each other, and also found mortal partners in visits to the mainland, and thus the Hyperborean race was born, all after the first generation being mortal, if somewhat longer lived than those not of the blood.

In time, Delphina knew, the people of Hyperborea conspired to kill their sire. They used their magical powers to guide and arm folks of the continent's then-great power, Tyrvad, and set those folks against the God that birthed them. It was not a difficult task, or at least the tales Delphina's mother knew claimed such, for that divinity had become the last to walk the world openly, and was a tyrannical sort, doing to mortals whatever it pleased, which very seldom pleased the mortals.

Any Hyperborean could be expected to know as much, and some of those stories, like the battle of the 'ancestor gods' of Tyrvad and a being of vast and evil power, were known in the rest of the world as well. What Delphina had never admitted to knowing was that the body of the god, not quite deceased, still rested in what had been its palace in Hyperborea, and that the Elder Council sought, ages after his fall, to claim the power that deity had wielded for their own. To this end they needed Accursed, breeding grounds for divine blood, because there was some missing part required for their magic to function.

What Delphina knew she had to hide that she knew were the ritual patterns for the Ascendance, the lines upon which power would be transferred to give the fallen god true death and the Hyperborean masters new power. She had faint sketches made under the guise of play and her mother's instruction, and she had committed them all to memory. Her mother had known them as one of Hyperborea's most promising students, and she had been certain that Delphina understood their inner workings as far as could be possible. There were precious few outside the Elder Council, Delphina was aware, who had even a fraction of the knowledge she had with regards to the actual magic to be done, and how it must have galled them when her mother defected with it.

But Delphina felt she had played her part well, the country bumpkin struggling for the table scraps of her better kin. They underestimated her, and that was exactly the way she needed it to be. The diplomatic escort arrived at the palace of Kalest with all the pomp and circumstance that was required of it and nothing more. Ulfr, it seemed, was being delivered back to her home at the same time as she was departing. That was worrisome – they would have sent him ahead if they meant to indulge her desire to punish the loathsome cur for failing to kill Esteri, and if he had managed to destroy the wretched child then surely the ambassadors, particularly Ormr, would have tried to leverage their eventual success to political advantage. With those options ruled out, it was evident that he was here on business, and Delphina doubted very much that the business was Esteri being back in the country.

On the other hand, she couldn't worry too much about the matter. Very soon, it would be immaterial. As would Esteri – Delphina would see to it. Ulfr himself might follow, depending on just how charitable a mood Delphina was in, which wasn't something she was inclined to give any mind to before events unfolded at least a little more.

The road from Kalest to Hyperborea was shorter than it might have been, thanks to another Hyperborean lie. The descendants of the god claimed that they had no territorial interests on the mainland, but that was not entirely true: they might not have territorial aims, but they did have a few, small holdings scattered throughout the world for their use. It was a fact that kings and queens did know – Hyperborea maintained secretive 'embassies' at the grace of past monarchs. Delphina herself knew of three throughout the world – one on the eastern edge of the Kalest-Tyrvad border, one on a small Indris island, and one deep in eastern Arynias. A few days of smooth travel and fine accommodations took her to the first of those three Hyperborean holdings.

It was a cold place, nestled in a shadowed depression, with

high walls all around so that no one who approached on accident could rightly say what was within. The walls were made
of gray stone, with no apparent seams for the bulk of the structure, topped with coils of metal wire that bristled with small
spines. It flew no flags nor banners, and the only indication
of its owners were small seals on the heavy, steel doors that
were the only ingress or egress apparent. The doors opened
for Delphina's carriage, and she was ushered inside. There,
there were several low buildings of a similar construction to
the wall, and between them the roads were packed dirt save
for one long, straight strip of dark stone, perfectly flat and
smooth. There could be no doubt on the interior of the magic
that Hyperborea possessed, whether it was one kind or the
other. Delphina suspected that what had let them construct
the space was simply hoarded knowledge, for as much as she
knew of the other she couldn't see it leaving this sort of lasting
impact, squat and dull.

Delphina was shown out of her carriage, and escorted
quickly towards the stone road. At the end of it was... Delphina didn't know how to describe the thing, a white, cru-
ciform object, larger than the carriage, though its main body
might have been smaller. It stood on three tiny wheels, and
its body had glass windows, which made its status as a conveyance obvious. The front came to a sharp point from which
protruded two small arms. The larger arms that gave the object its overall shape were long and broad but very flat, and
situated atop the bulk of the body. The rear end, beyond the
windows, featured what Delphina took to be a set of three
small arms like the ones on the main body, a mirrored pair to
the left and right and a larger one pointing straight up. It was
clearly her destination, though, so Delphina kept her head up
and did not show misgivings, treating the thing as though it
was as natural as any other means of travel.

Soon enough she was inside, a Hyperborean driver of some
description in the frontmost seat and an attache beside her,
when the conveyance roared to life. The entire structure rum-

bled, and the small arms at the front began to spin, so swiftly that they appeared to become a transparent disk. The contraption began to move forward, swiftly, and then jostled and, hesitatingly at first and thereafter with some measure of grace lifted into the sky.

A flying machine! Delphina did her best to not display any surprise, nor any unease at the discovery. It did explain how Hyperboreans sometimes seemed able to travel as swiftly as the wind. The flying machine wheeled in air, and set itself to the north. Delphina gazed out from the window, hoping to maintain a bored expression for appearances. Kalesti and Tyrvad, perhaps even Arynias territory raced by under them. There were no sharp distinctions, like the borders on the maps in the war room, just land, hilly, forested, mountainous and snow-capped, the bright sparkle of streams and the quilt-like outlay of fields. She could not see what banners they flew in the townships, tiny for their distance. Delphina supposed that it did not matter. Kalest's banner would fly over all, that was the plan.

Soon the sea was beneath them, a ruffled expanse of blue-to-black, vast and desolate. After a few hours of travel, while they were over water, the pilot of the craft picked up a small, black box connected to the glowing block at the front of the thing that Delphina had guessed were some of its controls.

"Control," he said, loud and clear into the box, "this is Diplomatic Escort Albatross, requesting landing. Over."

"This is Control," a distorted voice replied, echoing from the front of the flying machine. "Skies are clear, Albatross. You are clear for landing at field three. Over and out."

So, the vaunted Hyperborean distance-speaking magic Delphina's mother had spoken of. It sounded like the other person had their head in a cooking pot. Of course, the applications of even poorer communication across such gulfs of space were practically without number, but the artistry of its form left quite a lot to be desired, so Delphina was able to maintain her unimpressed veneer with only a little effort.

They banked over Hyperborea, and Delphina had her first sight of her ancestral land from the sky. And this land... it was far different than the countries of the continent. Its grand city, which was most of what she could see, was dark and glittering in the twilight, with what appeared to be tall towers that glowed like lanterns from countless... were those windows? Most of the towers seemed to have walls constructed almost entirely from glass. The flying machine gave the city a respectful distance in its circling and touched down, less gracefully than Delphina would have liked, on a strip of stone in a field bounded by fences of metal lattice. Delphina disembarked as well as she could, and was ushered to another conveyance, this one a somewhat obvious horseless carriage. The thing rumbled and roared like some angry beast, but once inside it Delphina found the means of transportation fairly luxurious, and by the way the landscape passed by when she looked out the window, incredibly swift.

They went up, mostly, skirting the city and heading along a winding road through the hills up to the Elder Temple, once the palace of the god and now the gathering place of the Elder Council of Hyperborea. That site was majesty she could understand – it was as though the whole top of a mountain had been carved and then further built upon, the pinnacle replaced with cyclopean towers and grand domes of stone, high and arching. According to Delphina's mother, the entire palace of Kalest might fit inside the grand rotunda, and seeing it from the outside Delphina did not doubt as much.

As majestic as it was, inside and out, it was also fairly austere. Hanging tapestries and colorful carpets couldn't entirely hide the the coldness of the stone construction. This was a place raised in an ancient age by a being that didn't understand human luxury to hold – perhaps imprison – its concubines and children. Every bit of it spoke of power, but very little of compassion.

Delphina decided very quickly that she quite liked the place. It projected the kind of grandeur that the world needed, and for the moment sorely lacked. The impression only became better when Delphina was shown where she would be quartered until the Ascendance – the room was furnished in a manner to which she was more accustomed. Servants attended her needs, bathing her in fragrant waters and bringing her deep red wine and fine food – fruit tarts, pale white cheese with crisp bread, roasted fish. Delphina saw that the servant who seemed wholly concerned with waiting on her tasted all of it, under the guise of generosity, for she had not been accorded a food taster. She doubted that her hosts would attempt anything so crass, but wasn't going to take chances.

The next morning was the day before the Ascendance would be attempted, and for Delphina that made it a very important day. She rose early, and the attendants that were placed with her did a superb job with her clothes and cosmetics, giving her the look of 'natural' perfection that she had so carefully cultivated. She made a show of applying a few wisps of her cosmetic magic. A minor fold in reality to bend light and give her face a subtle glow, ensuring her eyes weren't too shadowed, a little extra concealment for a blemish on her right wrist – the sorts of things that Ormr had already known she practiced. Hopefully, such a petty display of the Hyperborean art would distract from anything else she might do, put those who watched at ease, let them believe the Queen of Kalest nothing but a vain, preening creature.

Delphina could practically hear her mother's voice.

"They think of the great houses of this land as little more than fancy pets," she had said, "as something short of people. How aghast they were when I decided to join them, forgetting that it wasn't inability to do better that put the Kalesti where they are now."

That had been in some of her last good days. When Delphina was younger her mother had spoken more of the wonder of their ancestral homeland, but by the end she seemed to truly despise her former countrymen. A dangerous prejudice to hold at the best of times...

Well before most anyone else, Delphina found her way to the Grand Rotunda.

The second important thing about the Grand Rotunda was its size. It probably, Delphina considered, could hold the central structure of Kalest's palace as her mother had said, but not the outbuildings or the grounds. As befitted the Wanderers of the Birds' Wood, Kalest's palace was tight and tall, its corridors narrow and vaulted and its towers standing like mighty trees. The dome of the Grand Rotunda, however, might as well have been as high as the sky, especially as an orb like a silver sun hung suspended in air at its apex, filling the space with pale light.

The first feature to be noticed, though, was the Body of the God. It was gigantic, propped up on a stonework throne. The overall pattern of the body was human, though on a scale no human had ever existed upon, for it would stand, Delphina guessed, at least as tall as seven men. Fortunate, given his proclivities, that he could take other forms. Beyond the overall shape, though, the resemblance to anything human ended. The thing was as pale as fresh snow on the outside, and deep crimson where it was wounded, which was in countless places. Tendrils like strands of ivy thick as tree trunks spread from its back, flopping limply over the back and sides of the throne, their skin wrinkled and ash gray, The arms branched at the elbows, lesser forearms with gnarled hands branching away from the main arms, which ended in wicked talons. It was sexless, in a fit of irony, and its legs were like the legs of a bird with long ankles that almost appeared to be a second set of knees turned backwards from the proper way. Its shoulders were rolled forward and crowned with horns that looked almost like chimneys. And its face... that face was the stuff of nightmares. The lower half was dominated by a great, gaping maw, shaped like a downward-opened horseshoe, lined with curved and pointed teeth like a wolf's fang. And behind that row of teeth was another, and another, each with its barbs inward. There was no nose, nor hair nor ears, and the eyes were horrifically inhuman, wide like the eyes of a fish, and solid pools of welkin blue with a faded, dull sheen so that looking at them was like gazing through frosted windows at a winter sky.

But the feature that most drew Delphina's attention was the chest. It was splayed open, ribs pulled aside to expose viscera and nameless organs, and one part the nature of which was obvious: the heart of the creature, into which a massive sword had been buried to the hilt. As Delphina watched, the heart made a tentative attempt to beat, its pulse seemingly held in check by the weapon.

"There's no chance of reanimation, if that's what you're thinking."

Delphina looked to the speaker. It was a woman – no, a girl, she could not have been the senior of Delphina's hateful step-daughter – in a diaphanous dress of white silk, kneeling near where Delphina stood. In, Delphina noticed, a ritual circle. She looked at the lines drawn from that circle, which stood midway between a great circle drawn around the god, and one of a size between the two that surrounded a twisted lump of pulsating meat. She might have been cleaning up the place, but... was this slip of a girl the Conduit?

"Even if the blade were removed," she continued, "while the Godhead's biology might become more active, it lacks any mind or animating principle. It would, effectively, be coma-tose without hope of recovery."

"Interesting," Delphina said, hopefully in a way to get the woman to continue talking.

"That over there," she obligingly said, "is the missing piece. It's badly damaged, possibly not beyond repair because only mundane weapons were used to do the deed, but certainly be-yond its ability to repair itself in a timely fashion. Which is, of course, really all we need."

"I'm sorry," Delphina said, politely feigning ignorance of what she guessed, "you are?"

The girl stood and gave a respectful bow. "I am called Valdasa. And since I doubt that answers your question, I am she who will serve as the conduit of divinity. I shall mediate the power of this dead thing and redistribute it as needs be."

"Hm," Delphina voiced. "And may I ask how one so young got such a post?"

Valdasa shook her head, smiling. "It's not as though I petitioned for this duty. I was born for it."

"An interesting way of putting it."

Delphina knew the true answer, but only as one of many possibilities for the Conduit. Evidently, the elders of Hyperborea hadn't wanted to risk themselves with the possibilities of what would happen with the outflow of power after all.

"It's literally true," Valdasa said as though she recounted some vapid pleasantry about the weather. "My pedigree was carefully selected, and my mother and myself both received the best alchemical treatments that could be provided to enhance my ability."

"It sounds as though everything is prepared for," Delphina replied. Now, she thought, tell me something I can use.

Valdasa shrugged. "Nobody really knows what will occur tomorrow. After all, it has never been done, so the best guesswork of the Elder Council is just that. To the best of my instinct, energy from both parts of the Godhead will be channeled to this circle. When it interacts, it will attempt to form the True Godhead, but with myself as the flesh, it should coalesce within my soul, enabling me to take and then pass to others the eternal essence of the Godhead. In its current state, it should be incapable of gaining any cognition that would defy mine."

Delphina considered the girl's words. "That's a threat?"

"More now than when we had planned to use a Cursed One of sufficient potency to catalyze the reaction," Valdasa recounted, still unbelievably chipper. If anything she was becoming more animated as she discussed what was, admittedly, her life's work to this point. "But the tradeoff for the minuscule risk is that the proper reaction is nearly certain this way. Really, I hardly understand why the Elders bothered with ages of promoting the continentals to create Accursed and waiting for promising mistakes. I suppose no one knew it existed."

Delphina crossed her arms. "I hardly understand why they didn't simply use their own unwanted."

"Oh!" Valdasa said. "That's right... you would be Delphina of Kalest, correct? You wouldn't know – the potion doesn't work the same way on those of the blood. It can have a variety of effects, from poisoning to augmentation that reduces effective generation, depending on the Æther ratios and other preparation. There's been some success in serial treatment of those of the fifth generation and later to raise their potential to that of the prior generation to that of their birth. Assuming we still have a supply of Blood of the God after this, advances in alchemy might be able to render Second Generation like myself immortal like the First. Life Extension is an old pursuit in Alchemy, but only recently have synthetic reagents like..."

Delphina stopped listening. It was practically horrifying how much the girl loved to prattle on and on about such dry, technical details that Delphina didn't even understand. Eventually, Valdasa's recitation of some ungodly alphanumeric formula was interrupted by one of the quiet handlers, his presence sending her back to her kneeling position, no doubt worrying at the strings of magic, and ushered Delphina several paces away.

Delphina took the opportunity to inquire about her place of honor, and made no secret that what she was shown pleased her – a private box for her and a few servants to see to her had been placed near the central circle where Valdasa worked, facing the girl and, past her, the stands where the Elder Council of Hyperborea would assemble for their infusion of godliness.

Delphina didn't try to demand a share, a closer seat, a better view. A higher cushion, and a request for white wine were all the demands she made, petty things to keep up appearances. She talked plenty about her husband, about their aims for the continent, the small-thinking desires they thought were the limits of Delphina's ambition, the things of which Hyperboreans thought nothing.

It would be better if they continued to think nothing of her. Delphina was shown along through the halls of the great palace, filed past glass display cases holding artifacts of Hyperborea's past, gave only brief glances to the white-coated Hyperboreans who scurried through plain doors marked with colorful signs. She met briefly with Fjarri of the Elder Council and expressed pleasure with the honor being done her, imperiously as appreciation of what stoked her ego. There was ample time for leisure, and in those hours she seemed to simply recline and rest, languid like a well-fed cat, while in her mind she worked over every fundamental of arcane magic that she knew, focused her eyes to see the strings of reality, concerned herself entirely with the task ahead. Eventually, long after being left in darkness, she finally found some sleep.

The next day, Delphina was awakened practically at dawn. The scurrying servants attended her as they had before, and Delphina continued her show. She was shown to her place of honor as the Elder Council filtered into theirs, and other witnesses besides, farther out towards the walls of the Grand Rotunda. Food and drink were brought, and festivities were made. Musicians played, dancers performed, and several hours worth of speakers waxed dryly on about the significance of the day at hand.

Finally, Valdasa was brought forth, her entrance alone, all the trumpeters and attendants who were set to make it spectacular keeping a respectful distance from the girl, so that all eyes would be on her and only her. It wasn't a bad spectacle, and kept the focus where it ought to have been. Delphina would have to remember the technique for her own triumph. When she passed the throne of the old godhead, she cast aside her ornate train. Her hand plucked at the strings of reality like a harpist at her instrument and they parted, whisking the mass of fur, silk, and jewels away. Now that was a trick Delphina didn't know, and one that certainly would have been more useful than the strange corners of the art she intended to employ, just parting the empty air as though it were a stage curtain and tossing something unwanted through.

The girl might be a threat.

But then Valdasa stepped into the ritual circle and began her work. She teased the fabric of magic, nearly invisible even to Delphina, stirred it subtly, sent ripples along the tapestry of creation. It was slow, bitter work but Valdasa made it look like just more of the show, an exquisite dance as she directed energy here and there, using the circles of painted divine blood to help her direction. No doubt, it was the culmination of weeks of preparation, and Valdasa was totally absorbed in it. Blind, Delphina realized, to anything happening outside.

Delphina strained her senses to watch the flow of power, anticipating as the Elder Council no doubt did when the greater and lesser parts of a god would meet in the middle. Valdasa twisted them along the lines and circles, curving inward, feelers spiraling around each other tighter and tighter yet never touching. The eyes of the great body of the god seemed to glow as the silver sun dimmed with the shifts of power in the room, and the lesser body quivered faster, thrumming with anticipation.

Delphina stood up. Her timing had to be flawless.

Valdasa drew her hands inward, and the leading threads of power shot towards each other.

Delphina folded space. As best as she had ever imagined doing it, the trick would only last a split-second before snapping back to the way things had been before, maybe enough to dodge an arrow if you were lucky and your timing perfect. But here, a split-second was all Delphina needed. Reality reeled, and Delphina's eyes couldn't follow it fast enough. Fragments of her box, destined to recombine in a heartbeat, hung in air, Valdasa stood, clenched fists to her chest, about halfway to the elder council, the stone of the ground rippled and stretched like dough. Delphina stood in the center of the distorted circle.

The threads of power met. Delphina could feel them, inside her, and then a rush like a furious wind, icy cold yet burning like fire.

Delphina's heart beat. The heart of the god beat. The mass of flesh pulsed.

Reality snapped back into place and time seemed to start again, but Delphina didn't move as her place of honor reassembled. Valdasa was knocked flat at Delphina's feet, her eyes turning up as the last fragments crashed against one another with transcendent fury. Delphina could feel the what the god felt, the countless wounds, eons dangling between life and death on a stony throne. The dusty expanse of years without number. The patterns of the cosmos invaded Delphina's mind, along with a desperate awareness of countless new things that language was insufficient to describe.

Valdasa started to raise her hand, and Delphina sent reality trembling around her, shunting the girl behind its veil, through some netherworld to distant climes as her finery had gone before. The Elder Council fared far worse. As the Queen of Kalest turned her gaze upon them, they practically dissolved. "Here" and "there" became one and then separated again, trading bits and pieces, limbs sent across the Grand Rotunda or the world with equal ease. Some of the better sorcerers among them, or the quicker to action, escaped, the wise plummeting through the space behind the common world to none could know where and the less wise avoiding destruction at the first stroke only to be caught by the second. Fjarri stretched, thinning out to a thread miles long and fine enough to pierce the gaps in solid stone while Saga went tumbling upwards into black void. Echoes of the perturbation struck the distant walls of the Rotunda, and they seethed like boiling water. Delphina roiled to. What was a mortal body to this kind of power? Just a convenience, easily discarded She could be here and there, above and below, expanding spheres growing outward in unknown directions, intersecting the air of the rotunda like a hand plunging through the surface of a still pond, fingers given to frenetic motion.

Delphina focused. At once, the chaotically trembling threads of magic became still and solid as crystal, the walls of the Rotunda springing back to their old shape as though they had never changed. Delphina, as well, was instantly returned to the shape she had known. She breathed deep breaths of air full of the metallic scent of blood spread to every quarter, her heart pounded in her chest where the heart of the Body of the God was still and oozing from its ancient wound. But she was anything but unchanged.

Delphina Anu Metsaa Kalest was a god. She looked out across the grand rotunda, the silver sun above flaring bright. She gazed out over the crowd of guests and performers that remained. Many were running, others were cowering, and still others stared mutely at her. She walked forward, towards the gates of the grand citadel of the dead god, in no particular hurry, and those before her made way. The power inside her itched. It wanted to be released, wanted to spread, wanted to shake the world and make up for millennia of lost time. The roil was fierce, but it was subsiding. She conjured new finery around herself, elegant and luxurious garments of silk in forest green, and a black cloak woven from the night sky itself. What did she care for the scattering mortal fools?

One stood in front of her – Saga of the Elder Council, and some part of Delphina knew the two-hundred-thirty-seventh born of that First Generation. The woman was in horrible condition, seemingly afflicted with frostbite, burns, and lacerations. Blood covered half her face and stained her hair. She gritted her teeth, breathing heavily. In one hand she had one of the portable speaking devices, a large black box, and in the other she held a metal ball with a stem like fruit.

She may have escaped the void she fell into, but she now seemed determined to stand in Delphina's way.

"Move aside," Delphina commanded.

"You've lost... everything," Saga croaked. "A fitting price

for betrayal." She cast aside the speaking device and held the stemmed sphere out before her, knuckles white as she clenched it tightly in her trembling hand.

"I think you have me confused for you," Delphina said. "Step aside and I'll let you keep what tatters remain of your pathetic life."

Saga gave a bitter, rasping laugh.

"You don't get it. All you had to do was play nice and you'd have had the continent. Now you've done this, and neither of us will last much longer."

Delphina rolled her eyes. "Some personal grudge?" she asked. "Something to do with my mother? You are a tiny little speck. Let me show you."

Delphina reached out with magic, but Saga released her grip on the metal sphere before any spellcraft struck her. A split second later, the device exploded with fire and fury, sending burning shards of metal in all directions. The air between the sphere and Delphina crystalized at Delphina's least thought, harder than steel, directing the whole force back at the elder Hyperborean. When the smoke cleared, only a mutilated corpse remained, and Delphina was untouched.

"Pathetic," she declared. She looked up. She could see the sun in the sky, the front steps of the great citadel before her. With her next step, natural law unraveled around her, and Delphina rose into the sky, striding swifter than the wind back towards Kalest.

CHAPTER XXVIII

Piru

Piru tried to not think too much of his wife's visit to her ancestral homeland. It wasn't a hard task, because there was plenty else to occupy his mind. Lysama had been shockingly tractable after the death of Baudouin – the Merchant Association had been what swayed matters in the end, forcing the nobles who had wished to fight a war and civil war at once into line. Despite this, hours had to be spent with each draft of a treaty, and there had been at least two dozen drafts that had gotten as far as Piru himself. In all of them, however, he was acknowledged as at least a temporary sovereign of Lysama. Had there been a proper war, bitter fighting across an entire country, he might have demanded unconditional surrender, but now a more tangled web of political concerns were in play. The coup de grace, however, had been when occupation forces located Lysama's heir, the seven-year-old niece of King Baudouin. She was on her way to the Palace of Kalest, well within Piru's own territory already, and promised the key to legitimate rule. It was a fact Tuoni would have time to get used to, and hopefully appreciate.

Indris, in fact, had been the larger issue. The confederation had posed no military threat, but the continued occupation was a drain on resources. Many in Lysama saw Kalest's invasion as being at least with cause, and local forces were in charge of keeping the peace within cities. Indris folk, however, saw themselves as victims, and with no trustworthy local power, it fell to Kalest's armies to prevent riot and revolution. Daily, commanders wrote to Piru about having caught and executed insurgents, and the next day a letter would arrive making much of increased unrest. The area seemed almost ungovernable, unresponsive to a firm hand and unwilling to behave with less. Either a good deal of careful diplomacy or a good deal of bloodshed would be needed to subdue Indris, and the longer the situation dragged on, the more Piru worried that his diplomatic abilities would stay tied up with Lysama for the foreseeable future.

He knew Delphina wouldn't agree, but the thought of stopping here was looking ever more appealing to Piru. Tyrvad and Arynias were large, warlike, and had given Kalest no insult nor done his country any wrong in living memory. And what was more, now they were on high alert, mobilizing their armies in fear of a Kalesti invasion. The dream of a continent united beneath a single banner had been a beautiful one, but Ukko had urged caution from the first.

It was the mark of a wise man to know the limits of his ambition. To say you were without limits was to prepare for a fall.

It was while Piru was reviewing his situation, attempting to determine where his limits might lie and thinking that he might establish Indris as a nominally independent vassal kingdom, that Ormr and Ulfr, the hounds of Hyperborea, entered his study unbidden.

"What is the meaning of this intrusion?" Piru demanded. "Do you fools not know how to knock?"

"A thousand, thousand pardons, Great King and Emperor To Be," said Ormr, "but we carry grave tidings your majesty cannot fail to hear."

Piru sneered at them. Ormr was a dangerous ally at the best of times and Ulfr... He had done nothing wrong, as far as Piru knew, but his presence and manner set Piru on edge, so that he would certainly have dismissed the one-handed man if he could have.

"What is it?" Piru demanded.

"We come," Ulfr said, "bearing proof of treason against your majesty."

"Well, handle it," Piru said. "Show me the proof and then I trust you know the penalty."

"We hope Kalest holds to it," Ulfr said.

"And this is the first proof," Ormr added, handing a somewhat fancy document to Piru.

Piru looked at it. It was certainly a contract of some sort, and the signatures were former members of the Hyperborean delegation, and...

Delphina Anu Jokinen.

Piru read the contact, and felt his blood begin to boil. It was horrifyingly clinical, payments given for services rendered, but those services!

Piru had signed a contract not unlike it himself, before the Hyperborean poison had found its way into Esteri's goblet.

"How do I know this isn't a trick?" he demanded. "A forgery?"

Ulfr placed a hard-sided leather case on Piru's desk and opened it. Inside were many other documents. Piru sifted through them – manifests, invoices, transcripts of commands given signed and dated by all in the needed command chain and strange, gloss-surfaced pictures of Delphina years past and the Hyperborean agents meeting. There might have been magical trickery, but it was too much, documents scrawled in hasty hand, names Piru knew and thought he knew, a glut of evidence that the contract had been taken out and fulfilled.

In exchange for a ransom of gold and oaths of future consideration, which as far as Piru knew had been paid faithfully, Delphina had contracted Hyperborea's forces to murder Queen Aliisa of Kalest and make it look to all continental medicine like a sudden illness.

"If you need further proof," Ulfr said, "this is the toxin." He laid a vial of white powder on the table. "Test it on whatever living thing you would, have your doctors look after it, the same ones who attended your dear first wife. Ask them if the symptoms are the same."

"Why?" Piru asked.

"Your queen"-

"Why bring me this now?" he demanded. "What game do you play to turn me against my wife and queen?!"

"She has betrayed us as well," Ulfr said. "I am not privy to how."

"But she will be returning here," Ormr said, "for what would King Kalest think if his queen died in a foreign land? Instead, we give you truth, and deliver her onto your justice. We trust your majesty shall be fair in his judgments."

"If I may," Ulfr said, "that vial"-

"You may not," Piru said, cutting him off. "I shall not take the path of a skulking coward, whatever else I may do. Begone!"

"Majesty..." Ormr began.

"Out!" Piru bellowed. "Get out of my sight and do not enter it again without my permission! Go!"

Ulfr and Ormr hurried out of the study, closing the door behind them. They left all the damning evidence with Piru.

The king's heart was heavy, yet his rage hot, as though he were filled with molten lead. So much pain... losing Aliisa had nearly destroyed him, and how Delphina had stepped up to pick up the pieces. All old wounds, now torn open in knowing that was her aim all along, that he had suffered and his beloved wife had died just so she could step in. How she had wooed him, how she had played him... and it was on her damnable suggestions that Piru had lost his daughter as well! He blamed himself for hearing it, but he cursed Delphina for pouring such poison in his ear.

Part of him wanted to believe it was a forgery still, that Hyperborea had fabricated all this evidence, but it made too much damnable sense. How their agents had found themselves much more comfortable at the court of Kalest once Delphina was queen, how the woman's poorly veiled resentment of Aliisa had turned aside just prior to that sudden and terrible illness. Restless, he left his study, stalking the halls of the palace with a gilded sword in one hand and the contract in the other. Rage festered, driving away other thoughts as his bearing drove away any soul that crossed his path.

Then the trumpets at the gates rang, a clarion call for royalty that could mean one of only two possible arrivals, either Piru's treacherous queen or his son's queen-to-be, however little either was due. If it was the latter, Piru would be making no good impression, but he stalked down to the great entrance hall all the same, in time to see the iron-bound oak doors swing open wide and Delphina step inside. The fading light of the late afternoon was behind her, and it seemed as though she was enshrouded in a halo of silver and gold.

"My love," she said.

Piru threw the folded contract at her feet. The paper floated upwards by some arcana to her hands.

"What is this?" she asked, and then she looked to him. "My dearest, does this trouble you so?"

"Is it true?" Piru demanded. He would hear it from her own lips, and thought he would know if she were a lying serpent.

Delphina looked at the contract for a moment only, then cast it aside.

"Piru," she said, softly, not caring for appearances, "let the past be the past. Our golden future awaits."

She came forward, put her hands on his shoulders, smiled and looked him in the eye. She was radiant – literally radiant, but Piru would not see it. He did not care if her cloak was cut from the night sky or if the depths of her eyes now spoke to eons of power. However she presented herself to him, whatever trickery, she stood accused.

"Is it true?" he growled, demanding again an answer from her.

"You have me," Delphina replied. "And I have won for us a greater power than any king has ever known – look! I would move heaven and earth alike for you!"

The world around them seemed to spin while Piru was

standing still, light bending and shifting around him and Delphina.

"Answer me!" Piru shouted, caring not for illusions and promises. Delphina flinched as though struck, and looked away for a second before pulling herself closer.

"It doesn't matter," she protested. "Not now. Can't you see? I did it, yes, I did it for this day, for you! And now I can give you anything you want! I can place the sun in the palm of your hand! I can be anything"- And for a moment, her visage was Aliisa's, before returning to Delphina. "I can do anything! Simply tell me what you desire!"

Piru ran her through.

"Justice," he said. "That is what I desire. You can die for me."

Delphina's eyes were wide, horrified shock across her face slowly fading to a strange placidity. The air was stirred as though by countless great wings, rippling noiselessly.

"My love..." she whispered. She pulled herself up against him, driving the blade deeper through her chest.

"All that I am has always been yours," she whispered. "Take it."

She kissed him on the lips, and then Piru's mind reeled. He felt something ineffable course through his being, felt himself expand into unknown spheres, looked down at the scene for an instant from countless eyes poised in nameless angles and then crashed back into his body.

"For you, my love," Delphina whispered, "I would do anything."

The world righted itself. Delphina fell away from him, toppling back, her mantle of night becoming soaked in her pooling blood even as it faded away into wisps of nothing. She was stone dead.

And Piru? What was Piru? Who was Piru? He found himself disoriented, confused, feeling as though his memories were not his own, seething with unfamiliar senses, uncertain of their meaning. He raised a hand to his temple as though to steady his mind as it careened through black infinities that no witness to what had transpired in the grand hall could see. Slowly, the whole of Piru found its way back... and more beyond. His bones itched, as though ill-fitted to contain the reality that was all around them.

He looked back to Delphina. For a moment, she was unchanged, pale and beautiful, a spot of alabaster in the spreading crimson stain. Piru wished he didn't have to see it – hatred demanded a more gruesome sight while pain wished for her visage to be gone entirely. And even as he thought it, it happened, and Delphina's remains fell into utter darkness, the pool of blood turned black for an instant, swallowing her up. When it passed, only the marble floor remained, utterly without blemish.

And somehow Piru knew that he had not imagined that – he had done it. The corpse was elsewhere, drifting in darkness on its way to oblivion, but in the end she had given him something... something nameless, something powerful. Her words echoed in Piru's ears. Be anything, do anything.

It was the mark of a wise man to know the limits of his ambition, but Piru was not wise enough to say whether or not they existed any longer. What use did he have for political expedience any longer? He was not like other men. Not anymore.

Ormr approached, Ulfr just behind at his right hand.

"And so is justice served, great king," Ormr mused.

"You," Piru growled. "Give me one good reason why you treacherous worms should not be next, and all your misbegotten countrymen with you."

"We have ever served what is mutually beneficial," Ormr said, a hint of fear in his voice.

"You have great power now," Ulfr said. "We know of it. Your late queen stole it from our people, it seems."

"You knew?" Piru demanded.

"No," Ormr said quickly. "Only when we saw her. The message from home was... unclear."

"I still haven't heard why I ought to spare the poisoners when I have killed who hired them."

"We have always served as benefits us," Ormr repeated. "The world as it is... we see great benefit in rendering our service to you. Even if only to gain your grace, Majesty, let us be the first to proclaim ourselves your devoted servants."

Piru thought about it, but not long. Mercenary to the last they were, but at least a mercenary's loyalties were obvious.

"Done," Piru said. "Come. We have much to speak of."

CHAPTER XXIX

Esteri

As they approached the Tyrvad town, Radegond approached Esteri, and pulled her quietly to the side, speaking in a low voice.

"May I offer my opinion?" she asked.

"Of course," Esteri said, "though I can't say I'll agree."

"What do you think of these Kalesti?"

Esteri considered the question. "I think we can trust them," she said, "and I would rather take that chance than remain at odds with my countrymen and... my kin."

"That's not what I meant," Radegond said. "If they had ill intent we would not have come even this far peacefully. I was more speaking to their condition."

Esteri nodded. Of the lot of them, only Ukko himself was unharmed. Friendly Acacia seemed to be on the mend, her hurt a mere flesh wound, but Launo's arm was broken, and while Esteri found it difficult to muster sympathy for the woman, Seija's shattered ribs quite evidently made it hurt for her to breathe. As to Maria, the blonde woman who favored the massive two-handed sword, her condition had worsened day by day since the point where they met. Whether there had been poison coating Ulfr's dagger or simple but potentially ruinous infection was running its course, she was now delirious with fever, and required some assistance in walking so that Acacia, Launo, or Ukko were obliged to offer her a shoulder to lean most of her weight upon step by step, Seija not being able to take the weight and none among the Accursed

353

having been eager to step up to the duty.

"Fighting Erikis took much from them," Esteri said, conscious that not all had even survived that conflict. "Can you say we would have fared better?"

"No," Radegond admitted, "but that doesn't change the consideration. We reach relative safety today, and I suggest that those both willing and able to press on do so as soon as can be managed."

At the absolute least, that would mean leaving Maria behind, to whatever fate awaited her. Seija as well might be obliged to remain, and at that point would Launo or Acacia wish to press on? Esteri thought that even then she could count on Ukko's persistent support, even if she declared such an action necessary, but she doubted whether or not any of the others would follow. Of course, under the circumstances, there was a chance that Radegond saw that as a benefit... and a chance that she might be right.

"In short," she said, "you mean we should largely part ways with them. I'm surprised."

"Why would that be?" Radegond asked.

"Because," Esteri said, "I wouldn't have thought someone like you willing to sacrifice a long-term advantage for a short-term one. Wounds heal. If we leave them now we deny ourselves some potential allies who have proved themselves capable sorts."

Radegond frowned.

"It's true," she said, "they might be a help to us in the future. But right now we don't know what sort of time we have, and"-

"We know better than you give us credit. What do we stand to gain? Tyrvad's intervention against Kalest, or at least aid in our own endeavors if they are determined to see the matter as an internal affair. For now, Kalest's armies are spread very thin throughout Indris and Lysama. Even in the best-case scenario for Kalest, it will be months before my father could muster an effective offense to take matters out of our hands."

"That's true," Radegond said, "but what of Ulfr? We don't

know where he is going, to what end, or even how critical the situation may become if he achieves his aims. For all we know, it could make the matter of Kalest and your father and the Queen moot."

"And," Esteri said, "by the same token it may be as irrelevant as it is out of our hands. I suspect the truth will probably lay somewhere between those possibilities, though closer to which I cannot say."

"And so you think we can afford to delay? Or are you making this a debate solely to be certain?"

"I think..."

Esteri took a deep breath. There was a lot of wisdom in Radegond's words, but all the same it wasn't easy to leave someone, even someone Esteri didn't really know, behind. The people who would follow her... in the end they were all Esteri really had.

"I think that we can ill afford to turn aside any potential advantage. If we press on quickly and leave those who can't keep up behind, as well as those who would remain with them, we lose that number certainly. If, on the other hand, we take some time to allow them a chance to heal, we are risking costs that are unknown and may already be lost or may never become lost. Normally, I wouldn't believe in taking a chance where certainty would suffice, but in this case I think the risk is small enough, and the loss large enough, that we don't have a choice but to wait and see."

"How long?" Radegond asked.

Esteri looked away.

"A fortnight, at most," she said with a sigh. She knew that the term was basically random, but she also knew that 'as long as it takes' wasn't going to be an option. "That's not enough time for broken bones but it's still very possible to move under those conditions. It should, on the other hand, be enough time to know what will become of flesh wounds."

Radegond nodded.

"You know," she said, "I think you would have made a good

queen if you had the chance."

"Oh?"

"You care about your people, but not so much that you lose sight of the big picture. And more than that, you're decisive. Those who can't keep moving forward in times like these should never be permitted to reign."

Radegond's vehemence gave Esteri pause.

"Something about your mortal life?" she ventured.

Radegond sighed and nodded. "Yes," she said. "Back in my day, Kalest had a weak king who left matters to his generals and advisors. Of course, not all of those saw eye-to-eye, so the right hand didn't really know what the left hand was doing. It's a small wonder we did as well as we did, back then."

"When was this?" Esteri asked.

"Ah," Radegond said, trying to remember, "that would have been Veikko III. I might be missing my mark, but I believe he'd be your twice-great Granduncle?"

"That's right," Esteri said, "he's called Veikko the Dithering in modern records."

"I never met the king face-to-face," Radegond admitted, "but that was much the impression I received back then."

"Well, then," Esteri said, "at least history and memory are in agreement. I wonder though... knowing what we know, what do you think of my father's rule?"

"Personally?"

"As an expert on leadership and military, discounting our... attachments."

Radegond stood a little straighter, if such a thing were possible, and seemed to consider that.

"It's not easy to know," she said. "His plans have met real success, more real than has been seen in my lifetime, but it's almost too ambitious. I don't think you can really count the cost the world will pay yet, to say whether or not his reach exceeds his grasp."

"That's very... diplomatic of you."

"Like hell," Radegond said, "it's not about diplomacy, it's

about history. You want my unvarnished opinion, something about this is going to break whether we crack it wide open or not. And whether we crack it wide open or not, the question is still going to remain just how bad the break becomes. That's going to be the difference between a figure people struggle to find a consensus on and one that would go down in history as a legendary problem."

Esteri nodded. She hadn't really been sure what she had expected to hear or wanted to hear when she asked, but somehow Radegond's assessment seemed to put the matter into something resembling perspective.

Very shortly, the band entered town, waving wearily and bringing Maria to the fore in the hopes that someone would know how to treat her hurts. Esteri breathed a small sigh of relief when they were lead to a village alchemist, whose workshop was, while rustic, clearly very well appointed for handling the sick and injured. They laid Maria in one of the spare beds there, and produced such coins as it would be fitting to give the old alchemist for his troubles, and from there split their attentions to the other needs of the whole, some staying to see to their sick friend while others sought out provisions or lodging for travelers.

Those tasks accomplished, the matter of waiting began in earnest, and that was a situation that tried patience at the best of times. To the best of her ability, Esteri tried to see to everyone, and not simply allow herself the pleasant company of Tius or long conversations with Ukko. The remains of the first day, they mostly stayed separate, even those who had long traveled together going about their business separately, affording Esteri the opportunity to talk with each earnestly. The second day was much the same in that regard, with only breakfast and dinner being spent with the whole company, less of course Maria, together, and that with many of the locals. Those moments, however, showed the wear that the spirits of all those present had suffered. They ate in sullen silence, now and again glancing furtively to their friends or across the table to the knot of further enemies, looks that would now and again be returned by venomous glares. Acacia, Ukko, and Tius seemed more alarmed or offput by the air of hostility than they were participants, and Ukko and Radegond seemed able to converse with one another, but for the rest there was at least a moment where they seemed to be ready for a fight to break out, and looked as though they would not be displeased at something of the sort.

The third day, it rained, and the weather brought all together for the entirety of the day, with the slight exception of Ukko and Acacia each departing once or twice, separately, to check on Maria's state. The rest remained, and their forced cohabitation brought many quiet grumbles with it. The hostility Avina held for Seija was especially pointed, as could be expected, and the other woman seemed inclined to match her death-glare for death-glare until at last, in the mid afternoon, when none else were near, Seija broke the silence.

"Got something to say?" she demanded.

Avina crossed her arms.

"Because it looks like you've got something to say," Seija continued, "so just say it. If it's about that woman"-

"She was my mom!" Avina hissed.

The silence returned for a minute. "That's it, is it?" Seija asked. "And I bet you want revenge."

"And if I do?" Avina asked.

"I'm asking," Seija said.

"Maybe I do," replied Avina. Tius put a hand on her shoulder, but she brushed it off, though it looked as though doing so hurt her a little, and she whispered something Esteri couldn't quite hear, to which Tius nodded.

"So, what are you going to do, take my arm off? Limb for limb, that's fair."

"If you want a fight"- Avina began, but Seija cut her off.

"Fine," she said. "You can have it... after Her Majesty is done with us."

At that, Avina's eyes went wide. "What?"

"I said, when this is all done, you can take my arm. I messed up, and went after someone who was innocent, and I did it deliberately. But while Her Highness is still in danger I need that arm to fight the people who actually deserve it. When that's done, if it's still what you want, go ahead and take it. But until then stop giving me the damn stink eye, we're not going to get anywhere that way."

Avina's mouth opened, then closed again in silence. She closed her eyes, took a few deep breaths, then nodded sharply.

"Good," Seija growled. Then she coughed, and hugged herself, and swore from the pain.

Esteri, for her part, felt a little ill. It was a resolution, at least, and the matter was not, in principle, hers, owing to the fact that as much as those around her seemed to offer her deference, she did not see herself as their sovereign, or even more than a temporary leader. Thus, she held her tongue about the agreement, and hoped that Avina, who seemed shaken as well, might choose to offer mercy under the circumstances.

No one else said anything either, and while the air in the room had become less contentious with the decrease of tension between those two women, the mood was no lighter.

It continued as such for an hour or so, until Acacia came back in out of the rain. She wore a bright smile despite looking the part of a drowned cat, and Esteri could not help but smile back

"She's going to make it," Acacia declared. "He's pretty sure now. Her fever broke while I was there, and the wound doesn't look as bad as before."

Launo looked up, concerned. "Did he say how long the recovery could take?"

Acacia shook her head. "No," she said, "but I'm sure it can't be that long. It's just a flesh wound, after all, now that the infection looks to be clearing up."

Radegond stood, and walked to Ukko.

"I think we have matters to discuss in light of this, don't you?" she said.

Ukko nodded. "Of course." He stood from his place, and the two of them made their way to a more distant corner to speak in low voices. Esteri was glad such strategic minds were on her side, and as an attempt to open the floor somewhat better, waved Acacia over, and made room so that the sodden girl could sit closest to the fire.

Gingerly, Acacia took the offered place. A moment later, Esteri saw fit to strike up a conversation.

"Acacia, yes?" she asked, quietly and politely, wishing to be sure she did not have the girl's name wrong.

"Uh-huh," she said with a smile and a nod.

"There are a few things I'd like to ask you. You don't mind?"

"Oh, I couldn't, highness."

"There's no need for that title here... especially not if any of the locals might come within earshot."

Esteri was particularly eager to reinforce the matter for the latter reason, and because she had not the nerve, under the circumstances, to tell Seija as much earlier.

"Ah... yeah, of course. I'm sorry."

"It's alright. I was wondering... yours is not a military family, is it?"

Acacia shook her head.

"Not that I know."

"That you..."

Acacia shrugged. "I didn't know my mom and dad much and nobody ever told me what they did for a living, and my uncle was lame so he couldn't have fought. He was an architect, but he declared himself done with me... I guess it would be about five years past now?"

"That's terrible..."

Acacia laughed. "It's not that bad. I had a ton of friends in the city. Never a bad day."

Acacia smiled especially warmly, and Esteri could not for the life of her detect any hint of fakery. Yet the facts she laid out were the makings of a tragic tale, so how could she say that there had never been a bad day?

"Is that so?" Esteri asked.

"Pretty much," Acacia said. "Things weren't always easy, I guess. But what reason is that to get all downcast? I remember, it was my mom who told me, that even if bad things are real, letting them get to you, that's a choice. I may not know much about her, but I do remember that much."

Acacia looked away.

"A couple times, when it's something important enough, it's a choice I've made, because there are times when life deserves a few tears, but ah..." She shook her head. "Never mind, I've got no place lecturing you and that's what it's starting to sound like."

"It's quite alright," Esteri said. "You have a very... unique... point of view."

"Is it really?" Acacia asked, honestly interested.

Esteri nodded. "Most people rather keenly feel their problems, however grand or petty."

"And you?" Acacia asked.

"Me what?"

"Well, current business aside, what's weighing you down?"

Esteri blinked.

"Current business aside?" she asked.

Acacia nodded.

"I know what you've told me about the current mess, but that's something you're determined on. You know what to do, and we wouldn't all be together here if you didn't intend to do it. But that doesn't seem to really pick you up, does it?"

"Not particularly, I admit," Esteri said. "I just have this feeling..."

Esteri's voice grew soft as she realized what she was saying.

"This feeling like something terrible is going to happen, or has happened."

"Hey..." Acacia said. "If there is something, it's not anything you can do much about, is it? So we'll cross that bridge when we come to it."

"I suppose you're right," Esteri said. She thought back to

her nightmares, the ones in which her body warped, that were probably visions. Swords, darkness, blood... and at least one after the fall of Lysama, portending that there was more blood to be spilled.

"Was there anything else? You don't have to be ashamed if it's little. Sometimes little things are like a splinter, and bother you more than big ones."

"To be honest," Esteri replied, "I haven't had much time to think of little things..."

But, at the prompting, some thoughts came unbidden, and Esteri found herself thinking stray thoughts, on subjects that brought her little peace. Despite herself, she laughed, for she found that most of her troubles regarded the future, and its uncertainty, even now.

"Oh, something funny?" Acacia asked.

"Now that you mention it... there are a few things I wonder about, and I could just try to find the answer, like skipping ahead to the last page of a story to see how it ends, but it would seem like cheating, especially when life and death aren't at stake."

"What sorts of things?" Acacia asked.

Esteri shifted uncomfortably. She glanced at Tius, sitting very near, then looked back to Acacia. "I'd rather not talk about this... right here."

Acacia nodded.

"Well, if you ever do feel like talking about it, I figure I might as well make myself useful even when we don't have to fight."

Esteri forced a smile. "That's very good of you. Thank you."

But Esteri said nothing more, letting the matters drop for as long as they could be afforded to.

***

The weather cleared the following day, for better or worse, and thereafter Maria's condition continued to mend, and though when Esteri visited her she was still ashen and weak, she grinned.

"See," she said weakly, "told you all it was nothing."

Then she winced, and Esteri was swiftly ushered out of the room.

In all, it took a week from when the band arrived in the town until when Maria was deemed fit enough to travel. She was still weak, as were the other injured, save Acacia who seemed largely unhindered despite the bandages at her waist. At Radegond's insistence and with Ukko's support in the matter they were thereafter on their way. The path would probably take seven or eight more days, given that their pace was still reduced from what it might be had all been well and well-equipped.

On the sixth day, near evening, they once again reached a Tyrvad town, and found it in quite an uproar. Folk were not, it seemed, going around their business as usual. Nor did they seem to stir and consider the arrival of such a large band of travelers so clearly girded for and having faced battle to be the strangest event of their day, for as they told it a young woman had appeared near mid-morning with a calamitous bang and a brilliant flash of violet light. About this woman there were many rumors being freely told. Most said she was some sort of Hyperborean witch, which set Esteri on edge and had her considering pressing on as swiftly as possible, but it seemed that while those who had seen her did think she was of Hyperborean extraction, most were more concerned by her sorry state upon arrival, and whispered of what might have caused her wounds. That was an entirely different matter than if the arrival had been some favored sorcerer likely doing the bidding of their enemies. Perhaps something could be learned from her.

Thus, Esteri, along with Tius, Avina, and Acacia joined those waiting outside the house into which the Hyperborean had been taken, for the town's doctor to see to her hurts. There, many grumbled that they should be done with such a witch, while others espoused greater sympathy. Esteri, for her part, remained silent, seeing as she had no say in any debate of the locals, but felt the conflict very keenly. On one hand, she had seen some of their magic before, both in facing Ulfr and that which her stepmother was able to work. And while she had suffered for the former, she didn't see it being that terribly dangerous, and would trust her and the three of her friends with her against such magic. Of course, neither Ulfr nor Delphina had been able to create so great a stir as this Hyperborean apparently had.

Sometime about dusk the doctors emerged, and declared that while the young woman's case was very baffling, she could entertain the myriad questions that were no doubt held for her, so long as only a few would ask at a time. And to this, first a few elders of the village were permitted, and they remained for an hour or more before emerging, and promising what answers they had gleaned to placate most of the crowd. Thereafter, the next admitted was the family that owned the house, and from their protests at being kept out, found that the girl had evidently annihilated their flower garden with her violent arrival. Yet the woman of the house, a portly lady with a very red nose, did not seem distraught at the girl, and voiced a wish to bring her hot stew and hear from her own lips why and from where she had come so dramatically.

When they emerged again, and went around to another entrance, it was quite dark. The doctor went in again, and emerged, and by then everyone but Esteri and the three with her had dispersed. Esteri stood, and seeing as she and hers were all that remained, stepped up to take her turn.

The doctor, an elderly lady, tall and rail-thin like a scarecrow, stepped in her way.

"I'm afraid I don't know you, strangers," she said, severe but not too harsh. "Just what business do you have with my patient?"

"We just wish to talk," Esteri said.

The doctor folded her arms.

"Please," Esteri began, but then Acacia stepped up.

"It's for the sake of the world," she said

"Sake of the world?" the doctor demanded.

Acacia nodded. "Really! You have to admit weird things are happening. You heard the news about the war in Lysama, right? And now this lady appears here in a big purple bang! Anyway, you can come in with us if you don't trust us, and if you think what we've got to say is hurting your patient, well, then you can throw us right out, is that okay?"

The doctor frowned, and grumbled a little. "Very well, stranger," she said, "but be on your best behaviours, the poor girl has been through quite a lot."

And with that, they were led inside, through a small hall cordoned off from the rest of the house by a brightly painted door, and into a small bedroom. The Hyperborean witch was lying on top of the sheets. She was, Esteri guessed, twenty years of age or probably younger. She wore what must once have been an elegant dress, but it was stained with blood and charred about the edges. Her right arm was splinted and her feet, though bandaged somewhat, were clearly as black as soot. Her white-blonde hair was fanned out over her head in disarray, the tips of her fingers were blackened, and blood oozed from under her bandaged nails. Her left eye was covered with a cloth patch, but her right eye darted immediately to the door when the doctor entered, and soon rested on Esteri. Her gaze was not unkind, but when it fixed upon Esteri she felt a certain intensity.

"Valdasa," the doctor said, "these people said they wanted to speak with you."

"Ah," she said, "that's good. You should probably leave us."

"Do... you know these folks?"

"Perhaps," Valdasa said. "Can we talk in private?"

The doctor scowled a little, but left the room. Valdasa's gaze never left Esteri.

"You know," she said, once the Doctor was at least through a door from there, "I had never supported the Hrokrine Interpretation of Temporal Arcana, yet unless I miss my mark, here we are."

"Excuse me?" Esteri asked.

"Ah, yes, continental education... I suppose I should say that I was not a believer in Fate, yet I cannot think of much else that would precipitate this meeting."

Esteri cocked her head. "Do you... recognize me?"

"Well," Valdasa said, "you've a rather rare phenotype unless my eye deceives me. I think I'm in Tyrvad, so you're not outside its normal range, but your clothes are... Lysaman, yes? Two of those with you are Kalesti... and I was party to the Elder Council's considerations. So tell me, do I recognize you?"

"Yes," Esteri admitted. Valdasa had not, she noticed, uttered a name. In case the doctor was listening at the door, perhaps?

"I'm sorry," Valdasa said. "I thought yours was quite a sad story when I read the brief. That was when we thought you, and not the godflesh, would be the catalyst."

"Excuse me?"

Valdasa sighed. "And you don't know a thing about the situation in which you are a key part, do you?"

Esteri gritted her teeth, and Avina spoke.

"Could you stop with the cryptic nonsense? Who are you, and what are you talking about?"

Valdasa closed her eye.

"I am Valdasa, of the Second Generation, daughter of Skoll of the Elder Council, Conduit... I was supposed to be the Conduit of Divinity, she who would ensure the blessings of the god who sired our race onto the people of Hyperborea. The day of my destiny was today, in the wake of an agent's delivery of a mass of deathless flesh that had been the sentience core of the Great One. I believe you met."

"Erikis," Tius ventured. "Ulfr took the body."

"I wasn't told the agent's name. According to Saga, he was both irrelevant and unpleasant. Everything went wrong, though... Your stepmother was there, she... she stole what should have been mine, what was my destiny."

Esteri did not call the girl on having claimed to not be a believer in fate earlier. The story was still being told in a furtive manner, presumably, again, to avoid eavesdropping, but while the facts were either unclear or over her head, the tenor of the implications was grave.

"I was... thrown away, tossed behind reality like garbage into the waste bin. I got out, though the void is not very kind to living matter, as you can see. I didn't see what happened after that but I swear, even through the pain I could still feel it, the world stirring. Your most resolute foe has become more potent than anything to walk the world in millennia. Possibly by several orders of magnitude."

"Why are you telling me this?" Esteri asked, the shock of these pronouncements finally boiling over into vehemence. "Do you expect me to do something about it? I... this was all already over my head, it's been over my head since Baudouin. All I wanted, all I ever wanted, was a chance to live with the world at peace, and now the moment I dare to dream that I'll be free of gods and monsters it gets worse!"

Valdasa's expression then became very sad. "I'm quite sorry, but even if the Hrokrine Interpretation doesn't hold, I had assumed that under the circumstances you would have motivation and possibly means."

"To what?"

"To set things right," Valdasa said, "or to stop a great calamity, take your pick. What has been unleashed has wronged me and mine and presents a threat to you, so perhaps you would care to answer it?"

"How?" Esteri asked. "I'm... well, I am what I am, but you said yourself, I don't have the power."

"My father often said that a victory won through power alone was a victory not worth having. Granted, that may have been his way of encouraging me to fulfill my purpose when the time came, but in any case, the Old One himself was defeated, was he not? And by mortals, or those very near mortals. So

I doubt your task will be as difficult as one that has already been successfully accomplished at least once in the historical record."

"So," Acacia said, "that means we can definitely do it if we try." She smiled at Esteri, but Esteri noted that for the first time the smile seemed at least a little forced. Whatever her words, even she was at least a little frightened by the prospect.

"You'll need a few things," Valdasa said. "First, you'll need some arcane protection so what was done to me can't just be done to you. I could provide an alchemical formula, it's mostly based in green Æther. You don't have a pen and paper, do you? Everything here on the continent is so... rustic. More importantly you will need at least one enchanted weapon, and that will be much more difficult to procure, seeing as the conditions for their fabrication have a temporal component that won't be satisfied in a timely fashion. You'll be obliged to acquire, by some means, one of the blades of the Tyrvad Ancestor-gods, or at least another weapon of the same make. Without it, there's a chance that a being with the Old One's power in full would not be able to be killed by one such as yourself. Well, unless it was willing to die, but I don't suspect there's much of a chance of convincing someone who will see herself as a new-minted deity to simply accept her demise."

Esteri thought back to the azure sword. Something had told her to keep it, and she had. Was that another form of vision?

"I think that can be taken care of. What then?"

"Protected against the worst attack magic and armed with a weapon capable of properly killing an immortal being on the order of the Old One? You will simply have to employ the weapon and end the life in question. Unless said being takes on an extremely non-human form, the conventional approach should apply."

The sound of that caveat was not terribly comforting, but somehow reducing the monumental task to an assassination of Delphina was a relief. It should have been more of one, but Esteri's second thought, before the dream of revenge had even entered her mind, was of Tuoni. Her brother loved his mother, and why not? She had never treated him as anything less than her precious son. He'd be devastated... but if even a fraction of what Valdasa was saying was true, it wasn't even down to Esteri or Delphina, it was a matter of Esteri being in the right place at the right time for everyone's good.

"I'm not sure I understand all of what you're telling me," Esteri admitted, "but I think I get the gist of it. I have other friends in this town though, who'll want to – need to – hear what you told me, and better from your own mouth. You'll, um, still be here in the morning?"

Valdasa nodded. "I'm essentially bedridden for the time being, and despite the barbaric medical techniques you're limited to here on the continent, I don't anticipate that I'd expire, given the kindness of what I've received and the mostly surprisingly superficial nature of my injuries. Do be sure to bring a pen. And, um, maybe some spare paper?" She looked at her hands. "My penmanship may not be very good right now but it feels positively unnatural to not be making notes."

"I will," Esteri said. "Please tell the people taking care of you to let us in."

Valdasa nodded, and rubbed her throat. Esteri, for her part, went to the door and with muttered thanks and apologies departed, Acacia, Avina, and Tius behind her. In too many ways it still felt unreal, like the near-fugue in which she had first made her way to the Accursed colony... but at least, for a moment, the path forward seemed clear.

**

"If you want my opinion," Radegond said, "she talks too much while saying too little. But at the same time I can think of no reason why she would lie about something like this, given her condition. I want to say that she's playing us, but there's no game to be had."

By now, everyone had heard Valdasa's story from the girl

herself, taken notes, and now waited for some decision to be reached on what to do next.

"I agree," Ukko said. "Her story does manage to explain a number of matters that had been bothering me."

"Those being?"

"Mostly," Ukko said, "it relates to Hyperborea's endgame. We saw their meddling in Lysama, and heard more from Esteri, and though their deeds were clear, we did not have a motive for such actions until now. And when I think how their plots have arisen again and again, I must also consider that this end she speaks of, claiming the power of the Old One... it explains why they have done much of what they have done throughout history. And while it is, as Launo has said, a very fanciful story, I am myself too old to ignore fanciful tales. Often, they have more truth in them than stories that sound entirely reasonable."

The back-and-forth, mostly between Radegond and Ukko, had been continuing for an hour. Neither one of them seemed to value minutes, and thus they were perfectly content to bat a topic between them, saying the same things in slightly different ways in order, perhaps, to reach a different perspective. Esteri was tired and bored and not alone in that status. She looked around the room, and only Seija, who was seldom anything but sullen and alert, seemed more than half awake. Avina had actually given up and retired for the night. Under the circumstances, Esteri couldn't say that she was wrong.

"Perhaps if you told me more about what you knew regarding this Erikis," Ukko continued, Esteri having missed some of the interchange, "I might be able to piece together some of the methodology."

Esteri stood up.

"While I have no doubt this is a very engaging discussion," she said, "the task ahead of us is a different sort. And I'm asking you, because I don't know what to do... how do we go about it? Do we press on, hoping for Tyrvad's aid like before? I'd hoped that would forestall an invasion by exposing false pretense, but now if we do that, and Delphina must be dealt with, it will mean a full and open war. I... I want a better way."

Ukko seemed to contemplate the matter.

"Well, we all have some experience going behind enemy lines. If Valdasa's report is accurate, an assassination shouldn't be out of the question, and it could keep casualties to a minimum, assuming the problem actually departs with Delphina. That is the most practical answer."

"If it doesn't," Esteri said, "then was there anything we could do?" She looked to Tius, and to Radegond and Hathus. "I know many of you have no special love for Kalest, but would you see it burn for the crimes of a poor queen?"

The Accursed with her shook their heads.

"Then on that much I believe we are all agreed. So I want to hear, how would you pull it off?"

"Killing the queen..." Seija hissed. "It feels like treason, no matter the story about dead gods."

"I don't much care for the idea either," Launo said, "but in all of this – assassination, false flags, betrayal, gods... there is no honor in it. The question is not what is right, but what is worse, to raise our hands against royalty, or to do nothing while innocent people are liable to suffer to die. One is treason. The other is cowardice. We don't escape this with clean consciences, so what stain would you rather have on yours?"

Ukko nodded. "This is not a matter in which I can offer a personal perspective. The royal family is precious to me, even as I endure heirs who serve their people poorly. To think that as little as a year ago, it is likely I could have abided such dealings... walking the world is not always a kind proposition. As I find her to be of sound mind and good character, all I can do is advise Esteri on how to accomplish her aims. It is not for me to tell anyone here what those aims should be."

"Mine is clear," Ukko said. "I cannot abide matters as they are, so I need to return to Kalest and there learn Delphina's aim and what place I can take in or against it. But if needs be, I shall carry that burden on my own shoulders. I would only ask that no one try to stop me."

"You won't be alone," Tius said, and placed a hand on her shoulder. "I promise."

Esteri sighed deeply. She didn't want to admit it to the others, but she truly needed to tell Tius how much his faith and support helped her. Feeling as though she could stand firm, now, she spoke again.

"Tomorrow, I mean to make for Kalest. I... will do my best to discover what Delphina has in mind for the world and for me, and if it is for the worst, then what I choose to do will be my own will, and no one else will have to accept it. Anyone who wants to follow my path, at least for a time, is welcome."

CHAPTER XXX

Avina

The world was black, lit red, gleaming like iron, reflections illuminating a world that all twisted in one direction, flowing like a river towards a common destination. Avina felt herself pulled along with the flow, moving inexorably towards the center. If she moved, the center was ahead of her. If she stood still, the world flowed and closed the distance.

The center glowed. It was the light of this world, the only thing that gave substance, form. What the light didn't touch wasn't real.

Avina went forward willingly. Her black limbs stretched across the black land, along the flow, deliberately towards the red light.

The light was not steady. It pulsed softly, like a beating heart, rythmic, pleasant. With every pulse Avina lurched forward. Her claws dragged on the ground, her head fell from one shoulder to the other as each step raised and lowered part of her body. The world spun, and flowed. All that was steady was the light.

Then she woke up with a sharp shock. Avina flinched, and felt a surge of vertigo as the world grew massive around her. At once, she felt warm... someone was hugging her. She blinked.

"Tius? Hey, Tius, what's up?"

Then Avina looked around. Radegond was there too, and Hathus and Esteri as well.

"Why is everybody staring?"

Tius let her go and stepped back. "Sorry, it's okay... You

were sleepwalking."

"Sleepwalking?" Avina said. "Seriously?"

"Sleepwalking transformed, no less," Radegond said. "At least you weren't difficult to track.

Avina looked over her shoulder. The disturbed foliage did form a rather notable path.

"As far as we can tell," Radegond continued, "you wandered out of camp, shifted, and just kept stumbling southeast."

"Kept? How far from camp are we?"

"About an hour," Radegond said. "It's not quite dawn, but our human friends will be breaking camp quick as they can and catching up. Might as well move early."

"In the meantime," Esteri said, "I've gotten that this has never happened before. Do you remember anything?"

"Just a weird dream," Avina said, scratching her head. "There was this light, and I did feel like I was going somewhere.

Tius, Esteri, and Radegond's expressions all turned grave, while Hathus had looked away, towards the east.

"Do you remember what color the light was?" Radegond asked.

"Red, I think," Avina said. "Why?"

"Because I think I had the same dream," Radegond replied.

"Me too," Esteri said, "except it seemed more like a nightmare to me. I tried to stay away from the light, I don't know why."

"And me," Tius said. "I don't remember it so well, but a black place and a red light. Hathus?"

Uncharacteristically quiet, he just grunted and nodded assent.

"Well," Avina said, "we all had the same dream. That's weird and creepy, but what does it mean?"

"If I had to guess," Radegond said, "I'd say someone or something was calling."

"Delphina," Esteri said, grave.

"Why do you say that?" Radegond asked.

"A few reasons. First, I was afraid of the dream, and whatever its source was, so given my sight I doubt anything good would have happened if I followed it."

"You were't warped when you woke up."

"True," Esteri said, "so on to my second reason. Avina, you were walking southeast, a little more east than south. Follow that as a straight line path, and it would lead you through the heart of Kalest."

"And," Radegond said, "several other places. But that is interesting, at least."

"Third," Esteri continued, "I remember, you all said it was Erikis who found you. It's clear he had some sense for the presence of the Accursed, or someone like Tius would never have found your village or been found by it. For that matter, I found my way up there in a fugue. That might have been my sight, or it might have been something else. Whatever Delphina is now, Erikis is part of that, so you can't tell me she wouldn't have the means. I admit each element is individually flimsy..."

"But taken together, they do paint a picture that suggests enemy action. But for what purpose?"

"She know I'm Accursed," Esteri said, "and as long as I'm alive I'm a problem, however small. If she can't target me directly, but can target the Accursed..."

"It makes sense. And Avina was actually sent walking because she's more a part of that than the rest of us.

Avina scowled. "I'm right here, you know."

Tius smiled at her. "Don't worry," he said.

Avina smiled back. She probably would have snapped if it were anyone else, but for her big brother – which was still weird to think of, even if in a good way – she couldn't manage the bitterness.

"I'm not worried," she said. Then, trying to think of a way to cover her outburst, she continued, "I just want to give my own take on what, you know, happened to me."

"Okay," Tius said. He had clearly been honestly fooled, so Avina needed to think of something good.

"I think..." she said. "I think you're right, like it was calling to the Accursed parts in me, and that's more of me, but this all just means that we've got to deal with it, and make sure the others don't stab me or something. I'm not going home. Not yet."

"Not unless you want to," Tius said, and he shot Radegond a venomous glare for a second.

"Be that as it may," Radegond said, "Avina, you are quite right about requiring a more careful watch. I'd hate to know what would follow if this had occurred in a populated area."

And at that, Avina swallowed. Whatever the results, they wouldn't be pretty.

"In the meantime, I'm going to try to search her out again," Esteri said. "This sight has to be good for something."

Tius paced over to her.

"Do you need anything?" he asked, with the kind of tone that used to make Avina jealous.

It was amazing how much those few words between them had changed.

"Not especially," Esteri said. "Just make sure I don't fall down and hit my head or anything like that."

And at that prompting, Tius stood very close to the princess, and she closed her eyes.

"While that's going on," Radegond said, "I need to know if you remember anything else about this dream, or your walk."

Avina shook her head.

"No," she said. "I'm sorry."

Radegond grumbled, but declared the matter not Avina's fault, which was at least something of a relief.

A few quiet minutes passed, then Esteri openend her eyes, which were quite clear, and shook her head.

"It's just the same," she said. "I try to look into Delphina's future and I come up with nothing. I wonder if what she is, is blocking me somehow?"

"What about your own?" Avina asked.

Esteri frowned. "I've tried, over the last couple days, and

I've seen things, but... I'm not sure how to interpret them. I keep seeing this place, where sheer-sided mountains like glittering steel beehives cut the sky bloody. I can't believe it's a real place, a literal vision, but I don't know what it portends."

"Doesn't sound like anything good," Avina said.

"I know that much," Esteri replied with a heavy sigh. "I just wish it made sense, any of this."

Not much later, the humans arrived, Ukko (who Avina supposed was not exactly human) leading them., and with the whole of the group reconstructed, they set off to the southeast.

The very direction, Avina realized, she had been walking in her sleep.

***

After two weeks, the dream of going to the red light recurred often, but no sleeping person made more than a half-hearted attempt to get up and move. As for the rest of life, well, the long days on the road were mostly annoyingly quiet. Esteri was preoccupied with her visions of the future working or not working as the case was, Radegond was preoccupied with the conditions of the road, and Hathus... hadn't been himself since the Ancestor Gods. Who could blame him? For Avina, it still didn't feel quite real, like when she went home her mom and dad would both be there, not just her mom and bad news to deliver. It hurt, but part of her mind had pushed that hurt away, and she wasn't sure if she should be thankful or if she was supposed to hate herself for it.

Tius, despite being preoccupied with the princess, did keep making time for Avina, honestly more than she would have expected. But that was still hardly every hour of the day, or even every hour in which she might be bored. Which left, of course, the humans.

Avina had said everything she wanted to say to Seija. Sometimes, she thought about the woman's promise, an arm for an arm. Avina thought it would feel good, at least for a moment, but it wouldn't make her mother whole again. And she knew Tius and her mom both would want her to let it go, but that didn't meant she wanted to and certainly didn't mean she had to talk to that woman. Of the rest, it was still hard... True, Maria told good jokes, the rather dirty kind Hathus would normally have liked, and while Launo was pretty much cold, Ukko, though not warm in manner, wasn't unapproachable either. But for all her rare halting attempts at really striking up a conversation, few came to fruition.

Acacia was another story. Out of all the humans, she was the one who bothered to come up and say, "Hello." When she did, the talk was usually petty, but her friendly nature was, Avina had to admit, actually kind of endearing.

"Hm?" Avina replied after such a spontaneous greeting.

"Oh," Acacia said, "I just was wondering how you were holding up."

"Do you ask everybody that?" Avina asked.

"Pretty much," Acacia replied, "but most people have somebody else to talk to. You and Hathus, not so much... and he didn't really want to talk."

"So," Avina said, dubious, "what exactly did you want to talk about?"

"Well," Acacia said, "I was wondering, what is it really like to be, well, Accursed?"

Avina rolled her eyes.

"I mean, it's been a long time since the last great war, so being around for all those years alone must"-

"I'm sixteen."

Acacia blinked.

"Really? But you look sixteen, even Tius is thirty-four, and Hathus is past seventy. I know when it comes to history there's Ukko, but..."

"I'm sixteen," Avina said, now smug, "and if you want to ask what it's like for a human to be Accursed you're asking the wrong woman. I might as well ask you what it's like to be human."

"Well, do you want to?"

"Want to what?"

"Ask me about what it's like to be human, then," Acacia said, and she said it with such pleasant conviction that Avina couldn't help but be taken aback.

"Seriously?" Avina asked.

Acacia nodded.

"I don't know how much help I can really be," she said, "but I can try to guess what might be different, or important or... just human. Though you seem to have most of it down."

"I don't need a human-ness tutor," Avina said, recalling what her parents had sometimes jokingly threatened to get her.

"Okay," Acacia replied. "I'm sorry I misjudged you."

"It's alright," Avina said, "no harm done." And she smiled at the human girl, who smiled back pleasantly.

Maybe if planning to assassinate an evil god-queen wasn't what brought them together, they could be friends, despite the company Acacia kept. At the very least, she was proof that not all humans had to be stupid about things.

"You know," Avina said, "I was wondering a few things about Kalest..."

They chatted for the next couple hours, until fairly late in the afternoon. Their path was downhill, through pine forest, and none could say if they were still in Tyrvad, or had strayed onto Kalesti soil. Golden light filtered through the high needles, and the world felt at peace. Or at least it did until Esteri fell to one knee, panting. She lifted her head, and Avina could see black veins creeping out from the corners of her eyes.

"Something's coming," she said. "An enemy."

Those with weapons drew them, and Avina tensed herself to shift. A moment later she heard it, something rustling in the foliage, and caught movement out of the corner of her eye, something ducking furtive between the close-set trees to the side of the trail. Avina tried to remember what she could. If it was a wolf or a bear it probably wouldn't approach so large a group, but then Esteri's vision had recognized this thing as a foe.

Human soldiers, probably Delphina's Kalesti, Avina realized. Danger or no, Avina couldn't imagine them being that tough.

"Hey, you cowards!" she shouted as she fell in to put her back to her friends. "Why don't you show yourselves!"

The movement intensified, and it was clear enough that the figures were approaching, but when the first one came into sight, it was not at all what Avina had expected.

It wasn't human. Nor was it even a feral accursed. It should not even have been alive. The thing was practically a scarecrow, its body made of twigs and sticks from which haphazardly sprouted black feathers and dark pine needles, and atop its shoulders, instead of a head or a gourd or an empty hat, was a colossal bird's skull, a dark ruddy light emanating from deep behind the eye sockets. In one gnarled twig-claw, the thing held a hatchet. Others were emerging, and all bore arms, long knives, nets, polearms, and more.

"What the hell?!" Avina shouted. "What is this?"

"It doesn't matter," Ukko, who was beside Avina, replied. "They clearly bear us ill will, so the remedy is clear."

At that there was a rustling and one of the creatures leaped at the man, and he cut it in twain with a stroke of his sword, the thing falling apart into a pile of sticks, feathers, and pine needles crowned by that massive skull.

"Right," Avina said. The rest were charging, and as they did Avina stepped forward and into her other shape. The world around her seemed to shrink in an instant and she intercepted one of the things with each hand, grasped them and slammed them together, shattering their skulls to dry bits of bone, at which their bodies disassembled.

From there, Avina turned around. There were maybe nine or ten left, and she couldn't quite tell exactly how many had been dismantled in the first moment, and the majority of those left were in one knot. Two menaced Esteri, but didn't seem to know what to do with her and held their strikes while three more made vain attempts to cut at Tius or snare him in a net. The rest faced Hathus, Radegond, and the other humans who seemed to be doing well enough. Avina stomped over and gave one of Tius's attackers a swift kick, scattering its body and sending its skull rolling away. Tius himself got the better of a second and knocked its head from its body as Avina grasped the third and crumpled the twigs that made it up, watching it slip through her taloned fingers.

"These things aren't so tough," she quipped. And indeed, in short order all were subdued, and Avina returned to her normal shape.

"Wait!" Esteri cried, looking to Avina. Her eyes were still black.

"It's not over."

She stepped to the middle of the group, and all eyes turned about, looking this way and that frantically. Then, suddenly, she stopped.

"Hathus, jump!" she shouted, though she was not even looking his way.

"Huh?" came the reply

"Jump forward!" Esteri screamed.

In that moment, Hathus hesitated, and turned around instead, and then fell backwards. That was when Avina saw it, a half-formed one of those horrid things, grasping his legs with a gnarled branch, the other holding a knife.

"Everyone! They're coming!"

Avina didn't need to be told twice, and resumed her fighting state. However many times they needed to be-

Pain! Avina reeled, feeling a sharp shock in her calf. At once, she whirled, and saw another of the things had lept on her, and flailed with its broken spear. The stabs were like bee stings to her, but getting stung by a bee still hurt. No one had ever hurt her in battle before! Wildly, she kicked, eventually throwing the monster only to see another shambling forward, surprisingly quick. Avina grabbed that one and hurled it against a tree, only to see the monster she had kicked away literally putting itself back together and grasping a weapon from one of its fallen comrades to rush at her again. Avina kicked it back once more, and it shattered apart, but she did not dare to imagine it would be down for long.

Deftly, she turned back to where Hathus had fallen. Tius and Radegond were there, on either side of him, and though his clothes were blood slick, he had stood. Behind him was Esteri, who was doing her best to occupy the attention of one of the creatures. Avina turned her head, and saw Launo and Seija fighting together back-to-back, the latter with a long knife in either hand, parrying and holding at bay two of the monsters. Maria was beside them, holding her giant sword and gritting her teeth. Ukko faced one, and even as Avina glanced, forced it to give ground and sliced it apart.

Avina returned his attention to Hathus, where the fighting was thickest. She took Esteri's monster and launched it over her shoulder, to where the other two she was fighting were.

She saw one, grasping a boar spear, rise and run at Hathus, and Hathus changed his arm, and the thing was engulfed entirely by a gout of flame that blocked Avina's vision. Her spirit rose. They wouldn't get up if they were turned to ash!

And then her heart sank when a glowing, white-hot spear point erupted from the flames and buried itself into Hathus's chest. In that moment of horror, it was followed by the bluk of the monster, blazing like a bonfire, its jaw open as though screaming as silent as it was. Avina sprang upon it, and though its burning body scorched her hands she set to tearing at it. She ripped limbs away, and snapped them, and threw them this way and that.

Someone called her name. Tius, she heard him behind her, and the clash of metal on wood, but for a moment she didn't care. This thing, this monster, whatever it was, it had to die! She ripped its ignited innards out and scattered them, and at last dropped to a knee and slammed the charred skull of the monster into the road, shattering it. Near blind with fury she whirled, and nearly brushing Tius aside, sprang on two of the three monsters to that side, and grasped one with her hand and the other with the writhing strands of her hair and shook them this way and that until they flew apart, howling with an inarticulate, wordless scream of rage and grief.

Not again! Not now! She wasn't supposed to lose anyone else!

Then she heard Acacia's voice rise.

"The skulls!" she cried, "Break the skulls!"

And Avina noticed the skull of one of her latest victims, rolling away and coming to rest between two piles of twigs and broken bone that had been the very first two she'd crushed, skull to skull, that had never risen.

Avina sprang like an animal after it, and gripped the skull even as it seemed to lift plant matter and feathers to itself, and pried open and shattered its beak and jaw, and slammed what was left to the ground once, twice, thrice until all that was left was shards and the pain of the ones that had jammed into her hand. She turned, and saw Ukko cut his foe's head apart from skull to jaw, and before it hit the ground across at the level of its empty eyes, and the light went out of those damnable sockets.

In a screaming fury, Avina grasped for any monster she could see, to crush them, to tear them apart, to make something pay! She knocked Radegond, who was protecting the fallen Hathus, flat to grasp the woman's foe, and leaped at the next after, and when she was done with those and turned she saw, nothing but broken shards and scattered twigs.

Still, she made a wordless wail before collapsing down to her human self. When she did, tears came, and she doubled over, sobbing. Not again...

Moments later, she heard Ukko speak.

"I cannot say if he has a fighting chance," Ukko said, "but for now he lives. Radegond."

"Yes?"

"I would estimate that, with your wings, you would be the swiftest among us. Would I be wrong in that assessment?"

"No," Radegond declared.

"Then," Ukko said, "you should try to make your way to the next town in our path, and bring a doctor back here. Take whatever you need to make a better first impression and procure some haste on the return."

"And the rest?" Radegond asked.

"We shall try to tend to his wound as best we can. Tius?"

"Hm?"

"You are something of a woodsman where you come from, I gather. Could you, perhaps, search our surroundings for any medicinal herbs? Bay laurel, white willow, horsetail – whatever you can find that might be of help."

"I'll get right to it," Tius said. Avina heard one footstep, then another, and a snapping twig.

"No!" she screamed. She looked up, though she couldn't see straight, and fixed her gaze on the blurry form that must have been Tius pacing off into the forest.

"T-there could be more," she said. "I'll be right there, just wait a moment." She struggled to her feet. "Shouldn't go out there alone... nobody should."

"You're quite right," Ukko said, conciliatory, "though I believe Radegond will be fine in the air. Tius..."

Tius had stopped, and as Avina wiped her eyes and cleared her vision, she could see he was looking at her.

"Good," Ukko said, "the rest of us will do what we can here. Acacia, Seija, Maria, you should make sure no fires have been started in the brush, Launo, you, Esteri, and I..."

Avina had taken Tius's hand and followed him into the woods, ceasing to heed Ukko's voice. Soon enough, the sounds of the forest dominated all.

"Hathus is going to die," Avina whispered, "isn't he?"

"We're tougher than humans," Tius said. "I mean, you're not any worse off for having a spear through you."

"Don't lie to me," Avina said. "You know this is different."

"I do," Tius replied, "but he's not dead yet, so there's still hope."

"But there's still danger, too."

"Yeah," Tius said, nodding his head, "yeah, there is. And there might be nothing any of us can do about it. But as long as there's a chance, we might as well try."

"I know that," Avina said. "I- I'm just scared. That I'm going to lose him, and Radegond, and Esteri, and you. I can take care of myself, but I couldn't – didn't help him."

"You did everything you could," Tius said, "we all did. Sometimes that's just not enough, here as much as back when Erikis betrayed us. And I'm sorry you ever had to learn that, much less like... like this."

"... How did you?"

"You mean..."

"How did you learn... this. That the world doesn't play fair."

"Well," Tius said as he walked forward and here and there stopped to check the underbrush, "I don't know that there was one big moment, but if I had to guess, I'd say it was when I was around twelve. You know what a plague is, right?"

"Yeah," Avina said, "it's when a lot of humans get sick all at once."

"Well, back then, one came through the city I lived in. Not a really bad one, the kind that makes the histories, but most of the people I knew lived out on the streets, so we got sick a lot anyway. And a lot of them did. Some lived, some died, and some like me never got sick at all. And those were my friends, at least some of them, and there was nothing I could do for any of them except maybe try to score some food and clean water while waiting to see if they were going to make it."

Tius fell silent, staring intently at one tree before taking out his knife and starting to strip some of its bark.

"Tius?"

"This is willow," he said.

"Good for pain, right," Avina replied. She bit her lip a little, since it seemed he hadn't quite finished talking about the past.

Tius handed her some of the willow bark, and he clearly

saw the expectant look in her eyes.

"Those weren't good days, Avina. Most of my days before coming up the mountain weren't, but that time was worse than most. And a big part of it was because I was so helpless, and didn't understand why things happened the way they did."

"Did someone important die?" Avina asked.

Tius froze for a moment, then went back to cutting strips of bark to carry back.

"It's.... those days aren't important anymore. I've had twice as long to get used to things that happened back then than I'd been alive at the time."

"Alright," Avina said, and resolved to press the matter of the past no further. She probably shouldn't have asked as much as she did. "So... um... what do you think about now? Not Hathus, we'll try our best, I mean this whole killing a god-queen thing."

"Are you scared?" Tius asked.

"No," Avina insisted. "Well, I am, but that's not the point.

"What is, then?"

"These things that attacked us," Avina said. "They're all about birds and trees, so they've got to be Kalesti, right? And they're weird magic, so they're probably her fault."

"I think so," Tius said. "They didn't seem too eager to actually hurt Esteri. The rest of us weren't so lucky."

"So that means she's coming after us. We don't have a choice, and I could go for cracking the skull behind all of this."

"Are you sure?"

Avina stopped for a moment.

"What do you mean, am I sure?"

"About the skull cracking. I know it's got to be done, but I don't think you should be quite so eager. Hurting somebody isn't much fun, even when it's important."

"You're thinking about me and Seija, too, aren't you?"

"A little bit," Tius admitted.

"It's not your problem," Avina replied.

"Of course it is," Tius said. "I care about you, so I want you to think long and hard before you do something you could regret for a long time."

"Thanks," Avina said. "I'll think about it. But we've got to deal with the Queen, so that's not going to change no matter what I want."

"Guess it's not," Tius said, picking a few sprigs of something.

"Has Esteri ever talked about her – Queen Delphina – to you?"

"Only enough for me to understand that the queen always seemed to hate her. I don't know much else about her other than that."

"Why?"

"Why what?"

"Why does the queen hate Esteri so much?" Avina asked. It had been bothering her for a while, but asking questions about humans rarely met with straight answers.

"If I had to guess," Tius said, "it's probably about the royal succession, though who knows what's going to happen with that now, whether we win or lose."

"That..." Avina tried to remember what her parents had told her about the rulers of the outside world. "The King's oldest becomes the new king, right?"

"Yeah, that's it," Tius said, "which means that as long as Esteri is alive, no child of Delphina's was going to take the throne."

"But she already had it herself, right?"

"Not forever," Tius said, "well, not unless she was planning this whole mess the entire time."

Avina fell silent. It was a lot to take in. As best she could, she asked questions about the herbs Tius was collecting, and focused on remembering the trail they were following. After what felt like both too long and nowhere near long enough, Tius stopped.

"We should probably head back," he said. "We're not likely

to find a lot more very soon."

The return was swifter, and Tius went directly to where Ukko knelt beside Hathus with the herbs, bark, and other sundries in his arms. Avina stopped short. While the humans worked, slow though she knew they could do no better, she saw Esteri sitting down, hugging her knees, crying softly.

Then Avina saw that Esteri's eyes were jet black.

***

Hathus died in the night. One moment, he was lying at rest, his breaths soft, if unpleasantly wet, and the next the coughing fits began. Each one that wracked his body made the next worse and sooner. Blood flecked his face, and at last the frenzied gasps for air met with no success. Moments later, despite furious attentions, he was still. That was when Avina let herself cry again, as Tius offered his shoulder for the same, and though she was tired down in her very bones, she didn't sleep that night. Around noon, exhaustion finally claimed her, and she was awakened just before dusk by Radegond's arrival. Radegond had brought a doctor, and a cart, but of course there was burial to be done and not medicine. The weary company picked themselves up, and began the trek back to the town from whence the doctor had come. They made camp somewhat after dark, deeming it unreasonable to return without rest.

"I have to say, bad news this is," the Doctor declared. "Some folks, they'd seen these... things, stalking through the hills for days before now, but nobody was quite sure what they were seeing, nor had any trouble from them. Thought maybe there were advance scouts for the army, looking for a good passage into Tyrvad, but it seems like the truth is a lot worse."

"Is Kalest moving on Tyrvad, then?" Ukko asked.

"Well," the doctor said, "not that anybody knows. There's been no word of another war, but then the world's a crazy place, I'm sure you know."

"It is," Acacia said, "and we're very glad to be returning to Kalest... though the circumstances could have been much happier. But if you have any news of the kingdom, we'd like to hear it."

Avina's ears perked up a little. She was no tactician, but she knew that any news was good news for them. Better than not knowing, especially when Esteri's visions of Delphina drew blanks and her visions of herself were fixed on some distant hell.

"Strange things," the doctor said, "strange things indeed. But not all bad. Not, hm, not a week ago news came through that there's been an arrangement between Prince Tuoni and Princess Jeanne of Lysama, to marry the thrones when the two of them come of age."

"King Baudouin's niece," Esteri mused. "She would have been third in line before all that happened. It's a good match."

"All that happened, yes," the doctor said. "There's a story nobody knows the whole truth of. They say the King of Lysama turned into a giant monster, have you heard that one? Others said he was just the monster's first victim, which story do you hold to?"

Avina swallowed, but Ukko spoke very quickly and surely.

"The way I heard it," he said, "the monster had once been the King, yes, but Hyperborean spies turned him into the thing that smashed a goodly portion of his former capitol."

"Hm, hadn't heard Hyperborea named in that mess before, but maybe people just don't want to speak too much against them. That's another strange matter, they say many of those folk now have the king's ear, so much that he dismissed one of his generals for them. Now, the queen, I could understand, she comes from their stock doesn't she? Ah, but a queen would have a king's ear I guess. In any case, they're calling old King Lysama the 'Demon King' now, and if he became half of what they say, I'd say they were letting the monster off easy."

"The accounts are quite fearsome," Ukko said, "and a marker of days both strange and dark. Perhaps this dismissed general? That sounds like quite the shake-up above."

"It was the woman general. Can't recall her name rightly,

but the way I heard it, she was fairly unceremoniously re-lieved of her duties after some sort of disagreement with the Hyperboreans at court. Made quite a fuss, as I heard. News of that came in, oh, a few days before the royal engagement so I wonder if that's what it was over?"

"I doubt it," Launo said. "That doesn't sound like General Katri."

"Katri, was it? I'll try to remember that. Come to think, she might just be on forced leave or whatever you do to send a general to her room. At least, as the stories go, she's not got her head on the block or anything like that. So how about you lot? Travelers must pick up a few tales."

Here, Esteri took over for Ukko.

"Nothing as grand as what you've told," she said. "One or two versions of the fall of Lysama, of course. Other than that it's mostly Tyrvad news. Interested?"

The doctor sighed. "Well, if you think of anything worth telling."

"Now there is one story," Esteri said. "A town we were at a couple weeks back was all abuzz. They said there was a girl who just fell from the sky in a flash of violet light, can you be-lieve it?"

"It sounds pretty fanciful," the doctor replied, amused. "Go on."

"Well," Esteri said, "I was actually able to see the girl. She looked Hyperborean, but she could have been of Tyrvad blood. She didn't say anything about falling from the sky, but she did have some very choice words for the Queen of Kalest, which I won't repeat in polite company. It seemed a rather specific delusion."

The doctor shrugged. "Paranoid ravings often are, poor thing. Hopefully those mountain folk will take good care of her until she comes to her senses. They're a superstitious lot, though."

"Quite," Esteri said. "I must admit I have never seen as much credence lent to ghosts and goblins and omens of fortune or misfortune as I did in my time in that country."

Avina tried to resist the urge to laugh, seeing as they had witnessed nothing overtly superstitious in their time in Tyrvad. If anything, Avina thought Kalest's northern neighbors seemed a very practical people.

"Though of course," she said, her tone as honest as it was grim, "given what befell us, perhaps I had believed too little in ghost stories."

The doctor nodded.

"I'm truly sorry for what befell your friend. We'll see him laid to rest right... did he follow any god as his own?"

"Not especially," Tius replied, stepping in. "I'm sure whatever priest would be willing to speak for him would make him happy."

Avina wasn't so sure. Most of the Accursed didn't put much stock in gods, and as crazy as the world and the one that seemed to exist in it were, she didn't see much of a reason to start.

CHAPTER XXXI

Ulfr

This deal was getting worse all the time. It had been well more than a month, and no word had come from Hyperborea about what they were supposed to do with their God-King as he continued to flex his arcane muscles in new and terrifying ways. What had happened that day? They dodged a bullet when Delphina died, having already burned her, but nothing like that was anywhere in the canon of things that could happen!

The sole saving grace, as Ulfr hated to admit, was that Ormr had managed to ingratiate the Hyperborean delegation to the king, affording them, for the moment, a position of significant authority and the King's ear. Of course, even having that position showed how quickly it could turn around. When Katri had questioned the king's new stick soldiers, they had been quick to denounce her, and she had consequently been quickly on her way back to her family lands in barely sugar-coated disgrace. A victory, perhaps, since Katri had opposed the Hyperborean delegation at every turn, but it was not won by them but instead by King Piru's volatility, making such a sweeping change to his high command on a whim because she said the wrong word at the wrong time.

If they played their cards right, life could be fairly comfortable, but one mistake could see them up upon a pike, so as far as Ulfr was concerned he wanted to know how they were going to get out of the situation sooner rather than later.

Ormr seemed to agree, and what hours of his day he didn't

spend managing the king and his irrational outbursts, the ambassador spent waiting by the radio, making sure its battery was charged and hoping for some sort of reply from high command. Once or twice they had raised the local airbase, but that outpost was similarly out of contact with the motherland.

How long were they going to have to wait before they had to do something? And more importantly, what could they even do?

Around midday, one of the servants Piru had retained in the wake of his change, which was a fairly small number, appeared before Ulfr and Ormr and, trembling, told them that the King desired Ulfr's presence in the Grand Audience Chamber.

That chamber was one of the new additions to the Palace of Kalest. While the structure had retained its rustic aesthetic, Piru had been hard at work remodling. Rooms moved and distorted, and sometimes came into being or vanished entirely. Ulfr hadn't heard of anyone caught in a disappearing room, but he couldn't say that it wasn't yet another way in which this could end very badly for him.

But the Grand Audience Chamber had been one of the rooms to appear out of nothing, growing like a tumor, unfolding itself, and pushing the rest of the palace nicely aside to make room for its presence. It was a vast chamber – not compared to the Old Citadel in Hyperborea, where the Dead God had once kept court, but certainly cavernous compared to the close and high architecture of Kalest that reminded its barbarian people of the ancient forest they were so proud of. The vaulted ceiling nearly vanished to sight if one looked up, and the long, emerald-colored carpet that lead up to the high seat was broad enough that twenty men abrest could walk it, and long enough that while King Piru insisted no one advance within a hundred paces of him without his permission, that was most of the way from the great doors to the throne.

And that seat! It looked bloody uncomfortable, Ulfr

thought, but even he felt a bit intimidated. The dais on which sat the throne was greatly upraised, with some multiple of some sacred number of steps leading up from the floor to the level on which the king sat, and then comically another few steps were built into the throne so that Piru could rest his royal feet while still sitting in the chair.

That chair was gigantic. Like the ancient throne in the old throne room it was made of a single piece of carved wood, though Ulfr doubted whether any artisan had laid a hand on Piru's new seat and felt instead that its form must have been sculpted by the King's imagination alone. The back rose, to its highest point, at least thirty feet over the seat, and the thing would have been topheavy in the extreme if not for its colossal base, for it fanned out from side to side as it rose, giving it the silhouette of a massive tree. Ulfr would have called it a mushroom, at least in jest, but after the king's conjuring, Ormr had insisted on drilling Ulfr in all the symbology included, just in case King Piru happened to expect his servants to know and show some respect to a hidden meaning of the carving. He had used flash cards! Flash cards, as though Ulfr was back in primary school! It was absolutely insulting but also effective.

Thus, Ulfr knew, and resented that he knew, that the right arm rest of the high seat held the likeness of a stag and represented wisdom and pride, while the left had the likeness of a wolf and represented ferocity and power. The massive back was a great tree, and each of its nine great branches held a symbol and a meaning. The figure upon the crown of the tree, overlooking all, was a raven; held as the most sacred bird to Kalest, though the yokels had a healthy respect for anything that flew.

The raven, Ulfr reflected as he approached, was both unmistakable and unforgettable, though not so much thanks to its own design as to the presence of the guards in the chamber. They, too, were the king's creations: he had grown sour at the failures of his army, and had thus crafted the first as shambling things of twigs crowned with gigantic crow skulls and set walking with singular purpose. The second generation of those creations was more careful, and though they still presented the bare and rune-etched bird skulls, they stood straight, moved with care and intelligence, and their wooden bodies were both more refined and clad in armor.

Those hadn't bothered Ulfr; it was still just animation magic, if coupled with very high-level conjuring, which Hyperborea held in most regards to be wasteful compared to technological or mostly technological solutions to automation. Like the other wonders Piru had wrought, they were unknown only in scale, and scale was solely a matter of cost. Once someone at home made sense of whatever happened, they could match the King of Kalest, and solve the problem he presented.

The third generation of Piru's raven warriors, though, were cut from a different cloth. Half a dozen of them stood at attention, flanking the ascent to the high throne. They were not made of sticks and bones, but rather flesh and blood. The things were like ravens twisted into human form, and it seemed to every inspection that had been made that the creatures were actually alive. While the bare-skulled automatons stared blankly forward with their empty eye sockets, moving solely on commands or following what orders they were given with basic skill, the third variety watched Ulfr carefully and furtively, and executed their assignments in a manner not unlike human soldiers of great discipline, and when at times they were not bound to the dispatch of their duties, they gathered in black-feathered flocks and cawed quietly to one another about gods alone knew what.

Even if most of what Ulfr saw was smoke and mirrors, it was a better imitation of true life than he had heard out of any alchemy or magecraft. Ormr seemed disturbed by that development as well, and had spent twice as long as usual attempting to raise their homeland over the radio the day those things were unveiled and the day after.

For now, Ulfr reached the hundred pace mark, and kneeled.

He was granted permission to advance to within twenty paces of the throne, did so very carefully, and took a knee again, all under the watchful eye of Piru's raven guard, as canny and menacing as any of the Elder Council, even though they may have been literally born yesterday.

The king seemed to be in a pensive mood for the moment, for he did not have good moods, and he was something like his original six and a quarter feet in height, rather than the seven feet or more he now tended to present when he was agitated, or desired to inspire fear or flaunt his majesty. Ulfr regarded that as good, because despite the fact that he could change in an instant, it meant he was at least not beginning the conversation in a black rage. Probably.

"My liege..." Ulfr said, keeping his head down as he had been told to do.

"My birds have found them," the king said, his voice hoarse and breathy.

"I"-

"Dear Esteri... and her companions. Foolish things, knew not what to do, but I saw. They are on Kalest's soil once more."

"That is... good?" Ulfr offered.

"Good. Bad. She must be returned to me, but she knows, so much, too much. Lord Ukko is with her. That man is good, but if she proved what she knows? Why are they returning, and so in secret? Hm? No, mustn't mean happy returns. That is what we have divined. The north road, from Tyrvad, but no happy returns. Less happy for a poor welcome, pathetic things, should have begun with the best."

Ulfr could barely understand the king. Since it happened, he had been more or less lucid at times, but this was distinctly one of the less.

"This task was set to you before," Piru hissed. "To bring her here. Return... return my daughter to me."

"You wish me to acquire the girl? That has proved, ah, easier said than done."

"Ormr offered you. Return with her. Unharmed. Unperturbed. Her feelings are worth more than your life."

"Your majesty…"

"This is my will, beyond contest. Return with Esteri. Bring no harm to Lord Ukko. Depart by dawn. You will be gifted what we know before then."

Ulfr trembled. At once, he saw the problem with his situation. Given his previous clashes with Esteri, the princess would probably get him killed if he brought her back. He might be able to cut a deal with her, but how much would Piru learn anyway?

And Ulfr didn't have much of a choice, nor did he have the luxury of time to find one.

"Of course, your majesty."

"Go," Piru said, and the raven soldiers rustled menacingly, sending Ulfr quickly scurrying from the hall.

***

"You set me up," Ulfr growled, glaring at Ormr. He meant it to be threatening, but the ambassador clearly knew the threat was empty, because if Ulfr attempted anything as brazen as stabbing his treacherous supervisor, he wouldn't escape.

"You are a liability here," Ormr said. "When given the opportunity to position you farther from where you could get us both killed, and the rest of the delegation as well, yes, I took it."

"Is this about the damn flash cards?"

"It is not simply about the flash cards," Ormr said. "Frankly, you should be surprised you've lasted this long with your utter lack of decorum."

Ulfr fumed, and Ormr seemed ready to dismiss him, but then something happened, the first good news since this disaster had begun.

The emergency radio crackled to life.

"Ambassador Ormr." The voice had horrible static, but Ulfr still recognized it. The good news was that it was direct from Hyperborea itself. "Ambassador Ormr, do you copy?"

Ormr grabbed the radio, and then tried to hide his excitement.

"Yes," he said, "yes, I copy. This is Ormr, Ambassador to Kalest. Ah, to whom am I speaking? Over."

"Colonel Svanna, acting head of Covert Affairs and Special Operations. Over."

Ulfr's eyes widened. That was news, and very bad news especially for Ulfr personally.

"... Head of Covert Affairs? May I inquire as to the status of Councilor Saga? Over."

"Saga is dead," Svanna related, "and so is most of the rest of the Elder Council. We've found nine survivors of the First Generation, and don't expect to come across any more at this rate. How much do you know about what happened? Over."

"Assume we know nothing here. Over."

"Copy that. Long story short, Queen Delphina of Kalest managed to steal the Godhead Principle and promptly used it to annihilate the Elder Council. Something in her ascendance, attack, and departure caused a massive power surge. Most of our electronics were fried and at least 85% of the power grid infrastructure for Hyperborea was rendered inoperable, some of that on fire. We've been working hard since then to put some sort of order together and get the lights back on. Repairs on the Transcontinental Tower completed today, so we're talking to the rest of the world again. What's your situation, and the current status of the Usurper Delphina, as accurately as you can gauge? Over."

"Delphina is dead," Ormr replied. "You are aware of our standing mission for the Day of Ascendance? Over."

"I've been briefed. Over."

"King Piru of Kalest ran his Queen through on her return to Kalest, and she expired, but not before passing what in light of your report I believe to be the Godhead Principle to King Piru. Over."

Svanna didn't miss a beat. "Please provide a report on King Piru of Kalest's current status, then. Over."

Ormr took a deep breath.

"I will first endeavor to report on the powers and abilities displayed by the King of Kalest. He displays primarily Spatial, Conjuring, and Animation Arcana. As a matter of perspective, he's been literally inserting new rooms into the palace, physically between two rooms that already exist adjacent to each other without visibly distorting space. Also, I suspect the outer dimensions of the Palace have not been changing to account for these new additions. Also regarding spatial magic he seems freely capable of increasing and decreasing his own size. Further, he has endeavored in the creation of very sophisticated automatons, capable of following complex orders across vast distances, though in at least one known case with some disagreement as to the means of following said orders. Recent displays, however, have included what appears to be Life Magic on an unknown order. The automatons have been replaced with living things. They seem as clever as humans, or very close to it, alive and individually aware. I haven't had a chance to make a close analysis nor have I been provided any cadavers, so this is somewhat speculative in nature. Over."

"Copy that. Any psychological analysis? Over."

"In my personal assessment he's dangerously unstable. I say this having served in the court of Kalest for six years; this is not his natural state. King Piru had formally been a strong, resolute man, if sometimes conflicted. The current Piru appears to have multiple personalities between which he switches on a whim, including a bellowing, bombastic, and bloodthirsty sovereign, a whispering madman, a grieving widower, and an esoteric sorcerer. Unlike some supposed instances of multiple personalities there's full continuity between the modes, it is only his demeanor and outlook that changes abruptly and wildly. Over."

"Your statement has been recorded. Over."

"How does Covert Affairs desire we proceed? Over."

For a while there was silence on the other end.

"We had a theory for Delphina, that might have allowed us to re-attain the Godhead Principle if we brought her back here to Hyperborea, but the information you have provided may alter our intended plan and anyway it's not ready yet. If you can lay the groundwork for King Piru to come here without actually provoking him to do so of his own accord yet, it couldn't hurt, but just maintain observation and wait for further instruction. Copy that? Over."

"I copy," Ormr said, "over."

"Oh, and if Ulfr is still alive, get him out of there before he messes up everything. Over and out."

The radio fell silent, and Ormr turned to glare at Ulfr.

"Even the head of our department knows you're a liability now," he growled. "If you want to change that perception I suggest you do something about Princess Esteri that is to King Piru's satisfaction."

Ulfr felt his eye twitch, "But my previous encounters with that girl..."

"Are not my problem," Ormr said, "as I've told you a dozen times in this conversation. Now pack your bags."

***

The trek out to the frontier was miserable. Not only was it quite long and one more thing that Ulfr had to achieve one-handed, but he had been expressly forbidden from taking any of his usual entertainments with the continental rubes. Sowing a little death and discord may or may not have done anything for Ulfr's mood, considering it would not dispel the doom hanging over him but generally did tend to make him feel better. To be denied that release was certainly souring him even further.

As to the predicament, Ulfr had considered his options. He could not very well kill Esteri. If anything, that might well have been the worst option, because he was fairly certain that Piru could invent a fate far worse than death for one who actually managed that. Delaying success was also out of the question. Oh, Ulfr could simply go to ground in Kalest and claim to any human agents that he was looking but not finding. That would suit Ormr well enough, but on their second meeting the King had expressed a desire for haste, and at times Ulfr saw or thought he saw damnable raven guards skulking about. Whether they were on other errands or no, they would no doubt report if Ulfr was intentionally and obviously delaying his mission.

That left bringing her in, or at least making what would look like a good-faith attempt at the same. The king might forgive an honest failure, or something that could be played off as one. He might even place the blame on Ormr's head for suggesting the arrangement, which would be very gratifying. At the very least, Ulfr felt that this would be the least likely scenario to get him killed. It was, however, not without its risks; damned if he should not mime a convincing enough failure, damned if Esteri and her companions would show no mercy, and damned on Piru's whim if it fell out badly.

Better to honestly bring the princess in. Esteri, perhaps, could be reasoned with. Ulfr couldn't harm her, but she didn't know that. Thus was Ulfr's intention as he rode to intercept Esteri and his companions.

Once he came to their trail, which picked up about where Ulfr had been lead to expect, they were almost insultingly easy to track. Everyone had seen such a large, armed, and colorful group pass through town, and most had noted the road along which they had left. With a swift horse and a royal requisition for more, Ulfr had picked up the trail in a week, and in three more days believed that he had caught up to them, or else passed them in the night, which would be the better outcome.

And, indeed, none mentioned an earlier arrival of such a company as the one Ulfr tracked, and thus the agent of Hyperborea resolved to remain and await their arrival. That came some few hours later, no doubt due to the fact that they were walking, and had likely foraged in the wilderness for fresh water and food. The image of the prideful lot trying to scratch something from the dirt amused Ulfr so he decided to accept it as his personal canon of events.

For what they were, they were actually well-disguised; Esteri had been the most remarkable of them, but she was concealed very well, and drew the eye so poorly that at first Ulfr was not sure she was in their company. Ulfr himself kept concealed from their sight, for surely he would cut a memorable figure, as there were not that many one-handed Hyperborean men wandering about Kalest.

It was Ulfr's good luck that they seemed inclined to stay at an inn, having reached civilization. By his count, his former compatriots were at the same number and strength as he had left them with, while Esteri's band had lost one of their number; one of the ones who was neither the princess nor the miserable brat who had taken Ulfr's hand, though, so as far as Ulfr was concerned all was well. If he got a moment to claim a life in exchange for his limb, he would be sure to do it, but retaining his own life came first.

As such, Ulfr waited until after dark, and gained ingress to the inn through an open window on the first floor. In the common room, he heard footsteps upstairs. It was a fancy inn, where rather than a warm place by the fire they offered individual or small-group rooms to guests. Not civilized accommodations, but fair enough for being both on the continent and on the road, so Ulfr had gotten used to their sort. That meant that either someone was awake in the rooms, or moving in the hall between them,

Ulfr stayed silent and listened carefully to the pattern of the footfalls. Slowly, they paced forward, coming all the way to the point Ulfr judged to be the top of the stairs. There, they stopped, and rather than descending the stairs as someone on the way to the privy, turned around and continued back down the hall in the opposite direction. With the same steady tread as before, the footsteps came to rest what must have been against the wall farthest from the stairs, where a second floor window would admit some light in the morning. Then, after a significant pause, the steps resumed, on a path back to the stairs.

Someone had set a guard.

As such, Ulfr began moving again, but so as to not excite any squeaky boards born of shoddy workmanship, he resorted to creeping, and scanning the bare wood of the floor for nail-heads, showing where there might be sturdy beams below onto which he could place his weight without alerting the watcher above to his presence. Granted, given the heavy foot-falls of that person they were not versed in the art of stealth and were likely inattentive to stray sounds, but it didn't hurt to take care. In a lap or two of the guard above, Ulfr reached the stairs, and began his ascent. He found, greatly to his pleasure, that the steps were of an exceedingly solid construction, so that if he wished it he could probably advance up them with a simple quiet tread and remain silent.

Here, Ulfr ascended near halfway up the steps, before their switch back and the view of the upper landing, and paid renewed attention to the footfalls of the one above. He listened to the steps pacing away from the stairs, then towards, then away. He guessed that the one doing the walking was one of Ukko's band, but not the man himself, for the pace was absolutely regular except for the pauses at the end, but the incautious weight was not like the ancient man himself. That was good; Ulfr was not permitted to kill Ukko, and that man was the only person against which Ulfr did not fancy his chances even had it been an option. He counted the time it took to cross the upper hall, then waited for the footsteps to reach the top of the stair. There they paused, then turned around.

As soon as that motion began, Ulfr commenced his ascent, much faster now, counting each step as a matter of time he could not afford to waste. Cat-like he advanced and reached the hall before the guard, who was the hammer-wielding lord-ling of Kalest, had passed the halfway mark between the stairs and the far window. With bounding strides but quiet foot-falls Ulfr sprang upon him, and though he stopped at the end having no doubt recognized some hint of danger or disquiet, he was not swift enough, and Ulfr plunged his dagger into the back of the young man's neck, at the base of the skull. Blood flowed, and Ulfr caught the fool's body as it fell, with his maimed arm and interposed himself between the man and the floor, muffling the sound of any fall. The legs of whoever-it-was that Ulfr just killed twitched, and his death throes caused a scuffling scrape, but he could not scream, nor had he managed to raise any alarm, and if all in their rooms were sleeping it was very likely that the sound would not wake them. Once Ulfr was satisfied that the body was very still, and would be making no further sound, he withdrew his knife and stood.

There was, of course, the problem that he did not know what door the princess was behind, and the hinges were likely to squeak. In a flash of insight, Ulfr quickly reached to the body on the floor, and found the key on his person. Then, he descended the stairs with moderate subtlety and, with some poking, found a locked drawer behind the till. For this, Ulfr had a fine saw, which made quick and quiet, though not silent, work of the lock. Ulfr found inside some coin, which he ignored, and a single key, which he took, holding it to be likely the key to an unoccupied room.

Thus, he had a key to the room that the men of the party had rented, and a key to an empty room. Those could safely be eliminated, leaving four rooms in which the princess could be hiding. Ulfr made his way up the stairs, and quick work of trying the locks to discover which doors he could safely eliminate. Then, selecting one of the two rooms adjacent to the occupied room, Ulfr examined the lock.

Were silence not so paramount, he would have laughed, for he could see moonlight through the crack between the door and its frame, well wide enough for his dagger blade to lift the small latch on the other side. There was no bolt, nor bar, nor chain and in this way he didn't have to worry about snapping metal making a fatal sound in the room. Carefully, he started to move the door. It did make a sound, a subtle groan and a metal scrape, but not the high-pitched and ever-loud whine of poorly maintained hinges. Truly, the landlord's attention to detail had made Ulfr's job much easier.

Also part of that attention to detail was the fact that the women of the traveling party were rooming adjacent to the men, as Ulfr had suspected. There were two beds in the room, one closer to the window and the other nearer the door. In the bed at the window were the two women from Ukko's band, the one who wore her hair in black braids curled up and smiling stupidly in her sleep while the other, who had so often given offense, was on the other side, back turned, looking refined for a moment. In the nearer bed there was Esteri, and back to back with her the little Accursed girl.

The hair on the back of Ulfr's neck stood. There were two more missing – the older Accursed woman had still been with them, as had the girl with the big sword, but neither was evident in the room. Could one or both still be awake somewhere?

No, more likely they had taken worse accommodations. One even might, fearing her modesty less than that of the other women, be rooming with the men. And in any case neither had interrupted yet, even as the blood pooled in the hall, so interruption was unlikely in the immediate unless Ulfr's luck took a drastic turn for the worst.

The only problem that remained was how to obtain the Princess. It would be very difficult, possibly impossible, to do so without awakening the Accursed girl, since their backs were directly against one another. And there was very little doubt that Esteri's motion would not be the absolute most careful, so the alarm would be sounded the instant Ulfr took his move. At the same time, the longer he delayed, the more likely it was that something would go wrong and the alarm would be raised anyway.

Ulfr could not kill the princess. He could not even really hurt her. But Ulfr was the only one who knew that as a certainty. His course was clear, though it would have been easier with both hands. He crept close and then roughly grasped Esteri, gripping one of her arms with the elbow of his maimed arm and with his other hand firmly yanking her up by the collar of her nightgown, pressing the blade against her throat. The girl squawked in protest, and thrashed for a second before she felt the bloody steel, and the other women were quickly kicking sheets aside and awakening.

The eyes of the little Accursed girl were the first to fall upon him, and though Ulfr could have sworn he practically felt the air ripple around her, his voice stilled any attack

"Strike for me and she dies!" Ulfr declared. Esteri reached her free hand up and tried to grip his but he applied a little more pressure, just short of breaking the skin, and her struggles became quite still indeed, leaving Ulfr wishing that he truly had the freedom to have his way with her. The fear was practically delicious. Ulfr backed his way to the door, against the angered glares of the women in the room. He heard the other door open.

"If you value her life," he called, "you will not interfere." As he pulled Esteri another few steps back, he saw her would-be savior, and sneered at him.

"Having the upper hand only takes one," he said, and pulled the girl doggedly past him. Down the stairs, to the stables... that was as far as he needed to get. He made the passage, his foes following, clearly waiting for him to slip up, and when he reached the front door and made Esteri open it so he did not have to remove his knife from its position, he turned to them again.

"I suggest you remain here," he said. "Follow me before I'm out of earshot, and who knows what I could do?"

And swiftly he was into the night with his prize. At knife point he forced her to mount his horse, and that was the most dangerous moment when, mounted, she might have used that position to attempt to free herself. But Ulfr took his own place on the beast's back, and the time was finished. He spurred the horse onwards, hopefully towards a future in which Ulfr could keep his hide intact.

CHAPTER XXXII

Acacia

Acacia's whole body was trembling. Launo was dead and that man, that black-hearted villain, was making his getaway with the princess. For what end? Nothing good, of that Acacia was sure. Though lightly garbed, she was sweating, and she could feel her heart thundering in her chest. Beat. Beat. Beat. Beat.

The sound of fleeing hooves. Acacia steeled herself. One-handed, she doubted that Ulfr could keep a mortal threat against Esteri and control of his mount at the same time, which meant now was the time to move! She stepped towards the door, but Avina was faster. The air rippled, and a jet-black giant tore out of the doorway, taking the door, the frame, and a significant portion of the wall with it.

"Avina!" Radegond shouted.

"Where is he?" the girl bellowed. Citizens that emerged from their homes to see the commotion started to run screaming, and why not? They had no idea why there was a giant monster in their town, smashing the front out of a building.

Avina surged forward one way, straining her neck and leading with her ear, seeking hoofbeats over the din. Then she whirled the other way, to where spooked horses were running, and roared like an angry beast.

"Avina, stop!" Radegond shouted. "This is not how we are going to save her!"

Acacia stepped up as well. "Avina, please, can't you see

you're scaring people?"

Avina turned to Acacia, seemed to hear her words.

"They should be scared!" she bellowed. "That worm should be scared! The queen should be scared! I'll tear them all apart!"

"Listen to yourself!" Radegond shouted. Avina only growled. Then, unarmed, Seija ran forward. She grasped one of the writhing strands of what passed for Avina's hair and, with that anchor and lots of momentum, ran for a moment straight up the girl-monster's chest and delivered something resembling a kick to her chin before running out of steam. She kicked away as she fell, turning it into a backflip, and would have stuck the landing but stumbled and grasped at her chest with a wince.

"You!" Avina shouted.

"Yeah," Seija said, "me."

"You think you can fight me?" Avina shrieked. "Bring it on! I'll take that arm right now!"

"Much as I'd like to oblige," Seija said, "I don't have my hammer or even my swords and you're an idiot. Weren't you listening to your commanding officer? What the hell are you still doing stomping around like Baudouin?"

"I'm going to go after them! I'm going to get Esteri back!"

"You still aren't listening."

Avina tried to walk away, glancing to the horizons for some trace of Ulfr. Seija, however, wasn't about to let her. She ran forward, brought her hands together above her head, and slammed them down into the back of Avina's knee. Avina stumbled, and lashed out with her prehensile hair, but Seija rolled away and put her feet back under her before Avina could press any attack.

"You stupid little human!" she shouted.

"I'm not going to let you get anybody else killed tonight."

"I'm going to save Esteri! Am I the only one here who cares?"

Seija ran forward again. She ducked Avina's hair and kicked

her in the ankle. When the Accursed girl swiped a claw downward, Seija used the attack itself as a springboard to slam her shoulder into Avina's gut, and when she fell she rolled between Avina's legs.

Avina whirled and gave an inarticulate roar. Acacia simply watched. She had seen Avina fight, against the scarecrowthings that had killed Hathus, but now she was seeing Seija put into play every trick Ukko had talk them for taking on larger foes and then some; everything she could do alone to turn Avina's scale into a disadvantage.

"How are you so fast?" she demanded, probably not expecting an answer.

"Practice," Seija said, "and discipline. You might be a match for me if you had them yourself. As it is, you can't save the princess, because you can't even get past me."

Avina surged forward, and bent down in a lunge. At the last second, Seija dodged to the side, but this time Avina had expected it and her hair tendrils lashed around. Yet Seija wouldn't be caught, slung herself around like an acrobat, and threw herself boot-first into Avina's cheek. She kicked away, and hit the ground with a roll, but was slow to rise, clearly in pain from the broken ribs that hadn't quite healed.

"You can't dodge forever," Avina growled, "and if you're so good you should know I've got the upper hand. I'm more powerful than you'll ever be."

"And you of all people should know," Seija said, "what happens when a powerful warrior disregards her commander's orders and strikes out on her own. And if you're so much more powerful than me, how much damage are you going to do? And to who? Do you really want to repeat my mistake?"

To that, Avina had no reply, but met Seija's gaze. Acacia's friend stared down the giant, and didn't even flinch.

"I owe you an arm," Seija said. "What will your debt look like?"

For a moment, it looked like there was black mist against the night, and then Avina was back in her human shape, and human size, just a little young woman in her nightgown once more.

"Avina," Radegond said, stepping up, "go upstairs and fetch our things. We need to take stock of ourselves and get ready to move at once. For the rest of us... where are Maria and Tius?"

"I'm here," Tius called. He was on the rooftop. "I think I know what way that bastard went."

"Good thinking," Radegond said.

"Still alive," Maria groaned, stumbling from around the building. "What happened and why did I have to take the barn?"

Either she had never changed for bed or she had taken the chance to dress herself. And she had grabbed her gear besides, so that was... as good as any news could be right now.

"Maria..." Acacia said. It felt like it had been far too long since they'd really spoken.

Maria looked at her, at the ruined facade of the inn, at the faces of her friends.

"What the hell happened?"

Acacia stepped forward.

"Ulfr came back," Acacia said. "He killed Launo and took Esteri."

"That dastardly piece of garbage!"

"And, um, I think the good people of Kalest are likely gathering their torches and pitchforks, so we should probably get moving fast."

"Ready as ever," Maria growled. "So when are we sending him back to Hyperborea in a tinder box?"

"As soon as we are able," Ukko said. "He has a fast horse, but also an unwilling hostage, and if he meant her death he would have accomplished it already. And much like us, he has to sleep sometime."

Avina came down with an armload of their things, and when she turned around to fetch more, Seija went with her, silently putting a second pair of hands to the task. Tius appeared down among the rest of them.

"Southeast," he declared, "along the road, if the dust being kicked up there is any indication. He was moving at a hell of a pace, it won't be easy to catch unless he runs his horse down entirely, but that's a distinct possibility.

"Southeast would lead him back towards Kalest's capitol," Ukko noted. "It seems his aim is now different than a former threat to carry her off to Hyperborea."

"Or," Maria said, "some of his slimy friends have some kind of back door there. I for one don't want to find out. If we're going to be traitors, we might as well be horse thieves too. I'll see what I can find. Acacia?"

Maria waved her over, and Acacia hustled to walk beside her.

"Anyway," Maria said quietly, "sometimes I wonder where our lives went wrong, you know?"

"No," Acacia said. "What do you mean?"

"Well," Maria said, opening up the stables, "when we started this we were soldiers, out to fight the Accursed, rescue a lost princess, and win a war. I guess one of those things is still happening, but not the way we ever thought it would."

"I guess," Acacia said, "but I wouldn't say our lives went wrong. We've tried to do the right thing at every step of the way."

Maria shook her head and smiled.

"You're so naive, you know that?"

"Maria?"

The horses in the stable were skittish, but seemed to calm down amply with a little attention. It wouldn't take too long to be able to lead the five or six riding animals out into the night.

"It's part of what everybody likes about you, though. You don't see the same problems with the world that people like me can get stuck in. Like right now... we're aiming to fight our queen, and a god in one, and we're smashing up inns and stealing horses to do it. Anybody less naive would thinking about ending up on the end of a rope for their trouble."

"Well," Acacia said, tending to one of the horses herself, "maybe it's because I'm not a soldier, but when I think about what I wanted to be, why I wanted to serve my country, I think about all the heroes in stories, like the Chronicle of Kalest and the tales minstrels tell. A lot of them were like this, and did the wrong thing for the right reasons. And I guess we wouldn't be the first to meet bad ends for it, but if you live right, what does it matter how you die? I mean, I'd prefer old... but not old and full of regrets."

Maria laughed a little.

"I'd prefer not at all. Too bad Ukko doesn't know the recipe for his special reserve, isn't it?"

Acacia shook her head, and looked about for bit and bridle.

"Let's hurry up," she said. "We're going to make it through this, and when we do we'll see these people paid back. Then nobody will want to hang us."

Maria smiled again, shook her head, and started to lead the horses from their stalls as best she could.

***

Ukko had one last trick for when the village heads appeared, which was before the band could get going – a writ from king Piru granting him the requisition of whatever he needed. Hopefully, its promise of later recompense would be honored, and no harm come from their need for horses nor Avina's temper tantrum. At the very least, it bought them the right to leave without being pursued by an angry mob. They took four horses, and Tius and Ukko rode alone while Radegond flew above. Avina and Seija rode double, which Acacia thought was an odd pairing, while Acacia herself rode with Maria. They hadn't the luxury of staying to see Launo laid to rest, though since her friend had been of noble birth, his body would probably be treated well.

Ulfr had gained quite the lead, but it was far from insurmountable, and he made only poor efforts to conceal his movement from the air. The open plains, cleared of the Birds' Wood in times immemorial, did not offer him a lot of chances to hide, so the biggest struggle was in not alerting Ulfr to the fact that he was being followed, at least not any more than he no doubt already expected.

Acacia gritted her teeth. They were going to make this right, as much as they ever could. They would fight, and they would win. They couldn't bring Launo back, nor Taavi, nor Hathus for that matter. Nothing could. But they could well do their best to avenge him.

And as Acacia thought about it, she felt as though there was some cold fire burning within her. She had known that to be a soldier meant killing foes on the field of battle, but in her mind that had been a matter of unfortunate circumstance, and though she had yet to face it, excepting Baudouin's monstrous form, the hole in her heart told her that this was different.

This was personal, and emphatic. She wanted Ulfr to die for everything he'd done. She even might have wanted to do it herself. And that frightened her, but not enough to put away her hunger for revenge.

As dawn stained the horizon red, Radegond landed, and commenced to ride behind Ukko. She revealed that they were not far from their quarry, and would likely come on him not long after he might decide to rest, and suggested that all should keep careful eyes for where he might veer off the road. No doubt Ulfr suspected that he would be followed, and had every intention of evading pursuit if he could. The traveling party slowed their pace then, valuing care over speed, and just past mid-day it was Acacia who saw a trail of broken brush subtly veering left of the road, where the hilly landscape might afford some significant concealment despite the lack of tree cover.

And not long after, having left the horses behind and creeping through the brush as silently as possible, they discovered him, at leisure with Esteri, as best as their glance could tell, bound and gagged but by that token very clearly still alive. And at this, they began to attempt to circle the hollow with stealth, Ukko commanding with army hand signals, but as they were nearly about to emerge into clear line of sight, a great bang like a singular clap of thunder rang out.

"I suggest the lot of you emerge from hiding," came Ulfr's voice from the hollow. "If you are intent on ambushing and slaying me, I have no reason to not take dear Esteri with me."

Ukko looked to Acacia, and signaled her another path.

"We are coming out to parley," he declared in a loud voice, then stepped into the open.

The others followed his lead, but on order Acacia fell back and began to climb the small hill that had sheltered their approach from Ulfr's eyes, but evidently not his ears, or whatever other arcane senses a Hyperborean might possess. She crawled on her belly as best she could, to keep from being seen, and hoped that the sound of the others tromping out of hiding would be enough to conceal her.

"My, my, my, both sides?" Ulfr asked. "Well, it's no matter, except I must insist that you disarm yourselves and that the miserable cur who thought it was wise to wound me when we clashed in Lysama come where I can see him."

There was a pause, and a faint rustle.

"Good," Ulfr said. "While the rest of us can parley, you and I have a score to settle, rat."

Thinking Ulfr would be focused on his mark, Acacia pressed a little forward to see. Below, Ulfr was aiming his good hand halfheartedly at Esteri, while focused intently on Tius, who was in front of him with Radegond, Ukko, and Maria while Avina and Seija had gone the other way. They had all dropped their weapons, as Ulfr had insisted.

"I'll give you a chance to apologize and beg for your life," Ulfr said, "though I may not grant clemency no matter how piteously you plead."

Esteri, who Acacia could see had her legs tied together and her arms bound behind her back, squirmed against her bonds, piteously flopping a little in the direction of Ulfr and Tius... though Acacia thought she should be able to move a little better than that.

"For your amusement?" Tius said, sterner than Acacia had ever heard him. "No. I'm here for one reason, and that's to make sure Esteri stays safe."

"How very noble," Ulfr replied. "As for the rest of you, while you may have some objection to my vengeance, I can promise you this. Just surrender and disappear and Esteri will not be hurt by me. You can't win the fight you're picking, or do you not understand that you'll soon be in the hands of an angry god?"

"A god that walks upon the earth can bleed and die," Ukko said. "Tell us what you know, and let us decide for ourselves if we face an impossible quest."

"Bold words, Immortal," Ulfr replied, "but I don't think I'll go spilling state secrets just yet.

He turned his focus on Tius

"Frankly," he said, "I'm not sure I care if we have an accord or no. None of this matters, in the end. All that matters is that you'll go before me. I do hope you were prepared to die for your little crimson-haired harlot."

"... If that's what it has to be," Tius said, "but I think you underestimate her."

"I guess I'll find out," Ulfr said, and then he shifted his aim. But before he had Tius fully in the sights of his terrible weapon, Esteri flexed what muscle she had to sling her legs around, and she kicked Ulfr's feet out from under him. He fell hard on his back, and Acacia didn't hesitate; springing from her feet and leaping from the crest of the hill, she landed just a few steps from Ulfr. As he flailed to get his feet under him, Acacia pounced, and drove one of her blades through the shoulder of his good arm to pin him to the ground. Then she kicked his hand, and sent his weapon skittering across the stony ground of the hollow, and stomped on his fingers for good measure. Her heart was pounding, and the cold flame of hate turned to hot rage. She started to twist the embedded blade, and Ulfr howled in pain.

But then... the fire subsided, and she looked down at her enemy. Piteous, defeated. Perhaps he deserved to die, but that was not Acacia's right.

"The more you squirm," she said, "the more you'll bleed. Hold very still and you might survive, if her majesty has mercy."

Acacia looked, and Tius had recovered a blade and was cutting Esteri's bonds. He freed her hands, and then undid her gag, to which Esteri threw her arms around him and kissed him on the lips.

Tius looked shocked, but Acacia smiled despite herself. Decorum be damned, they made a cute couple.

A pained groan brought Acacia's attention back to Ulfr.

"You stupid... blundering... continental bumpkins," he groaned. "This won't save you. Nothing can save you."

"You should worry about saving yourself," Acacia said. "That's no small wound I gave you."

Ulfr just coughed. The others, including a brightly blushing Esteri and Tius, were converging around the Hyperborean now. Maria had recovered his weapon, and passed it down the line until it ended up in Esteri's hands.

She pointed it at Ulfr.

"Why are you doing this?" Esteri demanded.

"Put that away, you can't"-

"Holding it," Esteri said voice firm, "it's not that different from a crossbow. I can imagine it works much the same. Now talk."

"I was simply following orders," Ulfr said, "which you cannot hold against me, or is it now your way to ill reward loyalty?"

Esteri frowned.

"I know my history," she said. "That defense was fairly famously tried after the Ollerholm massacre. The Lysaman courts accepted it."

"You see"-

"The Kalesti did not."

Ulfr blanched from more than just his worsening blood loss.

"I want a real explanation. Give me one, and I'll consider letting you live."

Ulfr laughed bitterly.

"What magnanimity. Truly, Delphina raised you well whether she meant to or no."

"I'll overlook that. Who gave you your orders, Kalest or Hyperborea?"

"Kalest," Ulfr replied, "though my countrymen were quick to pass me into this damned endeavor."

"Why?"

"Why else but to do the duty that your fair-weather friends here have abandoned, and bring you home."

"You mock me, even now?"

"Under the circumstances," Ulfr said, "no. Of course, I don't know what would be done with you thereafter. Perhaps you'd have a very comfortable life, or perhaps you'd be cast aside like General Katri. Or maybe eaten. Really, why would I care?"

"Did you have any allies, anyone working with you to capture me?"

"I would say, hm... no."

Cryptic, Acacia thought. Esteri fell silent.

"Well, are you done? I could use a bandage sooner rather than later."

Esteri glared down at him.

"You said you would let me live," Ulfr protested.

"I said I would consider it," Esteri replied. Acacia knew at once what her answer was, and clearly Ulfr did too, as he surged upwards at her, wrenching Acacia's abandoned sword from the ground as he did in a final act of desperation. Esteri squeezed the trigger of his terrible weapon, and the hollow was wracked with another thunderclap, and Ulfr fell back to earth. Esteri did not let him try another assault, but brought both her hands together and, trembling, squeezed the trigger again. Thunder rang out one, two, three, four more times, and

417

the smoking, hellish device opened two more holes in Ulfr's chest, and another pair in his head, rendering his face an unrecognizable, bloody pulp. Then the weapon simply made a metallic click-click-click in response to the trigger, and Esteri stepped back and tossed it aside before collapsing to her knees.

Tius knelt beside her, and Avina and Acacia herself joined him as the others soon moved in around them. Maria, bless her foresight, stepped between the princess and the remains of Ulfr, obscuring the body somewhat from her view. All the same, they waited silently for Esteri to recover her composure. Which, at length, she did, standing slowly and turning pointedly away of what was left of Ulfr.

"Really," Esteri said, "I'm almost ashamed I didn't see this coming. Nor do I know what comes next."

"If I may offer a suggestion," Ukko said, "based on all we've heard I think we should pay General Katri a visit. Did you know her?"

Esteri nodded. "Passing well. She taught me a good deal of tactics and military history in days she found herself idle at court rather than handling her command."

"That's good. She seemed a prudent woman, and one who would not act in bad faith. If she has been dismissed from her post that both bodes ill for the right thinking of those giving the order, and well for the chance that she might hear you out."

"It's a wise course," Esteri said. "Katri could probably get us into the capitol unquestioned, possibly even into the palace itself, if she's disposed to help. Of course, if she isn't..."

"It's a risk," Ukko admitted. "I will, of course, defer to your decision."

"I did say it seemed a wise course... and right now I don't know what else to do... other than get away from this hollow. Could we?"

And with that, they began to make their way back to the corpse. No one spoke a word about leaving Ulfr to the crows, and what pity Acacia felt for such a fate was easy to quiet.

***

From there, their course veered, seeking out General Katri's homelands, where hopefully she would be in residence.

"I can't think of where else she would go," Esteri said on the matter, certain of their success in finding Katri. "Though she eschews her family name as a General, her brother is Yrkki, Baron of Talak, and thus she could find very acceptable lodgings in her ancestral manor."

"Have you been there, then?" Maria asked, eager as always.

"No," Esteri said, "but Katri spoke fairly highly of her brother, so they were on good terms. I can't imagine the matter to sour quickly, especially when the last story we heard was that she was relieved for her own good. Trust me, if there were a sordid tale to be had, it would quickly be the favorite."

And that began several hours discussing the peerage that Acacia didn't quite follow. For as outspoken as Maria was, Acacia suspected she was also not the best informed on the workings of the nobility, but all the same she seemed to be enjoying herself.

And, of that, the general pattern repeated nearly daily, with either Esteri displaying what she had earned from a royal education or Ukko or Radegond the fruits of their experience and most others listening patiently when they were close enough to do so. Tius rode with Esteri then, and if there was any discomfort in that they didn't let on, though neither did they reveal any special comfort taken in such company. Other than that, Ukko and Radegond went double, while Acacia herself remained partnered with Maria and Seija with Avina. Of this latter arrangement, Acacia was quite surprised, for the women had a natural enmity when they first met and made no secret of it. But, seemingly from the night that Esteri was taken, they had reached something of a silent ceasefire, possibly even a grudging respect, and though there were still few if any amicable words passed between them, neither was there vitriol, the tension between them seeming to have nearly vanished.

Acacia didn't pretend to understand why that would be, but she did have plenty of time to talk with Maria on their rides. It would have been nice, but as much as they'd become friends since that first day of training there was frustratingly little to talk about on this ride. Their fate was ahead of them, and nothing else felt like it mattered. So Acacia was happy for when they rode close to Esteri or Ukko and benefited from such an endless source of conversation as either of the two of them.

In four days, they came to the Barony of Talak. There, the lands were deeply wooded, and the terrain rolling so that one could crest a hill and gain sight of a sea of black-green forest threaded only by the gaps of winding roadways. Though Acacia had grown up in the city, part of her felt at home in such lands, for they were the kind of Kalest that its people dreamed of.

The barony's seat was itself a fairly small city, situated on a hill with a high wooden wall bounding it, though there were many outlying houses and cleared fields below the hill. The number of the people was similarly sparse, and few were in the streets when Acacia and the others rode through the open gates and made their way towards the manor at the center of the city. That house was quite recognizable, but at the same time it didn't have the scope or grandeur of the high manors in the capitals of Kalest or Lysama, looking more like the long public houses of Tyrvad with its scale and the festivities of its décor, though the architecture was very classical Kalesti.

When they arrived at the manor, Ukko stepped to the fore, and knocked loudly, as might be expected given the size of the place. Not long after, the door opened, and a fairly elderly man in garb that marked him as a butler answered.

"What is the reason for your visit?" he asked with a weary sigh.

"We seek an audience with General Katri," Ukko said.

The butler regarded him coldly.

"The Honorable Katri Talak is not receiving guests," he replied. "I regret to inform you that you have come in vain."

Here he tried to close the door, but Ukko put his foot in the way.

"This is no social call," he said. "We rode many leagues seeking her for urgent business. I bid you, tell her we are here."

"And," the Butler cut in before Ukko could give a name or rank, "Miss Talak bade me not disturb her for less than a royal messenger, to which she would be obliged. So unless you've come bearing King Piru's words, your wish for an audience will not be granted. You might present your business to His Lordship the Baron Talak, but His Lordship is on the hunt and is not expected for at least a week."

And before Ukko could speak any farther, Esteri stepped up, pulled away her shawl, and recovered what must have been her signet ring from her pack and held it forward.

"Tell General Katri that she has a royal visit, then."

The butler stammered for a moment.

"Impossible," he declared with awe.

"I'd rather let the general be the judge of that. If you will not announce us, then direct us to her. You have no authority to bar me and those who follow with me.

Silently, meekly, the butler nodded, and motioned them forward, into the manor, then lead the way into the northern wing and an assuming door. There, he motioned for them to wait, and knocked softly.

"Your honor?"

A sullen, slightly uneven voice from beyond the door responded.

"What is it now, Kyosti? I thought I told you to leave me be."

"You did, ma'am, however, under the circumstances"-

"Get to the point."

"You have guests, ma'am."

"I told you, no guests! I'm not entertaining anyone."

"Royal guests, ma'am."

And at that, there was silence.

"Ma'am?"

"I heard you," came the reply. "Just a moment."

There was rustling beyond the door, and then the dull clunk of the latch, after which it was allowed to creep open. Kyosti, the butler, stepped aside, and Acacia made her way into the room quick on Esteri's heels.

The chamber was very nice, but Acacia didn't really have a chance to admire it, because there was General Katri. Acacia had only seen the general in person a couple times, and never up close, but she had been a powerful figure for morale; even-handed, just, brilliant, and reputedly a tactical genius while also being no more than twenty-five years of age and report-edly very beautiful. Right now, though, she looked terrible – her hair was down and loose and tangled, her eyes had a dark cast to them as though she hadn't been sleeping, and she was clad only in a very oversized loose shirt and simple trousers. The general gaped openly at the group filing into her room. She said nothing, wide-eyed, but paced to a small writing desk, sat down, and began to pour herself a drink.

"My fair General," Ukko said, "I am sorry that the day finds you in worse spirits than when last we met."

"Cut the formalities," Katri growled. "Those are for court and fashionable nobles, and neither I nor this place would count as either."

"What happened?" Esteri asked. "I heard you had been placed on leave"-

"So that's the official story," Katri said. "I hadn't expected the mercy. As to what did happen, well, I should be asking you why Kalest's stolen princess is showing her face to a disgraced former general."

"That," Esteri said, "is a fairly long story, if you would care to hear it before telling your own."

Katri knocked back her drink, and replaced the small glass on the table with a loud 'clunk.'

"Time is something I have plenty of at the moment."

And from there, Esteri began the account of her own trials. How she was poisoned and became Accursed, how she fled blindly and, with what she believed after learning her possession of such power to be visions of the future, was led to the village of the Accursed. The travel to Lysama in the hope of stopping an unjust war. The fate of Baudouin. The travel through Tyrvad on the word of one who would betray them. And finally the journey home to confront Delphina for all she had done.

"There's something I wonder about," Katri said, "though I heard that the Queen returned to the palace, I haven't seen her since. In fact, there were some rumors that His Majesty slew her for some treachery, though there was no funeral."

"That's hard to believe," Esteri said. "If what Valdasa said is true, she couldn't be properly killed with mortal weapons unless she allowed it."

"I'm not saying she was," Katri replied with a heavy sigh, "but your accounts of what she might be capable of align more to the changes wrought in His Majesty."

"Changes?"

"He became withdrawn, nearly paranoid. At times, he seemed to lean on the Hyperboreans, which I had already thought to be a deadly mistake, seemingly for good reason. And of course there was the terrible power he held. He reshaped the palace grounds according to his whims, inserting rooms where there was no space, and that was just the start. I spoke out when the new devilry was to create the raven-things that accosted you. It felt wrong... unholy, even, if you'll excuse a less than faithful woman of the term. I though he might kill me for my temerity, because his temper had also become unstable, but he found worse to do. Stripped me of everything I had worked for and left me alive, with neither a purpose in being nor hope of redemption. And now I hear that even my suffering is denied – placed on leave, bah. I was stripped of my rank, ordered to begone, and defenestrated by those loathsome scarecrows to make the matter very clear."

Esteri shifted uncomfortably, and Acacia herself didn't know what to say to that.

"If you were hoping for aid," Katri said, "there is little I can offer."

Ukko seemed to consider that.

"Had your disgrace been open," he said, "perhaps that would be so. As it is, there are likely a large number of soldiers, even in the capital, who owe their loyalty to you, or believe they do. I believe you could probably get us close to the high seat with less incident than if I attempted to do so myself, given the matter of Ulfr and my status as a relative unknown within the armed forces."

"That is true," Katri grumbled, "but what you imply does not sit well with me."

Ukko nodded.

"In times like these," he said, "when the demands of one's honor are unclear, it is a matter of personal choice. I shall not hold it against you if you decline to offer aid, so long as we are permitted to depart as freely as we entered."

"In my brother's stead," Katri said, "I shall grant you that much. As for the actual matter"-

She reached for her bottle, but after a moment's hesitation, pushed it to the far side of the table.

"I'll need some time to decide," she said at length. "This is as shocking as it is sudden, you understand."

"Of course," Esteri replied. "Thank you, General."

Acacia noted that Esteri looked Katri right in the eye as she used the title, and for the first time felt of Esteri that awe-coated fear one would naturally hold for royalty.

***

Katri met the rest for dinner. By then she had cleaned herself up, and looked every part the general. A meal was served, poached fish and potatoes with cream, and Katri remained silent until it seemed that everyone was finished

"You know that what you're asking is, in a very technical sense, treason," she said, "and as such I should naturally do everything in my power to stop or thwart you the instant you leave this house and no longer have the protection of hospitality."

"I do know," Esteri said, "but there are extenuating circumstances, are there not? It has become quite clear that my father is sick of mind, and since he can no longer fulfill the duties of his kingship with honor and reason, proper authority, including the authority to remove him from his seat if necessary, falls to me as heir to the throne. So far as I've heard, even from yourself, I have not yet been formally disinherited."

Katri nodded.

"Such circumstances have happened before, but this is not the same as confining a senile old man to his chambers while those who can rule do so."

"But," Esteri countered, "if it's the legal principles that worry you, the case is as close to that as it would be to any treasonous rebellion. You've seen it with your own eyes."

"There are no principles or precedents for this," Katri said, "a king of Kalest becoming or consorting with some foreign god or demon. There is no procedure, nor easy answer."

"Then," Esteri said, "what is your answer? I doubt you meant to not deliver it."

"Though it may cost me my life and what tatters remain of my honor," Katri said, "I will assist you. I have given all that I am for my country, and cannot sit idle while it is in my power to see that it does not fall to dark magic."

Katri hung her head low, and Acacia couldn't help but feel a pang of sympathy.

"That settled," Katri said, "I shall make ready. We depart at dawn."

CHAPTER XXXIII

Esteri

When Esteri set eyes on Kalest's capitol, and the palace overlooking it, she felt sick and sorrowful. The day was as bright as any, but for her, there was a cloud over her ancestral home. Part of her wondered if it was a matter of second sight, for the sense of dread was almost palpable.

"I doubt we'll be recognized," Ukko said, very quietly.

Esteri shook her head. "That's not..."

Her ancestor smiled subtly and sadly. "I know. That is not the greatest consideration that ails you. I thought to allay that lesser issue."

"That is well," Esteri replied, "so forgive me my fears."

"Foolish," Ukko said, "not brave, is the one who does not know fear. At a time like this, especially."

"Do you ever give a straight answer?" Avina asked, evidently having overheard, and Esteri couldn't help but smile a little.

"Ah," Ukko replied with a smirk of his own, "I think I ran out of those long ago."

Avina seemed to mull that over, and then an impish smile crossed her face.

"Really, now?" she asked.

"Perhaps it is so," Ukko said. "Well"-

Katri cleared her throat.

"In any case," she said, "I believe I should ride ahead to the barracks. In case I am not well received, it may be best if we did not all go together."

Esteri took her meaning.

"Of course," she said. "Where should we wait for our rendezvous, then?"

"That," Katri said, "I had not determined. It would be best if it were somewhere easy to discover you. But then, it would also be best if it were not somewhere that a loitering group would be worthy of attention."

"The riverside market!" Acacia exclaimed.

"Excuse me?"

"I know that market like the back of my hand. I could find people there in a flash. There's always a ton of people, and there's lots to do so you won't really look out of place. As long as I go with the general, I can come and get everyone else when we're ready."

Katri seemed to consider this, then nodded sharply.

"I suppose having such a general area for a meeting place means that we couldn't give the rest of you up under torture, should we be arrested rather than heard out. At least, not in an effective manner that would deny you escape."

Esteri winced. "Do you really think that likely?"

"It's possible," Katri said, "and one does not succeed by accounting only for the most probable outcome, ignoring other possibilities. Painful setbacks and failures are especially important to account for."

"I see."

"As such," Katri continued, "I note that we will be entering the city quite early in the day. These dealings will no doubt take time, but if you have not heard from us before nightfall, you should assume that negotiations failed and any later appearance of myself or Specialist Suominen professing friendly terms means we have been compromised. At that point, I am afraid you must rely on your own strengths and wits to get any farther."

"We can still hope it won't come to that," Esteri said. "Any objections?"

None of the others said a word. After a moment, Katri

spoke again.

"I would leave you with as many as possible. Specialist Suominen and I will approach the garrison, the rest of you should make yourselves comfortable at the market."

And with that, Katri turned, and began down towards the city. Esteri followed, and the rest followed her.

***

Esteri had experienced much since her first flight from the palace, but the bustle of the riverside market, in the shadow of her former home, was unlike any of it. True, she might have found such sights in Lysama, had her reception not gone the way it did, but the sheer number of people, and their crowded motion, was something to behold. She wondered how Acacia could be so sure to find them in such a place, but the concern quickly passed as the sights, sounds, and smells bombarded her. That was the first strangeness of the experience – simply the senses themselves. The second, and by far the stranger, was that Esteri found herself feeling alone and isolated despite it all.

The flow of citizens was all around her, but people mostly went about their own business, and the bustle of their actions became a singular dull roar of which Esteri was not part. Even as much as she kept track of the others, they didn't seem to want to talk. Not that Esteri could really blame them... how much was there to really speak of that could afford to be overheard?

However, even such reasoning did wear thin, and Esteri found herself restless in her isolation at the center of the crowd. No, not quite isolation, she realized. The others may have been distracted, but Tius often looked her way, and the thought weighed upon her that they hadn't really spoken all too much since Ulfr's death and...

Esteri licked her lips nervously. Ever since acting on such an impulse, she'd been grappling with the shame of having lost her composure so. It was senseless – not only was it just a kiss, even if she had never kissed a boy on the lips before, but she didn't have to worry about status or succession any longer. She could do with herself what she pleased, and she knew that, but that didn't make it any easier to forget a lifetime of reminders that such behavior would be a stupid mistake.

She didn't make a mistake. She had done exactly what she wanted to do, but then she had tried to pretend she hadn't, and that was a real mistake. They'd barely exchanged a word since then, and true, they'd traveled hard, but...

If, she realized, she was only hurting herself, that would be alright. She had dared to look a little into her own future, and whatever was coming in the effort to face her father and, presumably, Delphina was chaotic enough that she could make neither heads nor tails of the visions. Would she live or die? Even if she knew some possible outcome, it was clear enough that the future could be changed, so what she felt before reaching that juncture wasn't of much concern. But she owed Tius better.

All the same, she waited for what seemed to be a good moment, with all the rest absorbed in the scene around them and unlikely to eavesdrop on a quiet conversation.

"Can we talk?" she asked.

Tius smiled back at her. "Sure," he said. "About what?"

Esteri shifted uncomfortably. Even now, she didn't exactly know how to broach the subject.

"First," she said, "I wanted to thank you. Through this whole ordeal, you've been by my side. You've lent me your strength when my own has failed and never asked anything in return. I've been... remiss in not telling you how much that means."

Tius nodded. "You're welcome," he said, soft and earnest.

"And," Esteri added, before the moment could flee her, "I wanted to say... about what happened in that hollow..."

Esteri hesitated.

"It's alright," Tius said. "You had been through a lot, and"-

"No," Esteri said, "that's not it. I wanted to say, what I did then... I meant it. I wanted..."

She raised her hands to her face.

"This is hard to say. I'm accustomed – was accustomed – to having everything laid out a certain way, and being free of that is thrilling and terrifying and I don't even know if we'll both be here come this time tomorrow, so I don't know if I even should..."

"Take your time," Tius said. "I'll listen."

Esteri took a deep breath, and struggled to regain her composure. She glanced this way and that to see that no one else was looking, at least not obviously.

"I don't know how this is done in circles other than my own," Esteri said, "what I may in good taste and with good grace say or do myself and what I must wait expecting, but if we make it through... I would greatly desire to court you, Tius, or learn how you would court me."

Gently, Tius took Esteri's hands, and cupped them softly in his own. He smiled softly, and Esteri's cheeks practically burned.

"I don't know if I'm going to be able to live up to what you deserve," he said, "but I'll do my best."

Esteri stepped closer. "Then I'm sure you needn't worry," she said. The anxious tension she had felt trying to spit out some confession was gone; the energy was still there, electrifying, but she felt for a moment light as a feather.

"So," Esteri asked, "how do we start?"

Tius shifted, blushing but not entirely uncomfortable. "Well, I'd say we could do something together. What would you enjoy?"

Esteri tried to think about it, looking for an answer that didn't seem too little nor too much, when very suddenly, Acacia appeared.

"Hi!" she exclaimed. The girl was hanging upside down, knees holding the hand rail of a stair landing just above, so that her head was about level with theirs. Esteri nearly jumped out of her skin as Acacia grinned and waved merrily.

"Not to interrupt," she said, "but there's good news! I mean, it's not all good news, but our friends were really reasonable, so we're ready for you."

"Thank you," Esteri said, trying to keep her voice from shaking, and largely succeeding.

"No problem!" Acacia replied. She heaved herself up a moment, grasped the edge of the landing, and vaulted effortlessly back to land on her feet without as much as a small hop at the end. The more Esteri saw out of her, the more she would have suspected the girl wasn't entirely human if she didn't know better.

"Oh," she said quietly, "if you're looking for a fun date, there's a little theater around here that belongs to a really amazing troupe. It's a bit hard to find, but I'd be happy to show you the way when this is all over."

Esteri could keep her face from displaying her shock. She could keep her words firm and level. But she couldn't keep herself from blushing, and felt mortified at that tell. The conversation had been private!

"Thanks," Tius said, clearly himself uncomfortable but managing respectable grace. And with that, Acacia waved to the two of them again, and bounded, practically skipping, in the direction of Ukko and the others.

***

Come evening, Esteri stared at the palace with dreadful anticpiation. She'd heard of her father's deepening madness, of the "Ravenguard" and other abominations, and surprisingly little of their true mark, Queen Delphina. Esteri supposed that she was playing from the shadows, but a sick feeling in the pit of her stomach reminded her that such a truth was what she wanted to believe.

She tried to push that worry aside. Whatever Delphina was up to, it didn't change Esteri's aim. She would take what chance she could to talk to her father, and appeal to the good man she believed he once was, but if that failed, she thought herself as prepared as was possible to bring the ever-growing nightmare to a halt.

She'd do whatever it took, she told herself, but that didn't stop her from feeling sick at the thought. She looked to the others around her – Ukko, Tius, Acacia, Seija, Avina, Radegond, and Maria were all there, and with them five more soldiers hand-picked by the commanders joined with Esteri and Katri in conspiracy, making the princess's escort a dozen in number. It didn't seem like many, but their purpose wasn't to storm the gates of the palace. Though the grounds were not, primarily, intended to weather a siege, the army of abominations that now protected that warped space was judged too difficult to overcome by strength of arms. Instead, the dozen-and-one of them would be brought in by a rear corner of the grounds while Katri herself would lead what volunteers she could find in open defiance at the front gate to distract the guard. They would only get one chance, and Katri's forces couldn't hold out forever against the rumored strength of the Ravenguard.

The distraction would begin as the sun dipped below the horizon, with little light left. Shadow would mask Esteri's ingress minutes later. From there, it was a matter of locating Delphina to put an end to her, Tuoni to protect, and Piru... Whatever would come from meeting with him.

The wait was tense and silent. If they were spotted or heard, the entire endeavor could fail, so they waited for the appointed time before daring so much as a word, much less breaking cover onto the open gardens of the palace grounds.

It seemed, at first at least, as though their endeavor was going well, for the lot of them crossed the open area and heard no indication they had been sighted before reaching the frosted windows of the conservatory, through which they could easily enter, but as Esteri slid a blade in to undo the latch and threw the windows open, she was grateful that she looked before stepping in, as the inside of the structure was not the pleasant walkway of the conservatory, but a high dome above a grand ballroom. She cried out in shock, and no little fear of falling in, and it was soon easy to see the reason why.

"Katri said that the palace had been changed," Seija grumbled, "but this is insane."

As Esteri stepped back, Seija crouched at the edge.

"There's a walkway just below the opening," she said. "We're in, but good luck getting around if it's all like this."

She hopped over the edge, hands holding the windowsill a moment before letting go to the sound of a soft thump echoing from not far below. Esteri peered in again and saw the outer edge of some upper balcony, its hand railing protruding into the room not far past the lower, outer edge of the window. Carefully, she followed Seija's lead, and the others came in behind.

Not only, Esteri reflected, was this room phenomenally misplaced, but it was impossible, for she could see other outward-facing windows on lower levels of the rotunda that would be beneath the earth. The others, one by one, followed suit behind her.

"Alright," she said, "it's safe to say that the layout is going to be even worse than the commanders thought. But that doesn't change that as best as we know my father seldom leaves his throne room, and if I know my brother he would be in what at least used to be the west wing. We'll just have to guess how to get there unless we can find a human servant to lead the way."

Ukko seemed to take that into consideration. "I believe, then, the time may have come to divide our efforts."

Esteri looked to him. "So soon?"

"I'd hoped to make our way deeper as a singular force," Ukko admitted, "but under the circumstances it would be better if we weren't all caught in the same snare."

Esteri thought about it, and tried to not betray her worry. Her eyes darted along the balcony. "I see two doors here," she said. "Please... find my brother. Make sure he's safe."

"As much as is in my power, I shall do," Ukko said. With no further words, he, Acacia, Maria, and three of the soldiers made for the door to their left. Esteri looked to the right. As likely as anything to take her to her father's throne, no reason to hesitate. Esteri strode forward, and the others followed.

Beyond was a hallway that Esteri recognized. It had been on the second floor, on the same side of the palace that Esteri had entered. So perhaps the palace would be more familiar than she had feared? She didn't have long to consider the situation before a screeching squawk reached her ears.

Esteri looked to its source at once. The creature... it was far from the most horrible thing she had seen, but there was something unspeakably loathsome about it... too real, too human, and yet nowhere near human enough. At once, deep in the pit of her stomach, Esteri understood why the "Raven Warriors" had represented such a dire rift between their creator and those who had followed him before. A split-second after, its cry stopped short, for Tius had appeared behind it and buried a long knife into the back of its neck.

"There will be"-

More soon, Esteri had meant to say, but she hadn't had the time before a side door burst open and a trio more of squawking, black-feathered fiends surged through, spears at the ready.

One of the two soldiers rushed the door. A halberd bit into his left shoulder, but he stepped inside the reach of the foremost raven warrior and stabbed at the creature.

"Go!" he bellowed, and Esteri snapped from her state as a horrified witness.

This wasn't what she wanted... but now that the alarm had gone out, there was only so much that could be done. Esteri broke into a flat-out run for the far end of the hall, and the others followed, save the one man holding their immediate foes back from pursuit.

Esteri wished she could remember his name.

When they reached the far end, they flung the double doors open, and entered a mercifully vacated gallery. The other soldier from the capitol garrison closed the doors firmly behind them, and threaded a long sword through the ornate handles to act as a bar.

"What about..." Esteri began. The boy – Esteri could hardly call him a man having gotten a look at his face – gave a frightening smile.

"He knew what he was doing," he said. "Me too, I guess."

"I don't want any more senseless death," Esteri insisted.

"Oh," the young soldier said, "I don't plan on dying today. But Lord Ukko put me on your team because I've got a few skills that should buy you a lot of time, provided I take the opportunity to employ them, and this seems as good a place and time as any. Interested or not?"

Esteri gritted her teeth.

"Alright," she said, "do what you must."

The kid smirked again.

"Well then," he said, "get moving. The farther you are from this room in a few minutes, the better."

Esteri gave a sharp nod, and started to make for the opposite side of the gallery, with the others moving at her sign. But halfway, she stopped, and called back over her shoulder.

"Wait!" she called. "What's your name?"

The boy just laughed, and then Radegond grabbed Esteri by the collar and pulled her forward into a run again.

Past the gallery, Esteri, Tius, Radegond, Avina, and Seija made their way through the twisted palace. Whenever they deemed it possible, they took the corridors meant for servants, rather than the broad halls that would be more likely patrolled. It felt like forever they ran in that blind maze, though it could not have been very long in truth. Esteri's heart thundered in her chest, and her body felt a newer, more acute strain than the long trail days she'd gotten used to. Some of the passages were familiar to Esteri, others were new, but every time they witnessed some space she had known, she became ever more sure that they were on the right path.

As they went, a distant din arose behind them, chaos of an unknown source echoing through the halls. Once, at the junction between a back route and one of the great halls, Esteri held a door ajar and watched a squad of raven soldiers move double-time back towards the wing from whence Esteri had come. That at least was mercy, for not a one had glanced to see Esteri peering from the cracked-open doorway, and when they had passed she and her friends were able to duck out and continue pressing forward.

But, Esteri knew, that couldn't last forever. She had heard some of how the throne room had been changed, the great hall that served as its antechamber and the cyclopean vastness of the site from which King Piru reigned. There was no doubt that there would be more inhuman guards there, that would not be drawn off by the futile assault at the gates nor whatever that kid had cooked up.

That, she realized, was what she had to rely on Avina and Seija for. They were the strongest fighters out of all thirteen who had made ingress to the palace, at least against large groups of foes in the comparative open. And having seen at least Avina fight, Esteri didn't doubt that she at least could give a fine account of herself.

Esteri just hoped that it could be enough.

At last, they came to a massive set of doors that Esteri did not doubt led to the throne's antechamber. Furtively, Esteri opened the door a crack, the portal gilding silent as a ghost on its hinges, and peered through.

Two groups of three ravens, clad in ornate, gilded armor, flanked the doors to the thone room, which would have been no concern if not for the rest of the hall. There, she saw what seemed to be a veritable army standing at attention, in file ten soldiers across, in rank ten deep, with bannermen standing beside at attention, and ornate champions before.

Esteri turned back to the rest, her face ashen, silently shutting the door.

"How many of those birds do you think you can handle?"

"Me?" Avina asked.

"Tell me, truly."

"At least a couple dozen," she said, "if I go all out and they don't fight like her."

Avina jabbed her thumb at Seija with those words, who took it as a chance to answer herself.

"Hard to say," she replied. "I've got my hammer again, but these aren't those things we faced in the forest. If they're as smart as they seem..."

"Esteri," Radegond said, insistent, "what's the situation?"

"There are a hundred," she said, "and more. A whole platoon of honor guards. They're lined up for show, but that doesn't mean they can't fight back."

"Are they between us and the throne room?"

Esteri shook her head. "There are some that way, but most are a little forward of here."

"Alright then," Seija said. "Course is clear. Make right for the throne, I'll keep that mess off your heels."

"What?" Esteri hissed. "Just you?"

"Well," Seija said, "would you rather leave more of us behind for whatever's in the throne room itself?"

"But can you"-

"If I can't, I deserve what I get. It'll be easier if I don't actually have to go through them, you know? Clearing a path is her specialty."

Seija jabbed a thumb right back at Avina.

Avina smirked.

"Just don't lose any limbs," she said. "I won't forgive you if you let some bird monster have the first crack."

Seija smiled back. "Wouldn't dream of it."

Avina stepped up, and everyone else back. The air rippled around her, and before Esteri even had a chance to register the monster replacing the girl, the sound of splintering wood and frantic caws filled her ears. No turning back.

Avina charged into the room, making a line for the grand doors of the throne room. Esteri, Tius, and Radegond followed in her wake, while Seija peeled off to the side. She practically smashed into the guards at the door, scattering the ones that stood at her right hand like tenpins. Those on the left made to block Avina's way, but she grasped one in each massive claw, slamming their heads together and tossing them aside as a petulant child would a disfavored rag doll, while kicking the third with such force that its armor rang like a bell upon impacting the stone of the wall behind it. In those moments, a mass of screeching black feathers and shining steel flowing up the hall. Avina threw the doors open and Seija took a stand between the rest and their foes.

"Get out of my backswing!" she barked.

Esteri needed no more encouragement, and followed Avina into the throne room. Once Esteri had passed the threshold, Avina threw the doors shut, and they gazed across the cavernous hall.

There were maybe thirty more guards, standing in ranks before the throne, halberds set against the intruders into that sanctum. They did not budge, however, and Esteri could see past them, to the high seat now so high and grand that its overlooked the chamber like a mountain peak rising above the clouds. And upon that seat, small and hunched as though stricken ill, was Piru.

"I'm home, Father," Esteri called. Slowly, she began to walk forward. The first rank of guards was a hundred paces forward, at least, and the accursed princess held her head high and advanced deliberately, forcing herself to make a stately and practiced stride.

"Though I have to wonder... what will the Chronicle say of these days I've been gone?"

The chamber was practically soundless. Her words echoed off the distant walls, and the ceiling that seemed as high as the sky. The sounds of battle, distant or otherwise, did not exist there, and as Esteri advanced, waiting for some reply, she could hear faintly as her father drew in ragged breaths.

Twenty paces from the first rank of guards, she stopped.

"Do you have nothing to say to me?" Esteri asked. "Has Delphina even taken your voice from you, to leave you the blame for this wickedness?"

For a moment, Esteri feared she waited in vain, but then,

Piru spoke. His voice was deep, like the rumble of thunder, but dry like a dusty tomb, the model of regal power but a far cry from what she remembered of her father.

"Delphina... the traitor... is dead," he proclaimed. "Aliisa avenged. This glory, her final gift."

Aliisa? What did Esteri's mother have to do with this? And Delphina, dead? The Hyperborean had seemed sure that was impossible, unless...

"I don't understand what you mean," Esteri said. "How did this happen?"

"She returned," Piru said, his voice now reaching a high timbre, echoing with wistful regret, transformed in an instant. "Her crimes revealed, she denied not a one. Not a one." His voice returned then to the booming majestic. "I ran the traitor through." And then it faded to a hollow rasp that, while still unlike Esteri's father, best fit the piteous figure he cut then atop his throne. "As another queen died in my arms, she said to take all that she was. For Kalest. For our son."

The creature Delphina had become could not be slain, they'd been told, unless a blessed weapon struck the mortal blow, or else she allowed herself to die. Esteri had not thought of it, but as much as she and Delphina had quarreled, as much as they hated one another... had Esteri ever doubted, earnestly and not in spite, that Delphina had loved her father? Could she really doubt that her stepmother would have died for him?

"And now," Piru rasped, "you, my lovely rose, whose fate I have lamented every moment since you were lost, you return. But you bring strangers and war with you, why?"

He sounded the most like himself then, his own voice even if in a tone she had only heard once before – wounded, full of sorrow.

"These people are strangers to you," Esteri said, "but they're my friends. As for bringing war? You still aren't making yourself easy to approach, father."

Esteri gestured to the guards before her, their beady eyes still fixed upon her, weapons ready and monstrous bodies tensed and waiting for the order to kill.

Piru raised his hand, though, and the guards lifted their weapons and broke rank, stepping to the side of the central path up to the throne and standing attention, all but the last half-dozen soldiers who stood tall at the throne's base.

Esteri began to walk forward again, and heard footfalls behind her. Tius, Radegond, and Avina again in her human form followed as she approached.

"Delphina didn't give you a parting gift," Esteri said, "she gave you a curse. Can't you see that?"

"Gift," Piru said, "curse, is there a difference? Your curse has gifted you, has it not?"

"But this isn't the same," Esteri said. "Look around you and tell me that this isn't wrong."

Piru was silent.

"Please... father... set aside what you were given. Let it end, before anything more terrible befalls you, me, Kalest, or anything else in this world. Let us be finished."

Esteri advanced beyond where the second rank had stood.

"I cannot," Piru said.

"Cannot, or will not?" Esteri asked. "Father, you were a better man than this, than all of this. How much poison was poured into your ears to bring us here?"

"I cannot," Piru reaffirmed. "Even if I wished it... one does not set this aside."

Esteri closed her eyes for a moment.

"Do you remember the story you told me, back before mother died, the tale of Dame Tuulikki?"

Piru made no sound. Esteri opened her eyes, and fixed them upon the throne.

"You said she was a knight in the early days of Kalest, when the Birds' Wood was freshly threaded and much still untamed... the days of gods and demons. There were so many stories about her adventures... born a peasant, chosen by the gods. How she fought against dragons, spoke with spirits, and won the heart of her prince. I loved those stories... but then you told me the story of her last adventure. How this hero who was loved above all others faced one of the last demons, an evil that could not die." Esteri's voice cracked, and she could feel tears streaming down her cheeks. "After many clashes, unwilling to let such evil run free, she permitted the demon to possess her body and then, before it could overcome her will, fell upon her sword so that when Teriana claimed her soul, she could drag the demon into death with her. I hated that story, father. I told you as much, and cried for a hero long gone, because that wasn't the ending she deserved. But, father, you told me that the lesson of her courage was important to learn. I still remember it, do you?"

At length, Piru replied, "She died as she lived, with honor and undefeated. It would have been wrong to shirk her duty to Kalest and its people to preserve a life sullied by Kalest. The principle our soldiers live by."

"You put it a different way to a child. You said that it was good, because no knight serves, nor king rules forever. So better to die with purpose, sparing the world an unspeakable evil, than unfulfilled and in her bed years later."

Esteri stopped where the last rank of soldiers had stood, twenty paces before the throne and its final royal guard. Vision dimmed with tears, she drew her sword. Steel rattled around her, a sudden shift as the soldiers to the flanks no doubt leveled their weapons at her. But, twenty paces away from even beginning the ascent, they did not strike. Esteri held the blade gingerly and then, its blue glow radiating all around, tossed it forward. The sword spun in air, then clattered against the stone floor, sliding along before finally coming to rest against the base of the throne, handle towards the high seat.

"I wanted to believe," Esteri said, not even attempting to conceal how she wept, "even if I knew it was impossible, that things could go back to the way they were before. But father, if there really is no other way... please, be the man who taught me, who talked so much about honor as he held me in his arms." She sank to one knee, head still lifted, pleading. "Be the father I loved, one last time."

For a moment, silence reigned, and a sick feeling grew in the pit of Esteri's stomach. She had asked such a thing without thinking, and now the weapon on which they'd pinned their hopes in case of a fight wasn't in her hand. How stupid could she be?

Slowly, Piru rose from his seat. Esteri's father looked down at her, and for a moment he looked... lost. Afraid.

Then, the air... no, the space around them pulsed, a wave of unseen pressure rolling through stone and flesh alike, disquieting. Esteri's vision blurred a moment as it passed over her, and when she thought she could see clearly again, her father was gone. In his place was a hunched, malformed thing that wore bits and pieces of his visage, and of others, and of monsters. It took a shambling step down, and there was another pulse, and in its wake Piru, but not as he was. Strong, tall, with an air of arrogance that reminded her of the monstrosity beneath.

"You dare?" he... no, it bellowed.

"I..." Esteri began. Her voice faltered. She had wanted this wrongness mended for so long, told herself that everything could be made right as long as Delphina was put out of the way. But now? What stared down at her had only one remedy, and she knew that, and hated it.

"I've given you a chance to regain your honor, father."

Step by step, what was left of Piru seethed down the stairs. He did not walk, exactly – he never moved, but approached all the same. The air turned hot as a summer day, and felt heavy as though with steam, but when Esteri breathed it in, the phantasmal, coppery scent of blood assailed her, even as boiling haze crept in on her vision. Rage had taken physical reality, and Esteri was forced to her knee.

"Just say the word." Avina grunted. "We'll-"

"Let me," Esteri whispered quickly. She looked up, and tried to see her father through the nightmare.

"This has to stop!" she called. "The father I knew would have seen as much. Look at yourself, at the taint of Hyperborea!"

The king stopped his roiling advance, and the air cleared some. A voice echoed from his figure, groaning deep and more felt than heard

"Hyperborea... From Hyperborea."

Esteri thought she caught a glimmer of her father.

"Where this curse came from," she said. "Yes. Please, if there's any part of you left, cast off"-

"My throne awaits in Hyperborea!" the creature bellowed. The human outline of Piru vanished entirely, and though the thing that had been lurking behind, like a mirage in shimmering air, could not be rightly seen, Esteri felt chill despite the oppressive heat, and could neither summon her voice, nor the will to move. The raven guards broke ranks then, and began a panicked flight from the room, departing through secret exits in the wings.

"I... will have what is mine!" the voice shrieked, fully inhuman, and then it launched upward like a shooting star in reverse, the roar of wind knocking all who still stood flat. In an instant, it was gone, only the hole torn in the ceiling telling of what had transpired.

CHAPTER XXXIV

Acacia

The hallway they stepped into wasn't anything that belonged in the palace. It was stretched, doors irregularly warped, as though the entire space had been made of wet clay and pulled until it nearly tore. Here and there, new egresses and ingresses stood in perfect form, untainted by whatever had happened to the rest of the hall, presumably added after. Halfheartedly, Acacia tried one of the warped door handles nearest, and found that it felt not just stuck but as though it were never even there, just a painted feature on the wall.

"This is all just messing with our heads," Maria grumbled. "Are we just supposed to guess where the prince is?"

Leevi, one of the soldiers from the city and seemingly not the kind of person to ever be anything but calm, stalked over to the first good door.

"Getting the job done," he said, "we can take rooms one at a time, or we can split up further. One of these options gets us a better spread, but also gets us killed if there are guards left in this area."

Aatukka, another of their new friends, flipped her hair and made an indignant sound. "I'd say let's not get killed. There's no way even the bird-brains are leaving the prince unguarded, right?"

Ukko stepped up. "If there are no objections, such aligns with my take on the matter."

No one spoke up, and the search began, checking each door carefully to see where it might lead. As they did, Acacia noticed Aatukka scribbling in some sort of notebook. After a moment, Acacia got a look over her shoulder and saw a mass of circles and lines.

"What's that?" she asked

Aatukka turned, gave her hair a flip, and spoke.

"It's a map, of course."

"A map? It doesn't look like"-

"Nothing in here fits, so if I tried to draw it literally, it would make a mess. Under the circumstances there's no need to represent the size, shape, or position of rooms accurately, only their interconnections unambiguously."

The girl's tone was positively withering. She couldn't have been less than a year Acacia's junior, would a little politeness really kill her?

Before Acacia could voice any reply, new signal horns, much closer than those at the gate, echoed through the hall.

"Fire, unless I miss my mark," Ukko said through gritted teeth. "They had to use their diversion so soon?"

"We need to hurry, then!" Acacia said. "He could be in danger, right?"

"That shouldn't..."

Whatever Leevi was going to say was lost when a panel in the wall opened, revealing a doorway that Acacia at least had not realized was there, and a white-haired man in formal robes scurried from it in a panic. Acacia might not have seen him before, but she knew him for, if not the Hyperborean ambassador, then some functionary beneath him.

That made the man Ulfr's master and, more importantly, someone who knew his way through the twisted labyrinth of the palace, to where the prince would likely be.

"Stop!" Acacia shouted, and began to run for him. For a second he did stop, and looked at her, but then he bolted in the opposite direction, getting maybe two or three steps before tripping over his trailing robe and falling flat face-first to the carpeted floor. Acacia was upon him before he so much as scrambled up to his knees, much less his feet, and seized him

445

by the collar of his robe.

"Hold on," she said. "We're not going to hurt you unless you make us, OK?"

"Ambassador Ormr," Ukko said. "Do you not find this meeting as fortuitous as I do?"

"You?" the Hyperborean near exclaimed. "Do you have any idea what has become of our world thanks to your damnable diligence?"

"If I do not," Ukko replied, "now is not the time for explanations. Instead, I have a request."

"R-request?"

"Lead us to Prince Tuoni."

The pale man went even paler.

"I will insist with whatever force is necessary," Ukko said, "so you should rise to your feet and begin at once."

Ormr rose, though Acacia kept a grip on him in case he tried more successfully than last time to run.

"What is your business with the prince?" Ormr asked hesitantly. "Depending on your answer, there are things here to fear more than even death."

Ukko nodded. "The madness that has claimed this land ends today, but as you may already have surmised, the palace may not be the safest place for such events."

And at that, Ormr laughed, showing obviously frayed nerves.

"You think fire and steel can end this?" he asked.

"I trust Esteri, and she believes it can be done."

Ormr glanced from side to side, as though looking for a way out of the situation.

"I am not feeling very patient, ambassador," Ukko said. "Lead on, or I will be forced to persuade you."

The ambassador hissed something under his breath and then pointed to a far door.

"This way, then... it seems I have little choice. Well, do you intend to hold me back from serving you?"

Acacia began to move forward, giving the Hyperborean

some slack, though with her free hand she drew one of her swords, hopefully to forestall what she feared to be an inevitable betrayal. He glanced to it, veered their course a little to a different way forward than the one she had thought he indicated, and Acacia felt a smile creep across her face.

As much as she wanted to believe in most people, she wasn't that naive.

Soon, they entered a wing of the palace that looked more normal. As they moved through, they caught sight of raven guards, and Maria, Leevi, Sampaa, and Ukko, and shortly after them, Aatukka leapt into battle and made swift work of the enemy while Acacia kept a good grip and a drawn blade on their coerced guide. At last, Ormr stopped them in front of a small set of fancy double doors that had been flanked by raven guards.

"Here," he said.

"Well?" Leevi was the first to say. "Open it."

The ambassador shrugged. "I don't have the keys to the crown prince's chamber, and see no reason why I should loot the dead for you."

Sampaa knelt next to the slain guard and began to rifle through its things, but Aatukka stowed her notebook, stepped over the scene, and with one swift strike kicked the door in.

"Come on out!" she shouted, stomping first into the room, a sitting room that had a desk and luxurious couch.

Aatukka stomped to the couch.

"I know you're there!" she bellowed, and thrust her hand into the space behind it. However, she withdrew her hand as swiftly, screaming bloody murder, as a pair of children leapt out from the hidden space and, in a blur, burst through the small door into the next room of the prince's chambers and slammed it behind. Acacia dropped her grip on Ormr and pushed him away, heading swiftly to where the children had gone, but before she got there, there was a huge crash on the other side, and Acacia found that the door only opened a crack before coming up against some obstruction that she guessed to be a toppled dresser.

"Little shit stabbed me!" Aatukka howled.

"It's what you get," Leevi said calmly. "You should really watch your manners, especially around royalty."

He walked to where Acacia was making slow progress on the door.

"Let me help."

He leaned his weight into it with Acacia, and the toppled furniture shuffled across the floor until Acacia felt herself able to squeeze through the gap, into the room.

This, she saw, was the bedroom, and the Prince and who-ever the other form had been were not in immediate evi-dence. There were two other doors, but...

"Prince Tuoni?" she called, and lifted the skirt of the bed to look under – from a safe distance, remembering the reason why Aatukka was still loudly cursing in the other room.

Again, two child-sized blurs of motion erupted, in this case from the other side of the bed, and through the left of the two doors. Acacia jumped to her feet, and caught it before it slammed shut. In that room, she finally got a good view of the kids. One was a young boy with pale blonde hair that she took to be the prince. The other was a brown-haired little girl, somewhere close to the same age. Tuoni stopped and stood between Acacia and the girl, arms outstretched, bloody letter opener in one hand.

"Easy"- Acacia began.

"Run, Jeanne!" Tuoni shouted to the girl, but she put a hand on his shoulder and shook her head.

"Alright then," he said, and gripped the little letter opener with both hands. "I swear I won't let anybody hurt you."

Acacia pushed both of her hands out in front of her and waved them frantically before she really registered she was still holding a sword, and dropped it like it was a snake.

"Whoa, whoa – gyah! I mean, we're not here to hurt you or your friend."

Tuoni glared at her with an intensity he shared with his

half-sister, and continued to hold the letter opener forward.

There was a shuffle and a muffled crash from the bedroom, and footsteps behind to tell that the others had gotten the dresser out of the way. Moments later, Ukko's voice echoed from behind Acacia.

"Perhaps I can explain," he said kindly.

"Sir Ukko?"

He lowered the letter opener a little, though Jeanne clung to him a little more fiercely. Despite herself, Acacia found she was smiling at the display.

"We came here with your sister," Ukko began.

"Esteri?!" Tuoni shouted. "Where is she?"

"On her way to... have words with your father, if all is well. In the meantime, General Katri is at the gates and I believe there is a fire somewhere near the conservatory, so if you'll forgive the rude introductions, it would be best if the both of you left the palace with us."

And to that, the prince took Jeanne by the hand, and went to Ukko without protest.

Ukko looked over his shoulder. "I trust you have no objection to accompanying us to the nearest egress from the building, Ormr?"

***

Though the Hyperborean was clearly displeased getting all involved to a window that overlooked the first floor grounds, safe to exit, he didn't fail to deliver an egress. From outside, smoke was clear, rising primarily from the vicinity of the conservatory, but also isolated windows or patches of roof elsewhere, blackening the dusk sky. Circling wide around the grounds, it seemed as though they would easily avoid trouble, the fighting concentrated before the grand gates, and the fire causing, no doubt, no little distraction. It took perhaps an hour, though it also could have felt longer than it really was, seeking covered paths that would not be easily spied out and moving with the constantly protesting Ormr, before they had made it behind the rebel line.

Austin Harper

The stink near the front was almost unbearable, and the sights were worse, enough that Acacia was not alone in moving to stand between Tuoni and Jean and the remnants of the fighting.

As soon as they found themselves among friendly soldiers, they were directed quickly to General Katri, The battle lines were eerily quiet when they arrived, and when they came in sight with her, on horseback though she was, Tuoni was the first to cry out.

"Auntie Katri!"

Katri turned at once, though her steed stayed still.

"Thank the gods, you're safe!" she said, and looked over the approaching crowd. "Ah, and Princess Lysama as well? But where is Her Majesty?"

"We had to take a different route from Esteri," Ukko said. "Unfortunate, but not unexpected. The front seems in better order than we had anticipated."

"You should have seen it at the start," Katri said. "Those monsters made an initial sally in the face of which I feared our enterprise would fail at once. But we withstood them, and they have seemed content to hold the gate since, which is proving damnably difficult to overcome without a proper ram."

"Is that so?" Ukko asked, voice full of concern. "The doors were imposing when last I visited, but seemed indefensible then."

"They were at the beginning," Katri said. "When Piru's birds withdrew, a portcullis and gatehouse grew around them.

"Meaning," Maria said darkly, "that even if you did bash it in, it might just grow back. Why don't we try a window? We've had pretty good luck with those."

"Three reasons," Katri replied. "First, if we peel off squads now to seek other ingress, our foe would likely notice. Second, our mission remains to serve as a diversion, not to take the palace by force. Third, if we were to"-

Whatever Katri had meant to say was lost when, with a

great roar, something erupted from the roof of the palace. A light streaked to the north, with a great wind that cleared the smoke in its wake, gleaming away in the blink of an eye. At the same moment, the front erupted into chaos. The gates flung open, and raven soldiers tore out of the palace, but their frenzied squawking did not portent an assault, and as soon as they were free of the portal they spread in all directions, clearly experiencing a total rout. More of the feathered fiends began to pepper the grounds, having emerged from windows, servants' entrances, and hidden sally ports to flee into the night. And at this Katri helped Tuoni up onto her horse behind her. Jeanne stepped up, and insisted to be allowed such a place, to which one of Katri's lieutenants took her, and while Ormr was deposited in the custody of more soldiers, Ukko, Acacia, and the others with them hastened to follow Katri forward, travelling the path from where she had waited to the front gate that was now open wide. Acacia hurried to keep up as the soldiers parted to make way for Katri and the royals with her. Near the front ranks, Ukko called out to her, and he and those that had been with him in the palace formed a vanguard to push into enemy territory.

Going forward, they met no resistance as they passed from the gatehouse, to the old vestibule, up to where the double doors of the great hall that stood before the throne waited, ajar. Acacia was the first to push those open, swords drawn in case some foes still waited, ready for a fight.

Acacia herself wasn't ready for what was beyond. There had been a battle there – or was it a slaughter? There were bodies everywhere, and the floor was carpeted with blood and feathers. Towards the end of the hall, especially, there were berms of corpses where two or three had fallen over one another. No doubt the press of battle had been harshest there, and those closer to the outer doors looked as though they dragged themselves away from the last twenty or thirty feet before expiring. Yet, all was silent

Acacia advanced cautiously, in case any of the downed

ravens yet lived, and tried to make out any sign of who or what they had thought against. The sun was down and the light in the hall had been snuffed, but as Acacia's eyes grew used to the dim conditions, she saw something. A few paces before the throne room's door, at the epicenter of all the carnage, there was a dark mound somewhat higher than the rest, and however subtly, it shifted, rising and falling with what was no doubt breath. Something was alive.

A moment later, as the throne room doors began to creak open behind that form, Acacia made out what, and couldn't hold her tongue.

"Gods... Seija?"

In the frame of the door, the others appeared, less the two soldiers who had gone with them, and Esteri cried out, an inarticulate squeal of shock.

"Get a medic!" Esteri shouted, looking past Katri to the others who followed behind. She locked eyes with one soldier. "Now! Hurry!"

The soldier broke into a run, and Acacia looked back. She didn't even register Esteri and her friends, Seija's surroundings and sorry state were too terrible to really take in anything else. Rows of dead raven guards, numbering at least a score in all, ringed her, outer lines falling back from the farthest reach of her meteor hammer, the two heads of which lay to the left and right, the rope between the weights cut somewhere in the fray. Within those rings the dead were even thicker, and bore gashes in their throats, or had their bare skulls split open, telling how Acacia's friend had drawn swords when robbed of her favored weapon.

As for Seija herself, she was hunched over, not quite on her knees, one leg skewered through calf and thigh alike by a broken spear. Her long blade was broken, and she leaned her weight upon the pommel, ragged remnant of a point driven between the tiles of the floor while her right hand, dagger through the wrist, rested limply upon the handle. The knuckles of her left hand were white, and she held tight to her arming knife, though blood from a deep gash in the outside of her shoulder rendered the arm slick. She had perhaps a dozen other wounds of note besides, and Acacia could not say how bad they were for the dim light and clinging, blood-soaked tatters of the woman's uniform. And yet, though Acacia did not think Seija could see much in her state, she still gazed forward with a hard glare, seeming ready for another fight.

Acacia's heart sank. Even if she lived, how much of a chance was there that she'd even walk on her own again? Somewhere near was the soured reunion of Esteri and her brother. Somewhere near was an account of what had happened in the throne room, and shouts to get a brigade putting out what fires might yet burn, but until the medics arrived, and ushered Acacia away from the scene, she couldn't hold onto it. Having seen friends dying and dead before didn't steel herself to watch what might be that same loss again.

***

It was settled without Acacia that someone would have to push on to Hyperborea. And when Esteri and her friends stepped up, Acacia did as well, mutely determined to see this matter through to the end. When the time came, as Ormr was arranging coerced or not, that was where she would part ways with Ukko and Maria, who would remain behind with Katri to act as Prince Tuoni's regent and bodyguard, respectively. Acacia stayed gathered with her remaining friends, waiting. In some ways, not knowing was the worst thing.

It was near dawn the day after the raid on the palace when a doctor appeared, Markku if Acacia was right, and said that 'given Her Majesty's personal interest in Miss Lahti's injuries, it might be prudent to come quickly.' And then he turned to Avina and said that, though under protest, he had done as Avina had asked, and handed her something. Then, at once, he began to lead the way

Acacia ran, and Avina and Esteri came with her, The doctor's pace was hurried, but Acacia herself frequently strained, getting ahead and then waiting impatiently to be led onward.

Seija had been placed in a private room. She was far from the only injured soldier, but having friends in high places had its benefits and she might have been the most grievously wounded to survive the first night. The doctor entered first, holding out a hand to insist the others wait, and shortly emerged.

"She's still awake," he said. "Normally I would have given her something for the pain, but she insisted she be allowed to speak before then, and the medicine would render her quite insensate."

"Is she..." Acacia ventured, hesitant. "Is she going to pull through?"

"Hard to say," the doctor replied. "She's stable at the moment but we will certainly have to amputate one arm and one leg before long... tourniquets may save a life but they do often cost a limb. If she makes it through the surgery there are half a dozen other wounds in which an infection could fester or where an incautious move could tear it open and end her life."

"Doctor," Esteri said. "These are her friends, please, be honest."

He nodded gravely. "I would treat this conversation as the last you are likely to have. Anything beyond would be a stroke of good luck," he said, and then gave Avina a dark and disapproving look, "or something like it at least."

And at that, they were let into the room. Even having seen her wounds, Seija looked bad – she was a twisted mass of bandages, many stained a ruddy brown, and whether that was from blood or some medicine used to treat her couldn't be said. Acacia tried to not look too closely, and focused instead on her friends bruised, pale face.

And then, before anyone else could, Seija spoke. Her voice was rasping, wet, and so soft that it was hard to make out her words.

"'s good for something," she said, as far as Acacia could follow. Then Seija locked eyes with Avina.

"You," she said. It sounded gruff at first, but Acacia thought it was also... desperate?

Avina stepped up. "You asked for me, right?"

The Accursed girl chewed on her lip, clearly nervous.

Seija took several deep breaths, then spoke with a little more clarity than before.

"It's time we settled that debt," she said, dead serious.

At that, Acacia nearly jumped out of her skin.

"You can't be serious!" she cried.

"I don't make a promise I won't see through," Seija replied, "and anyway, it's not like that hackbones can make my arms useful to Kalest again. Even if I live, I'm dead, he told me as much himself."

"But"-

"And you know," Seija said, waxing wistful, eyes drifting to the ceiling as her expression cleared from pain and determination to faint relief. "As deaths go? I can accept this. The enemy couldn't make me kneel in the end, so that's alright, and it's better to go out without any debts outstanding."

She looked to Avina again.

"So whenever you're ready," she said, utterly calm, "do your thing, and take whichever you want. Heck, you can have both, it'll go faster that way."

Avina looked away, head down. "That was the deal, right? When Esteri couldn't use you any more, an arm for an arm. You know, I thought it sounded like a really good deal."

Seija smiled, tiny and honest, and Acacia felt a little sick. Even if Seija could accept this, could anyone else?

"So I'll keep to it," Avina continued. "If you're as good as dead, I'll take your arm. It won't give my mom hers back, but it'll be fair."

"Good."

Acacia opened her mouth, but Esteri glanced at her, and her eyes were like daggers, so Acacia held her tongue.

"Honestly, I didn't expect you to keep to it, but nothing seems to happen like I expect it, so I'm used to it by now. I wouldn't even be surprised if the situation changed again."

At that, Avina withdrew a flask from some pocket and set it down with a heavy thud on the end table by the one arm Seija could move, next to a half-drunk glass of water.

"What?" Seija asked. She was breathless, and Acacia thought from more than just her wounds.

"If you weren't as good as dead," Avina said, back to everyone else in the room, "it wouldn't be time to pay that debt yet, because you'd still be worth more in one piece. In fact, if you recovered somehow, there might even be something else you could do instead, like apologizing to my mom on your hands and knees. I think she'd like that more than a dead, rotted arm."

Avina's fingers lingered on the flask, and Seija's gaze focused there too. Intent, staring exactly at it, exactly at the stopper, unblinking, considering. The implication slowly dawned on Acacia, and she realized why the doctor must have disapproved so fiercely. It was a choice rarely offered and more rarely taken, and the last time had resulted in quite the disaster.

"I've never had a rival before," Avina continued, withdrawing her hand. "I've always been the strongest, and nobody could match up, and nobody wanted to. In spite of everything, I don't know why... but I think I've liked it. So it would be a good surprise if we could keep on being rivals somehow. Ah, well... I'll... um... I need to go talk to Tius. I'll be back in an hour or so, and we'll see about settling that debt then, alright?"

And without waiting for a response, Avina fled the room, breaking into a run and keeping her face hidden away.

Seija scoffed, looking down at herself. Her mouth was set in a frown, but Acacia let herself hope – it was the same sort of grumpy face she had always made around Taavi.

"A monster like her's pity for a monster like me... I never asked for it."

"No," Acacia said, speaking before thinking, "that's not what you do. You can't demand to be cared about, it happens without your say, because despite one thing or another, you're both good people."

"You really believe that?" Seija asked, fixing Acacia with a glare. She wasn't angry, but she was intense, even more than usual.

Acacia hesitated. She'd probably said too much, but all the same, it wasn't untrue.

"I do," she replied.

"What a pain," Seija groaned. She looked to Esteri, "Did you see this coming?"

Esteri shook her head. "Not exactly, or probably the way you mean. I won't tell you what to do."

"Of course not," Seija replied, "it's a real pain." Her groan was exaggerated, and though she had much to moan about, felt at least a little fake.

Acacia waited a moment, the weight of holding back tears starting to be felt, but Seija didn't seem inclined to say anything else.

"So," Acacia ventured, "what are you going to do?"

"That's why it's so much of a bother," she replied, in a bitter mix of mock frustration and real frustration. She was low, that was sure, but there was something else too. "Everything was going to be put in order, but I just can't accept this."

"Seija..."

"I didn't ask for kindness," she said, "but am I supposed to think we're still even if I throw it back in her face? That's stupid."

"Do you want to know what I think?" Acacia asked.

"Maybe not," Seija replied, and Acacia thought she glimpsed a faint smile, "but I'm going to get an ear full, right?"

"Well," Acacia said, "you know I like to talk."

"And I don't hate listening."

"I think... I think you should pick whatever you can live with – ah, I mean whatever you can conscience."

Seija looked away, turning her head slightly to the side, probably as much as she could, hiding her expression.

"I think you may have said what you really wanted the first time. Can I be alone?"

Acacia hesitated.

"Of course," Esteri replied, and put a hand on Acacia's shoulder. "Do you want us to come back before Avina does? Perhaps let Ukko and Maria know?"

"Suit yourselves," Seija said, "as long as it takes at least a little while."

***

Esteri insisted on informing Ukko and Maria on what had transpired, and neither of them seemed particularly surprised by the situation. In truth, Acacia couldn't say that she was really shocked either. There was part of her that was just too lost to think of anything beyond that there was a chance Seija would live. Acacia thought she would, but she'd also sent them away... she didn't want them to see, and Acacia wished she could be sure what.

Ormr had been there as well, tinkering with some of the Hyperborean devices they'd brought over from the palace. Though Acacia was rather preoccupied, there was a certain fascination to the 'radio' that sent voices to distant lands faster than the wind, and watching intently as though she could discern the way its magic functioned almost numbed the worry of waiting.

"How very reckless," the ambassador said when he'd overheard, "but I suppose you need every sword arm possible, if you are to make this work."

Esteri stepped up, "Have you news, then?"

"Yes, unfortunately," Ormr replied. "The thing that used to be his majesty appeared and took up residence in the Council's citadel before beginning an attack on the surrounding environs with malformed puppets. The problem is, currently, contained, and the acting head of National Security should make a final call today on whether or not a pack of continental Accursed will be permitted to attempt to slay the beast, or whether the state of emergency will be resolved otherwise."

Esteri narrowed her gaze. "Do you think you can?"

"Probably," Ormr replied, "and that is the best anyone could say under such unprecedented circumstances. But the collateral damage would be quite substantial, so I suspect it will be deemed of negligible cost to send you in first."

"How very respectful," Esteri replied, acidic.

"You, like all those around you, are too ignorant to even comprehend the depths of what you do not understand," Ormr replied. He opened the drawer of his desk and withdrew a black box with a shining panel of stained glass inset into it, attached by a shining black rope to a metal rod. "For instance, I suspect when you have your new fighter, you will mean to waste time testing and divining what if any unnatural abilities have manifested, where as I could simply use this detector to compare the energy signature to the library of those recorded by Hyperborea, arriving at an answer in seconds rather than days if ever."

"More magic like your speaking box," Esteri replied, "useful, I concede, but hardly just cause for such arrogance."

"The fact that you believe a radio to be magic, and no doubt thought the same if that idiot Ulfr ever employed his service revolver, is entirely the point."

Acacia put a hand on the radio.

"So, how does it work, then?" she asked. As insulted as she felt by the ambassadors' insinuations, she tried to make the question sound at least as honest as it was.

"Excuse me?"

"If it's not magic, then how does it work?" Acacia repeated. She thought she would, in fact, rather like to know.

"Do you seriously expect me to sit here explaining the electromagnetic spectrum to you? You would not understand even the barest tip"-

"Try me," Acacia said. "We may not know a lot about your tools here in Kalest, but we aren't stupid. If you'd try talking to people, rather than talking down at them, you'd know that already."

Ormr scowled for a moment, then turned back to the princess. "You may not like our reasoning," he said, "but if the result is full cooperation with your personal crusade, do you truly wish to argue?"

"I'd like to be able to trust you and your countrymen farther than I could throw you," Esteri replied, "but I suppose that is a tall order, all things considered."

Ormr squirmed in his seat. "The next time I receive communication, I shall send for you, and you may air your grievances to the colonel personally, though I doubt she shall have time to entertain any foolish questions."

"In the meantime," Esteri ventured, "perhaps you should begin to explain the workings of that device? If it's not a unique Hyperborean magic, surely enlightening an ally as to its nature would be a gesture of peace."

Ormr gritted his teeth. "Very well. It's not as though anything will come of it. To begin with, electromagnetism is a blanket term for..."

***

In a little less than an hour, Acacia took note of the time, excused herself from the lecture about radio that had talked entirely too much about 'invisible forces,' and made her way to Seija's room. The door was open, and the first sign of what Acacia would find inside was a shout that echoed down the hall.

"There is nothing to inspect!" Seija barked. "Get out and don't come back without a uniform for me!"

Acacia entered the room. It was in total disarray, the bedside table toppled and torn bandages soaked with blood and chemicals tossed everywhere. Seija was still in bed, holding a sheet with one hand and waving a scalpel at some assistant of the attending doctor who was backed up next to the wall.

"Such a recovery is unprecedented, ma'am"-

"Stuff it!"

Acacia entered and put a hand on the boy's shoulder.

"Can't you tell when a lady is well and embarrassed?" she

asked quietly.

"I am not embarassed!" Seija yelled. "I am furious that this damn kid"-

Acacia smiled, hopefully disarmingly. "I'll take it from here, then." She grabbed the apprentice by the shoulders and quickly, forcefully, but hopefully politely ushered him out of the door before quickly shutting it behind.

Seija let out a heavy breath and, finding there was no bedside table for her to place the scalpel down on, simply tossed it to the side.

At first, Acacia didn't know what to say. Was she supposed to acknowledge what they knew had happened? Could she say how she was glad that Seija was alive and well, whatever she was now?

"It sounds like he didn't know about the potion," Acacia ventured. "It was probably an honest shock to find you up and moving around."

"Then he's an idiot," Seija grumbled, "at least the old hack-bones knows his business."

"So.... um..." Acacia shuffled a little, looking down uncomfortably. "How do you feel?"

"Honestly?" Seija replied. "I feel great. Like, it's kind of creepy, I'm not just in one piece – I'm not tired, I'm not hungry, I've got no little ache to piss me off. I don't exactly feel good either, but I can't remember the last time I've been... all together like this."

"That doesn't sound too creepy," Acacia said.

"Yeah," Seija said with a wry smile, "well now, remember that I haven't got a mirror in here, so I don't know if I've sprouted a tail or something. Some of them do, right?"

"I've heard stories like that," Acacia replied, trying to smile back, "but as far as I can tell, no tail."

Honestly, Seija looked the same as always. Acacia had never met any of the others before they took the potion, naturally, but she thought that wasn't really a rare outcome. At least, it didn't seem like it.

"Anyway, think you can stand?"

"Of course!" And to prove it, she shot up, but as she stepped triumphantly to the ground, her foot was caught in the sheet she was clutching, and she tripped and fell forward.

"Are you alright?" Acacia asked hurriedly.

"Speak of this to no one," Seija growled, picking herself up, "and I'll be just fine."

And Acacia helped her up, wordlessly as she would have been turned down had she just offered, made sure what little she'd been dressed in aside from all the wrappings was decent, which it was however barely, and suggested that Seija might wish to report to Ukko and Esteri personally.

"Like this?" Seija asked in an acidic tone.

"Sure!" Acacia said. "You might be the only person to formally petition royalty while in a nightgown and get away with it!"

***

Towards the late afternoon, Seija had found fresh clothes, and with Avina had found some grounds for a 'friendly spar' that, in Acacia's opinion, both girls were far too eager to engage in. But Radegond insisted on seeing, and with that Esteri and Ukko as well. Acacia had come, and Maria as well, in her own words to cheer Seija on, and Tius at the Princess's side. Prince Tuoni and Jeanne of Lysama were there as well, staying close to Ukko and Esteri. Acacia had thought to send a runner to Ormr, given his claims earlier, but he hadn't yet arrived.

"As ready as the two of you seem to kill each other," Radegond barked, "refrain from it. I want to see what the new girl is capable of, and I don't want to be cleaning up blood."

"Think you can handle it?" Avina asked.

"You should be asking yourself," Seija replied.

Radegond called for them to begin and... nothing happened. After a moment, Seija began to circle carefully around Avina. Even though Acacia knew what Avina was capable of, they really did look mismatched the other way around.

"Trying to get the drop on me?" Seija asked.

About then was when Acacia noticed Ormr appear with his box-and-rod that was supposed to answer what if anything Seija was capable of.

"Stop dawdling!" Radegond called. "Put yourselves through your paces."

And there Acacia got a good look at Avina's face, who seemed honestly surprised

"I... can't!"

"What?" Radegond demanded, indignant.

"Nullification." Ormr declared, holding up a tiny book. "The wave signature is a very near match to the sample." Here, he opened the book and began to read from a page he had marked with his thumb. "According to the guide, it interferes with arcane effects, including any abilities manifested by other Accursed, with an effective radius of suppression of new effects of ten meters on average, with a cubic drop-off in the intensity of disruption to standing effects compared to linear distance, coordinating with around a five percent instability at the limit of suppression. I dare say I might be able to supply more technical details as to your soldier's new capabilities in ten minutes than you could divine in ten years of ponderous trial and error."

Acacia found herself simply glaring at the man's arrogant condescension, and guessed from the silence that the others gathered were doing something similar.

"With the need for this spectacle met as such," he continued, "perhaps you would care to be informed that I am expecting contact from Hyperborea in approximately fifty minutes.

Ormr did not wait for a response, but turned and shuffled quickly back towards where his things had been brought. Esteri spoke quietly to Ukko, and then Radegond and all three moved to leave the area, Tius and the young royals in tow. Acacia watched them go, then turned back to the makeshift arena. Seija had found her way over to where a few training swords had been found and left to rest against a garden wall, then picked up two and tossed one to Avina

"What?" the Accursed girl asked.

"If you want to be my rival," Seija said, "it sounds like you're going to have to do it under your own power."

"I've never"-

"You'll learn fast," Seija replied in the same mock-gruff way she always did with her friends. "Pick it up and come at me like you want to kill me. Shouldn't be that hard, should it?"

CHAPTER XXXV

Esteri

"I'll be brief," the disembodied voice of a stern woman, Colonel Svanna of Hyperborea, said. "It's become abundantly clear that the final decision on whether you and yours are admitted to our lands to fight this monster lies with me. And personally, I couldn't care less about what you might happen to see, so the most cogent arguments against are nothing. I want to know one thing, though: what makes you think you have a chance? Over."

"A woman of your country, Valdasa, said that the weapons of the Ancestor Gods were the only arms that could truly slay what my father has become. I bear one such sword, and have no reason to doubt her."

After a moment, Ormr said, "Over."

"Valdasa lived?" Svanna said with no little surprise. "I'll want to know where that girl is, but if you say she's your source on that, you have a sword that can kill it. Now do you honestly believe you can get that sword to where it does its job or not? Over."

"I've seen a future in which the world lives on," Esteri said. "Though I cannot seem to witness the battle ahead of me directly, I believe absolutely that my father will be laid to rest, and I have faith in my friends that we can do it. Beyond that, if we fail, you have little to lose." Esteri's eyes darted to Ormr, and then she said, "Over."

"Very well," Svanna replied. "According to the ambassador, your proposed squad numbers half a dozen. I'll have a plane chartered for you a-sap. Details forthcoming. Out."

The faint crackle of the radio went silent, and Ormr crossed his arms.

"I hope you know what you're doing," he said.

"Spare me the false concern," Esteri replied, "and tell me when you'd expect us to depart."

Ormr fumed. "By morning, at the latest. I would not be so eager to rush to death."

"I don't intend to," Esteri replied. She straightened her coat, and turned away. "Don't underestimate me. That was Ulfr's mistake."

With that, Esteri stomped out of the room, and when she had closed the door allowed herself a sigh of relief. That had gone better than she had feared, but what was ahead was still unknown. It was only a moment later when a voice to which she had sadly ceased to be accustomed called out to her.

"Sis!"

Esteri turned, and watched Tuoni run up to her. He was alone, which was something of a surprise since nothing until now had pried him and Jeanne of Lysama apart. Which stood to reason, as unless Esteri missed her mark as to what the girl would grow up like, they'd end up married in the future.

"Tuoni? Is something wrong?"

"I just..." he said. "I wanted to talk to you."

"Alright," she said, lowing herself a little to his height. "Right here is fine?"

Tuoni nodded. "I heard... you were going to go after dad."

Esteri sighed heavily. This wasn't going to be easy for Tuoni to understand or accept at the best of times, and she knew she wasn't the most tactful person to try to do it.

"I am," she said. "If not tomorrow, then very soon. Believe me when I say I wish I didn't have to, but this has to be done and..." Esteri took a breath.

"Ukko told me that. I know you've got to go. But... you'll come back, right?"

That both made things easier, and was in its own way a

more difficult question.

"Tuoni..."

"Because mom went there, and she didn't come back," he said, clearly not aware of what Esteri took to be the truth of Delphina's ending, "and dad's gone, and he won't come back. But you'll be different, right? You'll come back for sure."

Esteri winced, then shook her head.

"I don't really know," she said, "and I don't want to lie to you when I do know that where I'm going will be very dangerous. I'll try my best, and I'm sure Tius and the others will help me make sure we can all come home."

"That's your boyfriend, right?"

Esteri felt herself blush, and looked away. "What gave you that idea?" she asked, though it wasn't something she wanted nor had the heart to actually deny.

"Miss Acacia," Tuoni answered. Of course.

"Anyway," Tuoni continued, "You've got to come back, because you've got to be queen, right?"

At that, Esteri shook her head again. "No... I'm afraid that won't ever happen."

"But why? You're home, and you're you, so you should be queen."

Esteri closed her eyes. "Father may never have taken me out of the succession," she said, "but the people will never accept me as I am. So instead, you'll be king when you're old enough. And you're going to be a good, wise king, I know it."

"I guess that's alright but... will you have to disappear?"

"I don't know that, either," Esteri admitted, "but if I come back from Hyperborea and can't stay around, I'll be sure to let you know where I've gone, so you can always find your big sister if you need her." She sniffled, not sure why this was making her hold back tears. "Will that be alright?"

Tuoni looked down, and Esteri softly put a hand under his chin to lift his gaze back to her. She forced a smile, and hoped it looked natural.

"I won't die easily," she said, "and I won't leave lightly. I promise, I'll do everything I can to make sure I can be here for you."

Tuoni was tearing up, and Esteri shifted and hugged her brother.

"Dry your eyes," she whispered. "A king can't cry over something like this."

"I... I can't help it."

"I know," Esteri replied. "Right now, what matters is that you try."

Tuoni hugged her back, and sniffled a moment, then stood straighter.

"I think I feel better now," he said.

"There you go," Esteri replied, though she was resisting the urge to cry herself. "If... if I don't get another chance before heading off, I want to say that I love you, and I hope you'll always be happy."

"I love you too, sis," Tuoni said with a sad smile. "Thank you..."

"I'm so glad," Esteri said, "that I've been able to see you again. And I'll do my best to make sure this isn't the last time. So do your best to make sure I can be proud of what you've been up to in the meantime."

"I will!" Tuoni replied. "I promise."

And then he hurried off, and Esteri stood and straightened herself out, let out a sigh, and thought about what do do with the time she had left.

***

Esteri wasn't ready. She put on a brave face when Ormr had declared that transportation had been arranged, but she wasn't ready. She had burned up all her time, and now only an uncertain future awaited. There were things she didn't say, things she didn't do, and though stern-faced and steely-eyed, she was terrified.

Esteri wasn't ready when the coach was boarded and she commanded its driver onward with practiced regal disdain and grace. She wasn't ready on the next day of travel, or the one after, and shamefully found herself unable to use the journey frutifully. She wasn't ready when the gray walls of smooth stone that marked the Hyperborean 'embassy' came into view, illuminated by strange lamps in the hours before dawn. And she certainly wasn't ready when, inside, she was introduced to the next leg of their journey.

It was a white... thing. It had a body like a stretched-out carraige, with small wheels beneath it, and arms that stretched from either side, and metal barrels above and behind. Esteri had been briefed – it was a Hyperborean flying machine called an "Airplane". Seeing the machine brought to mind existential dread, not of being in the air at the hands of a metal box, but at the fact that the journey forward was real, and Esteri wasn't ready.

As she walked to the conveyance, not quite hearing the countless questions about its function that Acacia busily asked and took down notes on the answers of, she wondered what more she could have done, to keep herself from feeling like her heart would burst free of her chest.

Could she ever be ready?

Magic, madness, and patricide awaited her. Gods and monsters spun around her. Who could be prepared for that? No one, she thought as the airplane roared, charged forward, and lifted off the ground. No one sane could have been prepared for that. No child should ever be ready to put her father to the sword. There was nothing, Esteri realized, that she could do to be better prepared.

But she had to be ready. This had to be done, and Esteri had sworn to see it through. As much as her heart raged against it, she told herself, she would be ready. Or at least, she would speak with a clear voice, fight with a determined purpose, and when the time came kill without hesitation.

Esteri didn't have to be comfortable with it. In her heart of hearts, she didn't really need to be ready for it. But this was her duty, and she had to do it in any case.

That would have to be enough.

Once she managed to steel herself with that thought, Esteri spent the rest of the aerial transit to Hyperborea trying to avoid gazing out of the windows. She had to fight a god, so being above the clouds supported only by roaring, rattling steel should have been no source of fear. Still, better to not tempt fate.

When the contraption finally stopped, Esteri was the first off. Standing ready for her was a group of Hyperboreans in what was at least recognizable as some sort of military dress uniform. Standing at the front of the formation with the most badges on her lapel and the largest crest on her cap was a severe-looking woman. Esteri guessed her to be about General Katri's age, perhaps a little older, though with Hyperboreans it was always hard to tell. Her ivory blonde hair was cut jaw-length and her icy blue eyes were entirely focused on Esteri, meeting her gaze and not wavering.

"Esteri of Kalest, I presume?" she said. Esteri recognized the voice, but the woman continued her introduction. "I am Colonel Svanna. In the current state of emergency, I speak for Hyperborea."

"Well met," Esteri said. She glanced over her shoulder to see that everyone was with her. "Perhaps you could enlighten us as to that situation."

"To the point," Svanna said with a little smirk. "I like you already. Follow me, then, some things are easier seen than explained." She turned, and motioned for Esteri to follow.

"I'll reward your frankness with my own. Immediately after the battle at Castle Kalest, the being we've designated Subject Two – Subject Zero being the original Godflesh and Subject One the former Queen of Kalest – arrived in Hyperborea and landed in the Citadel of the Elder Council. Since then, we've been monitoring the arcane energy flux from the citadel and have been attempting to devise a counter to terminate Subject Two. There are factors that make this easier said than done. We should have a view of that in just a moment."

There she pointed to the edge of a large building, and increased her pace to reach it.

"Suffice to say, we're nowhere near ready. Thanks to your information, we've made contact with Valdasa, but we've been unable to secure transport for her, so we're out the one living person who should have the best knowledge of the current situation. We did receive confirmation of your story of ancient weapons that could do the deed. May I see the one you've brought?"

Esteri drew her sword and held it out.

"... Glowing with a faint blue light, thought to be the result of exotic, high-energy Æther interacting with metal. Well, I can't say it doesn't fit the description."

They rounded the corner, and Svanna stopped. Esteri's attention was quickly brought to Hyperborea's grand city... and the fastness that was above it.

The city would have been something of unfathomable grandeur. Glittering towers, glass and steel, piercing the sky like a forest of gleaming swords. Red light glimmered through, though, and seemed as though that sky wept blood. At once, Esteri was horribly conscious that she'd seen this before, in her dreams – the prophetic dreams that warped her body and she never felt like she could be remembering rightly. Above it all was a massive castle, cast in crimson and black, and positively seething, like a loathsome giant snoring.

"Subject Two established a distortion zone around its residence – getting in and out on foot isn't impossible, though there are hostiles on the inside, but it messes with our instruments, which makes accurate readings of its energy signatures impossible. The lack of accuracy rules out a lot of proposed methods for defeating it. For instance, one group wanted to use massive generators to create destructive interference and literally cancel out the alleged god to static. There are only two options that we can honestly believe will work. Number one is a strike with a weapon like yours. If we could just give the same power to a guided missile, we'd do that, but it could literally be years before we could manufacture something like that, which means an ancient sword is our best hope for managing that method. Nobody's inclined to let Subject Two fester longer than we absolutely have to."

"And the second?" Esteri asked.

"Overwhelming firepower. If we ram a twenty kiloton warhead with a high-density green Æther shell down its throat, the resulting combination of heat, concussive force, high-energy Æther, and conventional radiation will, according to calculations, annihilate Subject Two utterly. Since the resulting problem probably isn't obvious to you, we're standing at about the minimum safe distance from a blast like that right now. Downtown and the core residential districts are all in the kill zone. We've been working to evacuate the city for a week, and it's still slow going. Even if we get everybody out and drop the bomb, that's not the end of it... we couldn't really move civilians back into the area around ground zero for decades, barring a miracle of cleanup. Naturally, that makes it Plan B."

Esteri didn't understand the events being described. She thought she understood 'bomb,' as the term was sometimes applied to fireworks, but kiloton? Leveling a whole city? These were nonsensical, unbelievable. But as she looked at the city, no doubt vaster than Kalest's own capitol, she thought she could imagine the human cost of losing it.

"It must have taken a lot to admit us here, then, given the origin of this disaster."

Perhaps, Esteri thought, Hyperboreans were different than Kalesti, but if it were Esteri, her pride would make it difficult to accept aid from the source of her woes. Not impossible, but hard.

"If you must know," Svanna said, "it's my opinion, and the public's, that the Elder Council's hubris is what brought us here. Of course, most of them died at the False Ascension, but those that remain are finished as a government. Most of us are decent, normal people, and if we all live through this mess I'd like to show the rest of the world that there are better ambassadors of our land than schemers and psychopaths."

Esteri nodded sharply.

"So," she said, "do we just try to walk in the front door?"

"There's not a lot of choice about it," Svanna replied. "There's a monorail from the beach to Citadel Park, which is inside the Distortion Zone and up on the bluff. From there, the transit to the Citadel's entrance should be short. You do already have warding Talismans, Valdasa said she saw to that. Hopefully that and the presence of your friend with Nullification will be enough to protect you from the Aberrations up in the Distortion Zone, along with the likelihood that they won't be quite so aggressive to someone more literally of the blood than most Hyperboreans. It's hard to be sure how intense their activity is going to be."

"When do we embark, then?"

"Well," Svanna said, "the sooner the better, but we want the best possible chance of success. If you need to rest, or want to be outfitted with flak jackets or assault rifles, we can arrange that. If you're ready, I could take you to the monorail and see you off right now."

Esteri gritted her teeth.

"I'm ready. Tius?"

"As I'll ever be."

"Radegond?"

"Sure," she said, "no point putting this off."

"I'm ready too!" Avina exclaimed.

"Count me in," said Acacia.

"Just tell me what to kill, I'll make it dead," said Seija.

"I think we're all prepared," Esteri told Svanna. "Please show us the way to the Citadel."

***

The humming conveyance stopped, and the door opened onto a different world. They were in a park, that was certain as they stepped out of the conveyance, for though the lamp-posts were strange and the benches of foreign style, it

473

certainly had the markings of manicured greenery. However, everything outside of a small boundary of gloomy gray was cast in crimson and shrouded with black fog. In the distance, there was motion in the haze, the writhing of giant append-ages that should have been visible from the beachfront but seemed to only exist inside the distortion. There was also smaller motion, scuttling and stomping in the black fog of things the size of dogs and of men and of giants, no doubt the Aberrations that Svanna had mentioned.

Esteri drew her sword, which still glowed despite Seija's presence, but the monsters didn't seem inclined to approach. Esteri could not see them clearly, but she might have wished that she could see less. Their skin was scabrous, and their forms twisted, countenances blasted. The Raven Men, for all the blasphemous evil their existence portended, had even in their crude forms been not entirely ignoble creations. These Aberrations, Esteri thought, were more like discarded mis-takes – they might have been living things, but that was only the same way as globs of clay could have been fine vases had they not collapsed on the wheel. Yet they lived, and breathed, and moaned, and bled from the sockets that might or might not hold eyes or cracks in their black skin, and it was the most Esteri could do to resist the urge to vomit.

Avina was less successful and was soon on her knees, heav-ing up her last meal.

Still the monsters ignored them. Some scratched near the edge where the mortal gray of dim light met hellish red, but none dared cross that barrier.

"Cowards," Seija scoffed as she helped Avina up to her feet. "If they're all like this, we should have an easy time."

The border of dim reality and darker hell moved with Seija. Staying close to her, it seemed that they had little to fear, and indeed the herds of abominations seemed to thin as they left the park and followed the cliff-side lane to the great doors of the citadel.

At last they faced it, the cavernous space, flanked by grand statues. Threads of flesh like the roots wrapped the statues, and those threads seemed to pulse with life. Or were the statues just more abominations, granted a stony shell over their hideousness? Black fog issued forth from the opening like billowing smoke. As they approached, wary of the flanking colossi, Esteri spoke.

"I'm sorry, Seija, but I'm going to have to ask you to hold the door again."

Tendrils of that dark mist threaded between them as they crossed the threshold, mercifully ignored by any intellect in the great beings, though they had been careful to thread between them.

"I managed last time, didn't I?" she said.

"You won't be alone this time," Acacia said, speaking up.

"Hm?" was all Esteri could manage to voice her surprise.

"I can fight just fine in this aura," Acacia said, "so I should, right? Two blades are better than one."

Esteri focused her gaze forward. She honestly hadn't thought of what Acacia was supposed to do, but then they didn't exactly know the shape of what they'd face.

"That's a good thought," Esteri said. "Alright. According to what Svanna said on the way here, we should have a straight shot to the Throne. That's where this thing rested dead for millennia, that's where it will be."

"Are you sure?" Avina asked. "I think it might be everywhere."

"What do you mean?" Tius asked before Esteri herself could.

"Look at the ground. All these threads."

Indeed, there was a carpet of something not unlike flesh, spread throughout the otherwise empty hallway.

"They feel like... it," Avina said.

"Well," Esteri said, "let's see."

She scraped her blade across the ground before her, carving a line through the scab-red mass, which blackened and pulled away from the wound on either side. For a moment, she tensed, having realized too late that such a thing might provoke a response.

"It looks like it's not vital, if it is," she said. "If there's nothing that seems... central in the Grand Rotunda, then we'll have to hunt for it."

Esteri sheathed her sword, and a gust of wind, warm and wet like breath, carrying black fog and the scent of blood, issued forth from the depths.

"I don't think that's going to be the problem."

With that, they strode forward, down the grand hall, to the shattered doors of the rotunda.

Esteri stepped in, passing the edge of Seija's nullification. The world was glowing red, and the air cloyingly thick with the scent of blood. At the center of the Rotunda was what Esteri couldn't doubt was their objective, the nucleus of the "godflesh" that permeated the Citadel.

There was nothing of her father left, and that was a mercy, but nothing else about it was merciful. The monstrosity reached from the floor of the rotunda all the way to the arching roof that looked as high as the sky. It was somewhat like a tree, more like a mushroom, and in places horribly like a man. One great, deformed arm hung from one side of the main stalk, muscular and brighter crimson than the scabbed red and black of the glistening core. It had three fingers and one more half-grown and vestigial, all tipped with obsidian claws that scraped against the floor as they hung from the flabby paw that could easily hold a human. On the main stalk, there was a maw, arch-shaped, hanging open with no hint of a lower jaw, and lined with fangs and teeth in all descriptions and titanic scale, row after row of gnashing pearly white and ivory yellow leading down the outline of a throat. Above that was an eye – one, single human eye, on the side opposite the flabby arm, giving the impression of a warped face. It stared lazily, welkin blue, half-covered by a bulge of warty flesh that seemed like a drooping lid. It was Erikis' eye, if now as tall as a man... was this what was really beneath his facade?

The maw belched another cloud of black fog. As it cleared, Esteri looked again. What were such an abomination's vitals? Would they have to fell it with her blade like the colossal tree it resembled?

A glint caught her eye. Above the eye, perhaps fifty feet above the ground, a lattice of flesh revealed a brighter orange light than the predominate bloody glow.

It pulsed. A moment passed. It pulsed again.

The monster's heart stood before them.

"There!" Esteri called, pointing it out.

"I see it!" Radegond called. "Looks like it's a good thing I came along."

Radegond's wings burst from her back. To the other side of Esteri, the air rippled, and Avina took on the monstrous form that seemed noble compared to their foe's bloated malformation. Esteri drew her sword once more.

At once, the gigantic eye focused upon it, and a hideous shriek welled up from the depths of the monstrosity's gaping throat, an impossibly loud high whine that conveyed fear... pain... alarm.

"I think it's noticed us," Tius said, one hand on Esteri's shoulder helping to steady her. "What now?"

Esteri held the blade out to Radegond.

"We end this quickly!"

Radegond took up the sword and leapt into the air even as the ground beneath Esteri's feet scuttled and writhed. Massive tendrils tore away from the walls and flailed wildly, and Avina stepped in their way, tearing away the errant chunks of flesh and tossing them this way and that.

Radegond ascended swiftly, beating her wings hard and fast as she grasped the sword in both hands. Nearly at the arch of the roof, she turned, and dove downward toward the monster's heart. Near the last moment, she flared her wings again, slowing her descent just a little as she raised the blade to stab deep into the monster's flesh.

Then, it happened in an instant. The drooping, flabby paw

Austin Harper

moved like lightning, faster that Esteri's eyes could follow, and snatched Radegond from the air a split second before she would have struck true. She plunged the blade into the monster's topmost finger even as its talons ran her through, and Radegond and the monster screamed as one.

"Radegond!" Tius called, but it was too late. The paw released her, and she fell limp, dropping thirty feet to the roots before the beast's maw.

Without a word to command him, Tius vanished, reappearing next to where Radegond fell. With one hand, he grabbed the hilt of the sword, and as soon as he did the eye locked at him, and the paw moved like lightning again. As smoke, he dodged its strike, again and again, leaping out of its reach and then trying to make his way back in to Radegond. At last, he tried too daring an assault, and was caught and back-handed by the beast, which sent him skipping across the floor. Esteri ran to him and Avina, far faster, leaped ahead to pick him up and drag him away from what might have been the monster's reach. Esteri came to him, and threw her arms around him.

"Tius!" she called. "Tius!"

He began to stir, and opened warped eyes.

"Ugh... what..."

With a pained groan he picked himself up back to his feet, and tensed, but Esteri caught his wrist, the hand that still held the glowing sword.

"Don't let it get you too," she said. She looked back to where Radegond had fallen. Slimy threads had tumbled from the maw and grasped her, forming the impression of a drooling tongue that now dragged her body back to the bulk. And yet the eye, that terrible eye, was still fixed absolutely on the sword that could undo it.

"We still have a chance," Esteri said, and she felt it was true. No – more than true, more than a chance. There was only one condition.

"From here on, you need to do exactly what I say," Esteri

said.

Tius looked to her.

"Your eyes..."

"Clear, aren't they?" Esteri said. "You just need to trust me."

"I will," Tius replied. "What's the plan?"

"I don't think it knows its own strength. I'm going to need you to get its attention to start. Just focus on surviving... unless I miss my mark, you've already got one broken arm, don't risk another. I'll call for the rest."

Tius nodded. He gripped the sword with his good arm, and darted into the monster's reach. The paw came for him again, but he was watching it, and each time he ducked through it. Esteri watched the beast's swings. No motion conserved, it followed far through where Tius had been each time.

But as he warped, Esteri thought he was getting slower, or the monster faster yet. There wouldn't be time to observe forever.

"In air!" Esteri called, and Tius followed. He appeared in thin air, and as he started to fall darted away again, across and around its vision. Here it flailed even more, with no ground to stop its swings. One, two, three, four.

"The eye! Now!" Esteri called. Tius looked to it and smoke darted to forward. Even as it did, Esteri called out.

"To me!"

For a split second, Tius appeared not a foot in front of the monster's eye. The taloned paw swung, and in the blink of an eye reached up, as Tius vanished not a heartbeat faster. A dart of smoke launched to Esteri, and formed into Tius, who sank to his knees before her.

The beast's paw didn't stop moving. There was a wet squelching sound, and a howl even louder and more terrible than the one before as the monster's talons pierced its eye. The organ ruptured, and blood and white bile poured from the wound.

For a moment, at least, the monster was blind.

Esteri knelt beside Tius. She took the blade from his hand

and kissed him on the lips.

"Leave this to me," she said, and she stood faster than Tius could protest, and turned to Avina.

"Throw me!" she called.

For a second, Avina hesitated, but then she grasped Esteri.

"You know what, princess?" she said as she tensed. "You're my kind of crazy."

Then Esteri was hurtling through the air. Her eyes focused on the pulsing brightness before her, and she brought up the sword, leading with the blade as much as she could. Avina's aim was true, and Esteri struck home with a wet thud that drove the breath from her lungs, and it was all she could do to cling on rather than falling back to the stone floor below.

The sword had been driven into the lattice of flesh above the heart, but as Esteri looked, though it seemed buried to the hilt and seared the flesh around it, it was not a deep enough strike. Gasping in pain, Esteri heaved herself up, arm trembling, strength threatening to fail her even as the blade threatened to tear free. Yet she caught a hand-hold, dug in at a foothold of deific tumor and raised herself up to the blade's level. With a cry, she thrust her arm forward, forcing the sword deeper into the monster's flesh – into its heart.

As the sword pierced it, the heart turned black and convulsed. Violet blood gushed over her as the world quaked in the thing's death throes, hurtling Esteri back into the air. She twisted in space, facing downward a moment. She saw all the roots blackening, graying, the crimson light vanishing.

She saw the dying monster's roots and the stone floor beneath them rushing up to meet her.

And then she saw a black blur, and felt a wrenching sensation, and in the next moment was sprawled on the floor, Tius beside her, coughing.

"Running time is now!" Avina bellowed. The girl stomped by them, grasping Esteri in one hand and Tius in the other. "Hey Rival! Get going or you'll be squashed by a roof!"

Esteri saw the blur of motion as they ran out of the rotunda, and heard a calamitous crash as the masonry that had been supported by the horror's sprawl began to come down. For a second, a vast sense of relief flooded her. Then, as the alertness of danger faded, Esteri blacked out.

***

Esteri awakened on a park bench, in a park that appeared to have seen better days, in the shadow of the Citadel of Hyperborea. The ruins were still shrouded in a cloud of gray dust, as shattered bits of petrified horrors littered the space around them, but it looked as though only the greatest dome had actually fallen inwards. The whir of Hyperborean machinery was behind Esteri's head, and she tried to turn herself to see only to yelp in pain at the suggestion of motion.

"I've just sent the monorail back for paramedics," Colonel Svanna's voice echoed from behind her. "I'd recommend you swallow your pride and wait for the gurney. And, Accursed or not, I'd also strongly suggest you avail yourself of a Hyperborean hospital before returning to the continent. In fact, I insist. I think you and the boy might have enough unbroken bones between the two of you for one person, and your right arm has some vile looking chemical burns. I'd ask what the hell happened, but that can wait until you've gotten treatment."

"It's dead, right?" Esteri said. "This is over?"

"I've got a Hazmat team picking through the rubble for any bits that are left," Svanna replied, "but the Distortion Zone went down and all malignant growths died and became gray and brittle, so I doubt they'll find anything. There's no energy signature we can detect from the outside, either, so I'd say it's not too early to declare Subject Two terminated, even if we'll wait and see a day or two before moving people back in from the evacuation. You did a heck of a job."

"... Forgive me if I can't quite celebrate," Esteri said. There had been far too many dead to reach this moment for her to appreciate it as a victory.

"I understand," Svanna replied, "but understand that the people of Hyperborea owe you personally, and arguably your nation, a great debt. As long as it's in my power, we won't be the kind of people to forget that. I suspect the world is going to change a lot in the coming years."

Esteri tilted her head back a little, looking up to the azure sky above, only a few wisps of white cloud hanging in the upper air.

"I want to believe it will be for the better," she said.

"Well," Svanna replied, "if you want to do more than hope, perhaps you'd care to provide some suggestions for that better future."

Esteri felt herself smile despite the aches and pains.

"I think I might, but first... how long until the medics get here?"

"Not long," Svanna replied.

Esteri closed her eyes. "I think... I'll rest until then."